Praise for the novels of Adele Parks

Lies, Lies, Lies

"Gripping, moving and elegantly written."

—Marian Keyes

"Brilliant, moving and deeply satisfying, Parks is the queen of the domestic dark side."

—Veronica Henry

"Compelling and suspenseful."

—Catherine Isaac

"I devoured *Lies, Lies, Lies*… [S]o engaging, well written. It is one of those rare books that earns the title, unputdownable."

—Sally Hepworth

"Engrossing and emotional, *Lies, Lies, Lies* had me gripped from the very first page to the final shocking finale. Adele Parks just gets better and better."

—Lisa Hall

I Invited Her In

"Packed with secrets, scandal and suspense, this is Adele Parks at her absolute best."

—*Heat*

"Wow! What a read. Intense, clever and masterful."

—Lisa Jewell

"A beautifully written tale of revenge and retribution, full of unexpected plot twists."

—*Daily Mail*

"A gripping read from the brilliant Adele Parks."

—*Hello!*

Also by Adele Parks and MIRA

The Image of You
I Invited Her In
Lies, Lies, Lies

Look for Adele Parks's next novel,
available soon from MIRA.

JUST MY LUCK

ADELE PARKS

Recycling programs for this product may not exist in your area.

ISBN-13: 978-0-7783-3173-5

Just My Luck

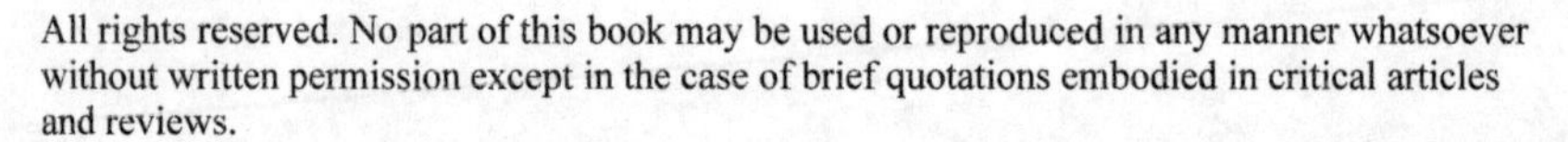

This edition published by arrangement with Harlequin Books S.A.

For questions and comments about the quality of this book, please contact us at CustomerService@Harlequin.com.

Mira
22 Adelaide St. West, 40th Floor
Toronto, Ontario M5H 4E3, Canada
BookClubbish.com

Printed in Italy by Grafica Veneta

For Jim and Conrad.

I won the lottery.

JUST MY LUCK

THE BUCKINGHAMSHIRE GAZETTE

November 9, 2015

Elaine Winterdale, 37, a property manager, has been handed a suspended prison sentence for failing to maintain a faulty gas boiler that caused the death of two tenants from carbon monoxide poisoning.

Reveka Albu, 29, was found dead with her son Benke, 2, by her husband, Mr. Toma Albu, 32, at a property they rented in Reading, on December 23, 2014.

Following an investigation by the Health and Safety Executive, Ms. Winterdale was today sentenced at Reading Crown Court for breaches of gas safety laws after she failed to arrange gas safety checks to be carried out at the property over a three-year period, despite assuring her employer, the owner of the property, that she had done so.

In June 2011, an employee of National Grid Gas visited the property to replace the gas meter. The boiler was labeled as "immediately dangerous" due to "fumes at open flue" and was disconnected. A report was left with Mrs. Albu and subsequently a letter was sent to Ms. Winterdale, which she failed to respond to or pass to the owner of the property.

The boiler was not repaired. For three years the only heating in the home was from one borrowed electric heater.

On October 22, 2014, Mr. Toma Albu was away from home overnight and returned to find the flat warm; his wife informed him that after repeated petitions Ms. Winterdale had finally arranged for the boiler to be reconnected.

On the evening of December 23, 2014, Mr. Albu returned home after a double shift to find his wife and son dead. Tests showed Mrs. Albu's blood contained 61 percent carbon monoxide. A level of 50 percent is enough to be fatal.

Ms. Winterdale pleaded guilty to seven breaches of the Gas Safety Regulations and was given a sixteen-month prison sentence, suspended for two years. She was also given 200 hours community service, was fined £4,000 and was ordered to pay costs of £17,500.

CHAPTER 1

Lexi

Saturday, April 20

I can't face going straight home to Jake. I'm not ready to deal with this. I need to try to process it first. But how? Where do I start? I have no idea. The blankness in my mind terrifies me.

I always know what to do. I always have a solution, a way of tackling something, giving it a happy spin. I'm Lexi Greenwood, the woman everyone knows of as the fixer, the smiler—some might even slightly snidely call me a do-gooder. Lexi Greenwood, wife, mother, friend.

You think you know someone. But you don't know anyone, not really. You never can.

I *need* a drink. I drive to our local. Sod it, I'll leave the car at the pub and walk home, pick it up in the morning. I order a glass of red wine, a large one, and then I look for a seat tucked away in the corner where I can down my drink alone. It's Easter weekend, and a rare hot one. The place is packed. As I thread my way through the heaving bar, a number of neighbors raise a glass, gesturing to me to join them; they ask after the kids and Jake. Everyone else in the pub seems celebratory, buoyant. I feel detached. Lost. That's the thing about living in a small village—you recognize everyone. Sometimes that reassures me, sometimes it's inconvenient. I politely and apologetically deflect their friendly overtures and continue in my search for a solitary spot. Saturday vibes are all around me, but I feel nothing other than stunned, stressed, isolated.

You think you know someone.

What does this mean for our group? Our frimily. Friends that are like family. What a joke. Blatantly, we're not friends anymore. I've been trying to hide from the facts for some time, hoping there was a misunderstanding, an explanation; nothing can explain away this.

I told Jake I'd only be a short while, and I should text him to say I'll be longer. I reach for my phone and realize in my haste to leave the house I haven't brought it with me. Jake will be wondering where I am. I don't care. I down my wine. The acidity hits my throat, a shock and a relief at once. Then I go to the bar to order a second.

The local pub is only a ten-minute walk away from our home, but by the time I attempt the walk back, the red wine has taken effect. Unfortunately, I am feeling the sort of drunk that nurtures paranoia and fury rather than a light head or heart. What can I do to right this wrong? I have to do something. I can't carry on as normal, pretending I know nothing of it. Can I?

As I approach home, I see Jake at the window, peering out. I barely recognize him. He looks taut, tense. On spotting me, he runs to fling open the front door.

"Lexi, Lexi, quickly come in here," he hiss-whispers, clearly agitated. "Where have you been? Why didn't you take your phone? I've been calling you. I needed to get hold of you."

What now? My first thoughts turn to our son. "Is it Logan? Has he hurt himself?" I ask anxiously. As I'm already teetering on the edge, my head quickly goes to a dark place. Split skulls, broken bones. A dash to the hospital isn't unheard-of. Thirteen-year-old Logan has daredevil tendencies and the sort of mentality that thinks shimmying down a drainpipe is a reasonable way to exit his bedroom in order to go outside and kick a football about. My fifteen-year-old daughter, Emily, rarely causes me a moment's concern.

"No, no, he's fine. Both the kids are in their rooms. It's… Look, come inside, I can't tell you out here." Jake is practically bouncing up and down on the balls of his feet. I can't read him. My head is too fuzzy with wine and full of rage and disgust. I resent Jake for causing more drama, although he has no idea what shit I'm dealing with. I've never seen him quite this way before. If I touched him, I might get an electric shock; he oozes a dangerous energy. I follow my husband into the house. He is hurrying, urging me to speed up. I slow down, deliberately obtuse. In the hallway he turns to me, takes a deep breath, runs his hands through his hair but won't—can't—meet my eyes. For a crazy moment I think he is about to confess to having an affair. "Okay, just tell me, did you buy a lottery ticket this week?" he asks.

"Yes." I have bought a lottery ticket every week for the last fifteen years. Despite all the bother last week, I have stuck to my habit.

Jake takes in another deep breath, sucking all the oxygen from the hallway. "Okay, and did you—" He breaks off, finally drags his eyes to meet mine. I'm not sure what I see in his gaze, an almost painful longing, fear and panic. Yet at the same time there is hope there, too. "Did you pick the usual numbers?"

"Yes."

His jaw is still set tight. "You have the ticket?"

"Yes."

"You're sure?"

"Yes, it's pinned on the noticeboard in the kitchen. Why? What's going on?"

"Fuck." Jake lets out a breath that has the power of a storm. He falls back against the hall wall for a second, and then he rallies, grabs my hand and pulls me into the room that was designed to be a dining room but has ended up being a sort of study slash dumping ground. A place where the children sometimes do their homework, where I tackle paying the household bills, and where towering piles of ironing, punctured footballs and old trainers hide out. Jake sits down in front of the computer and starts to quickly open various tabs.

"I wasn't sure that we even had a ticket, but when you were late back and the film I was watching had finished, I couldn't resist checking. I don't know why. Habit, I suppose. And look."

"What?" I can't quite work out what he's on about. It might be the wine, or it might be because my head is still full of betrayal and deceit, but I can't seem to climb into his moment. I turn to the screen. The lottery website. Brash and loud. A clash of bright colors and fonts.

The numbers glare at me from the computer—1, 8, 20, 29, 49, 58. Numbers I am so familiar with, yet they seem peculiar and unbelievable.

"I don't understand. Is this a joke?"

"No, Lexi. No! It's for real. We've only gone and won the bloody lottery!"

CHAPTER 2

Lexi

£17.8 million.

£17.8 million.

£17.8 million.

No matter how often I say it, I can't make sense of it. In fact, the opposite is true. The more I say it, the less real it seems. I can't imagine what it means. Not really. Our numbers are on the screen. They are still there. I've checked a thousand times, just in case, but they are *there*. And the other numbers, too. The numbers saying how much our winning ticket is worth—17,870,896 pounds. So much money! I rush to the kitchen and grab the ticket off the noticeboard, suddenly terrified that a freak gust of wind has blown it away, or that one of the kids has knocked it off when they pinned up their letters from school. Although this makes no sense because in the entire history of our family life, neither of our two kids has ever pinned up a letter from school. I'm much more likely to find them crumpled up at the bottom of their backpacks. I stare at the tiny hole made by the tack; the ticket is slightly creased at the corner. How can this scrap of paper be worth seventeen-point-eight-million pounds? It's unbelievable. It's incomprehensible. What does this mean for us? I turn to Jake to see if he is making any more sense of this. Jake beams at me.

It is the widest, most complete smile I have seen him wear for years. I'm reminded of our early days together. When we were nothing other than hope and happiness. It makes me splutter laughter through my nose.

"Are you sure this is right?"

"Absolutely. I've checked. I've watched the draw six times on YouTube. They've announced that there is a winner. Just one. Lexi, that's us! We are rich. Rich beyond our wildest dreams."

I giggle again because the phrase is crazy. *Rich beyond our wildest dreams* is something people only say in pretty dreadful plays or movies. My body is tingling. I can feel every nerve end. It is almost painful. "Wow. I mean *wow.* What shall we do?" I ask.

"Well, we need to call it in."

"How do we do that?" My fingers are cold, immobilized, but on the other hand I feel hot and no longer solid. I am melting. The two glasses of wine I downed now feel like six. Shock, I suppose.

"I don't know. It must be on the website or something." Jake starts to dart around the screen, hitting buttons. I can't believe it. Don't dare to. It can't be true. It's too lucky. It's too wonderful. I am quivering, Jake might be able to hear my teeth chattering. I notice his hands are shaking, too. "Here it is. The National Lottery winners' line. We have to call them." Jake pauses and stares at me, his eyes gleaming, bright but unfocused. He picks up the house phone and hits the buttons to dial the number on the screen. We almost never use the landline, but the occasion demands gravitas, and somehow the dusty, neglected phone on the desk feels more serious than a mobile. "I think we've won the lottery. The whole amount. The jackpot." The person at the other end of the phone must ask Jake if he bought the ticket, because he looks confused and a bit irritated when he replies, "No. My wife actually bought it. Well, yes, she paid for it... Yes, yes, she's here with me now." He offers the handset to me. "They want to talk to you."

I somehow manage to stumble through the security questions that confirm where and when I bought the ticket. I suppose some people might find winning tickets or steal them. The lottery company has to be certain I bought ours fair and square.

"Can you please write your name and address on the back of the ticket now, if you haven't already done so," advises the woman on the other end of the line. She sounds calm and measured, which I find comforting but bizarre. I wonder how many times this woman has spoken to winners, to people whose lives will never be the same again following this particular phone call. I wonder what it must be like to be her. I'm struggling to be me. I feel I'm having some sort of out-of-body experience. I can't concentrate or reason when she says, "Well, congratulations, Mrs. Greenwood. You are indeed a winner!"

"The whole lot?" I just can't believe it.

"Yes, Mrs. Greenwood. The whole lot—17,870,896 pounds sterling." The number, massive as it is, rolls fluently off her tongue. I start to giggle. It's impossible. Earlier on I thought this was the worst night of my life, but now the night has turned around completely. What am I talking about? My life has! "Now, Mrs. Greenwood, we have people here who'll take you through the process, and for us to do that most effectively we'll need to know, will you be taking publicity?"

"No, I don't think so." I imagine the lottery company like it if you take publicity. A good-luck story in the papers must mean more tickets are bought, but my instinct is to keep this to ourselves.

"You don't have to decide now," she replies smoothly. "One of our winners' advisors will be in contact with you shortly. They'll send an email or call you, and then they'll fix up a meeting. Probably for Tuesday next week. Usually it's sooner, but as it's a bank holiday on Monday, Tuesday might be better for you?"

"Yes, yes, whatever you think." I don't want to cause any inconvenience, make someone work on their bank holiday.

"You can talk through the matter of publicity with them and they will tell you everything about what happens next."

Jake grabs the phone from me. "Will he bring the check?"

Even at this distance I can hear the amusement in the woman's voice. "No, there is a tiny bit more paperwork to be done first. Bank account details, et cetera."

"When will we get the money?" I scowl at Jake. He is being crass. I am not sure what the elegant response to winning nearly eighteen million pounds is, but I doubt it is demanding the money like a highway robber.

"Our advisor will be in touch, but if everything runs smoothly, as I'm sure it will, you'll most likely have the money in your account by Wednesday. Thursday at the latest."

"This Wednesday?" asks Jake, beaming.

"Yes."

After the call finishes, we just stare at one another, amazed.

Then through some silent communication, developed after nearly twenty years of marriage, we simultaneously pounce on one another and kiss each other in a way that we haven't since the first week we dated. Urgent and jubilant, grateful and eager. Pushing away all other thoughts and just staying in the moment, we have fast, intense sex on the desk. For the past ten years—possibly longer—sex has been limited to the bedroom. The exciting, novel nature of this hungry and triumphant sex naturally means it is soon over. I pull up my joggers and laugh, a little self-consciously. "Now you really have hit the jackpot."

Jake holds me close and speaks into my neck, his breath tickling. "Actually, technically, *you* have hit the jackpot. You bought the ticket. This win is yours. That's why they wanted to speak to you on the phone."

I laugh. "What's yours is mine, though, right?" It has always been that way between us. It has for so long. We're a team. Husband and wife. Your spouse is your teammate, right? I shake my head, as a clouding thought enters it. It has to be addressed. "Jake, what about the Heathcotes and the Pearsons?"

Jake instantly moves away from me; he concentrates on putting on his jeans and won't meet my gaze. "What about them?"

"I just went to Jennifer and Fred's tonight. That's where I was earlier."

"Oh, so not delivering a book to Diane Roper like you said."

"No." Normally, I'd be mildly embarrassed that I'd lied to him about something so petty, but in the grand scheme of things it doesn't register. I hadn't wanted to tell him that I was checking up on Jennifer's story about them going away to Fred's sister's place this weekend. I thought he might have tried to stop me.

I thought he'd gently tease me, insist I was getting into a state about nothing.

Although he'd have been wrong.

"They are not away. Like they said they were going to be," I tell him.

"I see."

"I drove past their house. What do you think is going on? Why would they lie to us?"

"I have no idea."

"Don't you care that they've lied to us?"

"Not at all," he snaps. His tone suggests he cares quite a good deal. I stare at him; his head is bent. He must feel the weight of my gaze because eventually he straightens up and his eyes meet mine. Breathing fast and shallow, he says, "We've just won the lottery, Lexi."

"But the Heathcotes, the Pearsons?"

His expression changes to one that is smug and victorious, but there is also something about the way he moves his mouth that reveals to me that he is smarting. Concerned? He draws me to him. "Look, this is karma, after the way they behaved last week."

"It was just Patrick who was out of order."

"The others sided with him. It was humiliating. We don't need them," he whispers.

I lay my head on his chest and breathe him in. "Are you sure?" I ask. I want to believe him.

"Not now we don't, Lexi. We have everything." I try to heed his words. I want to feel absolutely safe, secure. I'd always thought being rich would make me feel invincible, but honestly, I feel apprehensive. I bury my face into his neck. He has always been my haven, and I will the feeling of dauntless unassailability to overpower me.

"We need to think how we are going to tell them."

"I'll buy a Ferrari and drive past their houses," says Jake. "Fuck them, Lexi, we are rich!"

I start to giggle because it is truly marvelous. "'Rich beyond our wildest dreams,'" I quote his words back to him. Then I kiss him, my handsome husband, and I hold him tightly, putting all thoughts of our former friends—who I thought were the best people in the world but now realize I hardly knew—out of my head.

CHAPTER 3

Lexi

Sunday, April 21

I wake up, and my heart is beating so fast and hard I can hear it. Adrenaline and excitement, yes, of course, but also a fairly clear conviction that someone is about to jump out on me and say, *Just kidding!* I can't believe we are lottery winners. I don't understand the amount of wealth that is now apparently *ours*. It's madness! As if to confirm the miracle, sunshine floods through the windows. It's an unbelievably beautiful day. I can't remember an Easter Sunday being warm before; I swear we had snow one year! How is our life such a miracle?

We've barely slept. How could we? We lie side by side, hand in hand, and whispered to one another about how this could possibly be happening. What it means. What we should do next. We made plans late into the night or actually early into the morning. The illusory feel is accentuated by the fact we fell in and out of consciousness and each other's bodies throughout the night. Clinging to one another in a new entangled, intense way. I'm left unsure as to what is real, what is a dream. *The* dream. All night Jake whispered into my ear. He told me he loved me. That everything is going to be perfect from now on in. That we have nothing to worry about. That we'll never have anything to worry about ever again. He repeated this over and over, like a hypnotist. And I want to believe him. I want that more than anything.

At seven o'clock we get up and go downstairs to make coffee. Jake takes the time to mess about with the old percolator, which he very rarely bothers with. In fact, I can't remember when it was used last, and the ground coffee is probably well past its sell-by date. Still, I understand; the aroma drifts through the kitchen, declaring it is time to indulge. Cornflakes just won't cut it this morning. We're going to have French toast. I crack some eggs into a shallow, flat bowl and hum to myself. A fluttering of excitement ripples through my body as I recall Jake's urgent whispers delivered in the dark, oozing seductive possibility. What an opportunity. How lucky we are. I am.

"Wow, Lexi, can you believe this?" asks Jake yet again.

"Nope, not really. I'm a different man!"

"Are you? How exactly?" I challenge gently.

"Okay, I'm the same man but, you know, better. Richer. Definitely richer." He laughs. "I can't wait until the kids get up. Shall we go and wake them? It's like a massively exaggerated Christmas morning, isn't it?"

For the past couple of years, we have woken up earlier than the kids on Christmas morning. Something I see as a bit of a bonus—it gives me time to listen to the radio, prepare the sprouts. For me, Christmas is about food, family time and, ideally, a little contemplation. Jake finds the kids' teenage lie-ins frustrating as he is always desperate for them to open their presents. He likes to spoil them and see their faces light up when they discover he has after all bought the latest must-have they've longed for and that we can barely afford. For him, Christmas is all about the giving and getting of stuff.

"I've been thinking about it. Maybe we shouldn't tell them straight away," I suggest carefully.

"What?"

"Let's wait until we are sure."

"We are sure."

"But it's complicated, isn't it? Because Emily is best friends with Megan and dating Ridley. She won't be able to keep her mouth shut. I thought we agreed the longer we can keep this from the Heathcotes and Pearsons, the better."

"How are you going to hide seventeen-point-eight-million pounds, Lexi?"

"I'm not trying to hide it."

"We'll have to tell our families."

"Of course."

"They'll expect a slice of the winnings. Well, maybe not *expect* but certainly they would *hope* for it, that is natural enough. How much is the right amount to give?" He is like an excited kid. I know he can't wait to start handing out bundles of cash.

I shake my head a fraction, trying to clear it. It is impossible to think straight after everything I discovered last night, after the poor night's sleep. I lost so much, then won so much. Their betrayal, his loving. My head and heart are about to explode. "I just think that it would be best to wait until the money is in the account. Just in case."

Jake stares at me. "I don't know how we can keep this from the kids. They'll be able to tell something is up. It's happening, Lexi. This is real." Jake is grinning so widely it looks like his face is about to split.

"But it's a big responsibility. This is going to change their lives forever. We need to think about what to tell them, give them ideas on how to adjust," I insist.

"How to adjust to what?" asks Logan.

I jump. Where did he come from? I want to kick myself—my

excitement had made me careless. I know, and usually remember, that one or other of our kids is invariably lurking, especially if they can smell food.

"We've won the lottery!" yells Jake.

"What?" Logan looks sceptical.

"Seventeen-point-eight-million pounds. We're bloody millionaires, my boy!"

"Jake!"

"Sorry, didn't mean to swear."

Actually, I was reproving him for his lack of discretion and caution more than his bad language.

"For real?" Logan asks, his eyes on me. He most likely thinks his dad is playing with him. "We're millionaires?"

"Several times over," I confirm with a shrug and a smile. "Most probably. Our numbers match and we've phoned to confirm it, but I—" My words are cut off because Logan starts to yell, actually squeal like a pig. He jumps up and down on the spot. Then he runs to his dad and launches himself, so their bodies smash into each other with a ferocious energy. A move that is somewhere between a hug and an attack. He doesn't know how to contain himself. He is literally overflowing. Effervescent. It's brilliant.

"What's going on?" Emily is in the kitchen, too, now.

Logan announces, "We've won the lottery. We're millionaires. We've won seventeen-million-and-something pounds!"

Emily looks cynical. "Yeah, right." Sluggishly she reaches for the cereal.

"It's true, my princess," says Jake, picking her up and twirling her around, just the way he used to when she was much younger and less self-conscious.

"Honestly?" Emily asks, caution and disbelief swilling in her eyes.

"Yes," I verify with a beam.

Emily bursts into tears, and then we all run to one another and amalgamate into a big mass of cuddles, screeches and happy tears.

We've been saved.

CHAPTER 4

Emily

Tuesday, April 23

"Emily, get up. Your alarm didn't go off. You've slept in." Mum is banging on my bedroom door, then she opens it and rushes in, carrying a freshly ironed school shirt. It's like this weekend never happened. "Come on, sweetheart, you'll miss the bus," she urges.

"Do I have to go in?"

"Are you ill?"

"No."

"Then of course you have to go in." Mum looks confused.

"But we won the lottery," I remind her.

"Emily, I'm surprised at you. Come on, get in the shower. Get a move on."

She rushes out of my room, and I hear the almost exact same conversation play out between her and Logan. He mutters, "What's the point of being a millionaire if I have to go to school?"

"He has a good argument," yells Dad from their bedroom.

I smile to myself. Dad is always on our side.

"Come on, people. I'm serious. Get out of bed," Mum insists. I stay where I am, thinking about how it is going to be at school today. The holidays are ridiculous this year anyhow. Who goes back to school straight after Easter? Who goes to school at all if they have just become millionaires? Mum and Dad have said we can't tell anyone about the lottery, which is going to be so weird because why wouldn't they want to tell the entire world? We are rich. Like super-off-the-scale rich! Mum says I just have to put it out my mind. Like, as if! How am I going to keep this from Ridley and Megan? We are lottery winners! Multimillionaires! Mum sometimes does this thing where she reads my mind; she does it now and swings back into my room. She hovers at the door looking uncomfortable.

"I know it's going to be hard keeping this from Ridley and Megan."

"Yeah, like, understatement of the year. Why do I have to?"

"Because there is a proper chance their parents are going to take this really badly. We were all doing the lottery together until just last week."

"Yeah, but they said it was lame."

"I imagine they'll feel very differently now."

"Can't we just give them some of the money?"

Mum doesn't answer me. She just looks torn. Mum has morals and makes a big thing of it all the time. If, for example, we are going into London to see a show in the West End and she sees someone sleeping rough, which is a given, right, then she insists we give the exact money we spent on one ticket to the guy on the street. Dad says it's a waste and that they'll just drink it or shoot it up their arms. But he says this at the interval when we are in the bar and he's drinking a glass of red wine, so Mum's counterargument is staring at his glass.

"We can't tell a soul until everything is finalized and your dad and I have had our meeting with the lottery company. Honestly, this will be for the best, for you, for Ridley and Megan, for everyone."

This is about the millionth time she has repeated this to prove she's *really serious* about it. Like there is any doubt. Mum is always *really serious* about everything, even winning the lottery apparently. It's a bit of a buzzkill.

I mean, I can see that the Heathcotes and Pearsons are going to be gutted. Can you imagine pulling out of a lottery syndicate the week before your numbers come up? Major fail! But Ridley and I will get through this. I know we are only fifteen, but we're really serious about one another. He is my One. We're soul mates. Megan, though? I'm pretty sure she will explode with jealousy. I mean, I love her, she loves me, but we are fifteen-year-old best friends so she also hates me sometimes and I hate her sometimes. Mum probably has a point. This shit is going to get real.

I hear the bathroom door slam. No! Logan got there first. He'll take forever and make it smell like hell. I pull on my robe and drag myself downstairs. I know there's no way on earth Mum is going to let me ditch school, lottery win or not. She values education above everything else. Thinks it's the biggest agent for change, etc., etc. Personally, I think maybe she *overvalues* education. I mean, clearly, a lottery win is a big agent for change, too, right?

As I pour myself a bowl of cereal, I glance over the lists we drew up yesterday. There's always a notebook knocking around the kitchen in which Mum scribbles herself little reminders of things she needs to buy. It also has the scores from our family games night when we play Monopoly or cards, and sometimes Mum and Dad write notes to me and Logan in there if they are going to be late getting home. Just stuff about what there is in to eat and how long to heat things up for, as though texting hasn't been invented. Yesterday, we used the ordinary little notebook to catch our dreams. I smile to myself as I flick through the pages. On one page it says: *red onions, gravy granules, bleach.* On the next it says: *Dad—Ferrari, Emily—holiday to New York, Logan—swimming pool (plus house),* which was written as an afterthought when it was pointed out to him that we don't have room in our garden to dig a swimming pool. *Mum—new sofa.* I don't think Mum has the hang of this game. Dad had said he'd get us anything we wanted, anything at all, and that was the best she could come up with. When we all laughed at Mum and told her to think bigger, she got a bit huffy and said, "Well, our sofa is quite lumpy, we really do need a new one." Hilarious.

Dad said he'd book New York in the next day or two. He would have done so last night, but he said the sort of style we want to do it in would more than max out his credit cards and the money from the lottery isn't in their account yet. We're going to fly first class. Obvs none of us have done that before, but Dad says that's the only way we are going to travel from now on. We looked at some amazing hotels, didn't know where to start. We put in the search "Best 5-star hotels in New York." We couldn't decide. They were all out of this world. Unlike anything we have ever stayed in. Well, we don't usually go on hotel holidays. Mum has a friend from work who has a flat in the south of Spain, we usually go there. She gives us ten percent off the price that's listed on the Owner Direct site. We stayed in a bed-and-breakfast when we did a city break in Edinburgh. It was nice, fluffy towels with a good-size TV in the room, but these luxury hotels that we looked at in New York are something else! They all have spas, rooftop swimming pools, club lounges and amazing restaurants in cool subterranean basements. They are so stylish I don't believe in them. We didn't know which to pick and just kept jumping around from one site to another. Sort of overwhelmed.

In the end we chose the Ritz-Carlton, because we'd all heard of the Ritz and know it means posh. Mum and Dad kept singing some crazy old song about "Puttin' on the Ritz." They didn't seem to know the song very well, though, as that was the only line they sang, but when they petered out, they just howled with laughter because it was a unique, unprecedented, amazing day when we all thought everything was funny! Maybe, and I *really* want to believe this, maybe none of us will ever be angry or sad or irritated ever again. Not for real.

The hotel is right next to Central Park. I have always wanted to go to Central Park since I watched this old show Mum likes, *Friends.* The Ritz-Carlton is the most elegant, chic place you could imagine, ever. Dad said Logan and I can have our own rooms; we don't even have to share. Mum and Dad will get a suite, so we all have somewhere to chill after we've spent the day shopping on Fifth Avenue, which features on like every chick flick ever. I literally can't wait!

Yesterday really was the most perfect day I've ever experienced. Dad quickly got bored of sitting around thinking about how we could spend the money; he wanted to get out and actually spend some. Mum made another call to the lottery company and once they absolutely, definitely double, treble confirmed that we had won, she said we could get a train into London and go to the big Topshop on Oxford Street.

You know, she still bought the family-saver ticket. Dad teased her about that. "No point in wasting money," she replied primly. In Topshop I just went wild. Dad said I could have anything I wanted in the entire shop. Anything at all. "We can afford anything and everything," he laughed. I tried on about a thousand things. We told the shop assistant we'd won the lottery. Once we convinced her that we weren't messing, she said I could take any number of garments into the changing room, even though the usual limit is eight. I can't even remember what I bought in the end. Loads of the Ivy Park's workout pieces, a little boxy bag that is so cute, earrings, a leopard print cap, some sundresses, shorts, quite a few tees. I lost count. Most likely over twenty pieces. Maybe thirty. I'm not actually certain where I'm going to wear it all, but I guess we'll be going to more fancy places now and so I'll have opportunities to dress up. Logan did the same in Topman. He bought the same T-shirt in four different colors because he couldn't decide which he liked best.

I finish my cereal, wash out the bowl, then pick up my mug of tea and drag myself up the stairs. Back in my room I lay out all yesterday's purchases on the floor and bed. I can't believe I have to put on my boring school uniform.

There's a tap at my door. I'm expecting it to be Mum, coming to tell me to get a move on, hop in the shower, dash for the bus, but it's not Mum nagging, it's Dad smiling. Logan is hanging around in the hallway, still wet from the shower with a towel wrapped around his waist. He's obviously not in a hurry, either.

"Hello, princess."

I beam. "Hiya, Dad. Just looking at my stuff again. I still can't believe it. Can you?"

"Not really." He grins and rubs his hair with his hand, something he does when he's really chuffed with life. Logan is punching the air, something he has done on a more or less continuous basis since they told us the news. "Look," says Dad with a reluctant sigh, "your mum wants me to remind you to keep this to yourself, at least for the moment."

"I know, I know. She's said."

"She's just worried about people's reactions."

"Why so?" asks Logan.

"Oh, you know, people can be jealous or just weird."

"Weird how?"

Dad doesn't directly answer. "She's worried about security."

"Security?" Logan looks fit to burst with excitement. "Like, in case someone kidnaps us?"

"No one said anything about kidnapping," replies Dad calmly.

"What then?" Logan looks crushed that his newfound wealth isn't going to place him in immediate danger.

"The lady who is our winner's advisor said she wanted to talk about how to deal with begging letters. You know, things like that. It's possible once the news is out people might just turn up and ask for money, I guess."

"Well, we've plenty of it so maybe we should just give these people some, if they need it," suggests my brother, showing that he hasn't got a clue.

Dad is kind enough not to say as much but just asks, "Yeah, but where would that stop? We will give to charity, of course we will. We just need to think it through."

"I can't wait for the moment when we can tell people, though," I add, beaming, thinking of Ridley and Megan's faces.

I. Just. Can't. Wait.

CHAPTER 5

Toma

Wednesday, February 6

"Do you want a cup of tea? I'm about to put the kettle on."

He didn't respond. Not coherently. His bones ached. He was so wet and cold that often when waking up, it took a few moments for him to process where he was. Who he was. What he was.

Homeless. Widower. Immigrant.

He stared at her, the woman asking the question. She looked kind enough, concerned. He had learned the importance of making quick character judgments. Still, it was too easy to trust people. Sometimes they looked kind and then they stole your shoes. This woman wasn't homeless, though. She was dressed in a trouser suit and had her hair tied back in a neat ponytail, suggesting she worked in an office, maybe the one he was sleeping outside. Still he remained aggravated, aggrieved, fearful. The homeless generally don't like being woken. Who does? Sleep is an escape. But when they are woken, the best they can hope for is that they are being moved on. The worst? They are spit on, robbed, assaulted. So he stared at her like a wounded animal, savage but impotent. She waved a bunch of keys at him and nodded toward the door he was obstructing, so he shuffled to the side to allow her to open it. She did and then she stepped past him, over the threshold.

It was a simple act, but he felt a twinge. He envied the fact she had a job to go to, anywhere to go to. The sign said Citizens Advice Bureau. A place set up to help, but to help people like him? He didn't know.

No doubt there was a protocol to follow, and naturally it was not a great idea for a woman alone to invite a homeless man into her office, so he was not surprised when she left him on the street. He might be dangerous. Desperation often leads to threat and menace. He didn't think he was a danger, at least not to her, but he couldn't be sure. He was no longer sure what he was capable of. He was surprised when she came back outside, carrying a mug of tea and a packet of biscuits, and sat down on the ground next to him. It had been raining—the wet would seep into her trousers and underwear. She was really trying. It was a nice gesture. Some would think it was patronizing, take offense. Not Toma. Toma hurt and he hated, but the man he had always been couldn't be angry at this woman for trying to find his level. It was not her fault that his level just happened to be in the gutter. She handed him the tea and biscuits and confessed, "I stole the biscuits, but honestly I think you need the calories way more than anyone in our office does."

He smelled bad—how could he not, living rough on the streets? The pertinent word in that sentence being *rough*. He saw her nose twitch involuntarily; she must be making a big effort not to pull away. He wondered whether she had enough dealings with street people to identify the length of time they had been homeless? He could grade them now. Those who had spent months or even years on the street smelled of damp and feces, alcohol and vomit, dirt that had penetrated past clothes and skin and into souls. It was almost unbearable. Not because it was the worst smell in the world—decaying rats in the walls smelled worse, death smelled worse—the sensory assault is accepting that the smell is made by another human being. A fellow human being.

People who had been on the streets for days or weeks, rather than months, smelled different. It was still overpowering, but it was just stale sweat, greasy hair, maybe urine. Other people's urine, often. Guys on their way home from trendy wine bars sometimes pissed on the homeless for sport. Toma knew this. It had happened to him.

"Thank you." He took the tea, made eye contact. It was important. Back in the day when he had a home, a wife, a child, people had called him handsome. He knew his large brown eyes were considered intelligent, even sexy. He wasn't trying to flirt with this woman. That was absurd. All that had gone. Those compulsions: desire, hope, fun. Now he existed, nothing more. And he existed to get justice. He made eye contact with this woman because maybe she could help, and she was more likely to help if she could see that his eyes were not clouded with drugs or alcohol. She would judge him. This nice woman with a wet arse who gave him sweet tea. She would try not to, but it was instinctual. She would feel hopeful if the eye contact was good.

"I'm Lexi."

"Toma Albu," he replied. "My authentic name." Few homeless people give a surname, and even first names are often made up. He wanted to show her he was different.

"So, were you waiting for me to open?" she asked. He shrugged, unwilling to expose himself by committing so immediately. He was scared to ask for help in case she wouldn't give it to him. In case she couldn't. This was his last hope. If this didn't work, he didn't know what else he could do. Find a tall bridge over a deep river, perhaps. Because why not? What did he have to live for? "Have you any plans for today?"

He shook his head, tutted. She left him to drink his tea, went back inside and then, about five or ten minutes later, returned clutching some leaflets. "There's a place you can go to get breakfast and a shower. It's about a ten-minute walk. Here's a map and the address, okay?" She was asking if he could read the leaflet. He nodded. "I'll telephone them, tell them you are on your way. Come back here afterwards and we can talk through some options." He slowly got to his feet, picked up his filthy, torn sleeping bag that was heavier than usual, bloated with rainwater. "I realize when I ask people in your position to come back to see me that there's only a ten percent or less chance of them doing so," said the woman.

"Then why risk it? Why not talk now?"

"We don't open until nine thirty, and you'll concentrate better if you've eaten something. Besides, I've worked with wilder odds. I'm secretly a bit of a gambler." She smiled. He liked her. She was joking with him, appealing to him. Treating him as a human being.

Toma spent the morning in the hostel she had recommended. He ate the breakfast they offered and took the opportunity to launder his clothes. As he waited for his clothes to wash and dry, he showered and then—standing in a borrowed, baggy tracksuit that countless men before him must have worn—shaved. He imagined how easy it would be to use the razor to slit his wrists. He thought that maybe he'd come back to this place and do exactly that tomorrow if the woman didn't listen to him. If someone didn't listen to him.

He returned to the office just after midday. He looked through the glass door and saw that it was a very small place, the desks practically on top of one another. He no longer smelled so didn't dread being close to people as he usually did, but there would be no privacy. He waited outside until she emerged. On spotting him, she said, "I can skip lunch if you want to come in."

"You shouldn't miss lunch. I'll walk with you to get your lunch."

She smiled again. She was definitely the sort who was fast to break into a beam. "Well, that's a strange inversion of the usual order."

"You mean a homeless man concerned that an office woman misses her lunch is comment-worthy?" He was suddenly irritated by her. Couldn't she understand that he used to be someone responsible, thoughtful, caring? Couldn't anyone imagine that?

She grinned. "I mean *anyone* being concerned with me missing lunch is an inversion of the usual order." He thought she was too thin. He imagined she regularly worked through her lunch break because she seemed concerned, committed. His irritation subsided. Her boss ought not to let that happen; her husband should encourage her to look after herself, as well. There was a husband, she wore a ring. He had checked. He hoped she had children, too. It would help.

They walked to Boots, and she bought them each a sandwich, crisps and a drink. They sat together on a park bench. It wasn't warm, but it wasn't raining.

"Where are your things?"

"Things?"

"This morning you had a sleeping bag."

"It fell apart when I washed it."

"Oh."

"It doesn't matter." He'd once had lots of things. Big things and small things. He'd had a life where he would sometimes be home from work in time to kiss his wife, tell her he'd take over. He'd carefully lower his son into a bath full of bubbles and toys, where the boy would babble, bathe and play. Toma would then gently lift Benke out, dry him carefully and thoroughly with a big towel, between the toes and behind the ears. Then he'd dress the child in Peppa Pig pajamas and place him softly in a bed. There was a night-light that threw out a golden light. It had small motifs twirling around the shade: cars, tractors and trains. Toma would read to his son from a colorful book, which lived with other colorful books on a shelf, until the son fell asleep.

They'd all gone.

The bath toys, the soft pajamas, the night-light, the colorful books, the wife, the child. Many things. Everything.

He should squirrel away the sandwich. He'd had breakfast. He didn't need it. Or more accurately, he might need it more later. Being on the street demanded constant forethought and planning. He bit into it anyway.

"Can you tell me your story?" she asked gently.

He took another bite. He wanted to tell her. He had to, but he hated pulling the words forward. At first, he had not been able to believe they were dead. For months he kept expecting to come home from work and find his wife behind the ironing board or in the kitchenette, his son in front of the TV. He would open the door and see them both instantly—there was nowhere to hide in their tiny flat. He would expect them to run to him, kiss him, hug him. It sounded old-fashioned. Him at work, her at home. But she was studying, too, a correspondence course in accounting. She had ambitions. She had plans to go out into the world. Be something. Do something. But Benke was young and she had to get the qualifications first, so she stayed at home, did her best to make the small, neglected flat into something that was not awful. They didn't have much. They didn't have enough. The place they lived in was a disgrace, really. Damp on the walls and in the beds, everything broken—locks, taps, cupboards, windows—and they couldn't get warm. Toma doubted an Englishman would have ever rented the place. It was all they could afford.

For months he had not accepted they were dead and so never looked for the words to say that they were. When he did finally accept that he'd never open the door to their smiles or sulks, their laughter or their grumbles, he fell into a profound, prolonged depression. He existed in a fug of antidepressants and alcohol. The months slithered by like black slippery eels. There were warnings at work. He was reluctantly let go. Someone who knew his story and felt sorry for him found him another job.

More tablets, more whiskey. The same solid grief. The warnings were more brusque the second time, the letting go less reluctant. He couldn't pay his rent. An eviction notice. Then there was a bed at the YMCA. No permanent address to write on application forms meant that there was no gainful employment to be had. Then finally there was another flat. Even worse than his home with Reveka, but better than the streets. He shared a bathroom. It was a cesspit. The place was horribly overcrowded. People and mold spores jostled for somewhere to rest. One day he tried to talk to the landlord about what needed to be done. That was the end of that, out on his ear, no notice period. Throughout this time, people asked him to explain himself. He wouldn't do it. He wouldn't trade Reveka's and Benke's lives and deaths for sympathy. For a bed, for an extra coin. Their names stuck in his throat, choking him, five years on.

The woman sighed heavily and admitted, "I Googled you this morning."

He was not offended; it was a relief. She was curious and concerned. She might be the right person. "Providing Toma Albu is your name—"

"It is."

"—then you are either a genius mathematician born in 1943, which seems unlikely because I'd peg you mid- to late-forties, or—" She left it hanging for a moment. He nodded stiffly. The pain, which people thought resided in the heart, permeated throughout his body. It throbbed in his legs, his neck, his arms. Everywhere. "Or you are a man who tragically lost his wife and child in 2014. Carbon monoxide poisoning, the result of a broken boiler."

"Yes, I am that man."

"I'm sorry."

People always said they were sorry. It wasn't their fault. What else could they say? It wasn't enough, though.

"How sorry are you? Sorry enough to help me?"

"Of course, I'll help you. There are ways to get back on your feet. I can't imagine what you've been though, but I do know that you are not the first person to find themselves on the street after such a monumental loss. I can make some calls to the Housing Advice Centre. I've seen enough cases to understand how easy it is for people who, one minute, are living fairly ordinary lives, to have a knock—not even anywhere near as profound as your loss, and then the next minute find themselves homeless. I can find you somewhere to live. I can help you find employment."

"I want justice."

She looked confused. "I read the newspaper articles about the incident, and court records. A woman, the managing agent, was brought to trial for her negligence."

Toma objected to her word *incident*. "They were murdered."

The Lexi woman looked uncomfortable. Her research would have told her that Elaine Winterdale was charged with negligence and several breaches of the Gas Safety Regulations, but not manslaughter and certainly not murder.

"The sentence might have seemed inadequate to you, and for what it's worth, I certainly thought it was, but if you think about it, Toma, even if she had been given a custodial sentence, no amount of time could bring them back."

"It wasn't her. She is just the monkey. I want the organ grinder. The bastard landlord that killed my beautiful Reveka and Benke but then wasn't held accountable."

"The landlord was exonerated. Winterdale lied to him about

the checks she was doing, and she didn't forward on the gas-board warnings to the owner. He was ignorant of all wrong-doing."

Toma shook his head. "No. I do not believe this. He has walked away and still doesn't change his ways, all these years later."

The woman weighed it up. On one hand, aggrieved people had bias and denied facts. On the other, mistakes were made. "What are you saying?" she asked cautiously.

"I accepted what the court said. I was too tired, too broken, to question. I thought it was this Winterdale woman. She said she was guilty herself. But later I stayed in another place. I discover same man is the landlord and I discover *he* is criminal. The laws, they are clear about a landlord's responsibility, right?"

"Right. Private-sector landlords are responsible for the safety of the tenants. The Gas Safety Regulations 1998 deal with landlords' duties to make sure gas appliances, fittings and flues provided for tenants are safe." It was clear the woman quoted this law frequently. Bad landlords were not confined to the Victorian era. She probably quoted it every day.

"But he doesn't do this."

She brightened. "We can investigate that. We can issue warnings. Have carbon monoxide alarms fitted by the council if the landlord fails to comply. We can stop this sort of tragedy from happening in another one of his properties. That would be something, wouldn't it?" Toma listened to her trying to sanitize the matter. Trying to rectify without rocking the boat.

"He still rents out slums," Toma insisted, his accent becoming thicker as emotion throttled him. "Since they died, I have suffered the pain, the grief, the loss, but I managed. Not lived, just existed. Never remarried although everyone said I should. Stayed loyal, stayed focused. Stayed here. How could I move back to Moldova to my sister and my cousins? I couldn't bear to leave my wife and son here alone. I have no choice but to stay. Then I lose my job, move into a hostel. End up on the streets.

Then last year someone takes me in. I work on a building site for a place to stay and food."

"No wage?"

"No. I know this is exploitation. I have no choice. I don't care. I stay in the place they offer me. It's better than the streets. But I notice the law is broken in this property. I ask who the landlord is. No one has a name but one day I stay off work. I pretend I am ill because I know that this day is rent collection and I see him, and then I recognize him. It is the same man. My old landlord. He was called into court one day during the trial, so I am sure. I would never forget his face. Then I start to wonder. Did he know after all? Is he responsible?"

"But why would Elaine Winterdale take the fall?"

"He pay her." Toma could see that the woman didn't buy into his theory. She was interested in helping, but there was a limit.

"Come back to Citizens Advice Bureau with me. We can look into this," she offered.

He understood what was happening here. He was a step ahead of her. She thought she was luring him in. She wanted him to trust her so she could introduce him to back-to-work schemes and find him better accommodation. She had enough compassion to want to see Toma on his feet again. Yes, undoubtedly she would issue warning letters about the carbon monoxide alarms to the bastard landlord, if she could track him down. She had a developed sense of responsibility and would want to stop this sort of disaster happening again if she could. She was good at her job. He nodded and stood up. He followed her through the park, back along the high street and into her office, certain that it was not him on the end of the line—it was her.

He would reel her in, a slippery, reluctant catch, maybe. But he would get her onside, convince her that his theory was a reality, and then he would use her office resources to investigate the bastard that had killed his loves. Toma would have justice. Or revenge.

CHAPTER 6

Lexi

Tuesday, April 23

I'm looking forward to the appointment with the lottery people. My family think my reserve is odd, but I'm not made of steel—of course I'm excited about this win. Over the moon. It is, as we keep saying to ourselves and each other, amazing, fantastic, spectacular. It is those and all sorts of other overused superlatives. However, I am a realist and I know that this sort of win comes with some complications and responsibilities, too. The timing couldn't be worse. I try not to think of the Pearsons and the Heathcotes because whenever I do the excited glow inside is extinguished. I feel cold and sour in my heart. I just need to understand the process, have everything locked down and agreed, and then we can really relax and enjoy our ridiculously good fortune.

Over the weekend, Jake and the kids drew up a list of stuff

they wanted to squander the money on. It was very general and included—but was not limited to—cars, property, clothes, parties, holidays. I groaned.

"Guys, that list is a lazy list." All three stared at me, uncomprehending. Both my children look a lot like their dad: dark curly hair, dark eyes. They are all beautiful to look at, compelling. They wore the same expression, too—excitement. No, scrub that—jubilation. "At least try and be specific. Don't just write 'holidays.' Write a list of places you've always wanted to visit."

Travel is edifying, right? Everyone knows that. I could happily sign off on travel. We'd do it together, we'd learn about different cultures, see what a big place the world is, after all.

"Disney Florida," yelled Logan. "Staying in, like, the best hotel. We'd fly first class, right?"

"We certainly would, mate," confirmed Jake. "I've always wanted to turn left when boarding an aircraft."

"And the Maldives. Scarlett Scott went to the Maldives last year and her Insta was amazing," chipped in Emily. "Oh, my God, no, scrub that, New York. Let's go shopping in New York! Actually, both. Can we do both?"

A few years ago there was this Irish couple who won an extraordinarily huge amount on the Euro lottery. I don't recall exactly how much. Over a hundred million. They immediately announced that they were going to be giving the bulk of it away to friends, family and good causes. A wonderful approach, very admirable, very sensible. Jake and I have agreed we'll pay off his brothers' mortgages and buy my sister a starter place. She has never managed to get on the property ladder as she is a bit of a nomad and has traveled all over the world for years. We'll send my parents on a world cruise. Something glorious and indulgent. Although, thinking about it, my dad suffers terribly with seasickness. We once caught a ferry to Calais and it was as nasty as a Tarantino movie, so a cruise probably isn't ideal for them. Maybe a safari. Or is that a bit too much now they are in their seventies? A couple of weeks in a posh pad in the South of France could work. Regret rips through my body. If only Jake's parents were alive to be part of this. They'd have been delighted. Thrilled. Well, everyone will be.

Won't they?

My mind is working one hundred to a dozen. Thoughts zap into my head, and I can't hold on to one of them for more than a moment. There are other people who can benefit from the win. There are endless worthy charities and individuals. Jake has agreed that we don't need to keep it all. We shouldn't. No one needs so much money, but lots of people need some money. My line of work starkly highlights that. I work at Citizens Advice Bureau. My job is to deliver easily accessible community advice. I'm a generalist, a sort of gatekeeper, who often simply takes notes and listens to walk-ins. I assess difficulties and point people in the right direction, toward a specialist like a lawyer, a doctor or counsellor. No problem is too big or too small to capture my attention. My average day might involve helping to stop payday lenders ruining lives or helping people fill out job applications. I am never bored at work. I enjoy the fact that I can't guess who I'm going to meet or help on a day-to-day basis. On the whole, I like how varied my work is and I certainly like the fact I can help, but sometimes it depresses me that people's vulnerabilities and needs are so far-reaching. Sometimes I come home from work exhausted, aware that no matter how many people I've met with and advised, I will never be able to help everyone or solve everything.

Still, I can try. I do. Day after day. And now I'll be able to do more.

I push the kids out the door just in time to catch the school bus, grab my handbag and hurriedly shove my feet into my work shoes. I glance around the kitchen. It's chaos as usual, but I'm running late and haven't even got time to stack the dishwasher.

It will be waiting for me later. Then I notice Jake sitting at the breakfast bar, still in his pajamas.

"Why aren't you dressed?"

"I'm not going to work today. The meeting with the lottery people is at three o'clock. There's no point."

"Well, I am."

"Apparently. Don't you feel like playing hooky, even for a day?" He smiles at me. His broad, charming smile that I've found irresistible more times than I can count. "We could go into London again, have lunch somewhere ridiculously swanky. Maybe The Shard? Nobu? There's plenty of time," he coaxes.

I have to steel myself against the temptation he's presenting. I should point out the flaw in his logic. If there isn't enough time to go to work, how is there enough time to have a long lunch? I don't. I just say, "I have meetings in my diary. I can't let people down." I quickly kiss him on the lips. He pulls me close and draws out the kiss. Being wealthy is obviously making him feel very randy. I giggle and gently move away, walk toward the door. "Hey, I've been thinking, when we talk to the advisor today, maybe she could give us some advice on how to choose which charities to donate to. You know, really get an understanding of which ones put money to work and which simply spend a fortune on advertising and their CEOs' salaries."

"Yes, sounds like a plan." Jake smiles affably.

"Because I was thinking, we can pay off our mortgage and then put some away for the kids. Let's say we keep two-point-eight million and then give the rest away."

"What?" Jake barks out a fake laugh. "Hilarious."

I freeze. "I'm serious."

"We'd quickly get through that amount. It would go nowhere."

"The kids bought everything they wanted in Topshop yesterday. Some of it didn't even fit properly, let alone suit them."

I was a bit startled with how greedily Emily and Logan had

behaved. I understand, of course, they are teens in Topshop, the equivalent to kids in a sweetshop. They were bound to get carried away. Being greedy is the normal reaction to a lottery win. Most people would think I am the one acting strangely by still thinking of purchasing items in terms of what we need. Jake and the kids have quickly swapped to only thinking about what they want. But, regardless, even during their high-octane retail frenzy, they spent less than a thousand pounds each. Admittedly, way more than we've ever spent in one go on clothes before, but only a tiny fraction of what we've just won. I can't imagine how we would use it all.

"Think bigger, Lexi," Jake urges. "Didn't you see that hotel in New York cost eighty thousand quid?"

"How much?" My voice comes out unexpectedly high and squeaky. Jake laughs. He's been ceaselessly laughing since our numbers came up. I don't recognize him. I am beginning to think he is technically hysterical. "I thought that was a mistake. It can't cost that much. I thought there was a decimal point in the wrong place because no one in the world would ever pay eighty grand for a weeklong holiday."

"There was no mistake, Lexi. Two superior rooms, one suite in one of the world's best hotels for a week, that's what it costs."

"That's ridiculous."

"It would have been ridiculous last week but now, it's a drop in the ocean," says Jake, grinning like the Cheshire cat. "It's a different world."

"Not our world."

"Well, it hasn't been, no, but it can be now. That's my point, sweetheart. We have an opportunity to live completely differently."

"But on Saturday night, we agreed we'd donate to charities."

"Yes. Absolutely. We will. But we can't give fifteen million away. What if the kids want apartments in London when they grow up? They cost a couple of million now."

I shrug. "Well, yes, I suppose some flats might, but it depends where you buy and—" Jake kisses me, silencing me. He cups my face in his hands. As he breaks away from the kiss, he holds eye contact. I feel dizzy. Woozy. I didn't sleep well again last night. I'm light-headed and struggling to think straight.

"You are going to be late for work if you don't get going. This is a lot to think about. Take a deep breath."

CHAPTER 7

Lexi

I've missed my usual bus, so have to take the next one and therefore I arrive twenty minutes later than normal, which still isn't officially late as I'm usually indecently early. I like a few minutes to myself in the mornings. Today, most of my coworkers are already at their desks. I throw out small, friendly waves and general greetings. I've made the right call. Being in the office, a place where I come week after week and simply try my best, is somehow reassuring. It is crazy to need reassurance after such news—after what is universally accepted to be the best news in the world—but I do. Everyone here is behaving in a dependable, ordinary way. And I like it. Jake and the children's frenzied excitement and constant chatter about what they are going to buy next is proving to be exhausting.

Rob is stirring some hot water into a pot of oats, the breakfast he always has at his desk. He stirs slowly, anticlockwise. Judy is vaping outside in the street. At all times she insists on keeping the door to the office open as she hates to miss out on any of the chatter. It is essential to her to know who watched what on TV on the weekend, even if it means everyone else catches a chill. Heidi still has her earbuds in. She likes to listen to audio books and hates stopping midchapter. Most of my coworkers simply have their heads down. The office opens at 9:30 a.m., and these fifteen minutes represent the calm before the storm. They are generally used to gather thoughts and breath.

I plunk down in front of my screen, flick open my diary and run through today's to-do list. This morning is drop-in clinic. I desperately hope Toma will come in today. Over the past few months I have been investigating his claim that the property owner was ultimately responsible for the appalling conditions in the bedsit he shared with his wife and child. Ultimately responsible for their deaths. Together, we have researched his hunch that Elaine Winterdale took the fall for her dodgy boss or bosses. It quickly became apparent that his hunch was likely to be correct. As soon as the trial was over, she moved into a brand-new, high-end apartment. We discovered that she didn't own it and that the registered owner was the same company as that of the property the Albu family had lived in. It looks a lot like a sweetener to me. More digging around led to the discovery that the same property company is responsible for a number of slum residencies, just as Toma claimed, including the one Toma lived in for a while when he was working for nothing other than food and a place to stay. So not only a slum landlord then, although that would be bad enough, but a modern-day slaver. This landlord had not learned a lesson. Far from it.

Through not entirely legal means, we've managed to find our way into three of these slum properties. I'm not proud of this. I do try to follow rules, and of course I respect laws, but sometimes the end justifies the means. It's not as though we were breaking and entering. I just flashed my business cards and said

I had been asked to inspect the properties. I should have been prepared. After all, Toma had told me he'd had no heating in his property for two-and-a-half years—other than one small electric fire that they only dared use spasmodically because of the expense—but nothing prepared me.

These places horrified me.

One of the properties had no carpets, just bare floorboards. None of them had curtains to offer privacy or even hide the cracked or missing windowpanes. In two of the properties there were no doors on any of the kitchen cupboards. I suspected that most likely someone, in desperation, had broken them off and burned them for fuel. There was damp on the walls in all three places and the shared bathroom facilities turned my stomach. It's disgusting expecting people to live this way. It's cruel, debasing.

None of the properties had carbon monoxide alarms, and one of them had a boiler that needed to be condemned immediately. I called the gas board. I've written to the registered owner and to the councils where the properties are located, stating the need for alarms and other vital improvement measures. I'm taking appropriate action where I can, but I am not getting very far. Until Friday I couldn't even attach a name to the property company. Corrupt landlords don't readily expose their identities. It's taken a lot of digging to finally find the name of the individual who is responsible.

I had planned to share that information with Toma straight away. I was desperate to, but now I'm not so certain. Would he be able to cope with the knowledge I have? What would he do with it? The sad truth is, I think it's unlikely that the landlord will ever be put away for a crime that Elaine Winterdale has already pleaded guilty to.

It isn't fair. Writing letters isn't enough. And I know Toma will think so, too. They are not going to get away with it. I can't—I won't—let that happen.

We have to be more creative in seeking justice.

Usually, I try not to get personally involved in the cases I work on. It doesn't help, not in the end. I'm compassionate—that's a given or I wouldn't do this line of work—but it's best to stay objective, efficient, clear-sighted. I do my best work that way. The past couple of months, since Toma Albu came into my life, that has been increasingly difficult. I can't help but admire his particular strength and dignity, his fierce loyalty and determination. I understand him. I realize I have become more involved than I should. It was hard not to.

And now it's impossible.

I pop my head around my boss's office door, knock as I walk in. The knocking is a courtesy. Ellie operates an open-door policy, and all the staff here think of her office as an extension of our open-plan space. Sometimes if the meeting rooms are full, Ellie vacates to give us and our clients some privacy. That's about the only time the door is ever closed.

"Hiya, Lexi, how was your weekend?" Ellie asks.

Where do I start answering that one? "Hot," I say lamely. Thank goodness I'm British and always have the weather to fall back on for conversational fodder.

"I know, right? Did you make the most of it?"

"Yes, thank you." She starts tapping her keyboard, always busy. "Ellie, I was wondering whether I could take the afternoon off. I need some personal time. Sorry about the short notice. Something has come up."

"Yes, fine. Of course."

"I'll work through my lunch but need to leave at two p.m., so I'll owe a few hours. I'll make it up this week."

"I know you will. Everything okay?" Ellie looks up from her screen. Her clever face, which is always set to host a smile, shows she is interested, ready to be concerned, but not nosy.

I nod, relieved when she doesn't probe. I don't want to lie and make up some excuse about a dentist appointment or something. I glance at my watch. "I better get at it."

"Yeah, enough slacking," she says with a grin, turning back to her own work.

My head is about to explode. The only way through this is to stay busy. I pick up the phone to set up a meeting between the head of community welfare benefit advice service and the local council's welfare rights unit. Then I set up a meeting of my own with the local branch of Age UK. There is a constant drip of people who need advice but no sign of Toma. With every client I see, I realize that writing a check will solve, or certainly ease, their problems. I have never been so conscious of the power of money, and despite my effort not to think about everything, I am. The responsibility is making me feel nauseous. At about eleven, I stand up from my desk, stretch and walk to the room that is not much bigger than a cupboard but serves as the staff room. Rob and Judy are hovering over the boiling kettle.

Judy exclaims, "Lucky sod, I wish that was me! Did you hear, Lexi? Someone local has won the lottery."

I freeze. I don't know how to reply. Luckily, Judy doesn't really expect me to. Like many of Judy's questions, it is rhetorical, and she is comfortable answering herself. "Bought the ticket on our high street, can you believe? At WHSmith. Exactly where I buy mine, when I bother. Which I don't often, just when I'm feeling lucky. I didn't this week, but I wish I had! It could have been me."

"Well, only if you'd picked the same numbers," points out Rob. Judy continues, not sidetracked by this fact. "Isn't it unbelievable to think the winner might be someone we've passed in the street. Brushed up against and we wouldn't know. Seventeen-point-eight-million pounds! Can you imagine! Lucky sods."

"How did you find out that the ticket was purchased locally?" I ask, a sliver of something uncomfortable gliding up and down my spine. I'm not used to keeping secrets. I'm normally an open book, available for anyone to read.

"Said so online. The local news feed on Twitter."

"But how could anyone know?" I ask sharply. "I mean, unless the family are taking publicity, then those details are kept private." I know this from my conversation with the lottery people on Saturday. Judy eyes me intently, and I blush. I'm not usually sharp and it must seem odd that I know the procedure so well. Have I given myself away? I'm relieved when Judy laughs.

"Are you jealous? Well, if you're right about that, then I'm guessing the winner is taking publicity." I shake my head. That's not what we agreed. Has one of the kids said something? Already? They've only been out of my sight for a few hours.

"I expect they'll announce the name of the winner soon. Just think, it might be someone who has walked through these doors and we've helped."

"Sorry to interrupt," says Heidi. "There's some Eastern European guy here to see you. I asked him if I could help, but he was pretty insistent he only wants to speak to you."

I dash out of the staff room, keen to get away from Judy and her speculation. I see Toma, sitting at my desk, with his now-familiar expression of solemnity and determination, and I feel a wave of territorialism and affection sluice through me. It's not strictly professional, but I tell myself it's not wrong, that it is manageable. My body goes hot then cold, the feeling my granny would have described as someone walking over my grave. A warning. I am suddenly certain that I can't share the knowledge I gained on Friday. Even though we have been hunting for it together, even though he is desperate for someone to blame. Because of that, I can't tell him. The knowledge would overwhelm him. Knowing the landlord's name, and also the fact he won't be brought to justice, could cause Toma to do something stupid. He might want to attack the man, kill him. It sounds extreme, but Toma, like me, believes in justice and doesn't care how unjust he has to be to get it. I have a solution. I can protect Toma. The money I've just won can be put to good.

"How are you?" I ask.

Over the past ten weeks, besides investigating Toma's claims about the slum landlord, I have also helped him find a room in a decent house. He now lodges with an elderly couple who like having him around the place because he acts like a surrogate son—their own lives in the States and calls just once a month. Toma changes lightbulbs, cuts their grass and makes them feel secure.

I can understand that.

Whenever I am with him, I, too, feel safe, assured. Even when we are creeping about grubby properties, meeting people who are unsavory through choice or circumstances. It's not his huge physical presence, it's his deep, poignant calm. I guess when the very worst thing that can happen to you has happened, nothing ever scares you again.

"I am good. Thank you." He's a man of few words.

"I'm glad you popped in. I think I may have found a lead on a job for you."

"Yes?" He looks keen. He doesn't like to be idle. He's been busy enough whilst we've been playing detective, but that has to stop now. A job might distract him, at least temporarily, from his hunt. "It's in an industrial laundry. It doesn't pay brilliantly. It's shift work."

"Could I take double shifts?"

I smile. "Well, yes, if you want to, I guess."

"I want. I've never been afraid of my own sweat. What else have I to do, besides work?"

"I hope you might find some level of community there. Many of the workers are Eastern Europeans."

"Good. Sounds good." Toma nods. "I had hoped you called me in because you tracked down the name of the landlord."

I shake my head. "Sorry." My stomach turns. I don't like lying to him.

"It's okay. I know you are trying. I know you are doing your best for me."

I am. I want to reassure Toma that everything will change for him very soon, but I force myself to keep quiet. Sometimes staying silent is the right thing to do. "Let me dig out the application form. It's a formality, really. They are keen to get labor as soon as possible. You could be at work by the day after tomorrow."

"Or maybe sooner if I walk my application to them right now. Those at the top of the mountain didn't fall there," Toma says, and then he flashes me a rare smile that beams into my core.

CHAPTER 8

Lexi

The people from the lottery company said we could have the initial meeting anywhere we liked. We decided it was easiest and most discreet to have them come to our home to go through the paperwork. I can't help but feel nervous. Once we accept the check, our lives are changed forever. No going back. But then I ask myself who would want to go back when so much good can be done going forward? Going back is crazy talk.

I pick up a carrot cake from the supermarket on the high street. I also feel the need to purchase some speciality teas. I don't want to look flash, but I do want to be welcoming. I buy teapigs, a brand I consider a treat, but I'm regretting choosing liquorice and peppermint combined. It might be challenging, could seem pretentious. What was I thinking? Still, I can always brew a regular cup of builder's tea.

I arrive home to bigger challenges than exotic tea bags. I am surprised to find Emily sunbathing in the front garden and a startling yellow Ferrari parked on the road in front of our house, incongruous against the leylandii hedge that needs trimming and the recycling bins that need emptying. I don't know much about cars, I have little interest in them beyond getting me from A to B, but even I recognize the black horse on the badge.

I'm unsure which I should ask about first: the surprise presence of my daughter or the car. Jake takes the matter into his own hands and calls out, "I treated myself!" He laughs, delighted. His hands on his hips, his legs wide, manly, triumphant, he doesn't take his eyes off the car to glance my way but adds, "And I picked up Emily because she texted me to say she was feeling unwell."

"How did you buy this? We haven't got the money in our account yet."

He beams at me now, pleased with himself as though he's just done something brilliant like got a promotion or won the fathers' race on school sports day. "I just took the winning ticket into the garage and waved it about. It was amazing. You should have seen their faces." He's giddy, not himself at all. "I'm not sure they believed me at first, but I told them we've been doing it for years and that we always use the same numbers. That we—you—buy the ticket from the same WHSmith on the high street every week, during your lunch hour. They loved the story. Lapped it up. Everyone loves a winner, right?"

Well, that solves the mystery as to how the knowledge that the winner is local was leaked onto the internet. My own husband blabbed to a sales rep who obviously couldn't resist sharing the scoop. "You took the lottery ticket into the garage?" I'm amazed at his audacity, at his stupidity. I drop my handbag to my feet and gawp at the car.

"Yeah."

"What if you'd lost it?"

Jake clocks my expression, which is no doubt a mix between

concern and irritation. "Oh, right, sorry. It was stupid of me. I shouldn't have done that. I'm just so excited!" He puts his arms around me, hugs me tightly. He murmurs into my ear. "Sorry. My bad, but don't worry, I didn't lose it." His breath is warm and his touch familiar, and I can't help but sink into it. Emily looks embarrassed at our PDA, and so Jake breaks away and starts to enthusiastically recite facts and figures about the car that make no sense to me. "Isn't she a beaut? This is the 488 GTB. It has a three-point-nine-litre engine, five hundred and thirty horsepower. The performance is outrageous, the chassis is sublime." He strokes the bonnet, practically caresses it. "This model is a big deal for Ferrari. It represents a change of philosophy for the company's mid-engine supercar." I stare at him. He could be speaking a foreign language for all I understand. Or care.

"This car doesn't actually belong to me," Jake adds. "It's on loan."

"Oh, thank goodness." My relief is short-lived, though.

"Mine won't be ready for a few weeks. Mine is red and I'm getting some customization done. That takes a bit of time. I found it hard to make a call between leather or carbon fiber door cards. I wish you'd been there to help pick. She's sensational, right?"

"How much?"

"Hey, if you need to ask, you can't afford it, and as we can afford anything you don't need to ask." He grins at me. His irrepressible, charming grin. Normally I find it overpowering; today I manage to remain focused.

"How much?"

"Well, this model is from 195,000 pounds, but we're getting a convertible and they are a smidge more."

"Two hundred thousand pounds for a car!"

"Ours will be nearer two hundred thirty." Jake sounds proud.

"You can buy a house for that."

"Yeah, if you want to," he agrees, obviously not getting my point. "Maximum speed is 205.1 mph."

"That's an illegal speed."

"Well, I won't ever actually travel that fast, of course—it's just there as an option."

"Isn't it stunning!" chips in Emily. "Although I think Dad should have gone for British racing green with a red interior. I've just been looking at the colorways online."

"Why aren't you at school? What's wrong with you exactly?" My tone is harsher than I intended. Emily looks to the ground. Bringing the shutters down.

"Period pain," she mutters grumpily. "Or maybe a stomach bug?" She then shoots her father a look. I'm too busy processing the fact a car can cost over two hundred thousand pounds to notice if Emily's expression is one of embarrassment or one pleading for secrecy. It's shifty. She's obviously just skiving.

I don't want to throw cold water when Jake is so buoyant. He loves cars, and I did expect him to buy a new one with our winnings. Of course. Throughout our marriage we've made do with reliable secondhand hatchbacks. This was bound to be a moment for him. I just hadn't expected him to select one so quickly. And so *expensive*. But in the spirit of keeping the show on the road, I say, "I treated myself, too. I bought teapigs tea bags."

Jake and Emily burst out laughing. Emily recovers first when she realizes I'm not joking. "I'll put the kettle on," she offers.

"No need, I have champagne on ice," says Jake. "It's Cristal. It cost two hundred quid a bottle."

"I don't want champagne. I want a cuppa," I say.

"Yeah, but when the lottery lady gets here, she might want a glass," says Jake. With a sigh, I accept this might be true.

CHAPTER 9

Emily

I don't know if it's just because Dad is jazzed about his new car or if he has actually forgotten, but I'm massively relieved that he obviously doesn't feel the need to tell Mum the details of why I am home.

I walked out of school. It was as simple as that. Then I texted Dad. I don't want to be here.

Coming, princess. Wait until you see my chariot!

The car is awesome. It's just like this great big daffodil-colored pile of perfection. You can see it a mile off and hear it from even farther away. Dad sat at the school gates revving the engine. Since I was skipping lessons, I should have been keeping a low profile. That would have been the wise thing to do, but it was pretty cool to see kids with mouths hanging wide-open. Ridley was one of them. I pretended not to see him but I could feel his glare on my back. I flicked my hair over my shoulder and then Dad zoomed away. It cheered me up a bit after my fallout with Ridley and Megan. I just can't believe the way they acted! It was like we'd never been friends! Like we weren't a thing! So jealous.

"Did you see their faces, did you?" I asked Dad as we sped away.

"Sure did." Dad started to give me lots of info about the car then. I didn't take much of it in. I got the gist. Bottom line, the car is fast and expensive. We drove around for a bit. Neither of us wanted to go straight home—we drove past Ridley's house and Megan's house. Not, like, on purpose, that's just the way home, although I think the revving outside their homes was deliberate. Dad is definitely being more crazy since we won the lottery. I think I saw someone at the window at Ridley's house. Probably Jennifer, she's usually at home. We decided to drive on the big A road.

"Just to let her open up a bit," said Dad.

It wasn't just schoolkids who turned to look our way—every other driver stared enviously, tongues lolling. He didn't say anything for a bit, we just drove enjoying the warm feeling that comes from knowing you have it better than anyone else. Then he turned to me and asked, "So what was up at school?" I should have known I'd get grilled. Yeah, Dad is the fun parent, but he's still a parent and so always wants to know what's going on in my life.

"It sucks," I muttered.

"I thought you liked school."

"Nope."

"You used to."

I shrugged. "Ridley and I had a row. Megan, too."

"About the lottery win?"

I shrugged again because technically I wasn't supposed to talk about the lottery win but on the other hand Dad has just driven a great big, bold Ferrari up their street. Not exactly subtle.

"I know you won't believe me now, but you are young and there will be other boys, other best friends." I looked out the window. He's wrong. Every emotion I have ever felt wanted to explode out of my body right then. I am, like, obviously really, really happy we are so rich but I just can't believe Ridley and Megan! How could they act like that? It feels like they've punched me. I can't explain it. Even if I could, Dad wouldn't get it. He's too old. Because I didn't say anything he carried on, "And maybe it's for the best. You are going to be busy in the next few months."

"With my GCSEs," I said with a groan. I'm in Year 10 but my GCSE mock of the mocks are in a couple of months' time. Honestly, the results make zero difference to precisely anything but my parents still talk about those exams approximately every thirty seconds.

"Busy spending money," laughed Dad. "We'll be moving to a new house, going on holidays." I beamed at him, relieved. To hell with school. I don't need qualifications now! We are rich!

It was brutal today.

Ridley and Megan went schizo. They were pleased for me for like a split second when they thought that the win was between all three families but as soon as I told them that their parents had chucked in the syndicate before the win, they went proper mental. They kept saying that it wasn't fair, and it wasn't right. Megan said—and I quote—she "hated fucking rich bitches." She said we weren't going to be able to be friends anymore. Just like that. An actual lifetime of friendship, like, binned.

"Ridley, what about you? Do you feel the same?" I asked, pulling him by the arm to make him face me. You know it's weird, even in the middle of a big row the touch of him floors me. I feel him all the way through my body. Like I've swallowed him whole, or something.

"Em, this is hard."

He is the only person who calls me Em. My mum is pretty keen that I get the full Emily thing as her homage to Emily Brontë and corrects most people if they dare to shorten it. She doesn't do that to Ridley, though. She has some boundaries. He calls me Em and I call him Rids. It's our thing. And even though he wouldn't look me in the eye, his gaze bolted to the floor, he did call me Em so I was melting. Megan had stomped off, but was doing that annoying thing she sometimes does when she's in a mood; she doesn't disappear altogether, just keeps herself in our periphery, so we'll chase after her. She can be quite the attention seeker. "I mean, I'm pleased for you," he added. "It's great news but I didn't know my mum and dad had ditched the lottery. Probably Megan didn't know, either. So when you said you'd won, I thought we'd all won. You know?" He kept glancing over at Megan as he explained this. "She's upset. I'll go and talk to her."

"I'm upset, too."

"Yeah, but you are rich upset and that's never as bad." He flashed me a fast grin and then ran off to catch up with Megan. It was confusing because in that moment I sort of thought I had everything and nothing at the same time.

Driving in Dad's new car was fun, but I couldn't get Ridley and Megan out of my head. "Can I leave school, Dad?"

"Maybe. You could take a year out, get tutors as we travel. Or just take a year out and drop back a year when you return. You're young in your school year and, anyway, there's more to life than classrooms. Your mum and I need to flesh out a plan. You can certainly change school if don't like the one you are at. We can send you to a private school if you want."

"Yeah, I think I do."

That's when he said we should loop back and pass the Heathcotes' and Pearsons' houses just one more time. God, that engine is loud.

CHAPTER 10

Lexi

I instantly like the lady from the lottery, Gillian. She looks just like someone who could work alongside me at Citizens Advice Bureau. Sensible, bordering on mumsy. She has dyed blond hair; her roots are a mix of a darker color and some premature gray streaks. She probably does her own color in the bathroom at home, like I do. This is somehow reassuring. Gillian wears secretary glasses and carries a large handbag that is functional rather than beautiful.

"Would you like a cup of tea?" I offer. I've laid out the cake, plates and mugs. I would have put out cups and saucers if we had any—we don't. Emily says maybe we should buy some now. I also forgot to buy paper napkins.

"Oh, yes please. Just straightforward builder's with milk, no sugar," says Gillian, in the tone of a woman gasping for a cuppa after a long car journey.

"I thought champagne would be more appropriate." Jake is holding the bottle aloft.

Gillian flashes a fast look between the two of us; we are being weighed up. I do the same when sat opposite clients at the CAB. The advice I offer is always the same, but has to be delivered in a myriad of ways depending on what sort of person I am talking to.

"I'll have whatever you're having. Champagne is always lovely, but I'm driving so only half a glass for me. I have a lot of information for you, so I guess it depends how good you are at keeping a clear head," Gillian replies with a diplomatic chuckle.

Jake is already twisting the wire that encases the cork. He bounces into the kitchen to pour. Gillian and I sit in silence until we hear the pop sound. Then Gillian smiles. "You have so much to celebrate."

"Yes, we do."

We toast. Jake downs his as though it's going out of fashion, then immediately refills his glass. Gillian begins to pull documents and files from her large handbag and sets about pegging our dreamy unreality into something that approaches a practical proposal.

"We need to set up meetings with accountants and financial advisors. As you can imagine, it wouldn't do to pop this sort of money into a high street bank. You can get it to work harder for you if you talk to the wealth management arm of your bank."

"Wealth management arm?"

"Looking at who you currently bank with, I'd suggest Coutts. Have you heard of them?"

I think of the elegant branding on the side of a massive, seemingly impenetrable building I sometimes pass on the Strand, in London. Only ever pass—I've never dreamed of going in. Curly, rich-looking black lettering on a creamy background. Coutts is the royal family's bank. "Will they accept us?" I ask.

"Without a doubt," Gillian says, and smiles.

"Money talks," chips in Emily.

"Money shouts," laughs Jake.

I'm uncomfortable with Emily being privy to this conversation about finances. In the past, we've always avoided talking about money in front of the kids. Although that was because previously all our discussions were about whether we had enough and if not, how could we make more?

"My notes say you are undecided about publicity, but we've been online and there's already a leak that the winner is local to this area. Is it to do with...?" Gillian tactfully trails off, but swivels her eyes to the front garden where the car is parked.

"Yes," I confirm. "My husband lacks discretion."

"Ah, but I make up for it in enthusiasm." Jake taps his fingers in a way that imitates someone hitting a cymbal. Emily laughs. Gillian smiles politely. I swear the man doesn't take drugs, but he's as high as a kite.

"Well, I suggest you take publicity now. With the leak and a Ferrari parked on your road, it will only be a matter of time before the local press reveal who has won the seventeen-point-eight-million pounds. If that happens, you can't easily control the narrative. If we take the lead, then we can help direct and manage the publicity so that it's the least intrusive."

"Control the narrative?" I ask, bemused.

"Well, there's a lovely story to be told here," says Gillian with a reassuring smile. "Family of four, big win, people will relate." She means ordinary family. We're quite ordinary. She's just too polite to put it into words. She could, I wouldn't mind. I am okay with being ordinary. I smile. If it's a little stiff, Gillian doesn't seem to notice. "We can introduce you to publicists and even image consultants if you want." I have no idea what an image consultant is, but I nod anyway. I want a team...support. "In that case, if you are taking publicity, we need to set up a little ceremony to hand over the enormous check. That can be a lot of fun. How about this Friday? Does that work?"

"Yes, I only work a half day on Fridays, I'm sure I can swing it," I say. Again, Jake and Emily giggle between themselves. Clearly work and school are not considerations for their availability.

"It can take place wherever you want, but I'd suggest not in your home. Maybe at a local country house, somewhere grand for the photos. We'll invite the local press and radio stations. We'll talk you through the sort of questions they are likely to ask. We can practise answers if you like. There's nothing to worry about. It won't be huge. This isn't a national story."

"It's not?" I'm relieved.

"Not really. You'd need to have won sixty million upwards to make the national press."

"Imagine that," says Jake in awe.

"I took the liberty of scouting around the area this morning, in case you did want to go in this direction. This manor house hotel looks lovely. Just the ticket." Gillian hands over her iPad. "I've already spoken to the events manager there. They can accommodate us, if you like it." There are pictures of the stately home hotel, Camberwell Manor. I know of it; they host big weddings and corporate balls. I've never visited, but somewhere in the very back of my mind I've always thought it might be the perfect venue for Emily's wedding in, say, fifteen years' time.

"Very nice." I nod.

"Yup, great. I always wanted to take the publicity. I think it will be fun," comments Jake. "Only one thing. Will we have to wait until Friday to get the actual money? We were originally told it could be in our account by Wednesday."

I close my eyes, embarrassed by his greedy keenness.

"The check is symbolic. You can't actually cash it," points out Gillian.

"No, thought not."

"However, of course we can get the money in your account sooner if that's what you want."

"It is," replies Jake firmly.

CHAPTER 11

Emily

Friday, April 26

The lottery company arranges for a car to pick us up so that both Mum and Dad can have a glass of champagne at the press conference without anyone suggesting they will be driving home under the influence. Dad says he could have "just the one" and still drive and that he wants to drive there in the Ferrari. Mum says he can't because even if he is technically under the limit, it will make a very bad story if any of the journos notice. Dad says Gillian said we're not as big a story as all that. He sounds disappointed by this. Mum says we don't want to become a bigger story for the wrong reasons and anyway we can't all fit in the Ferrari. Logan says if Dad is driving then he wants to go with Dad because the Ferrari is dead cool. Mum pushes us all into the lottery car, which is a stretch limo and not too shabby anyway. She says she doesn't want to hear another word.

Final!

Camberwell Manor is pretty grand in an old-fashioned way. There's a graveled, tree-lined driveway. Inside there are lots of ancient, scruffy rugs on the wooden floors and lots of paneled walls. Posh people like both things. It's not how I'd decorate a country house if I had one. I'd go all modern, channel the surprise of the unexpected, but I can see its appeal. We are shown into a high-ceilinged room that has pictures of strangely proportioned horses and insipid country scenes hanging on the walls. There are about twenty chairs set up facing a lectern. We are offered drinks. I ask for a cappuccino, but someone brings both Logan and me Coke—full fat so I don't touch mine. A few journalists start to arrive. They are polarized; they either strut hastily through the door, sweating because they seem to think they are late and want everyone to know they are busy and therefore in demand, important, or they saunter, clearly prepared to linger over the elevenses on offer and make the "job" last all morning. Dad says it depends entirely as to whether they are staffers or freelancers. A couple of them are struggling to carry lots of equipment—tripods and real cameras—as though the iPhone hadn't been invented. None of them are sharp and sassy like I thought they'd be. I guess they are all slightly disappointed that the internet has been invented and Fleet Street is no more. I know that Fleet Street was an exciting journo hub in the ancient past from some novel I read by Evelyn Waugh for English, and also from Dad, who often talks about disappointing careers.

The journos are all local and it's obvious that they know each other. They happily chat among themselves, asking after one another's kids and partners. It sort of starts to feel like a party. Not my kind of party but a parent party. They smile at us, and we shyly smile back, but Gillian, the woman from the lottery company who seems to be our sort of rich-person babysitter, has made it clear it's best not to say too much to the press until we make the announcement, then there will be an open-floor question-and-answer session. Whilst the journos tuck into the cakes that Gillian has arranged, our family largely holds back. Only Logan bothers. He eats three éclairs and a doughnut in about five seconds. I think the rest of us are a bit nervous, even Dad. When the journos have taken up most of the seats, Gillian stands behind the lectern.

I listen as she tells the world—okay, the dozen journos that work on local papers, mags and radio stations in just one of England's counties—that we are lottery winners and, suddenly, hearing her say that makes everything seem really real and brilliant. This last week we've been on shopping sprees, Dad has bought his badass car, we've booked a holiday to New York, all of this stuff has been absolutely bloody awesome. But somehow, unreal. I think Mum in particular has been worried that someone was suddenly going to take it from us, and her worry has sort of hung around in the background for everyone else. She is a constant worrier. Gran calls her worry bones, Dad calls her worry head, basically her entire anatomy is devoted to worrying. I beam at her and she beams back. Suddenly and simultaneously, we believe it. We are okay. We are winners.

At that exact moment, Carla and Patrick Pearson and Jennifer and Fred Heathcote bustle into the room. Carla's voice rings out, loud, brash, confident and—to be honest—a bit annoying.

"We're close friends, we've come to congratulate. Let us in."

It's a command, not a request. The guy we met when we arrived at the hotel, who was standing behind a desk that said Concierge, is obviously not heavyweight security. He politely steps aside and allows the Heathcotes and Pearsons access. All eyes are on them. Gillian waits patiently for the newcomers to find a seat. But they don't sit. I glance about for Ridley and Megan. There's no sign of them. Since our row on Tuesday I haven't heard from either of them. Not a word! Unbelievable! I haven't been into school this week. I can't face it. There's literally no point to school if I don't have Ridley and Megan. Mum has gone nuts with me practically every day because she hasn't really bought the excuse of my having a bad stomach, but Dad has backed me, so in the end she's given in. Before the win, there was no way on earth she would let me go shopping on a sick day, but that happened. I wish Ridley was here. I look pretty hot in my new midcalf-length pink dress from Boss...probably supposed to be on the knee but since I'm vertically challenged it is a little longer on me.

I glance at Mum and Dad. They are not smiling. They are both stone-still and bone white. I know Mum didn't want the Heathcotes and Pearsons to know about the win yet; she's going to go ape when she finds out I told. Dad cared less. I guess he accepts we have to face their reaction at some point. Will the parents be jealous, like Ridley and Megan? Or will they be more reasonable? They said they were here to congratulate. I hope so, then perhaps Megan, Rids and I can make up.

Jennifer and Fred are Ridley's parents. Ridley looks like his dad, but he has the same smile as his mum. She's not smiling now, though—her jaw is set with a grim determination. The Heathcotes are dressed as they dress most of the time: smart. Not fashionable but somehow decidedly suitable. Classic. Jennifer has expensive-looking caramel highlights in her hair, and I think she's probably just had a trim to sharpen things up. She always looks as though she's just stepped out of a hair salon. Fred has a beard and it makes him look like some old royal duke or something. I can't quite describe it, but they've nailed the look I'm pretty sure Mum and Dad were hoping to discover when we were trailing around New Bond Street, money burning a hole in their pockets. Mum has told me before that Jennifer and Fred are actually very posh in a way that none of our other friends are. They both went to boarding school and she had a pony when she was a kid. I think maybe Carla and Patrick are actually richer now, they certainly live in the biggest house, but despite this Jennifer and Fred are the ones everyone admires the most, I think. Because they are so proper and different. They are very nice. Polite, you know?

I glance at my parents. They look cool, younger than either the Pearsons or Heathcotes, but they also look a bit too shiny. They are undoubtedly people wearing new clothes, which is never a good thing. Except maybe on holiday. My mum is basically pretty but doesn't do anything about it and as neither Carla nor Jennifer work, they both have a lot of time to go to the gym and beauty salon. Maybe now we are millionaires, Mum can even things up a bit. I remember once joking with her that when me and Ridley get married, she'll have to work really hard not to let the mother of the groom outshine the mother of the bride. All she said to that, though, was, "You're too young to be talking about marriage." Mum isn't really very competitive.

Is Ridley still even my boyfriend? The thought scuttling into my mind sends actual shots of pain through me, like someone is repeatedly flicking at my flesh. This has to be a blip. It has to be! Patrick, Megan's dad, is wearing his usual weekday uniform, a suit and tie. I briefly wonder why he is not at work. Usually Patrick is permanently attached to his phone and talks about nothing except work. Not something my dad is guilty of. In fact, shouldn't both Patrick and Fred be at their offices? It's got to be a good sign that they've taken time off specially to come to this press announcement, hasn't it? They must want to be supportive. Or at the very least, to suck up to us. I'm pretty sure that now they know we are lottery winners they'll want to scam a free holiday when we rent some amazing chateau somewhere. Everything is going to be okay. Once they see how generous we'll be. I'll get my boyfriend and my best friend back. Things will be okay.

Carla basically looks better than I've ever seen her look. She is wearing a green-and-blue midcalf, slim-fitting but not vulgarly tight body-con dress. Green and blue shouldn't work but it does. The season is all about the bold colors. A woman in

Armani told me that when we were on our shopping spree. I have to admit it, Carla has upstaged Mum. Honestly? She always kind of does upstage everyone. Carla likes to be the best at everything. She has to be the slimmest, the chicest, the fastest if they go on a run. Her kids certainly have to be the cleverest. Look, that's just my opinion. Mum likes Carla a lot, but I think she's a bit full-on. You know, she's one of those mothers that can tell you exactly what percentage Megan got in her mid-week Physics test and who played defensive fullback in Megan's last hockey match. Megan has two younger brothers, Scott who is twelve and Teddy who is nine. Carla watches them all like a hawk. She constantly complains how exhausting it is being a mother of three, but I wonder what would she do with herself if she wasn't living through them?

At least I can't complain that my mum lives through me.

Gillian politely asks the Heathcotes and Pearsons to take a seat two or three times over, but they still don't. Instead, Patrick marches up to the microphone. "Ladies and gentlemen of the press," he says, which is a bit over-the-top, but he can do that. He knows that a slow, posh voice makes people sit up and listen. "We are thrilled that the entire syndicate of winners are able to be here today after all, for this photo opportunity, rather than just the syndicate representatives, Mr. and Mrs. Greenwood."

What? I don't get it! I turn to Mum and Dad, who look like a bus has just hit them. No one seems to know what is going on and there's a confused murmur throughout the room. The words "syndicate" and "team" are repeated by the press people, over and over, the words are stones, the pond is rippling. What is he on about? There *isn't* a syndicate anymore. They dropped out!

Mum opens her mouth, but no words come out, just a little *phut* sound. She reaches for my hand and puts her other arm around Logan's shoulders, but her gesture isn't comforting, it's freaking me out. She's behaving like when she had to tell me

Grandpa Greenwood had died. And I'm behaving a bit the same, too. My brain is heavy and slow, like wet cotton wool.

"Fuck off," says Dad. "You are *not* the fucking winners. We are *not* a syndicate."

The "ladies and gentlemen of the press" suddenly turn from lethargic doughnut-eating sloths into twitching, hungry beasts sniffing out a story. So much closer to the journo stereotype I had imagined, but also quite frightening. They leap to their feet and start yelling questions at us. "So, this is a syndicate win? The six of you are winners?" one journalist shouts loudly. It's basically the same question that everyone is asking, so people pipe down and wait for a response.

"No, there are not six fucking winners," my dad yells back. It's not like him to swear so much. I mean, if he hits his thumb with a hammer the air turns blue, but mostly, in front of Logan and me, he's pretty careful not to say any of the words that we hear constantly at school. I don't like to see him losing control. I don't think it's helping, and I get the feeling we do need help. A number of journalists scribble something in their books. I can't think that's a good thing.

"We have all been doing the lottery together for fifteen years, four months," says Patrick loudly, although no one asked. He sounds calm and smooth. Authoritative. "We, as a group, have bought a ticket every single week for all those years." He has hold of Carla's hand. She is smiling at the cameras, she is very photogenic.

"That's not true," insists Dad.

"What's not true?" asks Patrick. He turns to my dad, smiling. But it's a bullshit, so obviously fake smile. How could anyone be convinced by it? "Have we, or have we not, been a syndicate for over fifteen years?"

Oh, no. I can see the train wreck that is coming. This is such a classic move. I see it at school all the time. But I can't warn my dad. He walks right into it, admitting, "Well, yes."

"And have we, or have we not, always used those exact same numbers?"

Dad nods and tries to say something else. He's stuttering. His spittle makes it into the room but not his words, because Patrick smoothly turns back to the journalists, smiling triumphantly, point seemingly proven.

"But you pulled out of the syndicate the week before we won," Dad protests.

The Heathcotes and Pearsons pull their faces into textbook expressions of confusion and incredulity. Carla tuts, shakes her head. Jennifer looks to the floor as though she's embarrassed for my dad, shyly tilting her head. Then Fred slaps Dad on the back, quite forcefully, "Good joke, old man, but enough is enough now."

"I'm not fucking joking," yells Dad.

Mum touches his arm. "Stop swearing, Jake."

He stares at her murderously. "Is that all you can say? You are worried that I am swearing when these bastards are up here trying to steal from us?"

"Okay, okay, that's enough now." Gillian is on her feet. She signals for help and suddenly the hotel manager swiftly ushers us out of the press conference into another room. The Heathcotes and Pearsons follow us, as do a couple of the hotel staff, sensing that all sorts of crazy is about to go down. They probably haven't had as good a day at work ever. The journalists are being ushered by security into the foyer. Gillian seems to be talking to everyone at once.

"We will release a full statement before anyone goes to press. If I can ask you to refrain from reporting anything, either online or in print, until you get that statement that would be a great help." I suppose she's appealing to their better natures, hoping that the local press will be generous as they've enjoyed the doughnuts, but I wonder what the legal position is. Everything that has been said has been said at a press conference. Probably they can report what they like and at least one of them most likely will.

The moment we are out of the journalists' sight, Patrick pounces on Dad. It's really scary. "What's the fucking game, Jake?" he demands. He pushes Dad up against the wall, holding him around the neck. Patrick's face is puce. He's a really good actor. He keeps glancing around the room to ensure all the staff are seeing him put on this performance. They seem scared. I look around for the two security guys but they are busy escorting the journos off the premises. Patrick looks genuinely wild. I've never seen such unadulterated violence and anger in a person's face. Dad is way fitter than Patrick and I expect him to just push him away, but he doesn't—he glares with contempt. This seems to infuriate Patrick more. He tightens his grip around Dad's throat.

"Let him go!" yells Mum, lurching forward. I wrap my arms around Logan, restraining him from piling in, but also because I really need to hug him. Then Fred leaps into action. He roughly grabs Patrick's shoulders and pulls him off Dad. I guess he's effective because none of us expected Fred to become embroiled physically, he's a pretty mild-mannered man. My body relaxes as I feel a huge wave of relief and gratitude. Fred has calmed things down. But then—shocker—Fred punches Dad in the stomach! "You bastard," he growls.

Dad goes down like a sack of potatoes. Mum rushes to him and covers him with her body. "Jesus, Fred, what are you thinking? Stop this!" she yells. Neither Jennifer nor Carla say anything to their husbands. Jennifer walks calmly to the table that is set up with ice water and glasses. She carefully pours a glass and then hands it to my dad.

Adults are un-fucking-believable.

Mum stands up and steps away from Dad. I suppose she thinks it's over and he's safe now, but Patrick grabs my dad by the collar of his suit and hauls him to his feet. Dad is struggling to breathe properly, winded by the punch, but he tries to appear ballsy. "Easy, easy friend," he says, putting up his hands in appeasement, showing the room he is surrendering. That he is reasonable and wronged. I look around in desperation. Why isn't anyone helping? Patrick tightens his grip, shakes Dad viciously, a bit the way a terrier shakes a rat.

"We are not friends," he insists. He draws his fist back and I think he's going to hit Dad, too. Fred's punch was shocking, it took Dad down because he was not expecting it. I fear Patrick will land something far more malicious and damaging. He's a stocky man. Right now, he looks like a brutal little barrel that could roll over anything in his path and destroy it. His face is contorted with a filthy anger. I scream, everyone turns to look at me. They seem surprised that Logan and I are here. I think they'd forgotten about us. As though I've pulled them to their senses, the hotel manager dashes out of the room. I hope he's gone for help.

"Stop it, please. Let go of him," begs Logan, who's crying now.

"This is what you get if you mess around with the big boys," snarls Patrick. "You should know that." I think Patrick is talking to Logan, but his eyes are on Dad.

At that moment, Gillian enters the room. The hotel manager is hovering at her side, unsure what to do with himself. I want to be sick.

"Let go of him at once or I shall call the police," Gillian instructs.

"Why don't you do that?" bluffs Patrick, but he does immediately step away from Dad. Logan and I run to him, wrap ourselves around him.

"Lexi, Jake. I've called you a lawyer, she'll be here in twenty minutes," says Gillian.

"Oh, I don't think we need lawyers, do we?" chips in Jennifer. "We're all friends here, aren't we?"

"Are we?" snaps Mum. "How was your trip to Fred's sister's last weekend?" Jennifer holds Mum's gaze, but doesn't answer her. Mum turns to Fred. "Your wife told me you were going away but that's not true, is it? You didn't go away." Fred looks confused, unsure how to answer.

"Is that why you are lying about the syndicate?" Carla asks. She doesn't seem fazed by the fact her husband has just acted like a basic thug. I mean, it was so outrageous, so disgusting! Why isn't she more riled? She just continues interrogating Mum.

"Your feelings are hurt because they didn't invite you to dinner one particular night and so now you are trying to cut us out of the syndicate. Lie about us. Steal millions from us."

"No!" says Mum hotly. "Well, yes."

"Yes, you are lying!" Patrick throws a triumphant look Gillian's way. "Well done for admitting it, Lexi, now let's get this sorted out fairly."

"No, no, I am not lying. I'm just saying yes, my feelings are hurt. You left the syndicate. You are not our friends. I know you for what you are." Mum isn't shouting, but she looks wrecked, I'm pretty sure she might cry any minute.

Gillian puts her hand on Mum's arm. "Okay, Lexi, Jake, I am advising you to stop talking until your lawyer gets here and we can get to the bottom of this."

"You think you can get away with this?" demands Dad, ignoring Gillian to the max.

"We're just claiming what's rightfully ours. We're not trying to get away with anything," says Carla primly.

"But you pulled out of the lottery. You said it was common," stutters Mum. I can hear the righteous indignation in her voice, but I wonder if other people will recognize it as that or just think she sounds a bit squawky.

"That's not how we remember it," says Patrick with a sneer. "I'm surprised at you, Lexi. Him—" he points at my dad "—him I expect this sort of low thing, but not you."

"Lexi bought the ticket," insists Dad.

"There was an implied contract," argues Fred. He stares right at Dad. "I am owed a great deal." He is the color of a tomato, most probably this is because he is lying. I don't imagine that comes easily to Ridley's dad, but somehow the color works in his favor. If you didn't know him, you'd think he was pretty sincere. "You may have actually purchased the ticket, Lexi, but there was a kitty. We all chipped in, as usual."

It's unbelievable. I watch as my parents' former friends all manage to pull their faces into complicated expressions that somehow communicate their regret and disappointment in Mum! They look totally innocent and credible. Honestly, they must have been rehearsing this! Mum looks like she wants to pull her hair out in fists, she probably wants to bang their heads against the wall—I know I do. The lying, thieving con artists!

Mum turns to Dad, collapses against his chest, she's becoming increasingly unstable, hysterical. She bursts into frustrated tears and yells, "Just because you say a thing often enough doesn't make it true."

And I think of Ridley. His hand on the inside of my thigh. His chest rising and falling, as he took in fast, excited breaths, pushed them out again, as we moved together. *I know what I'm doing, we're safe.*

I've never felt more alone. My mum is right. Just because you say a thing often enough does not make it true.

CHAPTER 12

Lexi

Tuesday, April 30

The room is full of suited and booted men and women. It's a small space, airless. Too many expensive perfumes and after-shaves clash up against each other. It's cloying. They all flash me efficient, practiced smiles that are so brief they have gone before they've fully arrived. They hold out their hands for me to shake. No one has sweaty palms, or irritatingly weak grips, and no one tries to assert their dominance by crushing my bones. It is all very sleek; these people know how to do things properly. That makes me feel more nervous, not less. I wish someone would make a mistake. I look for laddered tights, low flies; of course, there are none.

Our lawyer is Ms. Walsh. She is a slight woman in her thirties. She looks as though a strong wind could blow her away, but when Jake and I met with her on the day of the dreadful press announcement, I was struck by her fast mind and her no-nonsense approach. She remained calm and cool with us, I admired her for that. She's someone who just wants to get on with the job at hand. Since we've become lottery winners, people mostly seem flustered around us, either sycophantic or resentful. It is refreshing to meet such neutrality.

There are two people from the lottery: Gillian and a man who I don't know. "Mick Hutch. My boss," says Gillian, pointing her thumb at him whilst pulling her face into a fake grimace that suggests they like and respect one another.

A man in his fifties, who is a poster boy for pale and stale, introduces himself as "Terrance Elliott, old family friend of Fred and Jennifer Heathcote." He is their lawyer. Yes, a family friend, too. I met him last year, at their twentieth wedding anniversary party. We spoke for several minutes about ambulance chasers, but he obviously doesn't remember me. The Heathcotes' family friends are all accountants, solicitors, doctors.

There are three more lawyers in the room. They all have a haughty, complacent air about them, undoubtedly the sort of people who are used to winning. Mr. Piper-Dunn, Mr. Caplin-Hudson and Ms. Chen-Ying all say they are representatives of Patrick and Carla Pearson. Whilst I am good at remembering names, I don't commit these three to memory but instead dub them Double Barrel 1, 2 and 3. Three. Three! They have *three* lawyers. We are the ones with millions in the bank and they have three lawyers. I feel exposed and underprepared.

"Do you mind if I record the interview?" asks Double Barrel 3.

I look at my lawyer. She smiles encouragingly. "Lexi, this is entirely voluntary. You must keep that in mind."

Gillian chips in, "You are not under arrest." Her tone suggests she is joking but my eyes widen. Gillian sees I'm frightened and quickly adds, "No one is. We're simply trying to get to the bottom of the matter." She squeezes my arm.

I take a deep breath and try not to panic. This inquiry is serious. I have never been on the wrong side of the law, and I don't like the merest implication that I am now. I have to stay calm and focused. I have to tell my story to the best of my ability. Sort this mess out. I wish I was wearing one of my new dresses—after all I've bought three this past week. But this morning I just put on the first things that came to hand: jeans, a T-shirt, trainers. Suddenly I am struck by the concern as to whether Ms. Walsh, *my* lawyer, is even *my* lawyer at all. She is someone the lottery company sourced for us. Is she representing me or is she really here for them? Is there a difference? Before the press conference I would have said not. Now I'm pretty clear the world is always divided into them and us. It's just a matter of working out which team everyone is on.

I need to step up, get back in control. Behave as I would at work where I constantly fight for the underdog, fight for what is right and fair. Justice must have its day. That's all that matters. They have to believe me. "Okay, I have nothing to hide. I'm happy for you to record my interview."

Everyone looks relieved. I've given the correct answer.

I know I am not under arrest, but I have a lot to lose. *A lot.* People are lying. Cheating. Desperate. It's dangerous. Liars undermine everything. You can't trust or know a liar. It's exhausting trying to. A waste of time. People do bad things, they make mistakes—that bothers me less. As long as they own their mistakes and failings. If people own their mistakes, you at least know what you are dealing with, and you can make a move toward forgiving them.

Maybe.

But lying? Well, lying destroys reality and histories. And futures. Besides being small and plain, the room is a bit grubby. It's nothing like the lavish room from which we made the press announcement on Friday. This place is much more like the sort of room I take my clients into at the CAB. Functional. Low budget. I ought to feel comfortable as it's so familiar, but I feel

I am on the wrong side of the table. Have I already got used to being in more splendid environments in just ten days?

The table is wobbly and scratched. Not with legible graffiti, just mindless defiance or careless neglect. There are hard chairs around it and plastic cups on top of it. These have been filled with water from the cooler in the corner. I disapprove of single-use plastic, but don't feel it's the moment to go eco-warrior. My palms sweat. My throat is dry. I take a sip of water. "So, what do you need from me?"

Gillian smiles encouragingly. "In your own words, with as much detail as possible, please, can you give an account of the evening of Saturday, the thirteenth of April 2019? That is, the week before the lottery win."

"The week you allege the Pearsons and Heathcotes dropped out of the syndicate," adds Double Barrel 2. I don't like his use of the word *allege.*

"Where do you want me to start?"

"Anywhere you like. Tell us anything you think is relevant. Set the scene if you think it helps." She presses Record on her phone. I don't know how far back to go. Our friendship group stretches way back, and my belief in the magic of Saturday night goes further back still. And Jake? Well, Jake has been forever, really. We met at university, where I was doing a degree in sociology and social policy and he was studying industrial economics. I was eighteen, he was nineteen. He and I have been an *us* all my adult life. I love Saturday nights. Always have. Since I was a teenager. To me, they represent untold opportunities, freedom. Not that I had a wild youth, far from it. Throughout school and college, I was consistently bookish and conscientious. I studied during the week and then babysat on Friday evenings. On Sundays I visited my grandparents. That is precisely why I lived for the outlet, the release from conformity, which Saturdays offered. What could be better than house parties where I snogged boys and drank cider and blackcurrant until I was ill or stupid? Where I danced to Take That and Mariah Carey and dreamed of a future which I was sure would be happy, meaningful, important?

Even when I was in my twenties, I rarely took advantage of weeknight happy hour deals. Jake and I preferred to go to bed early while our friends dashed around the city looking for people to get off with. We had each other and no interest in scouring pubs and bars to meet sexy strangers. Not that we were boring—we were young. In those days early nights did not mean sleep. Enough said.

We both savored Saturdays, though, when we got dressed up, went out with a gang and danced at various low-rent nightclubs until my feet hurt. We'd drink enough to make singing in the street on the walk home seem like a good idea. Everything changes once you have children. It's not worse, it's just different. For the past fifteen years, weekday evenings have been swallowed in a never-ending round of cooking, bathing, storytelling and then, as the kids got older, in homework supervision, ferrying them to and from their friends' houses, household admin. Basically, adulting. But Saturdays have remained fun. Largely because of our friendships with the Heathcotes and Pearsons. Our best friends. Where do I begin explaining all of this?

"Saturdays is when our gang—the gang—get together. We have dinner, a few drinks."

We tell one another hilarious stories about our bosses, our families, the other school parents. Actually, we tell each other pretty run-of-the-mill stories, but because we usually put away a week's worth of units in three hours the stories became hilarious. The incidents recounted may have originally been frustrating, saddening or aggravating, but they became amusing anecdotes. It is then that my shoulders loosen, I stop worrying about Jake's inability to find a job that he is truly inspired by, or whether I've missed the optimal time for Emily to get braces, or whether

Logan will be picked for the school football team and I just... relax. And laugh. Out loud. Sometimes until my sides ache.

"Who exactly is in this gang?" The way Double Barrel 1 says "gang" makes it sound like I head up the Mafia.

"Carla and Patrick Pearson, Jennifer and Fred Heathcote, Jake and me. We are good for each other. My frimily," I add.

"Frimily?" He raises an eyebrow.

"That's what I call us. I think I coined the phrase. We've often said we were more like family than friends. We met at childbirth classes when we were all preparing for the birth of our firstborns, over fifteen years ago now."

"Wow," says my lawyer.

I nod. I'm used to people being impressed by the longevity of our friendship. In a world where things are fleeting and unstable, where news is received in 280 characters and national treasures only expect to be flavor of the month for a week, longevity is coveted. A fifteen-year friendship means something.

Or, at least, it is supposed to.

"Time flies when you are having fun," comments Gillian.

I agree. "Gone in a blink of an eye, and yet none of us can even remember a time when we haven't known one another. You know? Sometimes it seems odd that we weren't together at college, let alone at each other's weddings."

"So, it's safe to say you are close?" asks Double Barrel 2, his posh ink pen poised to make a note.

"Yes, we're close. Or at least we were up until—" I break off. We've helped one another through childbirths, miscarriages, promotions, redundancies, house moves, new puppies and even losing parents. Every triumph and heartbreak. Even though the sitcom show *Friends* played out its final episode a year before we even met, the influence of the show was still profound. We would never say it aloud as it sounds daft but, on some level, I think the six of us have always seen ourselves as older, British versions of the twentysomethings who bounced around Manhattan. Frimily. All the eyes in the room are trained on me as I fight tears.

What's happened is so sad. Money is glorious. Money corrupts. Ruins things. I need to go further back. The past is safe.

"When we met, we all lived in London. Clapham. The six of us formed the lottery syndicate when our first babies were very young and we were housebound because finding reliable babysitters in Clapham on a Saturday night was about as likely as finding the elixir to eternal youth." I look up hopefully, but no one responds to my small joke. I make jokes when I'm stressed. It's a much-misunderstood habit. I push on. "It was then that we started taking turns to host suppers. The evenings were often frantic juggling acts involving crying babies and badly prepared food, but we didn't care—we called it a social life. Then Jennifer and Fred announced their intention to move back to Buckinghamshire, just before Ridley's first birthday."

They had persuasively cited the many advantages of doing so. We all lived in one- or two-bedroom apartments in London. Jennifer kept saying that in Bucks we could buy decent-sized semis or even a detached doer-upper. Plus, Bucks had impressive coed grammar schools. Sort of private school, without the fees. At the time, I was struggling to get my head around Monkey Music class admissions, but Jennifer insisted that it was important to think ahead. The rail links allowed efficient commutes into London, which meant the career ambitions of the men—and any of the women who wanted to continue to work (just me)—didn't have to be curtailed by geography. Jennifer and Fred had family on the doorstep, so would have access to reliable childcare and whilst this didn't apply to the rest of us, Jennifer swore her mum was ready to be "Everyone's Granny."

"Patrick and Carla moved out just six months after Fred and Jen. They settled in the same village, Great Chester. It was only when we couldn't get a decent infant school place for Logan that we decided to join our friends and move out of the city, too," I explain.

Unfortunately, the property market was booming at the time of our move, and we really didn't get quite as much bang for our buck as we'd hoped. We settled in Little Chester, a couple of miles away which is, in every way, slightly inferior to Great Chester. Still, it has a pub, a post office and small convenience store. True, we don't live in one of the pretty wisteria-clad cottages in the high street. We live in a 1990s three-bedroom semi on the outskirts of the village, but I've never regretted the move.

Or, hardly ever.

Admittedly, there isn't quite so much to do as there was in the UK's throbbing capital: fewer shops, theaters, galleries, but we make our own entertainment.

"We fast fell into routines. When the kids were little, we frequently got together for impromptu playdates through the week. That doesn't happen now. The kids make their own arrangements and I work. But we've continued our tradition of meeting up most Saturday evenings, with the dads, too. Sometimes we throw what has to be recognized as a dinner party, other times we pick up greasy bags of fish and chips. Keep it low-key."

"How often do you meet?"

"Three weekends out of four. We rotate between each other's homes. One weekend in a month, we do something separate, just as families or with other people."

The weekends off are healthy, essential, so we can continue to appreciate each other.

"And you did the lottery on those weekends you had supper together?" asks Ms. Walsh.

"We did the lottery *every* week. It was one of my favorite things about the weekend. Even though I always thought it was sort of silly, dreamy, impossible. Probably *because* of those things."

"Well, not impossible," chips in Gillian. "You've proven that." She beams at me.

"Improbable," I correct myself.

"Have you ever won anything before?"

"We've twice won twenty pounds."

"How did you share the winnings?"

"We put it towards the takeaway the following week." I see what Double Barrel 1 is doing, but it's irrelevant. The past is irrelevant. I push on, trying not to allow him to derail me. "When the draw was still televised, we'd all watch the show together. Just for the fun of it. It was a tradition."

At least it was to me. It was one of our things. Like watching the fireworks on Guy Fawkes Night or seeing in the New Year, something we'd always done. It proved we were solid. A unit. "Now that it's not televised, sometimes someone remembers to put the news on and wait for the numbers to be announced at the end of the program, but the news is a downer and invariably brings our evening to a close. So more often than not, as dessert is being served, Jake has a sneaky peek on YouTube and then he'll announce, 'Not this week,' which generally solicits a round of playful groans and assertions, 'Next time!'"

Double Barrel 1 coughs and says, "So let's focus on Saturday the thirteenth, in particular, shall we?"

"I was hosting." We'd had a few days of dry weather and it really felt as though summer was around the corner. Summer is my season. I unfurl. Winter just has to be got through, best hope being not too many bouts of flu and not too many unwanted gifts that need returning after Christmas. "I was planning on serving drinks on the patio. I'd themed the night. Mexican. I'd made margarita cocktails. Strong ones. And I'd bought Corona and Sol."

"Sounds like quite the party."

I sense criticism in Double Barrel 2's comment and say defensively, "This sort of attention to detail is my way of showing I care. I'd even got Emily to download some Mexican tunes." It was the sort of music that makes people want to sway their hips.

"The tunes were blasting out when Carla called to say Megan wasn't coming along."

"Megan being one of the Pearsons' children?"

"Their eldest. Carla and Patrick have three children. Megan is fifteen like Emily and then they have Scott and Teddy. Twelve and nine. Emily and Megan are best friends. The Heathcotes' son is called Ridley. He's Emily's boyfriend."

"Very cozy," comments Double Barrel 3.

It doesn't sound like a compliment. It sounds like she is accusing us of incest or something. So my daughter's best friend is the daughter of one of my best friends, what could be more natural than that? And her boyfriend is the son of my other best friend. How wonderful! That is a good thing.

Or at least it was. Poor Emily.

"Sounds like a really jolly evening," says Gillian, encouragingly.

"It wasn't actually," I admit with a sigh. "Despite all my efforts, to my disappointment and—at that time—mystification, I don't think my guests were particularly comfortable. The evening had stuttered along, rather than flowed."

"And why do you think that was?"

"At first I had no idea. It wasn't as though the stilted conversation was a result of adults watching themselves around the kids. We hadn't been expecting Megan, but Ridley also failed to show up. Because neither of her friends were there, Emily hadn't bothered coming to the table. She'd shut herself in her room with a plate of toast and her phone. The younger ones had stuffed down their food as fast as humanly possible and then dashed off to play video games. Jake tried to strike up a conversation about work, but Patrick said as it was the weekend, he didn't want to think about 'the bloody office.' There was definitely an atmosphere. Something was off."

"And did you have any idea what was off?" prompts my lawyer, Ms. Walsh.

"No, not at first. No idea. But it became very apparent. The atmosphere was off because they had ganged up and decided to pull out of the lottery."

"And that was a big deal, was it?" asks Double Barrel 1. He throws out a laugh that is shot through with incredulity. Double Barrel 2 and 3 joins in.

I glower at them. "Clearly, since we are all here." I enjoy watching the smiles slide off their faces.

"But before the win, why was it such a big deal? It's just a game," insists Double Barrel 1.

Gillian coughs and wiggles on her seat. She and her boss throw a look between them. Working for the lottery company, they know, more than any of us, that it's never just a game if money is involved.

"Them wanting to leave the lottery was symbolic," I explain.

"How do you mean?"

"They were dumping us, as friends. At least that's what it felt like."

"Let's stick to the facts, should we? Rather than feelings."

Double Barrel 1 is a smug toad. I remind myself I can buy and sell his butt now, and it's some comfort. Still, I do as he asks. The outcome of this meeting will determine just how many times I can buy and sell his butt. I need to cooperate. They need to hear my story and they need to believe it.

CHAPTER 13

Lexi

"Fred was talking about, oh, something or other, I don't remember, his car engine? Tire pressure? It wasn't interesting, then Jake interrupted to announce we weren't lottery winners. Like he does pretty much every week. But that week, his interruption created an odd mood. The air was sort of heavy. I guess no one likes to be reminded that they've lost at anything, even if there was never any real expectation of winning." I shrug. Who knows? People are strange. "I broke the silence by reminding everyone it was time to chip in to the kitty again. I collect a fiver off each couple every few weeks. As each game cost two pounds, the kitty lasts a little while."

"And does everyone always pay in advance?" asks Ms. Walsh.

"Sometimes I forget to ask for the money, I just buy the tickets anyway. I'd done that for the preceding two weeks as it happened. It's just a few quid. I only mentioned the money for something to say. But then Patrick demanded, 'Why are we even doing the lottery?' His face was flushed, his voice booming. 'What's the bloody point?' he asked. He sounded angry. I couldn't understand why he wasn't just reaching for his wallet and casually handing over the cash. I guess it was the drink. I don't want to be mean about this, but facts are facts. Patrick had downed two cocktails and polished off a bottle of red before I'd even served the main. By this point in the evening he was drinking whiskey straight. It was a bottle that my mother had bought Jake for his birthday." I look at Gillian and Ms. Walsh. "I was wondering if maybe Patrick is misremembering things because of the amount he had to drink. I want to think the best of him, you know."

Gillian squeezes my arm again. My lawyer nods and asks, "In your estimation, did Mr. Pearson drink more than usual that evening?"

"Yes, I think he did. Not an unprecedented amount—we've all seen each other quite the worse for wear at some point or other over the years—but yes, thinking about it, he probably did drink more than usual. Fred, too, actually. But he's such an easygoing drunk. Just sort of dozes off in his chair."

"And Patrick isn't an easy drunk?" probes Ms. Walsh.

"He gets a bit edgy with alcohol." I pause and then admit, "Or even without it. We've all got used to his short temper. His belligerence. Jake and I have privately wondered if perhaps Patrick is a tad stretched."

"Stretched? Do you mean at work? Workload? Financially?"

"Possibly both. I don't know for a fact. It's just rumor at the school gate."

"Can you elaborate?"

"I am reluctant to speculate. When I first heard the whispers, I dismissed them. It is hard to imagine. Patrick and Carla have always been financially successful. Big house, two family holidays a year. Patrick has his fingers in many pies, he talks about his investments a lot. Jennifer and Fred are comfortable, too, although they talk about money less. Fred insists his job is dreary and rarely mentions it beyond saying his boss is a wanker. Until our numbers came up, we simply got by."

"What happened next?"

"We all started to talk about what we would spend our money on if we won. Just joking about, you know. That's when Patrick turned quite nasty."

"Nasty?"

"He shouted, 'Will you cut the crap. All this talk about lottery wins is doing my head in.' The more I think about it, the more I believe maybe he does have money issues and that's why he's making this stuff up. I almost feel sorry for him." I stare right at Double Barrel 1. "You need to know, even if the money was split three ways, that's an enormous amount to us. We wouldn't keep it from them if they were due it. But I'm not a pushover. I'm not going to cough up the cash after the way they insulted Jake."

"Insulted him?" asks Ms. Walsh.

"Patrick said the lottery was common, that it was for losers." I glance apologetically at Gillian and Mick Hutch. "He wouldn't let it go. He said he only had ever done it to humor Jake. He was quite patronizing. Quite personal. Going on about Jake liking a wager, as though Jake was some gambling addict. He kept coming back to the common thing. He was behaving like a real snob. Going on about people on benefits, 'doleys' he called them, and he compared doing the lottery with taking your shirt off in public or having a tattoo."

"Well, none of those are criminal offenses," comments Gillian tartly. She has a tattoo on her wrist, a small bird.

"I know that. Jake has a tattoo. It was clear what Patrick was saying. He was saying *we* are common. I tried to reason with him. I pointed out that the school's Parents Association runs a raffle every term. It's the same thing. I challenged him on why he'd suddenly had a change of heart, after all those years."

"Yes, the exact question I was going to ask," challenges Double Barrel 2. "It doesn't make sense."

"Well, I suppose people change." I take a deep breath and stare across the table at the gaggle of lawyers who are opposing us. "Look, there's no room for confusion. He was very clear about the matter. He said he didn't want to be a killjoy, but they were going to pull out."

"They? Both Mr. and Mrs. Pearson resigned from the syndicate?"

"Yes. She always goes along with him. She said, 'It's not as though we're ever actually going to win big.'" Those were her exact words. Ironically."

"And Mr. and Mrs. Heathcote?" asks their lawyer, Mr. Elliott.

"They'd largely been quiet throughout the row. Fred kept dozing off in his chair, but as the Pearsons left, they stood up to go, too. Jake explicitly asked them whether they were still in."

"And how did they respond?"

"I remember it clearly. Fred said, 'I think it's had its day, old man.' I remember it clearly because the phrase was annoying, a ridiculous affectation. Jake isn't an old man and Fred isn't a 1940s cad in a B movie. I offered to get his coat."

CHAPTER 14

As Carla Pearson entered the room, all the men rose from their seats. This meant the women felt compelled to do the same. Carla was a very attractive woman, the sort that people held doors open for, packed shopping for, went the extra mile for. She had a flat stomach, silky hair, a suspiciously wrinkle-free forehead. Nothing about her admitted that she was a middle-aged mother of three. "Mrs. Pearson, thank you for agreeing to speak to us," said Gillian.

Carla smiled at her bank of lawyers. Patrick had insisted that they employ three; he said it would intimidate the Greenwoods. He pointed out that they might as well—they had lawyers on retainers anyway as his businesses demanded a lot of legal attention. He said he knew what he was doing, and she had to believe him. "Call me Carla, please. We don't need to be formal, do we?"

"Well, actually I think it is best if we stay formal," replied Gillian, politely determined. "You understand this is entirely voluntary."

"I want to be here. I want my say." Carla sat down and crossed her legs at the knee. Her flowing skirt had a split in it, which fell open to reveal toned, tanned flesh. "Although why there has to be a huge inquiry is beyond me. It's not complicated. We were in a syndicate. The money should be split six ways."

"Six? Not three?" asked Ms. Walsh.

Carla waved her manicured hand. "Whichever."

"Can you tell us about Saturday the thirteenth of April? We've established there was a dinner party at Lexi and Jake Greenwood's home. We know who was in attendance. What we're looking for is your account of the evening."

"It was very jolly," Carla said firmly.

"Throughout?"

"Yes. We ate a lot. Talked a lot. Laughed a lot."

"Can you recall what you talked about?"

"Oh, the usual things. The kids, goings-on at their school, our holidays."

"And was there an altercation?"

"No, nothing of the sort."

"No cross words exchanged?"

"No, none." Carla shrugged her skinny shoulders with a chic insouciance. "Why would there be? We've been friends for years. There's rarely a cross word between us. We're more like family."

"The families I know do have cross words," pointed out Mick Hutch. Everyone turned to him. These were the first words he had spoken throughout the proceedings. People had forgotten he was in the room. Or wondered why he was. However, the point he made was a fair one.

"Oh, but you know what I mean. We're friends who are practically family. That's why this is all so upsetting, actually. I just don't understand them. I don't understand how money can have come between us. Why won't they just share it?" Carla's eyes became watery. The men felt varying levels of sympathy for Mrs. Pearson, ranging from mildly uncomfortable to genuine concern; the women in the room wondered how she could do that on command.

"Was the lottery mentioned at all?" asked one of the Pearsons' lawyers.

"Yes, actually it was. Briefly. Lexi said she needed us all to chip in again, that the kitty had run out. She buys the tickets, you see. Always has."

"And did you all chip in?" asked another one of the Pearsons' lawyers.

"Yes. Yes. The moment she asked for it, I reached for my bag. Patrick doesn't carry cash. I paid. I contributed to that winning ticket."

"And was there a contract confirming this syndicate exists?" asked the Greenwoods' lawyer. Carla didn't like the look of the woman. She was the sort who didn't bother to make the most of herself, which Carla thought a waste.

"No, of course not. Friends don't draw up contracts between each other."

"Any written correspondence at all? A text? An email?" the woman lawyer with the frizzy hair pursued.

"Well, no," Carla admitted.

"And is there any similar correspondence to suggest the contract has been terminated?" asked one of Carla's lawyers.

She smiled at him. "No."

"I'd have thought a fallout of the scale the Greenwoods described would have merited a text at least." He raised his eyebrows.

Carla thought the retainers Patrick paid were well worth the money. "There were no texts about a fallout because there wasn't a fallout."

Mr. Elliott was the first on his feet when Jennifer Heathcote came into the room. He rose with such speed that he made the other lawyers look tardy, even though they were all in the process of standing, too. "Jennifer, always a pleasure," he said, leaning over the table to kiss her right cheek, then her left. The movement was graceful, synchronized, their glasses did not clash; they had been greeting one another this way for years without self-consciousness or a collision. He was clearly half in love with her, in that way certain men were always half in love with English roses. Women they felt duty-bound to protect and defend. Women they underestimated because they had bright eyes, rosy cheeks and didn't wear a lot of makeup.

"Thank you for agreeing to see us today, Mrs. Heathcote," intoned Gillian with significantly more neutrality. She made the introductions.

"Anything I can do to help," gushed Jennifer. She beamed broadly, seemingly less aware of, or at least less troubled by, the gravitas of the occasion than the other two women who had been interviewed. Jennifer liked people to know she had a sunny disposition. She kept her steely core hidden.

"As you are aware, there is some discrepancy about what was agreed on the night of the thirteenth of April at Mr. and Mrs. Greenwood's home. We are talking to everyone who was present in order to see if there is any level of consensus."

"Gosh, yes, obviously. Is this an actual criminal inquiry?"

"What do you mean, Mrs. Heathcote?"

"I mean, am I under arrest?"

"Should you be, Mrs. Heathcote?" asked Ms. Walsh, looking up from her notes.

"Oh, don't be silly? Me? No. *I'm* not the criminal here."

"Well, that is to be determined," Ms. Walsh muttered.

Mr. Elliott coughed. "Shall we get on? So, what do you recall about the evening?"

Jennifer made eye contact with everyone around the table as she began to recount the details. "Lexi had made a huge effort. That was a bit unusual. Sometimes she just buys an M&S supper, you know, dine in." She dropped her voice to a discreet whisper. "They watch the cash a bit more than the rest of us. I'm not being a snob about it, I'm just saying. They always have had to be a bit more careful. Jake just hasn't found a job he's especially committed to, yet. He's always chopping and changing. He sells ergonomic chairs at the moment, or is it photocopiers? I'm not sure. But they do struggle financially." Gillian made a clicking noise with her tongue. It had the desired effect of moving Jennifer on. "Anyway, that night Lexi had really gone for it. She themed it a Mexican evening. She made chicken chili tostadas and pinto bean salsa salad. Delicious."

"Sounds lovely, but Mrs. Heathcote, if I can bring you to the point," said Ms. Walsh decisively.

"The point?"

"The syndicate. Do you remember anything specific being said that evening with regard to the syndicate? Or the lottery?"

"It's talked about every week. That week was no different."

"What was said?"

"The usual. That we hadn't won. Lexi said that we all owed money. That she'd bought the tickets for the past couple of weeks, that she couldn't be expected to cough up every week."

"Cough up?"

"Her phrase."

"And how did people react?"

"Am I under oath?"

"Would it make a difference?"

"I wish I could tell a lie."

"We'd rather you didn't."

Jennifer paused. Took in a deep breath. She had the room's full attention now. "I was in the loo."

"Sorry?"

"They were getting spiky with one another, grumpy. I don't like scenes. I never want to be involved in their tussles."

"Whose tussle?"

"It happens from time to time. Rarely, but often enough that we can all identify it for what it is and see it coming. Jake and Patrick lock horns. It's never over anything big—not politics or religion—but they hold opposing views about whether the school should save or demolish the old cricket clubhouse. They often disagree on the school hockey coach's tactics. That sort of thing. It can get a little tiring, you know? So, that's why I went to the loo, to avoid it the moment I realized they were squaring up."

"They fight?"

"Not exactly. It is fair to say they have heated debates." Jennifer giggled, apparently uncomfortable with the idea of anyone having a disagreement. "They are both rather competitive," she confessed. "Still, some might think it's a testament to the strength of their friendship that they never shy away from disagreements. They bash it out. Verbally, of course, and once they've said their piece, they move on. Generally."

"Mr. Pearson didn't contain his actions to verbal onslaught on the day of the press conference," pointed out Ms. Walsh. "I understand he throttled my client."

"That was a first. I'm sure he regrets it. Everyone was so wound up."

"And does your husband get involved in this—" Ms. Walsh broke off and checked her notes "—this tussling?"

"I'm so glad my Fred stays away from that sort of macho posturing."

"The day of the press conference your husband assaulted Jake Greenwood," pointed out Ms. Walsh.

"Well, yes, as I said, emotions were running very high." Jennifer looked embarrassed, apologetic. "I really wouldn't call it an assault, more of a scuffle."

"I heard that he threw a punch."

Jennifer colored. "He's not normally a confrontational sort. But he feels cheated." She paused, lowered her eyes. Gillian thought of Princess Diana. "You know this is all terribly difficult for me."

Mr. Elliott nodded sympathetically, leaned across the table and patted his client's hand. Gillian raised an eyebrow and wondered whether the man had slept through the #MeToo revolution.

"I think everyone involved feels this is a testing time. Why difficult for you in particular?" asked Gillian.

"Well, I wasn't in the room, so I'm in the same position as you are. I'm wading through the quagmire of claims, trying to work out who said what. I mean, I *know* I didn't resign from the syndicate *personally* and I'm sure if my husband had, he would have admitted as much. He's a very straightforward sort of chap. But, on the other hand, Lexi and Jake say he did resign and why would they lie? And as for the Pearsons? Well, I don't know what to think." Jennifer shook her head sadly. One of the men handed her a handkerchief. "I just wish I'd been in the room. Not being so has put me in a uniquely vulnerable position."

Gillian wondered whether it had crossed Jennifer's mind that she was in fact in a uniquely powerful position. By not alienating the Greenwoods, but still tactically supporting her husband and the Pearsons' claim, she stood to benefit whichever way the pendulum swung.

Jennifer dabbed her eyes and asked if it was possible to leave now. "I do voluntary work at a local school on Tuesday afternoons. Nothing too arduous. Just teaching children to read." She giggled self-consciously. "Well, not even that, just giving them extra practice time. It's very rewarding and they've come to depend on me. I don't want to be late if I can help it."

Everyone stood up as Jennifer left the room. They basked in the sense of calm dignity that she left behind, like perfume floating on air.

"Do you see who you are sitting opposite? Do you understand that I have lawyered up to the fucking hilt and I'm going to have those bastards for every penny they owe me? Do you understand?"

"Would you take a seat, please, Mr. Pearson."

"They owe me nearly six million pounds. Are you listening? Six million pounds. The man is a thief. I might have expected it from *him*. But Lexi? I can't understand why she would lie. She's always been a Goody Two-shoes. A little bit holier-than-thou, you know the type. Turns out she's just another bitch."

"Thank you for seeing us, Mr. Heathcote."

"No trouble. Best get this all ironed out pronto." Gillian and Mick tried not to exchange a look of mild amusement; neither had ever met anyone outside Italy who said "pronto" without any sense of self-consciousness or irony.

Mr. Elliott took the lead. "Fred, I was wondering, has the syndicate always used the same numbers?"

"Yes, indeedy."

"And how were those numbers chosen?"

"We chose one each that first time we did it. I chose eight, my lucky number. Jennifer chose one, to celebrate our firstborn. As it happened, Ridley is an only child, so I suppose the number one has taken on an even greater significance. I think Lexi chose twenty-nine because she was twenty-nine years old when she had Emily, or maybe it's her birth date. I'm not sure. Something very meaningful. Jake chose twenty, their wedding anniversary, I do remember that. Or do I? Maybe that's his birth date. Or Lexi's? Anyway, you get the gist. Everyone picked something personal. That's why we all feel committed to the lottery. Not just the money, but the history behind it."

"Including the Pearsons?"

Fred nodded, a single decisive movement of the head. "Yes, they feel committed, too."

"No, I meant, did they pick their numbers for personal reasons?"

Fred chuckled to himself. "Funny story there. Carla initially picked twelve, her birth date, but Patrick, her husband, shouted her down."

"Why?"

"He said most people pick their birth dates, so numbers under thirty-one are more frequently chosen. Therefore, if you did win the lottery you were more likely to have to share your winnings. He said we'd want to win with different numbers, so we would be less likely to have to share. Patrick picked fifty-eight and Carla changed hers from twelve to forty-nine because she likes to keep her husband happy." Fred smiled fondly. "That was typical Patrick. Not only expecting to win, despite the crazy odds, but also gunning for the biggest win possible. You have to admire him. And he was right of course. A clean win." Suddenly Fred's face darkened. "Except for the Greenwoods, trying this shady stuff."

"You maintain that the syndicate was still active at the time of the win?"

"Yes, I do. We chipped in to the kitty that very evening."

"You did?"

"Yes. I threw in a tenner, took Carla's fiver as change. There was no suggestion that we didn't want to play anymore. Why would there be? It's a bit of fun."

"And your wife saw you put that money in the kitty, did she?" asked Ms. Walsh. "She saw you recommit to the syndicate."

"Yes, she did. She was sitting right next to me."

"Interesting," murmured Ms. Walsh. She couldn't resist. She flashed a look at Gillian and Mick to be sure they had spotted the inconsistency.

"How so?" asked Fred.

"Well, your wife says that she was away from the table at the time of the discussion on whether or not to recommit. She says *she* definitely didn't pull out of the syndicate but perhaps you did." Gillian watched as color, vitality and hope drained from Fred Heathcote's face. She looked to the floor, fully expecting to see a puddle underneath his chair.

"She said that, did she?" Fred's voice choked in his throat.

Mr. Elliott jumped in. "I really don't think we should be discussing other witnesses' statements."

Heathcote glared at Elliott. They had gone to school together, endured masters and bullies. But Fred knew his friend was vaguely infatuated with his wife and would not be able to stop himself siding with her. Fred's godfather was a lawyer—he should have gone with him.

Fred paused. He appeared to be weighing up something important. "I'd like to change my statement please."

"You would?" Ms. Walsh looked delighted. The Pearsons' lawyers all steadfastly held their faces in studied expressions of neutrality, waiting to see what would come next.

"Yes, I'd had a fair bit to drink. To be honest, and I don't know if I do recall everything as clearly as all that. I think I did put the money in the kitty at the beginning of the night, but towards the end of the night perhaps there was talk about pulling out of the lottery."

"Perhaps?"

"Almost definitely. Sorry if I'm a bit vague. I didn't want to admit to how much I'd had to drink, you can understand, didn't want to appear like some sort of alki." He laughed self-consciously. But then he stopped laughing altogether and in a strong, confident voice that did not catch in his throat, he declared, "I recall it clearly now. Jennifer agreed with the Pearsons, she said the lottery was common. She said Jake Greenwood was common. She was quite particular about that and I wanted to support her. So, yes, we all pulled out. Jennifer is not owed a penny and nor am I, regrettably. I'm afraid I can't bring myself to support her story or the Pearsons'. It's not fair on Lexi and Jake."

"Do we even need to interview Jake Greenwood?" Gillian asked her boss, Mick. "I mean I think it's quite obvious what's happening here. It's open-and-shut. I believe the Greenwoods. These so-called friends of theirs are a bunch of sharks. There are more holes in their stories than there are in my kitchen colander."

Mick weighed up the situation. The money was already in the Greenwoods' account. Some of it spent. The lottery company did not have a legal responsibility to do any more than pay out to the ticket holder, providing there was a reasonable proof that the ticket holder had bought the ticket. That was not in doubt. The lottery company was involving itself in an effort to de-escalate this situation. No one wanted a scandal.

All the lawyers in the room shuffled their papers. Gillian was right: there were a number of inconsistencies and now a mid-interview statement change.

"I agree we can all go home right now," said Ms. Walsh. It was a hot day, her shirt was sticking to her back. She was imagining a long, cool shower.

Terrance Elliott, the Heathcotes' lawyer, looked pained. He clearly thought they probably should call it a day, his clients having been the least reliable throughout the inquiry. He was disappointed. He had become embroiled in this because he thought the Heathcotes were good sorts—the type that paid their taxes, never cheated on insurance. Jennifer baked cakes for the school fair, Fred loaned out his power tools to his neighbors. They followed these rudimentary human standards. He hadn't wanted to see them cheated. However, it soon became apparent that their morality was vague and untested. When Jennifer claimed she was in the loo at the most significant point in the evening, he'd gathered it was because she didn't want to tell a lie but nor did she want to sell her husband up the swanny, either. Mr. Elliott had rather admired her for that. Even if she wasn't being scrupulously honest, she was being loyal. But then Fred changed his story, admitted he'd had a few and that they had left the syndicate after all. Rather embarrassing for all concerned. Terrance Elliott didn't want to judge, but he also didn't want to risk his own reputation. It was obvious that the Heathcotes and Pearsons had pulled out of the lottery. Damned bad luck, but there you had it.

"I'd like to interview Mr. Greenwood," insisted Piper-Dunn. "There still might be a case." He was an experienced lawyer and knew that perhaps the Heathcotes' unreliability could work in the Pearsons' favor. Confusion could be a friend of the lawyer. Results could stand very proudly apart from either justice or truth. Clarity was the killer.

Mick Hutch sighed. "I think you are most probably right, Gillian, but we ought to talk to Jake, if only to be seen to be fair and consistent. We've spoken to everyone else."

Gillian stood up and opened the door to the hot, stuffy room. Jake Greenwood was sitting on a bench outside. She beckoned him in.

"Mr. Greenwood. Thank you for your patience, and thank you for agreeing to talk to us about the night in question."

Gillian was being playful using the hackneyed phrase "the night in question." She thought Jake was a bit of a joker. Not a joke. He was too attractive for women to think of him as a joke but certainly someone who liked to have a bit of fun. She wanted to put him at ease in order to get the best from him. She wasn't certain he would be his own strongest advocate. She had been able to depend on Lexi to present herself well, but Jake was less careful. She sensed he played things a little fast and loose; she wondered whether this was a new thing—since the lottery win—or was an established trait. People interested Gillian. Through her work she came across different sorts from all walks of life.

Jake flung himself into a chair and leaned back in it, like a boy who didn't want to be in a maths lesson. He listened to the introductions with a barely disguised sense of impatience. "You've already spoken to my wife, Lexi," he stated.

"Yes, we have."

"Then you know exactly what happened. I can't imagine I can add anything more. We were both there. She's good on details."

"Well, yes. But we have interviewed the other two couples separately."

"Because you are trying to catch them out?"

"Because we are trying to get to the bottom of this."

"Same thing. They'll trip themselves up. I bet their stories didn't line up. Or if they did, that will just be because they have rehearsed." Jake scoured the faces of the lawyers for clues as to what had been said, but they remained inscrutable.

"Okay, well, as you can imagine, we're not in a position to tell you what they said just yet," Gillian replied. "Not until the inquiry is over, but we would appreciate it if you could give your own account of Saturday the thirteenth of April."

"They pulled out of the syndicate."

"As simple as that?"

"Well, that's the important bit, isn't it? They are greedy monsters who are kicking themselves because they pulled out and then we went on to win. And win big. You want the facts?"

"We do, indeed."

"Here are the facts. Yes, we have been in a syndicate for fifteen years. And yes, we chose the numbers as a group, way back when, and it's true that we haven't deviated from the numbers ever. But none of that matters. The only thing that matters is the fact that they pulled out the week before the win. They clearly expressed a distaste, no, a *disgust*, with the whole concept of the lottery, so they are not due a penny."

"Can you be more specific?"

"They called it 'common.' Well, they were calling us 'common,' really. They said they didn't want to be part of it. They were very specific." The room was silent. Suddenly everyone felt the unexpected heat of the long day. Shirtsleeves were rolled up and the window was open, but there was no relieving breeze. Everyone sweated, like cheeses on a board. Limp and indolent, the lawyers fought the urge to loll, forced themselves to stay upright.

"What is going to happen now?" asked Jake. "The money is already in our account."

"Yes, it is."

"Are you going to force us to hand some over to them?"

"That's not in our power."

"Then why are we even having this conversation?"

"Because there might be private legal action. It's our duty of care to report if we believe there is any misappropriation of cash."

"And do you?"

Mick Hutch took the lead. "As far as I can see, there is no proof that you were in a syndicate at the time of the win. No written contract, no informal notes. It's a case of their word against yours."

"So, we are done here?"

"No, not quite," said Mr. Piper-Dunn. "I think the Pearsons may very well pursue this matter. There's likely to be a private investigation, independent of the lottery. I'm certain they will want to pursue all legal routes. We'll be requesting a second interview with Mrs. Heathcote. If she stands by her statement, we're still three voices against three. That's still a case."

"Three?"

"Mr. Heathcote has admitted he did pull out of the syndicate," said Ms. Walsh.

"He did!" Jake could hardly believe his ears.

"But he also admitted to consuming copious amounts of alcohol. His testimony isn't consistent or reliable," added Piper-Dunn.

"And Jennifer?"

"Mrs. Heathcote was in the bathroom at the time of the altercation," stated Mr. Elliott.

"Jennifer was?"

"As you were no doubt aware."

Jake looked confused. "Well, yes, of course, but I never imagined for a second she'd admit that."

"Well, she has. She says she didn't pull out of the lottery and even if her husband did, she'd still have a claim. Three against three," commented one of the Pearsons' lawyers. "This is not over, Mr. Greenwood."

CHAPTER 15

Lexi

"We need to get at that woman."

"Which woman?" The limo driver is holding the door open for us. Jake sweeps past in—it has to be said—an imperious manner. I fling an apologetic smile at the man. He's been waiting for us for three hours. As we couldn't all fit in the Ferrari, and Jake wouldn't travel to the inquiry by train or in our old Volvo, he booked us a car and driver for the day. An actual chauffeur with a limo, a bit like the one that collected us on the day of the press announcement. It seats ten people and there are chilled drinks in the bar. I guess it is usually hired to ferry indulged girls to their prom, or wild guys on a stag. It's embarrassing. He wouldn't tell me how much it cost when I asked. At least it was somewhere for the kids to sit and play on their screens whilst we answered questions. We brought them along because we thought they might have to contribute a statement to the inquiry. I'm pleased and relieved that, at least, didn't happen. I shuffle in the leather seat, uncomfortable with the phrase "get at." My husband sounds thuggish, ruthless. I just want everyone to calm down.

"Jennifer," he states.

"Jennifer?" I'm surprised. I glance at the kids, who are sitting facing us; Jake's gaze follows mine. Emily and Logan are wide-eyed, pale, and worry pours from them. They've been anxious since the press conference blew up. Naturally. One minute they are at school moaning about the lunches and homework, the next in New Bond Street hell-bent on a shopping spree to end all shopping sprees, and then they are witnessing their father on the wrong end of a punch. It's a roller-coaster ride.

Jake throws out a smile. "Hey, it's going to be fine, right. There's nothing to be concerned about." Emily rolls her eyes, Logan shrugs. They both turn their heads and look out of opposite windows. Unconvinced. It was easier when they were babies.

"Why do you need to get to Jennifer?" I ask quietly. "She's on the fence. Her testimony was ambiguous."

"Ambiguous how?"

"She said she was out of the room when it was discussed. I guess she could fall either way."

"But she wasn't."

"No."

"Why would she say that, rather than stick to her story? Doesn't that weaken their case?"

We are whispering, aware of the children. "It does, which suggests to me that she's open to some sort of deal."

I fight a surge of anger that is simmering and threatens to boil. "And Fred?"

"That's the strangest thing of all. Fred has admitted that they pulled out."

"He did!"

"Yes, isn't that odd?"

"I can understand it. Did he say he heard Carla and Patrick pull out, too?"

"Maybe. Yes, I think so. I don't know. I need to talk to Jennifer."

"Do you, though?" I ask.

Jake doesn't acknowledge my comment as he pulls out his phone and sends a text. Presumably to Jennifer. I glower. We haven't been in touch since the thirteenth of April. She was once one of my best friends. It's unbelievably sad. Jake must see the grief skitter across my face. "Look, don't worry about it. Leave it to me." He stares purposefully at the kids, and I know he's trying to remind me of what we are in danger of losing. He's reminding me of my loyalties and duty.

It is frustrating that neither of them has their earbuds in. Usually it is virtually impossible to get their attention, but I know that whilst they are pretending to be focused on the cars and tarmac whizzing by, they are no doubt acutely tuned in to what we are saying. Maybe this is why rich people have to drive around in such big cars—so they can whisper about deals, wins, pacts and treaties. "What a mess. It's all so grubby," I mutter.

Jake plays with the cuff links on his shirt. They are new (Deakin & Francis). His suit is new, too (Tom Ford), as is his shirt (Brioni), and tie (Stefano Ricci). Even his socks and underwear are new (Calvin Klein). He looks crisp, sharp, expensive. "I'm a whole new man," he said gleefully as he got dressed this morning. I had to root through the discarded receipts in order to establish how much this new man had cost. Unbelievably, over ten grand. I guess that is far from grubby. "Surely we should just leave this alone now. Let it all die down. The lottery company will believe us as Fred has backed up our story."

"That's not going to happen. The Pearsons are still going to fight us. We need Jennifer onside. I have to talk to her. You can't just hope for the best, Lexi. You also have to plan for the worst. There are millions at stake here." Jake reaches across and squeezes my leg. The squeeze sends a thrill and a throb through my body. It's weird, even after all these years, I'm still basically putty in his hands. Carla and Jennifer used to say I was really lucky that my husband could still make me feel that way. Sometimes I'm not sure. For a few moments neither of us can trust ourselves to speak. Eventually he says, "I'll drop you and the kids off at home first and then go straight to Jennifer's."

"Without me?"

"Yes. This will be better if I handle it."

We drive home in silence. The thick soupy miserable sort that floods homes with grief and regret.

When we get back to the house the kids go to their separate rooms. Close the doors behind them. I guess Logan will be playing Fortnite and Emily will probably be indulging in another round of online shopping. I sigh. I know I need to get them back to school and into a routine, but I'm getting no support from Jake on that, and obviously they are reluctant. I haven't got the energy to fight them all.

Whilst Jake is out, I text Fred and thank him for his statement. He texts straight back and we swap a few messages. I pick up a magazine and try to read it. I find my mind wandering and I read the same three lines of the same article about twenty times. I hunt about for my old copy of *Mansfield Park* by Jane Austen. I studied this text for A level and have reread it about ten times since. It's reassuring, civilized, orderly. I've always liked the message Austen advocated: decency prevails. This novel is comfort food for the brain, and I need to get out of my own world. Odd, when I'm living the dream.

When Jake finally returns, he's carrying a number of cardboard bags, the fancy sort that are fastened with ribbons and have rope handles. The driver helps him unload the car. Clearly, he's found time to indulge in another shopping fest. The kids dash down the stairs to see what goodies he's bought. I can't talk freely in front of them but am desperate to know what's gone on. "Did you talk with Jennifer?" I whisper.

"Yes."

"And?"

"I offered them a million pounds each if she changed her testimony and confirmed our stories. Close down the Pearsons completely."

"You did what?"

We've been together long enough for me to know that he always goes on the attack when he feels guilty or wronged. "It's not what I wanted, Lexi. But I don't think we have any choice." Jake dumps the packages he was carrying on the floor and storms out of the room.

Our house isn't big, there aren't a huge number of places available to go to sulk or rage. Jake slams a few doors as he stomps around the house, but his vehemence needs more space. It needs to be exercised out. He goes outside into the garden and to my utter surprise starts digging in the vegetable patch.

I watch him. I hear the shovel hit the earth and then my husband's grunt, the earth being thrown to the side. What is he doing? The vegetable patch needed turning over, but he is shovelling with such force it looks like he's on his way to Australia. I know him, he's very physical. When we were at uni, he played a lot of team sport every weekend and on Wednesday afternoons. But, besides that, if ever he was stressed by an assignment or upcoming exam, he would have to find another physical outlet. He'd go on a run, go to the gym, have energetic sex. I guess today he'd rather dig into the garden than me.

I sigh and force myself to fill the kettle, open a cupboard, find a couple of mugs. I root out the tea bags and milk.

I take two steaming cups of tea out to the garden. "Fancy a cuppa?" It is the universal peace signal, everyone knows that. Jake slows down, then nods, throws his shovel onto the ground. We both sit down on the low wall. That's when I notice that he hasn't even changed out of his suit. His brand-new, cost-an-arm-and-a-leg suit. There is mud caked on his trousers, all the way up to his knee. I'm angry with him but picking my battles. We're teetering, unstable. I'm not going to row about something that the dry cleaners can fix.

"Is it going to be okay?" I ask.

"Of course," says Jake. His tone isn't as confident as his words. "We're winners, Lexi. You have to trust me."

CHAPTER 16

Hearing the door open, she turned and glared at him. She wasn't sure why she'd agreed to meet him at all. The text finally arrived. It simply said, Usual time. Usual place. It was insulting in its brevity. It was tardy and isolated. She wanted to ignore it. But it was too tempting. She needed to hear what he had to say, how he would justify himself. So yes, here she was, usual time, usual place. They had met at this hotel almost every Tuesday afternoon for over two years, exceptions being Christmas, spouses' birthdays and last week. They had picked this particular hotel because it was convenient for him as it was not too far from one of his big clients; his boss thought he put a lot of hours into securing their ongoing profitability and loyalty. "Long, boring meetings," he always claimed. She didn't work at all. Tuesday afternoons were handy for her because she had her hair blow-dried on Monday, her nails done Tuesday mornings. On Wednesday she liked to swim at the club, Thursday was yoga classes. She often shopped on Fridays or met a girlfriend for lunch. He fitted in perfectly to her life on a Tuesday afternoon. Just another treat.

At least that's what she thought at the beginning. A sexy, charming, handsome treat. She'd always admired him. For years. She realized it wasn't quite the right thing fancying your friend's husband, but despite appearances she'd never been particularly hung up on doing the right thing. She thought it was overrated. Anyway, she might have left it alone if he hadn't made it clear that he wanted her, too. He had instigated the affair. Hadn't he? Or was it just one of those things? Inevitable? She didn't believe in fate or anything dreamy like that. She was not a romantic and fate was the excuse for those too idle to cut their own paths. She thought that there were identifiable patterns in life that led to predictable outcomes. She thought his wife was a tad sanctimonious. He was competitive with most men, anyone who earned more than him, which her husband certainly did. He had a chip on his shoulder about that. Throw in a basic attraction. Ta-da! On some levels it went back a lot further than two years, a lot further back than the sex. There had always been a little flirtatious spark, just waiting to be lit. Often, he would agree with her opinion even if it meant disagreeing with his wife. He'd listen attentively to what she had to say, whereas her own husband sometimes cut her off midsentence or, worse, actually fell asleep. It was so nullifying. When the three families went on holiday together, and she was wearing a bikini, his eyes would roam her body. Explore. Challenge. If she ever asked for help putting sun oil on her back, he'd jump to lend a hand. On New Year's Eve, what should have been a friendly peck on the cheek had always been a firmer kiss on the lips. Just brief enough to pass as pally, just long enough to suggest something more. He started to squeeze her tighter when saying hello or goodbye.

Something shifted from friendly to fuck me.

It finally happened at the end of one of their infamous Saturday night suppers. She'd hosted, which meant she'd been up and down from her seat all evening, seeing to other people's needs. She'd hardly had time to take a bite. The drink had gone straight to her head. Evidently, it hit a different part of his anatomy. Hard. People were talking about leaving so she went to get their jackets. He was in the downstairs loo, just next to the coat cupboard. He emerged as she was rooting around. Had he been waiting for her? He didn't mess about, didn't ask with his eyes or his voice, he just put his hands on either side of her face and started kissing her. Not tentatively. Not apologetically. With real intent. She wasn't a child or a prick tease. If she kissed a man, it was because she wanted him. Completely. There was no going back. They slipped into the downstairs loo and he took her from behind whilst their spouses were finishing their coffees.

A sexy, charming, handsome treat.

He was the one who first started talking about love, asking for more. Talking risks. Talking chances. At first he limited his declarations to specific parts of her body. He told her he loved her breasts, her arse, her eyes. Then he said he loved her laugh. He loved her cruelty. Finally, he said he loved her. That he was in love with her. No room for ambiguity. She had believed him. She had always been the sort of woman that men wanted to declare love to. And because she believed him, she allowed herself to think that maybe she loved him, too. Or at least if she didn't love him, he didn't annoy her quite as much as her husband did. But then last week, he didn't show up. Last week of all the weeks, after her husband had found out about the affair and told her to pack her bags. He didn't show up when she needed him most because he'd won the fucking lottery.

Now she loathed him. He'd deserted her. She wanted to hurt him. Very much so.

But she loved him. Could she get him back? She'd never hurt him.

She didn't know if she was coming or going. She might still be able to keep him onside so she had made an effort. She was wearing a figure-hugging dress. She'd had a wax and was wearing lacy, claret-colored underwear, just in case. Because there was a chance, wasn't there? That he'd offer an explanation of some sort, that he'd still want her. Or at least take her. There was a lot of money at play. A *lot*. Nothing was clear-cut. And although it should have been a straightforward case of four voices against two, the two had stolen the march and so she had decided to make a two-way bet, cover off all bases. She had put on quite the performance today for those lawyers, but she wasn't sure the people at the lottery were convinced by the claim she and Fred and the Pearsons were making. She had to use all her intelligence and charms to ensure everything turned out as she hoped. By saying she was in the loo, she was sending a message to Jake. When she received his text, she knew he'd got it. Loud and clear. She had never considered leaving her husband for Jake. When her husband discovered their affair and screamed at her to "just fucking leave, get out of my sight. Go to him," she'd had no intention of doing so. She'd planned to stick around, see if things calmed down. She wasn't the sort of woman who could live with a poor man. And Jake had, up until very recently, been a poor man. She could play with a poor man nicely enough, but she needed to be married to a man who was comfortably off. She liked living in Great Chester and could never have managed in Little Chester the way Lexi did. She didn't want to have to work and chip in on covering the bills. She enjoyed having manicures, pedicures, blow-dries.

Of course, Jake was now a very wealthy man. Obscenely rich, in fact. She had a lot to play for.

Last week, when he hadn't turned up to their usual rendezvous—when there was no call, no message, nothing—she had sat in the hotel bedroom and worried about him. The thought made her rage now. She'd seriously considered that he had been in a car accident, imagined him unconscious, his face bleeding and smashed against his steering wheel. She'd wondered about calling hospitals.

But then Ridley and Megan came home from school and told their parents about the lottery win.

She'd still waited for him to call or message. Still believed he would. Each time the tiny icon to say a message had arrived flashed on her phone or laptop, her heart leaped. But the messages were never from him. The silence stretched and physically tormented her as though she was being pulled apart on a medieval rack. She needed to speak to him more than ever. It was clear that he was trying to hide the win from them all. Even her. He had said he loved her. But people say all sorts of things.

The betrayal burned.

It frightened her to think that he didn't need her now. A man as rich as he was would have his pick of lovers because there was always someone willing to buy and sell. Many someones. That was the problem with being a mistress—it was a transient role. Everyone knew that. The wife had some power, was propped up by children, society, shared history. Even if a mistress ever became a wife, she knew she had just opened up a vacancy. A more devastating thought was that he wouldn't want a lover at all now. With this newfound wealth, maybe he'd settle for his wife again. Maybe he'd find he could buy up enough excitement and pleasure without having to have illicit sex on Tuesday afternoons. Perhaps all she'd ever been was the equivalent of an exhilarating thrill ride at an amusement park. He could certainly buy bigger thrills than that now. He'd driven his Ferrari right past her house, for God's sake.

Despite promising herself that she'd be charming, she found the moment he pushed open the hotel bedroom door and she set eyes on him—in his new expensive-looking clothes, with his new smug-looking expression—that her anger surged. Impulsively, she reached for something to throw at him. The first thing that came to hand was a hardback book about mindfulness.

She flung it at him; the irony wasn't lost on her. He ducked and the book sailed above his head, hitting the door behind him. He looked amused.

She let loose a cry of frustration and humiliation. He moved swiftly across the room toward where she was sitting on the end of the bed. She was not lying on it or in it, as usual, but she had not sat on the desk chair, either. He would know that by sitting on the bed she was showing that she was still open to negotiations. He knelt on the floor in front of her. Leaned toward her so that their lips were just a fraction away from touching. She lurched forward and bit him. "Fuck, that hurt, you bitch," he yelled, standing up and swiftly moving away from her.

"It was supposed to, you bastard."

Jake looked at his mistress: exciting, expensive, explosive. Secretly, he liked a show of passion. It turned him on when she was uncooperative, difficult. He had fully expected her fury. He hadn't treated her well since the win, but they were not nice to each other. That had never been part of the deal. Not what they wanted from one another at all. They were always saying so. Even when he'd told her he loved her, he'd almost resented her for it—for making him weak and needy.

"You fucking bastard. Where were you last week?"

He admired her for starting with that question, the least expected. The most personal. He had failed to show up for their rendezvous and she was upset. Or at least paying him the compliment of pretending to be so. What a joke, considering everything else that was going down. He loved it that she was ignoring the question of the lottery when really it had to be all she was thinking about. She was such a game player. So exciting! "Buying a Ferrari."

"Fuck you."

"I'd rather fuck you," he said, and smiled. She glowered.

He shrugged. She wasn't ready for him yet, but she would be. She'd wanted him when he was a loser. How much more she must want him now he was a winner. She was probably wet for him right now. This was just a game.

"I suppose everything has changed now your wife won eighteen million pounds," she muttered sulkily.

"Nothing has changed." She looked wary, vulnerable. He'd never seen her like this before. "And my wife *and I* won eighteen million pounds—give or take."

"She bought the ticket." He shrugged, careless of the technicality.

Relationships were all about power, who has it, who wants it. The balance, the imbalance. All longing was in the gap in between. She had always had the power. And now he did. Or at least, he had the money, and that was more or less the same thing.

"What's going on, Jake?"

"I'm going to divorce her. I'm going to get nine million. Not as much as that of course if I have to split it three ways predivorce." He watched her carefully, amused at how she was trying not to react. Something about her mouth betrayed her, though; it flickered as she suppressed her smile of triumph. He knew she'd never felt happier, more victorious.

"I see, and if we had a third per family and both divorced, we'd still only have six between us." It was a big sentence with all sorts of promises and lies enfolded into it. They stared at one another, long and hard, wondering whether they could trust each other. Or not.

"You're always a step ahead. Clever girl. So you see how important it is that you drop this silly claim that we were all still in a syndicate."

"What will you do with the money?" she asked, looking at him from under her eyelashes. It was a cliché but Jake didn't care. It was a sexy as hell cliché. They were both breathing heavily.

"I will do anything I like. And I like you."

"You used to say you loved me."

"Don't split hairs."

There was a beat and then they jumped at each other. Clamped their lips and hands down on one another with a complete and visceral passion. His hands slid over her body—her full breasts, her tight waist, her delicious arse. He felt the muscled firmness of her through her clingy dress, he felt the exciting mounds and curves, he felt her nipples stiffen. She'd wanted this all along. Her anger was an act. A risk. A gamble. Her boldness caused his cock to harden. She arched toward him, slunk into him. He broke away, but only to pick her up and throw her back on the bed. She fell flat, lips and legs slightly open. Inviting him. His fingers slipped up under her dress, hers laced into his hair and drew him toward her again. Their mouths banged heavily on one another, almost painful, totally delicious.

With a swift, practiced confidence he undid his trousers, pushed her dress roughly up her thighs and pulled her knickers away. He was inside her in a second, her hot flesh accepting him completely. He put his hands on the tits he said he loved and went at it. Victorious.

CHAPTER 17

Emily

Wednesday, May 1

Bloody fecking hell, this is the worst. I can't believe the Heathcotes and Pearsons are trying to screw us over like this.

It's all my fault.

Because I blabbed to Rids and Megan, they all had time to rehearse their stories and come up with some crap that is halfway convincing. I hate Ridley and Megan now. I do. I do! Mum looks really grim. Dad is trying to keep the shit together. He says everything is going to be fine and that the investigation will undo the Heathcotes and Pearsons. I hope so! They need to be exposed as the cheating lying shits that they are. Dad says we can tell whoever we like about the lottery win at school now, that we should take ownership of the win. Even without press coverage, I reckon people will believe me because of Dad picking me up last week in a Ferrari but, for the avoidance of doubt,

Dad went out and bought ten Michael Kors Gemma tricolor pebbled leather totes yesterday. TEN!

"They are big enough to get A4 books in," he points out helpfully, as though that was the thing that excites me about them.

"Yeah, they are gorge!" The leather is soft and smells amazing.

Expensive. Everyone in my year talks about Michael Kors all the time, but only Evie Clarke has one and I'm not even sure if it's genuine. "But why did you get ten?" I ask.

"You can give them to your friends. You want them to feel part of the celebration."

As if I have ten friends. I had two. Ridley and Megan, and we kept to ourselves at school. We arrived at Glenwood Grammar a readymade gang, so we didn't bother with anyone else. Thinking about it now, I'm not sure how wise that was, but it wasn't a conscious decision at the time. We were glued by our parents and none of us thought to spread ourselves about. We were just grateful that we weren't the ones desperately dashing about begging people to sit next to us or scanning the playground hopefully for someone to talk to during break.

Plus, you know, we liked each other. Loved each other.

I could never have imagined a time when that would change, a time when I'd need someone else. Rids did make some other friends, through his rugby mostly, and also because he's pretty musical and plays in the orchestra (which he pretends to think of as lame but actually loves) and a band (which is just all-out cool). But even when we are playing hockey, Megan and I have each other and don't need anyone else. We always partner up for the exercises, we chose each other for teams, etc.

At least we used to.

I don't suppose that will be happening anymore. Jesus, I better make friends quickly or I'll end up passing the ball backward and forwards with Miss Granger, the PE teacher who needs to wear a better sports bra. Social death.

Way back, there was a brief time when I did sometimes try

to mix. It was when we were about thirteen and people started having parties. I thought it would be cool to be part of that, you know, have a bigger group to arrive with and dance with and stuff, but Megan didn't like it if I spoke to other girls. She said we didn't need their dumb-arse mixer socials, and then when Rids and I got together I really never again questioned wanting to spend a moment with anyone other than the two of them.

Rids.

Ridley. Is he even my Rids anymore? I don't think so. I have sent him, like, a thousand messages and he hasn't answered one of them. I know I should be acting cooler and I should be the one ignoring him, but I can't! He, apparently, can ignore me, though, which suggests he's not my Rids. In any way, shape or form. I have to get used to that, I suppose. Yet. When I think of him, I sort of swell and sweat inside. I know that sounds so gross but it's actually awesome. Or at least it was. Now my physical reaction is more like feeling someone is holding me under freezing water. I'm panicked. Flaying. Drowning.

I guess that's Dad's point. He knows Mum won't let me be off school forever so he's sending me to school with ten totes so I can find ten new friends. I am not above buying friends. Monarchs have bought armies in the past. History doesn't have a problem with that. Whoever says money doesn't buy happiness is simply not shopping in the right place.

"How is she supposed to get those to school?" asks Mum. True, Dad could barely get them through the doorway. I can't quite see myself waltzing into maths with them bundled under my arms. "It's a crazy idea," she adds with a tut.

"What did you get my friends?" asks Logan.

"Video games," replies Dad. He holds up a game bag that is bulging with blue and green plastic boxes.

"Cool!" It sometimes makes me feel sick with envy how easy Logan finds life, but I also love it about him.

"I got a selection because I didn't know which of your friends had what."

Mum takes the bag off Dad before Logan can even get his hands on it. She peers inside. "All of these are certified for over sixteen or over eighteen," she grumbles.

"That's what they're all playing," points out Dad.

"Maybe, but there is no way you can hand them out to his friends. Leave the goodies at home, kids."

"What, we can't give them to our mates?" Logan, who actually has mates, does the thing he always does when he's fed up—his body sort of slouches extra-strength, basically it collapses in on itself.

"Maybe, at some point. Their birthdays or something, or after I've discussed it with their mothers. Now get a move on, you'll miss the bus."

I pack one of the Michael Kors totes with my schoolbooks—I pick the pink/fawn combo—and then I hide two more in my sports bag.

"It's not PE today, is it?" asks Mum. Her vigilance is usually spasmodic and always infuriating.

"Taking my kit in in case I decide to go to training," I lie.

She beams at me. "Oh that's great, Emily. The sooner you get back into the usual rhythm, the better it will be."

She's like one thousand per cent wrong about this. Things can never be as they were before. It's stupid imagining they can. The usual rhythm is dead and gone. Because the usual rhythm used to beat around Ridley and Megan. Why can't she see that? I don't enlighten her. I smile at her, kiss her on the cheek and dash for the door.

When Logan and I get on the bus, I swear it goes quiet for a moment. Everyone is gawping at us. For a split second I panic, I daren't breathe. Maybe the silence is ugly, and everyone is going to react the way Ridley and Megan did to the news of our win. But then Logan's friends start cheering, whooping and chanting,

"Rich boy, rich boy!" I read the energy on the bus, concerned that we are going to get ambushed or something, but the mood is definitely celebratory. Logan's mates are mentally happy for him. Like real mates are supposed to be. They can't sit still but are up and down off their seats like they are on speed. Logan punches the air over and over again and other people start to do the same. He raises his hands above his head like a champion and people start to sing the *Rocky* theme tune. Even though none of us were born when the film was made and none of us has ever seen it, we know it's sort of the iconic song of winners. He walks toward the back of the bus and as he makes his way down the aisle, people clap him on the back and shout out, "You lucky bastard!" But in a good way.

I follow him, riding the uncomplicated tide of happiness. I'm thinking he'll still be the only person I can sit with, but halfway down the bus, Scarlett Sorella says to me, "Cool bag. I love it." She's smiling in a really friendly way, so I don't think she's being sarcastic.

"Thanks," I mutter cautiously. Scarlett Sorella is in a few of my classes, but we haven't really spoken much before. She's pretty and cool. She's an excellent hockey player.

"Hey, sit with me." She is sitting with Liv Spencer, one of her two best friends. Scarlett throws Liv a move-your-ass look, and Liv gets the hint. She scurries into a seat in front, but she doesn't do it in a sulky way; she beams at me, as though she's happy to be kicked out of her seat for me. I slide in next to Scarlett.

"You can have one, if you like," I offer. Scarlett and Liv don't follow me. Not surprisingly. It's not every day you get gifted a two hundred and seventy quid bag. I reach into my sports bag and pull out the totes. They look particularly shiny and special next to our school uniforms, which are pretty ugly.

"For reals?" asks Liv. I nod. Her eyes widen, but she doesn't hesitate, not wanting to risk me changing my mind, I suppose. "Dibs on the butternut one."

Scarlett smiles. "Works for me. I'll have the pink and fawn

one that matches Emily's." We grin at each other. Handbag twins. It feels good. A relief. The three of us chat and laugh for the rest of the journey. I don't look around, but I feel eyes follow me. I guess everyone is curious and any number of people could be staring, but I sense it is Ridley and Megan sending the evils. Their loathing can't touch me, though, because I'm protected by an invisible barrier a bit like the one Violet in *The Incredibles* throws over her family all the time. I guess my mum did just that. She created a protective bubble when she bought that winning ticket.

By lunchtime word has got around that I am giving away designer handbags to my friends, so I have plenty of friends. In the dinner hall, everyone is jostling to be on my table but Scarlett stays close, like a best friend. I'm not an imbecile. I know she's not my best friend yet, but I'm not going to lie—it feels awesome to have the possibility that there might be new friends on the horizon. No one mentions Ridley or Megan or asks what the beef is between us. All anyone wants to talk about is the lottery win.

"Do you want to know what heaven is?" I ask. "Heaven is all the shops on New Bond Street, the moment after you've told the assistant that you've won the lottery." Everyone gasps and laughs.

I tell them what I learned. "Dolce & Gabbana is just out there. Maybe one day I'll go to some event, like a ball or something, and being so out there will seem like the right fashion choice but it's not okay for me right now. Miu Miu is crazy chic, Loewe charges over six hundred quid for a pair of khaki trousers. One word. Gap." My new friends laugh again.

"Although, you totally won't be shopping in Gap anymore," points out Scarlett.

"I hadn't thought about it."

"No, you totally won't. You'll be all about brands like DKNY and Boss."

"I did try some of theirs, but all their stuff is way too long for me."

"They'll have tailors or something that do the alterations," points out Scarlett, who I think is taking to me being rich faster than I am.

They want to know exactly what I've bought so far and what I'm planning on buying next. We're not supposed to have our phones on in school hours, but I pull out my brand-new iPhone and flick through various sites so I can show the girls what I've got. They ooh and ahh appreciatively. I practically drown in a chorus of, "You are so lucky!"

"That is going to look so cute on you!"

"Do you think I could borrow that?"

I show people the hotel we are going to stay at in New York. Not the one that cost 80K because Mum vetoed that, but we're staying at one that looks really good anyhow.

"When are you going?" Nella Wang asks.

"The week after half term."

"Term time?" Everyone looks surprised, a few gulp in a melodramatic way. It's to be expected, we are fifteen-year-old girls and, yeah, we are excitable! Term-time holidays are a rebellion, maybe even an act of war because the Head is dead strict about people taking time off during term. I still can't believe Mum agreed to it. I think she only did in the end because the people at the lottery recommended that we get away "to take stock, take a breath," and Mum couldn't get half-term week off school because nearly everyone in her office has kids and they take turns about who gets to go on leave during school holidays. The ones with younger kids get priority. Mum said she's going to call the Head today and explain.

"Do you think you'll get permission?" asks Liv.

"What can Coleman do? He can't chain me to the desk." Everyone laughs at this and we start to make jokes about whether the Head and his wife like bondage sex.

Basically, I've become a very funny person since I've become a very rich person.

I don't see anything of Ridley or Megan. They are probably skulking about somewhere, keeping out of my way, drowning in their own jealousy. For the first time in years I don't care what they are doing. And realizing I don't care is a huge relief. The win has freed me from needing them. And I tell myself that I don't want them, either.

None of my new friends are taking the bus home because they really are staying after school to train for hockey or netball. As I had no intention of doing so, I don't have my kit with me, my bag was full of luscious totes, so I have to travel home alone. I don't mind because it's been such a fantastic day. A bit of alone time is bearable after being center stage all day. I decide to pop into the toilets, even though the bus drive is only twenty minutes. It's been so hectic I honestly haven't had time to even wee.

I never sit, I hover. Opinion is divided on this one. I don't really believe you can catch any germs from the seat, not unless your bum has an open wound on it, but why risk it, and putting paper all around the seat is bad for the environment. Mum says I should just sit because I'm more likely to get an infection by not emptying my bladder properly. I literally pretend she hasn't spoken when she says stuff like that.

I hear them before I see anyone.

There's sniggering and the door of the cubicle next to mine swings back on its hinges, bangs. Suddenly, Ridley is peering over the top of my cubicle. I am so mortified because my knickers are around my ankles. Not that he hasn't seen that part of my body, but he hasn't seen it peeing. Rushing to cover up, I straighten up a moment before I stop peeing. You can guess how that works out. I pull up my pants but he's already taking photos. It's just stupid. Totally fucking stupid. I'm humiliated and angry at the same time. Pissed off that he's ruining my perfect day but also terrified that he's pranking me to this level. Photos of you drunkenly falling over are bad, photos of you pissing your pants are so much worse.

He's laughing his head off.

I burst out of the cubicle and try to grab the phone off him, but he is tall and easily holds it above my head. Then I see Megan.

But not just Megan, there are three other girls with her—Evie Clarke, Shayla O'Brian and Madison Aidan. They all rush at me. They push me back into the cubicle I've just come out of, and their combined force is overwhelming. I bang the back of my legs against the toilet, they throb. But as I register that pain, I realize someone has grabbed my hair and is pulling my head backward. Someone else, Megan I think, slaps me across the face. Once, twice. I've never been hit before and bloody hell it hurts. I cry out, but then a hand comes over my mouth and I don't think I can breathe. They pull my blazer off my shoulders, down my arms, so it acts like a restraint. I'm wriggling and struggling but can't actually fight back. There's no room to move and besides they outnumber me. I'd like to throw a punch but mostly I want to get away before they can really hurt me. Will they?

My phone falls onto the tiled floor and I hear it smash. Shayla bends down picks it up. "Oh, fancy." She drops it down the loo.

Megan leans close to me and growls, "There you go. Your shit is going down the toilet with your actual shit." Her friends laugh. I can smell her breath. It smells of the burgers we were served at lunch. "The money your mum and dad stole from my mum and dad can't make you safe, Emily. Remember that. You are fucked."

Someone yanks on my hair again. Madison? What have I ever done to her? Or any of them, come to that? It's so painful I think she must have actually pulled hair out. Someone kicks me. Maybe Megan, maybe another girl. It's a muddle of arms and legs in the cubicle. I'm too confused, sore and scared to be sure.

Ridley has been standing by the bathroom door throughout this, keeping watch for teachers. Presumably he feels squeamish about beating up a girl.

Me.

Someone he once said he loved.

"Okay, let's get going, we don't want to miss the bus," he instructs.

And they melt away.

CHAPTER 18

Lexi

"We're in the kitchen," I call through unnecessarily. The children and I have an after-school ritual that has been long established. On Wednesdays and Fridays, when I only work mornings, I am always waiting for them in the kitchen. On hot days I am there with sliced fruit, iced drinks, and on cold days I offer hot chocolate and biscuits. It's one of my favorite times of the day. I love the quintessential old-school mothering aspect of it. It balances out the times I'm dashing for the door because I'm late for work, and just scream instructions at them. "Don't forget your glasses." "Have you got lunch money?" "Did you do your homework?" Waiting in the kitchen for their return seems like something mothers have been doing for generations. Plus, if I greet the kids as they walk through the door, I'm most likely to find out how their day really has been. On the three days a week that I arrive home after they do, I cheerily ask, "So how has your day been?" I am usually greeted with a perfunctory "Fine." At six o'clock their school day is old news and they think I am annoying for asking about it. On Wednesdays and Fridays, I get the lowdown.

Logan will remember to tell me about the parents' night we're due to attend, or he'll talk about how his football or rugby game went, and who he considered man of the match. He'll tell me what he had for lunch and maybe which teacher is getting on his case. I listen carefully and try to decipher how much of the "unfair hassle" he has asked for or whether a teacher really is nitpicking. I use this time to try to unobtrusively guide and advise him.

This is, if he can get a word in edgeways.

On Wednesdays and Fridays, Emily lets it all out. She gives me a running commentary of her entire day, including not only who said what to whom, but also who sat next to who, who side-eyed which teacher. Emily tells me who is dating, who is drinking, who is smoking dope. I really found that quite the shock but pretended to take it in stride; if you judge, they clam up.

Today, Jake waits with me because he isn't working anymore. Oh, yes, that's news. Jake has officially handed in his notice. Well, that makes it sound more civilized than it was. This morning he sent his boss a text, it read: I've won the lottery. Please use my outstanding holiday leave in lieu of me working my notice. All the best. I thought he should have written a proper email at least, but he just shrugged and said his boss wasn't especially formal and that he'd understand. I can't say I'm surprised he ditched his job. I hope now he'll finally find something that he really wants to do with his time. Whilst he doesn't need to work for a salary, he could find something in the voluntary sector, or maybe set up a business. I can't think of anything worse than endless days that need to be filled stretching out in front of him.

When Jake graduated, he landed a temp job in a glitzy advertising agency based in Carnaby Street. The work he did was menial, the hours long and no one ever remembered his name, but he learned such a lot. He loved every moment of his six-week contract and it was his dream to get a position on a graduate program in one of the big agencies. No, not just his dream—back then, it was his ambition.

It didn't happen. He applied to at least a dozen ad agencies and was not offered a position. There was rent to pay so he got a job working for the sales department in an electrical company; he thought it would be good experience, a CV builder. He didn't plan to stay forever, but time passed. Not a lot of time, just long enough to somehow disqualify him from following a career path into advertising because when he reapplied for jobs in advertising, he was told his experience was irrelevant, not helpful, if anything a hindrance. "We're looking for innovation." "We're looking for fresh."

His next job was selling branded appliances into large retail accounts. It wasn't a terrible job. We got huge discounts, and the washer-dryer we owned when we first married was top-of-the-line. But he didn't love the job, so after a couple of years he moved again and started selling software. It required some retraining. At first, he found that interesting. Then boring. Next it was office supplies, and then physiotherapy and sports equipment. Jake has sold something different every three years. He has not progressed to an international position or even a senior position here in the UK because he simply cannot retain the love of his products.

He still comments on clever adverts. He often gets excited about electronic billboards.

Obviously, as I am passionate about my work, I realize he has been in an unenviable position. He was good enough to be paid enough, but not ambitious, fulfilled or content. Maybe with this win, and the freedom it affords, he'll find satisfaction. That's my hope. I'm pinning a lot on that.

The kids trail into the kitchen, their arrival home quieter than usual, and before I even see their faces I know something is up. "Oh no, Emily! What happened?"

My baby girl is black-and-blue. Her lip is bleeding and her right eye is cut, bruised and swollen. My first thought is that she's been injured at hockey training and we need to get to the hospital as soon as possible.

"I'm fine," she mumbles, and then promptly bursts into tears.

I can't believe what she tells me next. Megan and Ridley beat her up. They threatened her. Her best friend, her first love, the babies we've known since birth, punched and kicked and slapped her. As she recounts what she's been through, I feel like I've been assaulted. I wish I had been, me rather than her. Every parent feels this when their child is hurt, either emotionally or physically. They'd do anything to take that pain. But this is worse because we've caused it. This fight has come to her door because of the trouble between us and their parents. I also can't help thinking this might not have happened if she hadn't taken designer handbags to school, which she has confessed to. I want to thump someone. Maybe the kids who have hurt her. Maybe Jake. Maybe myself. Instead, I hold her in my arms and let her sob. I try to find the words that will comfort her, but there are none. I am silent, my head is full of the blood on her shirt, the bruises on her face and legs. When she finally stops crying, I lead her upstairs, run her a bath, add lots of soothing bubbles, and then I leave her to soak. The minute I'm out of her sight my wrath—which I've been suppressing whilst I comforted her—erupts. "Those bastards are going to pay for this! Those animals! I'm going around there right now and I'm going to have this out. Fuck Jennifer and Fred's deal. They are not getting a penny. Not one of them."

"Hang on, Lexi. This isn't really anything to do with Jennifer and Fred, or even Carla and Patrick. Ridley and Megan did this to Emily, not their parents," says Jake with a reasonableness that only fans my fury.

"They are animals and they have bred animals," I spit.

"Okay, well, let me just check."

"Check what?" I stare at him, confused. Why isn't he just reaching for the car keys?

"Check that Jennifer has spoken to Gillian. That she has amended her testimony."

"What?" My blood freezes.

"I'm not saying you can't speak to them at some point, but the important thing now is that Jennifer has changed her story. Then, even if she changes it back again, or Fred does, they will look like unreliable witnesses."

"Fred won't," I snap.

"But if he does, if this ever goes to court, they will be doubted for shilly-shallying. We don't want to upset them before we know that the revised testimony is in the bag. Hang on, I'll call Gillian."

"Jesus, Jake. Are you listening to yourself? Ridley and Megan beat up Emily. Your daughter is bleeding. I'm going to their houses. I'm going to the school. I'm going to the police! They are not getting away with this." I am raging. Sounds are whooshing in my ears and I think it is actual fury whipping up a storm. This means it takes a moment for me to realize what Jake is saying. "I think we should just pull her out of the school. Walk away from them all. We don't need the police involved. We don't need a scandal. We're just getting through one investigation."

My mouth is hanging open. "You can't expect me to ignore this," I splutter.

"When she gets out of the bath, we'll ask her what she wants us to do. Take a deep breath, Lexi, I'll pour you a glass of wine."

"I don't want to take a deep breath. I don't want a glass of wine!"

"Think what is at stake here."

"Our daughter's health." I glare at Jake, but can't say any more. I'm conscious that Logan is still in the room with us. He looks shaken enough. I put my arms around his shoulders and pull him into a hug, kiss his forehead. He's clearly upset because he allows this, uncomplaining.

"Will I have to change schools, too?" he asks.

Jake and I answer at once. I say, "Your dad wasn't serious about that. We'll discuss it."

Jake says, "Yes, you're changing schools. Fact."

When Emily emerges from her bath, wearing candy-striped pajamas, she looks about ten years old. Vulnerable, overwhelmed. Her skin is pale. There's a film glistening on her upper lip and her forehead. My heart aches for her.

I am making pasta arrabiata for supper, it's her favorite. She sits down at the kitchen breakfast bar and watches me. "Okay, so we have some options. As this attack was on you, I want you to be comfortable with my response so your father and I can go to their houses right now. We can have it out with them and their parents."

"Then what?" She slouches forward and rests her head on the breakfast bar.

"Well." I'm stumped. "Demand apologies at the least." I can hear how inadequate I sound.

"Their parents won't even care. I mean, they hate us, right?"

I'm not prepared to give up at the first hurdle. "We can talk to the school to have them punished."

She shakes her head. "What do you think will happen if you go in to school and get them into more trouble? Are you going to get me bodyguards?"

"Then the police. We'll go to the police, press charges."

"They can't follow me around 24/7. They can't make me safe. Besides, Dad isn't pressing charges against Fred or Patrick and they assaulted him."

"Well, no, but that's different."

"How?"

I don't know what to tell my daughter. Maybe Jake should press charges. We just don't want a scandal. Have we set a bad example?

"Well, what do you want to do?" I try to swallow my exasperation. I'm not angry with Emily, but my sense of injustice is so ferocious I'm not able to keep a lid on it as well as I'd like.

"I want to watch TV." Her eyes swim. She's fighting tears.

"What?"

"I want to leave the school. Go to a private school where everyone is rich and they won't hate me for it."

"Sweetheart, I'm not sure that running away is the answer."

"It is."

I drain the pasta and slowly stir in the sauce. "Are you saying you don't want me to do anything?" I can't believe my feisty little daughter would respond like this.

"Yes."

"You are content with them getting away with this?"

"Don't make things worse, Mum." She walks through to the sitting room. Jake shrugs. He doesn't look as surprised as I am. I wonder whether he talked to her before I did.

"That's that settled then," he says. "Shall we eat this in front of the TV?"

"It's spaghetti, it will get everywhere."

"We're getting a new sofa soon anyway, right, and I think the important thing is to cuddle up with Emily and Logan." He's right about that at least.

Somehow, I hold it in while we eat dinner and watch a Netflix movie, all together as a family. Ostensibly. The thing is, I know we are in the same room, but I don't feel we are very together. I have to concentrate to try to ignore the issue of our daughter taking a beating, since she is here with a split lip and bruises. If Ridley or Megan were stood in front of me, I would push my thumbs into their eyes until they popped. I would rip their heads off and use them as footballs. Instead, I put my arm around Emily and reassure her I won't do anything to "make things worse."

She lets me tuck her into bed. I kiss her forehead, and despite the trauma of the day she's out like a light. She's always been a good sleeper.

I sit on the floor by her bed, surrounded by bags of shopping and makeup. I lay my head on the side of her bed. I remember back to when she was a baby, and the fact that she always slept so well had Carla and Jennifer believing I was some sort of baby whisperer with a special knack. Carla used to get me to put Megan to bed whenever she could. I remember this and I cry, silent, fat tears that dampen my daughter's duvet.

CHAPTER 19

Fifteen years ago

"I don't know what I'd do without you," Carla commented as Lexi sneaked back into the sitting room. "Is she asleep?"

"No, but she's calm. I think she'll drop off soon," replied Lexi.

"You are the baby whisperer, I swear it." Carla scooted up next to Jennifer so that there was room for Lexi to join them in front of the TV. Lexi had noticed that Carla always positioned herself in the middle of things. No one minded, it was just what felt natural. She was physically the tallest and somehow also the biggest metaphorically in their threesome. Lexi collapsed onto the sofa, grateful to put her feet up. Baby whisperer or not, pacing the floor for forty minutes with a screaming infant, even someone else's screaming infant, was knackering. She enjoyed the fact Carla turned to her, believing she could soothe little Megan because Lexi's own baby girl was a good sleeper. The best of the three babies, actually. Emily hit seven consecutive hours of sleep at just ten weeks old, practically a miracle, and now she regularly slept twelve hours at night as well as taking an afternoon nap. Lexi didn't brag about her daughter's sleep patterns—she knew that exhausted mothers would find that really annoying—but her two best friends, of course, knew the facts.

It was flattering that Carla thought Lexi could work some sort of miracle on baby Megan, who was fractious and agitated, day and night, and had never slept more than three hours in a row, but truthfully Lexi didn't think she had any special powers over Megan or anyone else's baby. Perhaps she had a bit more patience.

Lexi was constantly being told that she was lucky her baby was a good sleeper, and a good feeder, too, as it was turning out. They'd all three recently started weaning. Emily would eat anything that was offered up. Was it luck? Lexi swore by routines, blackout blinds and home-prepared food. Carla didn't believe in those things.

Jennifer leaned forward and picked up the bottle of red, poured a glass for Lexi and refilled Carla's and her own. "Is it wrong of me to be glad I'm no longer breastfeeding, so I can enjoy a guilt-free glass of wine?" she asked, grinning.

The other two women smiled lazily and didn't bother to reply. It was a rhetorical question. They felt the same. They were all good mothers, devoted even. Their eight-month-old bundles of joy were their worlds, but no one ever told a new mum just how exhausting and relentless the whole mothering business was. A glass of wine, a bar of chocolate, the occasional whinge to each other were necessary coping methods that kept them functioning.

"Where are the men?" Lexi asked, looking about her.

"They've popped out for the takeaways," replied Carla. "Thai tonight."

"Oh, goodie. Did you order me—"

"Crispy prawn tempura served with sweet chili sauce and jasmine rice. Yeah."

Lexi nodded, grateful and content. It was amazing how close they had all become in the past ten months. Close enough for them to each know one another's favorite dishes on the takeaway menus, whether they were opting for Thai, Chinese or Indian. They had met at a prenatal class and had clicked immediately, brought together by fear of the unknown as much as excitement. Bound by their swollen bodies that had seemed a long way from the desirable blooming, bonded by talk of intermittent incontinence and depressingly low sex drives.

A sound emitted from the baby monitor. They all froze and listened. Collectively holding their breath, they waited to see if it was a sleepy murmur, or a precursor to a full-on wail. "That's Ridley," they chorused in a whisper.

Close enough for them all to recognize each other's baby mews. Lexi and Carla turned to Jennifer. She was perhaps the most anxious mother of the three. Ridley was the result of four rounds of IVF. All the babies had been wanted, of course, but Jennifer had waited the longest. Lexi hoped Jennifer wouldn't dash upstairs to see her son. He'd most likely go back to sleep if left alone. All three babies were in the same room, two in travel cots. Chances were, Emily would sleep through if Jennifer did go in the room, but Megan would almost certainly wake and wail. They waited a beat. Nothing. Relieved, they smiled at one another. Then, suddenly, there was noise at the front door. Baritone laughter and chatter. The men back with the food. It was somehow primal and satisfying. The women leaped to their feet. Opened the door. Hushing their husbands, they began dashing around the kitchen, hunting out plates, cutlery, trays.

"Did you watch the lottery?" Jake asked as he landed a light kiss on the back of his wife's neck. He was comfortable with giving public displays of affection. He fancied his wife like mad, even when she had baby food in her hair and hadn't managed to put makeup on for a week. He liked to show his desire. Lexi smiled at Jake, paused for a fraction of a second and leaned her head back to rest against his.

"No, I missed it. I was helping Carla out, putting Megan down."

"We caught it, though," said Carla. "Sadly, we did not become millionaires this week."

"Did any of our numbers come up?" asked Patrick.

"No, not one," replied Carla with an air of amusement. This wasn't a surprise. They'd been playing the lottery for about four months and they'd never had a number come up. It had become a running joke between them that they were defying the odds in managing to be so unlucky. Jennifer reached for the kitchen roll and efficiently snapped off six squares. They didn't bother with napkins. It only caused more laundry and they were long past the stage of feeling they had to try to impress one another. In fact, they had simply skipped that stage. It was hard to be the sort of person who might impress guests when all your conversations centered around cushion rings for piles and putting cold cabbage leaves in your bra to ease the pain of cracked nipples.

"I'm not resigning on Monday then," laughed Fred.

"No, darling, you're not," said Jennifer, playfully nudging her husband in the ribs. "So, make yourself useful and open another bottle of wine."

The babies all slept through until it was time to carefully carry them home. The parents drank five bottles between them. More than they'd had for a while, but not as much as they once used to put away. Luckily, they all lived close to one another, and no one had far to walk, just a few minutes up the road. Lexi and Jake stood at the door, waving their friends off. The couples excitedly whispered plans for the next meetup and tried to smother the drunken laughter that erupted from one or the other of them. They all felt light-headed. Lighthearted. Lucky. As they closed the door behind them, Jake pulled his wife into a hug. He kissed the top of her head. He didn't try to kiss her lips because he was aware that sleep was a higher priority to her than sex at the moment; if he'd kissed her lips, she might have thought sex was what he was hoping for.

"Who needs the lottery millions when we have everything already?" he asked sleepily. "Great friends, loads of booze, a beautiful baby and each other."

Lexi lifted her head, met her husband's slightly unfocused gaze and whispered, "Shag me."

Their life was perfect.

CHAPTER 20

Lexi

When I'm certain Emily is fast asleep, I pick up my phone and hit Carla's number. I know I gave Emily the impression that I'd follow her wishes, that I wouldn't say anything, wouldn't "make things worse," but you know what—I'm the adult. I'm the parent. I get to decide what a suitable response to a beating is.

Carla picks up after just three rings. I imagine her in her immaculate Nicholas Anthony kitchen. The tobacco-dark wood units that beautifully contrast with the luminously pale, high-gloss lacquer surfaces. The ultimate in minimalist chic. Her cleaner comes in twice a week. She'll be holding a glass of wine, perhaps. Red. There will be a bowl of fruit, all ripe and ready to be munched, nothing browning or past its best. I don't bother with any sort of greeting, I launch straight in.

"In case your lawyers are just thinking about their retainer and not keeping you fully briefed, I thought you should know

Jennifer and Fred have changed their stories. Initially, he maintained he and you had recommitted to the lottery. She double-crossed you from the off, said she was in the loo at the pertinent moment. Anyway, now they are both saying that they were present and aware and that they do remember pulling out of the lottery." I have to be honest, delivering this news gives me a certain amount of satisfaction.

"I see."

"So, you have no case. They've let you down."

"What did you offer them?" she asks coolly.

"None of your business. I just want you to know, they are not your friends."

"What happened, Lexi? When did you become this person?"

I ignore her comment. Don't rise to it. "I had been planning on giving you three million."

"Patrick and I are due six."

"Why are you keeping up this pretence?" I ask. "Do you think I'm recording this call?"

"Do you think I am?" she counters. She's good, I'll give her that. I sigh.

"Well, I'm not recording it, don't worry. I just wanted you to know I have been planning on giving you three million for old times' sake. Jake doesn't agree, of course, but I thought you were owed it."

She's quiet, so quiet I can hear her breathing down the line. It's crazy to think you can interpret breathing, but I can. I know her that well. I've heard her breathless after a hard run, then her breathing is raspy, labored. I've heard her breath catch in chortles because she's laughed so wildly, often at something I've said or done. We'd roll around the floor, our stomachs cramping in hysteria, unable to spit out words because we were laughing that hard. I've heard her breathing become ragged with shock when she took the call to say her brother had had a stroke. I've heard her fall asleep next to me on airplanes and in cars, after late nights out: gigs, parties, childminding. She doesn't snore exactly, but she breathes heavily. I know how Carla breathes.

Her breath right now is expectant, hopeful. I continue. "With that sort of money, you could do a lot of things, Carla. You could move to a new house, go back to London." I know she's secretly hankered after the bright lights of the metropolis for a while now. She's become bored of the countryside and misses the hit of being at the heart. "You could start up your own business, buy that beauty salon you've often talked about." Carla once put together a really impressive business plan to buy a high street salon, which she insisted on calling a spa. For a time, she was extremely excited about the prospect of working, being her own boss. Patrick vetoed the idea. Wouldn't even let her petition the bank. He said salons were common. I think he likes having a little wife at home, being the big "I am." I pause. "You could leave your husband. Take the kids and go somewhere very far away."

She gasps. Shock? Excitement?

"But I'm not going to give you a penny now. Not one. Go and ask your daughter why."

Then I put the phone down before she can respond.

CHAPTER 21

Lexi

Thursday, May 2

Neither of the kids are going in to school today. I can't risk a repeat of yesterday.

"But I don't need to stay off, do I?" asks Logan. "Ridley and Megan are hardly likely to try to beat me up."

"We don't know what they'll try," I mutter ominously.

"I'm not scared." He looks frustrated. He thinks he's being treated like a baby and he hates it.

"No, I know you are not."

"I think we are giving Megan and Ridley and their apes the wrong message. You should stand up to bullies, Mum. That's what you've always said. What's going to happen every time someone crosses Megan? She's going to think it's okay to kick the hell out of them. Fail."

My heart swells with pride. I try to hug him, but he dodges

it as he's annoyed with me. He stares at me with that particular brand of accusation that only children can muster when they quote back to their parents their own words.

"I'm surprised to hear you arguing for going to school."

"I'm bored of shopping, and that's what Dad and Emily are going to do today, most likely."

"Actually, I think they are looking at new schools."

He sighs. "My friends are not arseholes. I shouldn't have to change schools."

"Don't say arseholes, Logan."

"Why not? Dad does."

He walks out of the kitchen. I feel for him. I understand from Emily that Logan's friends were apparently thrilled for him. He is in a gang of five boys. I use the term "gang" as loosely and innocently as possible. They are still at the stage where the most rebellious thing they do is fart loudly in maths classes and then deny it. I bet they forgot all about the lottery win by lunchtime. When Emily was being beaten in the loo, Logan was waiting at the bus stop, exchanging Fortnite strategies with his mates as usual.

I also understand why Logan might crave normality—I certainly do. I leave Jake in charge of the kids and catch the bus to work. It's a bright spring day, birds are chirping, some spindly branches of trees, defiant and lush, reach, bend and bang against the side of the bus as it trundles along the narrowest part of the country roads. I enjoy the relentlessness of nature that somehow seems eternally hopeful and exuberant. Although, of course, soon the council will be out to chop back the branches before it becomes dangerous for vehicles taking a bend. I'm running a little late, but I'm sure Ellie will understand. I told her about the win after the press conference. I also told her about the Heathcotes' and Pearsons' hijack, so she understands how emotionally complex everything is. The CAB team were excited for me. Judy kept exclaiming, "You dark horse! You dark horse!" To celebrate, they bought me a Victoria sponge from M&S and we shared a bottle of cava. We ate and drank at our desks, chuckling and chatting much as we do when one of the team has a birthday. They asked me how I was planning on spending the money. "Jake seems to be handling that," I replied wryly, which got a laugh. Then, after about ten minutes or so, it seemed we'd said all that we could say about the lottery and soon we were asking one another about the status of various clients. "Did Aliya Habeb have any luck with child support?"

"Has anyone circulated the details of the firefighters' education program to the schools?"

By the time I was washing up the plates in the tiny sink in the staff room, I'd almost forgotten why we were eating cake to celebrate.

It's a five-minute walk from the bus stop to my office. I can do it in three if I try. I walk at the sort of pace that makes me feel waxy on my lower back. As I turn the corner, I instantly know something is up. Usually this is a fairly quiet part of the high street. The neighboring retailers include two vaping shops, a betting shop, a tattoo parlor, a curry house, a kebab shop and a fish-and-chip shop—it's the place to come if you're hungry. Some other retailers are boarded up, there's a lot of graffiti. Not the cool sort, just people's names and expletives. I don't judge. People have a primitive need to be noticed. At this time of day, only the CAB is open and so it's never a busy street, but today there is a queue of people outside the office. As I approach, I hear people murmur, "There she is."

"That's her."

And then, with more insistence, "Mrs. Greenwood, can I have a word?"

There are too many of them to be the usual clients looking for a drop-in appointment. Initially, I fear they are journalists, but I quickly understand that they are people petitioning not for advice or a story, but for money.

"He said he'll change the locks if I can't get the money to him today."

"My son needs a new electric wheelchair, we're fundraising."

"Excuse me, can I talk to you about the Byson Centre for MS?"

I realize instantly that I can't, and shouldn't, try to manage any of these people; client interaction outside the office is frowned upon. Although I've broken the rules on that before, I feel this queue and the number of requests might overwhelm me and decide I had better stick to protocol. I smile briskly and stride toward the office, nodding at everyone who pulls at my arm or tries to talk to me, but effectively brushing them off. "Do make an appointment. Can you just bear with me? I just need to get inside. I have meetings."

Inside the office is not much calmer. Every one of my colleagues has a drop-in client. There are other people filling the chairs in the waiting area and many more are standing about. As I step inside, everyone seems to pause and turn to me. I don't know what to say. One woman breaks the silence. She is sitting at Judy's desk, but quickly and dismissively turns away from Judy. "Thanks for your help, love, but it's her I want to see." In an instant, the woman is up on her feet and pushing through the tightly packed desks toward me. Her initiative seems to give everyone else permission to move, and suddenly six or seven people surge toward me. I recognize a couple of the faces: Laura Atkins, who has a brutal partner that she is too scared to leave; and Vicky Lavin, who has fallen foul of an exploitative payday lender who regularly threatens to break her arms. I see hope in their eyes as they clamor toward me. Someone knocks over a chair in their haste. It clatters to the floor, but no one bends to pick it up. The air feels volatile. It's chaos. I instinctually retreat from them and then feel trapped when the back of my thighs hit my desk.

I'm so grateful when Ellie's strong, calm voice cuts through the demands and disorder.

"If everyone can just take a seat, please. We're going to form an orderly queue. Rob, if you can give everyone a number, you know, like at the supermarket meat counter. Lexi, can we have a minute in my office, please?"

I hurriedly and gratefully follow her into the office, embarrassed that I didn't handle that well. I've never backed away from someone in need in my life before. I normally run toward them. I close the door behind me, but the pleas of the crowd can still be heard, although muffled. They pull at my conscience.

"Well, this is unprecedented," says Ellie. I think we both wish we were in some sort of nineties cop show where she could open the drawer of her desk and pull out a bottle of whiskey and a couple of glasses. She sits down, but doesn't offer me a seat. I hesitate, unsure why there is suddenly a formality between us that there never has been in the past. I continue to hover.

"The people at the lottery company said there would be petitions for charity," I point out.

"Did they tell you how to handle it?"

"Well, usually the winners hire an assistant to open the post, answer emails etc. Then the winners can buy some time before they make considered choices about who they want to donate to." I shrug apologetically. "But I guess I'm much more accessible."

"Yes, you are. Almost everyone you see and work with on a daily basis is in some sort of position of vulnerability."

"We are going to donate to charities," I rush to reassure my boss.

"I don't doubt it." Ellie smiles, but it doesn't seem entirely natural or relaxed, and it seems to require more effort to muster than usual. "Sit down, Lexi." She suddenly seems impatient with me. I hastily pull out a chair, which scrapes along the floor, lets out a howl. We both wince. "So, what are we going to do? You know you can't give any of these people money, right? I mean, that's not our job. Doing so would be short-termist. It would cause a lot of trouble for the bureau."

"Of course," I sigh. It's impossible not to think how easy it would be to go back out there and start to dish out cash. It would ease countless concerns.

"Because you know once you started doing that, it would be impossible to know where to draw the line. Our job is to give advice, guidance, not cash."

"Yes." I nod. Ellie studies me to see if I'm really listening, then shakes her head.

"I'm not sure you'll be able to refuse them, though. It's not in your nature. You always struggle to draw a line." I glance at her, guilty. I don't think she is aware of the out-of-office help I've given Toma, how involved I have become, but I suppose she might be. He's not the first client I've bent rules for. I have delivered clothes that my kids have grown out of directly to families I know are in need, when strictly speaking I shouldn't visit clients in their homes. On one occasion I paid for a client's supermarket shop because I knew she was too proud to go to a food bank and her kids wouldn't eat that week if I didn't. I'm not a natural insurgent—Jake is the maverick in our family—but nor will I adhere to red tape for the sake of it if I think it's standing in the way of the right thing being done.

I sigh again. Ellie is right. I will struggle not to dish out cash willy-nilly, even though logically I understand it's not the proper way to go about things. Or even, I admit, the most effective.

I look around the office. I am reminded, not for the first time, how insistently Ellie is resisting the digital age. Her shelves heave with lever arch files that are overflowing. Many of the cases date back ten or even twelve years. She is always promising herself that she'll catalogue them digitally one day. They could probably be binned, but Ellie won't do that because she's too conscientious and also somehow respectful; the troubles those people had shouldn't be entirely forgotten. Until she can preserve them digitally, the heaving files will remain. I read the posters that advertise the signs to look out for in a loved one if they have depression, others that advertise websites and phone numbers that people can call if they need help with certain legal or health matters. I don't want to meet Ellie's gaze. I think I know what she's going to say, and consequently tears of frustration have welled up in my eyes. I don't want them to spill. I have never cried at work. I've heard and seen many difficult things here, but it doesn't help anyone if I cry. People come here looking for clear and confident guidance, not emotions. I can't let the first tears be ones of self-pity.

"Are you sacking me?"

"No, no, of course not." She pauses. "But I do think it will be best if you take a period of absence. No one can get on with their work with this sort of disruption and they have to work, Lexi. What we do is vital."

"I don't know how people found out where I am."

"Word gets around, I suppose. You have been in all the local press. Many of our clients no doubt simply recognized your face." I'm not certain, but I think I hear disapproval in Ellie's tone. She probably thinks we shouldn't have taken the publicity. She's most likely right. It was never my intention. I wasn't left with a choice. "Yesterday afternoon was quite tricky. There were fewer people here than there are today, but it was still disruptive. There was this one young guy, he can't have been more than twenty, has Tourette's syndrome. Apparently you are helping him find work." She looks at me, waiting for me to identify him. She trusts me enough to know I know the names of all my clients.

"Dave MacDunn."

"Yes, that's it. Well, he didn't believe it was your half day. He just thought we were stopping him seeing you. He got agitated, lashed out, knocked some elderly chap clean over. The elderly chap hadn't even come to see you. He just wanted to talk to someone about his heating bill. It was very tricky."

"Oh, no. Was he okay?"

"Banged his elbow and thigh as he went down. It really was

quite a violent shove. His daughter has already made a complaint. We're going to need to write it up."

I shake my head. This is the last thing Ellie needs. We're always thinly stretched, and a complaint investigation will add significantly to the workload. "I'm sorry."

"Well, it isn't your fault exactly." She sounds grudging.

"Was Dave okay? I know him. He won't have meant any harm."

"Maybe not, but he caused some. And of course, the Tourette's didn't help. Once he started swearing, old Mr. Ryan just thought he was a terrifying thug."

"It's a very much misunderstood condition," I interject.

Ellie looks impatient. "I know, Lexi." We sit for a moment in silence. I feel chastised, she feels patronized. I don't like the gap that's widening between us. I fear I might fall through it. Ellie eventually lets out a long sigh. "After a few months, things will calm down and we can talk about you coming back."

"A few months?" I gasp.

Ellie shrugs. She's not committing. "It might be less. I don't know how long these things take to blow over. You are going on holiday soon anyway, aren't you?"

"Yes."

"To New York, right?"

"Yes."

"I've always wanted to go to New York." She says this with what I think is a note of envy in her voice. "Staying somewhere lovely, I expect?" I nod. She studies me as though I'm an insect behind one of those glass domes the Victorians were so fond of. A curiosity. "You should just try and enjoy your good luck, Lexi."

I leave her office. There's nothing more to be said.

I walk to the local greasy spoon that's just ten minutes from my office. I expected some people from the queue at Citizens Advice Bureau to follow me, but they don't because I lie, reassuring them I'll be back in a minute and urging them to stay put. "You don't want to lose your place in the queue." They trust me so don't follow. I feel squalid and selfish ignoring their requests, being one more person who is prepared to lie to them and let them down, but what can I do?

At the café I order a mug of tea. It's served stronger than I usually drink it. I swallow it quickly anyway, scalding my mouth in my impatience. I check around, but no one is paying me any attention. The place is full of builders on their morning break reading tabloid newspapers, their bottoms spread over the small wooden chairs, their stomachs rolling over their belts. Not for the first time I think the real win in life is being born a man. I pull out my phone and hit the number that is now saved in my favorites. It rings two, three, four times before he picks up. "Toma Albu," he declares. I have always liked the way he owns his name, not afraid to state it. Even when he was on the streets Toma claimed his name, held on to himself, despite the odds. "What would you do with three million pounds?"

"Lexi?"

"Yes." I repeat the question.

"I read about the win. Congratulations!" I hear amusement in his voice, which warms me. "You are ringing me to ask how to spend it?"

"No, I won nearly eighteen million, not three. I'm ringing you to ask how *you* would spend three. If I gave three to you."

"Why would you do that?" I can hear talking in the background.

I guess he's on his tea break, too. Like the builders, he also starts early. I imagine the bustle in the factory staff room as people jostle for mugs, tea bags, milk. I feel his stillness. His seriousness and calm as he waits for me to explain myself. Which I can't. Not really.

"I want to. Is it enough to allow you to return home?"

"Well, I suppose I could exhume my wife and son and have

their bodies flown home if I had that sort of money. Is that what you meant?"

"No, not exactly." I feel mortified because I've been clumsy. He told me he couldn't leave the UK because he couldn't bear to be so far away from them. To leave them behind. He has never said the problem was money. I suppose I hadn't really believed it. I suppose I still thought money could help him start again. Have I started to think like Jake? Do I believe money can fix everything? I'd be an idiot to believe that when the evidence is stacking up to say the exact opposite.

"Yesterday, my daughter was beaten at school," I explain.

"I'm so sorry to hear that. Is she going to be okay?"

"Yes, in the grand scheme of things I know she's not—" I break off. Change tack. "I know things could have been worse." He makes a sound, not a word exactly. I find it soothing. "Before it happened, I thought I understood how you felt. That I understood your loss. Your sense of anger and impotence. Or at least almost—" I stumble again. I take a deep breath and admit, "But I see my empathy was limited."

"It still is. Your child was hurt. Mine is dead."

"Yes."

I feel fury and shame. Fury that she was hurt. Shame that I didn't protect her. Toma must feel something a hundred thousand times more daunting, more dreadful.

"My problem isn't your problem, Lexi," says Toma quietly. "I can't take your money. You have done a lot already. Thank you. You are a very good woman." His thanks are heartfelt and steady, not gushing. "Thank you. You've helped me get back on my feet, the lodgings, the job."

It still doesn't seem enough. "I don't want you to lose any more time."

"You can't control that. Even with millions you can't control time."

"Right." I sigh and it sits between us. The boundary of my abilities.

Toma seems to understand my sigh, my frustration. I can hear the smile in his voice. "But Lexi, I'm nearly there. Things are changing for me. You did that."

"I want to give you this money," I insist.

"Three million pounds is a lot of money, Lexi." He whistles. "A lot."

"It's a fraction of what we won. Really, Toma, I want you to have it. Go and do some good with it. Or go and blow the lot, I don't care. I know it doesn't bring them back," I mutter apologetically.

"Nothing can."

"No. But it might help with other things." For a moment he is silent, and I am afraid he's not going to let me do this. "Please."

He sighs and then says, "Okay," and he gives me his bank details. I feel breathless. Light-headed. I make a call to my bank, trying not to think about how Jake will react when he finds out what I have done. I am taken through security by someone at the bank who is terribly well-spoken and efficient. In just a few moments the transaction is complete. As easy as that. I'd expected that moving such a monumental amount of money might be difficult, but things are made very easy for the rich.

None of it seems very real to me. It's like playing with Monopoly money.

CHAPTER 22

Emily

Dad and I spend the morning trawling through various sites like Oliver Bonas, Anthropologie, Zara. Click, click, click. I buy lip balms, jewelry trees, bracelets, photo frames, handbags, hair clips and clothes. I didn't want to do real-life shopping because I don't want to stare at my bashed-up face in the mirror in changing rooms and I certainly don't want people staring at me. Dad sits next to me while I shop. Before the win, if I was browsing online, he'd be all like, "Wait 'til you see it in the shop. They make stuff look better online." Basically, massively discouraging. But now he is worse than me.

"Get it, get it. Why not?" He gently strokes my cheekbone, which is the color of a thunderous cloud.

Logan buys two different football kits. Manchester City and Real Madrid. It doesn't take long at all, but he seems mad happy. Mum has gone to work, but I don't think she'd have joined in on the spree even if she'd been here. Other than the clothes for the press conference, the only thing she has expressed any interest in buying is a book from The Folio Society. Apparently, they publish special-edition books with cool illustrations. She got one last Christmas off Dad: *Atonement* by Ian McEwan. She said she "might start collecting them." What is she on? *Start* collecting them? Doesn't she realize she can afford to buy the entire lot in one drop? We don't need to eke anything out anymore. I don't know how Mum can exercise so much self-control. I have no idea why she would want to. I tell Dad he should buy her the lot to surprise her, but he buys her just one, *Wuthering Heights*. "Your mum secretly loves a bad boy, and Heathcliff is the prototype," he says, grinning. I grimace. That is not information I need. Then, just as he's at the checkout, he pops *Mansfield Park* into the e-cart and murmurs, "It's her favorite book. Two isn't over the top, right?" My favorite book is *The Fault in Our Stars*. I don't know if Ridley knows this. Ridley says his is *Catch-22* but he's never actually read it, it just sounds cool. His actual favorite is *Harry Potter and the Chamber of Secrets*.

Dad is buoyant today because last night he took a call from the lottery company who say Jennifer and Fred have now confirmed that not only had they pulled out of the lottery but that the Pearsons had pulled out of the syndicate before the win, too. He looks smug. I'm just relieved. Hearing their names makes me feel weird. As they are Ridley's parents, up until very recently they were always associated with fun, happy times and specifically access to Ridley. Ridley has been part of my life forever and I can't remember a time when I didn't love him, one way or another. At first just as a friend, and then… Well.

People say we were like siblings because we shared paddling pools and chicken pox, but that was never true. I was always more aware of him and in awe of him than anyone is with a sibling. When we were tiny, I thought he came up with all the best games and plans. I followed him up trees and through streams.

We built every Minecraft world to his specification. He is the first boy Megan and I ever kissed. We both kissed him on the same night. It was a long time ago, when we were younger and all just working out whether we were—I don't know—people who might want to kiss or be kissed, I suppose. It was experimental and the experiment turned out to be conclusive. For Ridley and Megan, their kiss was just a bit of fun, a practice. For Ridley and me, our kiss was everything. We started to acknowledge that we saw each other differently. I don't understand the raw need he lights in me. I just know that when I'm not with him, I'm not really anywhere. I don't exist. I'm just flat. Then he walks into a room and I'm all the dimensions.

At least, that's how it was.

Now money is the new Ridley, I guess. The things we're buying, and the things we can do now we are rich, excite me. It's not the same, obviously. I can't kiss and suck and breathe in money. Money can't cause me to burn. But somehow, one edged out the other. It's just the way it is.

I didn't think I'd have to choose.

I still think spending the money *with* Ridley would have been the best. The old Ridley. The boy I thought he was.

I *hate* Jennifer and Fred for messing everything up. For trying to con us and pretend a third of the money was theirs. If they hadn't done that, Ridley and I would have been fine! We'd have got over his initial reaction and he'd never have done what he did to me in the school toilets. And yeah, they've had a fit of conscience *now* and at least had the decency to do the right thing and come clean *finally.* But so what? It's too late. It's all too late. I wish there was a button, though, that I could press and just turn my feelings off completely. I have played Rihanna's "Love the Way You Lie" basically on loop. 'Cause #EvenAngelsHaveTheirWickedSchemes.

How could he have stood by and let them hurt me? And the photos he took!

I can't forgive him. I switch up my playlist. Now I am all about Ariana Grande: #IWantItIGotIt.

Dad is distracted by admin. He announces he has made an appointment at a private school. They are prepared to see him this afternoon. I think Mum will kill him for going without her, but he doesn't seem to care when I point this out.

"Do you want to come?" he asks me.

"No, you're all right. I don't think this face makes the right first impression." I try to wink, to pretend it's not getting me down, but it backfires because winking hurts like hell.

"Fair point," says Dad. He kisses the top of my head, carefully, to avoid causing any twinges. "Will you keep an eye on Logan?"

"Yeah." The minute Dad has gone I beg Logan for his phone.

Mine is obviously done for since it was flushed. He is at his computer, a blue glow shining on his nerdy little face. I have to tap him on the shoulder to get his attention and get him to take off his headphones. Like any normal teenager, he hates handing over his phone.

"What will you give me?"

"I don't know," I admit. In the past, I'd offer a pound. We stare at each other for a moment and then simultaneously realize that we can no longer bribe one another with cash because we have loads of it. This makes us laugh and Logan gives me his phone.

"If you post anything on my accounts, I'll kill you."

"Fair."

I dash to my own room and then set about logging in to all my social media accounts that I can. By flushing my phone, Megan basically pushed me overboard and left me bobbing in the sea without a life jacket or even a crappy little whistle. Since we fought on that first day I told them about the win, I have been hopelessly and compulsively checking every form of communication about every three minutes to see if Ridley might contact me privately. Snaps, Insta, WhatsApp, Twitter, basic text messaging and even old-person Facebook. Since she flushed the phone, I can no longer feed this obsession. I guess Megan has done me a favor even though that's the last thing she intended. She knows—everyone knows—how vital a phone is. She's basically hacked off a limb. The thing is, I have not told my parents about the photos Ridley took in the loo. I just couldn't bring myself to do so. They think that the worst he did was stand guard for teachers and they fecking HATE him for that. Especially my mother, I think she would rip him apart with her teeth if Dad and I allowed it. I don't know why I'm protecting him. Or maybe I do. I have to know what he plans to do with them. Is he going to humiliate me and post them? Has he already done that? Or is it enough for him to know I know he has them? Does he just want to feel powerful again? I can't imagine he's wanking over them. I keep wondering, and this is bad. Are they a thing now?

Ridley and Megan? Just the thought, just the suggestion, makes it difficult for me to breathe. No, surely not. She's never fancied him. Or has she? I guess she wouldn't tell me if she did. And he's gorgeous. Why wouldn't she fancy him? Megan always had this big thing about us telling each other everything about everything. Like we talked about period pain, how fat our thighs looked versus how fat they really are, what we'd like to do with our lives, the fact she gets a recurring blackhead in the middle of her back (which I always squeezed for her) and I grow a single persistent hair out of my nipple and even though I pluck it, it comes back. What is that about? Who gets tit pubes? That's the sort of question we used to put to one another.

There were things I didn't tell Megan about Ridley.

It became impossible to put into words the things we did to each other. The pleasure we got from one another. I didn't hold back telling her about that bit of us because I'm ashamed of it—the opposite! I didn't tell anyone because it's so brilliant, so amazing and special! I'm protecting us. Other people would ruin it. Even Megan. They'd say we were too young. They'd gasp, be shocked, horrified. They'd say once he got what he wanted, he'd leave me.

Maybe they'd be right about that bit.

Ridley wouldn't go there. Would he? With Megan?

Here's the truth about Megan. She isn't super pretty. I mentioned she didn't get her mum's looks. Well, she's not even super funny, either, which is a shame because her dad can be quite a laugh. She is, however, super clever. Cleverer than I am and she's all science-y, which is cool, especially for a girl (it should not matter, but it does because we're not living in the future yet and people really do stereotype). I love—loved—seeing people get blown away when she talked about the space-time continuum or black holes or whatever. When we were eleven or twelve, that was just the best. Some dumb and arrogant boy would be going on about *X-Men: Days of Future Past*, naming all the mutants' skills or something tedious, and Megan would casually start talking about the possibility of time travel, for real. Quietly arguing that if it was going to happen, moving forward in time was far more likely than back. Their faces! We'd practically burst, laughing about it.

I loved Megan. And then Ridley. Oh, God. Help me.

It wasn't that I left Megan behind or moved on. I loved them both. It was just that what I feel—felt—feel for Ridley was something so different. So more.

Like, everything about him gets to me. The way he smiles, laughs, eats an apple. Ridley moves in a way that is somehow both purposeful and also slack. It's not that he learned this posed strut as a cool teen, it's intrinsic to him and always has been. He's a great sportsman, and boys who grow up being told they are brilliant at throwing and catching and saving and hitting balls just ooze a different, inimitable confidence and a trust in their bodies that nerdy kids never have. He knows where he wants to put his hands, his mouth. He knows where I want him to put them. It hurts. Thinking about it, his hands on my body and the fact that they won't be again, that I'm no longer entitled to that, it causes me actual pain. Way more pain than when Megan's thugs tried to rearrange my face.

There is something I know I need to do. Like, very much more important than my nails or my brows, yet I haven't. I daren't. I can't. It's better this way. Not knowing for certain. Limbo is pretty liberating when you think about it. Being on the fence you get a view of everything. Once you jump down on one side or the other, half the world is inaccessible. Right? The point is, although I'm not the science geek, I'm not an idiot. Time travel is not a thing. You can't undo the past. Time moves in one direction only and that relentless march has never been more poignant than now.

I fight the overwhelming lethargy that invades my body whenever I think about this and stand up, walk toward the large number of shopping bags that are scattered on my bedroom floor. I haven't got around to unpacking everything we've bought. I'm not even sure if I have enough hangers and space. Even in among all this mess, I know exactly where it is, though, and I'm drawn to it like a magnet pulls a needle on a compass. It's nestled in a skinny plastic bag, hidden inside a quality cardboard bag, right at the bottom, below a pair of Guess jeans.

The pregnancy test.

CHAPTER 23

Lexi

I come home to a silent house. Logan is reading.

"Where is my son and what have you done with his body?" I ask the alien invader.

"Ha-ha."

"What's the book about?"

"A postapocalyptic world where a bunch of teens survive without parents but have an army of zombies to fight."

"Sounds great."

"It's awesome, really gory and actually the kids do much better without parents."

"Funny boy." I'm just pleased to see he's reading, rather than playing video games as usual, but know better than to say as much. If I support an activity, I am condemning said activity to certain death.

Emily is in her room. It isn't clear what she is doing; she claims to be watching a YouTube tutorial on how to apply eyeliner, but there's no sign of a screen. She's just staring at the ceiling.

"Everything okay?" I immediately want to kick myself. It is too general a question, unlikely to elicit an informative or a specific response.

"God, yes, Mum. Why wouldn't it be? We've just won the lottery."

"Right. I was thinking of doing some baking. Do you want to help?"

"Bad day at the office?" I applaud her perception. She hasn't noticed I'm home five hours early, but she does know that I often bake when I feel wobbly. There's something about the rituals of weighing, sifting, stirring that I find extremely therapeutic. I cross my fingers, hoping that she'll agree to bake with me. "Don't fancy it today, thanks." Her gaze stays focused on the ceiling.

"Not even brownies? Or cupcakes? We could make those bake-in-the-mug cupcakes."

"Actually, Mum, if you fancy a cupcake you should probably just get some from Lola's, you know, in Selfridges? They do delivery. They're very on-trend."

"Okay, maybe I'll look into it." I won't.

I've spent most of the afternoon clock-watching because I figure six o'clock is an acceptable time to open a bottle of wine. The kids tell me that Jake is seeing a new school but neither of them know which one, and although I call him he doesn't pick up. I assume it's the local private school he's visiting, but I don't know for sure. For all I know, he might have made an appointment at Eton or Cheltenham Ladies' College. Nothing would surprise me anymore. I'm irritated. He shouldn't be looking at schools without me or the kids. He doesn't get home until I'm a third of the way down the bottle of wine.

I tell him about Ellie forcing me to take a leave of absence. I expect him to be insensitive and go on about how it's a good thing because it will give me more flexibility and we can take more holidays. He blindsides me with understanding and thoughtfulness when he says, "Oh, Lexi, I'm really sorry about your job. I know it mattered to you." I'm at the breakfast bar, nursing my glass. He stands behind me and massages my neck. He leans close and kisses my nape with extraordinary tenderness.

"Thanks." I realize this is the moment I should tell him about giving three million pounds away. I stay silent.

Jake pulls away and claps his hands together. "Okay, right. Who feels like cooking tonight? No one. We need to go out for dinner." He's out of the room and calling up the stairs before I respond. "Kids, come on, we're going to London. We're going to find a really great restaurant and eat and drink too much." They don't need to be asked twice. I hear them scampering above me, running to bagsy the bathroom. Jake comes back into the kitchen and beams. "Emily needs an opportunity to wear some of those new clothes, right?"

As is quite usual in our family, the teens are never simply compliant. After the initial excitement about the prospect of eating out at a cool restaurant, Logan is disgusted to hear he might have to wear school shoes because some of the places Jake is thinking of taking us to have a footwear policy that specifies no trainers. Then Emily has a mini confidence crisis because of her injured face and won't believe us that her makeup covers the bruises. "You can hardly tell." She's right not to believe us. Her attempts at caking makeup over the wounds just draw the eye, but both Jake and I are well aware that to say so, whilst ticking the box of honesty, would backfire and escalate her panic.

"I think it makes you look edgy," says Jake. "Kind of heroin chic."

"Jake, that's not a thing anymore and it's hardly aspirational for our daughter, is it?" Jake winks at Emily and whether or not she understands that her dad is alluding to an anarchic vision of beauty, signaling drug addiction, she grins and dashes for the door.

We call an Uber and as we are driven into London, Jake makes some phone calls and secures a dinner reservation at a restaurant called @, not "At" or "Arobase," just @. The name alone tells me the place will be so trendy it will be terrifying. Jake says that at the moment @ is reputed to be the most expensive restaurant in London. He beams. "It is fair to say that it is the sort of restaurant that only oligarchs and those with expense accounts visit. There's a waiting list that's three months long, but when I told them we were lottery winners they found us a table."

"Cool!" comments Logan, although I wonder what he'll find on the menu that he'll like. He's a burger and chips boy, steak and chips on special occasions.

It's impossible not to be impressed. The ceiling towers metres above us, and the floor is vast, a place where people come to see and be seen. All the tables are round. And we are shown to a circular booth, which affords privacy. My guess is that this one table is always kept aside for the trail of pop stars, actors and VIPs that must want to drop by every night. The leather booth is dark blue, the round table is gold. It should be awful, garish and obvious, but I have to admit it's stupendous, luxurious and startling. The room is swathed in various shades of shimmering fabrics that suggest a bygone era.

"It's like being on the set of *The Great Gatsby*," says Emily, giggling. She's completely forgetting to be a teen and showing her enthusiasm in spades. I can't help but be thrilled by this. Any parent of a teen knows that a child's mood dictates the success of the evening and it's a relief to see her happy. There's a lot going on in her world and I need to spend some time unpacking it, but there's a lot going on in my world, too, so I haven't quite got to the bottom of it yet. The large cardboard menus are as thick as magazines. In each dish there is at least one ingredient I don't recognize, but we manage to order anyway as we largely depend on the recommendation of the staff, who are incredibly friendly and thankfully not the breed of waiters who feel their job is to rudely intimidate.

Jake insists on ordering champagne. He hasn't drunk anything else since the win.

"Let's buy by the glass, then we can switch to wine if we want to," I suggest. He shrugs, but doesn't object. He just throws me an odd look that suggests I'm bonkers and then catches himself, tries to put his face back into neutral. I know, I know we can afford champagne, we can probably bathe in it, but I want wine. Once we have our drinks and whilst we wait for the main course, I turn to Jake. "So the children tell me you went to look at a school today. That was quick off the block."

"Why hang about? I called Coopers and the Head there said she'd see me." Coopers is the local private school; I'm relieved that at least he hasn't been more ambitious and thought of sending them to boarding school without consulting me. "I thought it was worth striking while the iron is hot. I know you don't like me just hanging around the house."

This is true so I can hardly object to him showing initiative. "What's it like?"

"Beautiful. Amazing. The facilities are out of this world. They have a theater, language labs, science labs, a music room."

"Sign me up," says Emily.

"We have all that stuff," points out Logan, not willing to keep the reluctance out of his voice.

"Yeah, you do, but this is all just bigger and better and shinier." Jake laughs and downs his glass of champagne, signals to the waiter for another one. He offers me another, but my glass is still full. "Their theater has dressing rooms and the light-and-sound kit is amazing. The language and science labs are state-of-the-art. I've never seen as many instruments as there were in the music rooms. The sports facilities are spectacular, son."

"Really?"

Jake knows which buttons to press, I'll give him that. "Honestly, they have everything. An Olympic-size swimming pool, full-size football and rugby pitches, 4g AstroTurf, cricket nets, squash courts, tennis courts, a gym. You should have seen it."

Yeah, he should have. We all should have.

Our starters arrive and the conversation is put on pause as we all ooh and aah at the plates in front of us, which are basically works of art. The waiter asks if we need anything; Logan asks for ketchup. To give the man his credit he doesn't blanch. It's only after the chorus of appreciative noises has died down that Jake says, "There are places available. You could start straight after half term."

"What? The week after next? No, that's not possible," I say instinctually, although I haven't really fully formed a reason as to why I'm objecting.

"Why not? It makes sense to get half a term under their belts before the summer. That way they can make friends who they can see over the long holidays. The right sort of friends," adds Jake, looking pointedly at Emily's bashed face.

"How come there are places? I thought a school like that would have waiting lists. It should have if it's any good."

"It does." Jake grins. "The headmistress mentioned her plans to extend the library. I made a sizable donation."

"You did what?" I bristle.

"It's how it works, Lexi."

"If we start the week after half term, does that mean we can't go to New York?" asks Emily. "That was when we were planning our trip."

"I think we should cancel that," says Jake.

"What? No," Emily objects vehemently.

"Well, postpone. We can go in the summer. Your mother is right, we need to get you back in a routine. Start our new life as soon as we can." The kids glare at me and I'm unsure how the blame landed at my door.

"If we cancel the holiday, will we get our deposits back?" I ask.

"For the hotel, yes."

"What about the flights?"

"I'm not sure."

Emily looks broken. I want to fix her. "I suppose now that I'm not working and don't have to worry about getting leave at half term we could bring the trip forward. Go next week," I suggest.

"I thought about that, but then thought maybe it's all a bit too much. Maybe we do need to take a breather, like you said. Take time to really let it all sink in. I mean, we'll need to organize buying the new school uniforms and such. It will be hectic," says Jake. I am gobsmacked by his U-turn and I must look as startled as I feel because he adds, "What's up? I thought you'd be pleased."

I am. Deep down, I think. I do believe we need a breather and I wasn't really looking forward to the orgy of shopping on Fifth Avenue that I know Emily was planning, but I had been keen to visit Ellis Island and see the Statue of Liberty. Besides, I just don't like breaking promises to the kids. Reading my mind, Jake assures me, "The kids will get over it. I'm not saying never, I'm just postponing." Turning to them, he flashes one of his best smiles. "When we go in the summer, we can stay longer or fly to the West Coast, too, and go to LA."

"LA! Really?" Emily is instantly mollified.

"We could visit Universal Studios," adds Jake. And that hooks in Logan. He doesn't need to say anything more—they are placated, compliant. The holiday forgotten. A new school agreed to. Like lightning. Jake has secured everything he wanted. Yet he pushes on regardless. "You know what I've been thinking?"

"What?"

"We should throw a party."

"A party?"

"It's no one's birthday for ages."

"You can have a party without it being a birthday, Logan,"

points out Jake. "I was thinking we should throw a party to say goodbye to all your old school friends and we could get the class list off your new school and invite your new friends, too."

"Have you lost your mind? That will never work," I interject. I think it's so obvious I don't even feel I have to explain. Two sets of teens from different schools and different scenes. Half of whom we've never met. Why would they even agree to come? I'm absolutely blown away by the fact that Emily isn't closing down the idea immediately.

"*All* my old school friends?" she asks with what sounds like curiosity.

"Yes. A huge blow-their-minds sort of party." He doesn't say it, but I can't help but think that far from being a celebratory occasion—the subcontext is to rub other people's noses in it. To smear our wealth far and wide.

"And my friends?" asks Logan.

"Sure, yeah of course, buddy." Jake ruffles Logan's hair. "And mine and your mum's. We'll invite everyone we know."

I hate being thrust into the role of realist bad cop, but feel I have to point out the flaws in the plan that seem so obvious to me and are apparently eluding everyone else. "And do you think everyone will come?"

"Well, my old mates certainly will," says Emily, presumably discounting Ridley and Megan, who are unlikely to RSVP in the positive even if we did ask them, which I never would, not in a million years.

"I see that, but your dad mentioned inviting your new classmates. I'm not sure about that. We know nothing about them. We don't know how they roll."

"Everyone loves a party," interjects Jake.

"Well, no, teens don't. Not always." He's a very involved dad; I know he is aware of cliques, gangs, fashions, trends, socioeconomic status, cool status and just plain old-fashioned self-consciousness—all the factors that can cripple a teen party.

"I think if there is enough drink, everyone will enjoy it," insists Emily.

"Emily, you are fifteen. Any alcohol served will be limited and, besides, you don't even drink."

"Yeah, you're a freak," chips in Logan.

Emily throws him a searing look of irritation and I automatically say by rote, "Don't be rude to your sister."

"I'm not being rude. I'm being factual. She's two months off her sixteenth birthday and she doesn't drink. Everyone else her age does. She's a freak and I don't just mean everyone else considers her a freak, which they do, she is an *actual* freak. Statistically proven." Logan continues to dip skinny fries into the ketchup and then pushes them into his mouth, seemingly unaware of the offense he is causing.

Jake rescues the situation. His ease and charm are always really helpful when it comes to defusing the kids' spats. "I think everyone will come to the party if it is cool enough. And yeah, that means some drink," he says, smiling encouragingly at Emily, "but dished out responsibly." He shoots me a reassuring grin. Jake has a way of making everyone love him even when they are on opposite sides of the fence. "This party needs to be awesome. And when I say awesome, I mean awesome. A recognized DJ. For starters."

"Really!" Emily squeals.

"Yeah, like someone who plays on Radio 1. They gig out at unis, don't they? We must be able to secure someone your mates will know. We'll have lights, a dance floor, smoke machines, all of that."

"Wow." Emily's eyes are wide with expectation. "Also a theme. We need a theme."

"Like *Stars Wars*!" exclaims Logan excitedly.

Jake and Emily don't dignify his comment with a direct response. Jake continues, "Like a color theme, or underwater world, a carnival," and looking around him for inspiration, "*The Great Gatsby*."

"A carnival could be good." Emily is grinning. "We can hire rides, like a Ferris wheel and a merry-go-round."

"A bouncy castle?" Logan is beaming, enough of a kid to want to bounce on a castle for the sheer joy and giddiness of jumping up and down. I think Emily might caustically shoot him down, but she maybe is still enough of a kid to appreciate that joy, too, because she nods.

Or maybe she just knows impulsive uncontrolled bouncing up and down is a great way to flirt.

Is she even thinking about flirting with someone new? What is she thinking and feeling about Ridley and Megan? I don't quite know, and I should. Yesterday she was adamant that she hates them, but that sounds too simple to be true. She's had a strange feverish edginess about her tonight. What does that mean? Does she fear them? Teens are surprisingly resilient and horribly vulnerable, sometimes simultaneously. I can't help but wonder if she's purposefully stuffing back emotions she can't comprehend.

"We could get a candy floss machine, bunting, festoons of lights. A marquee in the shape of a circus big top."

It's lovely to see my daughter so excited by something, especially after what she's been through. I feel mean throwing cold water on the idea, but I just think this is all moving too quickly. I don't know for a fact that the gifting of the designer bags inflamed Megan and her thugs enough for them to instigate the beating, but I have a feeling that it did. Jealousy is an insidious, pervasive disease. I'm concerned that throwing a look-at-us, full-on, show-off party isn't going to have the desired effect of getting all our friends, neighbors and associates to celebrate with us; it may just turn into something that will cause further resentment. "We haven't got room for any of these things. We can't fit a Ferris wheel in our garden."

My family turn to me and laugh loudly. Even Logan. "We'll rent a venue, a field or something, *obviously*."

"Obviously." I down my glass of champagne and make eye contact with the waiter. I think I might need to order a bottle after all. This is likely to be a long night.

CHAPTER 24

Lexi

Friday, May 10

The days of the week explode like fireworks, tumble, shine and then disappear now that we are lottery winners. The days have no order to them, and time seems irrelevant, almost awkward. Routines are abandoned, surprises are abundant. Friday is no longer a day when I see the kids off to school, my husband off to work and then go to work myself, partially excited that it's a half day (home by two o'clock—the freedom!) and partially panicked (how I will fit a day's work into a few hours?). Only one of my kids goes to school, and neither my husband nor I work. As my days are no longer divided into thirty-minute appointments, they stretch out, endless and indolent. This Friday I'm pleased to have something to do, somewhere to be. We are meeting with a financial advisor to decide how best to manage our millions. Unbelievable.

Jake and I sit in the huge glass atrium, staring at an eight-metre-long reception desk at which sit four receptionists of exceptional beauty. There is a living wall of plants behind them, reaching up at least ten metres and yet still not hitting the ceiling. There are a number of conversations I want to have with my husband. They hang in the air around us, like overly pungent incense: silent, colorless but intrusive all the same. This morning I received a text from Hugh, Jake's eldest brother. It detailed how much was owed on Hugh's mortgage and his bank account number. I wasn't aware Jake had asked for either thing when he called to share the good news but maybe he did. We do plan to pay off both of Jake's brothers' mortgages, but I'm a little put out by Hugh's expectation that this is a cert, and I'm irritated by the fact that he requested we make the payment in full before the end of the month, as he has apparently already canceled his direct debit. IN FULL was written in capitals.

I loathe texts that are written in capitals.

I have been a lottery winner for twenty days. I had no idea how exhausting it would be negotiating other people's emotions: the envy, disbelief, incredulity. I constantly feel a degree or two warmer than usual as I absorb the heat of everyone's gaze.

I want to tell Jake about Toma. All about Toma. Our secret mission to discover who was ultimately behind the deaths of his wife and child, and the relationship that has developed as a result of our shared undertaking. I want to tell my husband about the respect I feel for another man, because if I do that, then surely I disarm the ticking bomb. But I don't know where to start. Most importantly I *have* to tell him about the money I gave to Toma. I know Jake will be furious, and he won't understand. He'll point out that I can't right other people's wrongs, can't offer compensation. Can't play God. And even though I know what his argument will be, I find I don't know how to present my own.

Instead, I look at the wall of plants and ask, "Do you think they are real?"

"That's why it's called a living wall. We should get one."

"Why do we need a wall of plants?"

"I don't know. Why do these guys need one? It looks cool." Jake sees that I am unimpressed and so adds, "Oxygen? Imagine how much oxygen it's producing."

"Well, I can't see that in our front room."

Jake laughs, "Which is why we need to move. We need somewhere that reflects who we are now."

I am still me. The same person I was before our win. For good or bad.

I'm not anyone different and can't really imagine living anywhere different. We don't need to move. Maybe we could extend our own house. When we bought it years ago, we sometimes bandied around the idea of adding a sunroom by extending into the garden and building an extra bedroom above, if things ever picked up for Jake at work. That would be lovely. The extra space would certainly be useful.

Gillian meets us in the reception. As ever, I am delighted to see her. She is going to chair the panel of advisors, which I find reassuring. There will be a financial advisor, a solicitor and an accountant. I am dimly aware we're paying for the service of at least the latter two, maybe all three—I don't know how it works with the financial advisor. Do they make commissions off whatever products they sell? But then, everyone keeps stressing that this financial advisor is independent, so maybe that just means we pay for his expertise up front. I have no idea what these professionals cost. A lot, if the scale and style of this office is anything to go by. Jake has pointed out we can afford it anyway, so there is no need to worry about it, which I suppose is true. I almost envy the easy way he has adapted to our new wealth. He's straightforwardly overjoyed, not in the least bit overwhelmed. No twinges of conscience, no concerns about responsibility. I'm not being difficult on purpose. It is just after a lifetime of knowing what costs what and being excited when there was a two-for-one offer on at Pizza Express, it's surprisingly difficult to feel entitled to so much cash. I've always been the sort of person who shopped about, got estimates and compared quotes. I was a woman who regularly handed over coupons in supermarkets and Boots. I collect points on at least a dozen loyalty cards. I've always had to be that person, and I don't really know how to stop.

Apparently, we're to expect a different solicitor from the one that was present at the inquiry as they all have areas of expertise. I'm glad. I want to put all that business behind me and am not in a hurry to be face-to-face with Ms. Walsh again, even though she's very good at her job.

The receptionist approaches, her heels click-clacking on the marble floor. Her skirt is so tight that she has to put one foot directly in front of the other to move at all. As a result, her hips sashay left and right. She is mesmerizing: of Japanese descent, she has alabaster skin, and her long black hair falls down her back in waves. I've noticed how many beautiful people are connected to the wealthy. Without exception, the shop assistants in New Bond Street were stunners. Male or female, they were shiny, groomed, tall, symmetrical. I wonder, is that another privilege of being rich? The fact that the only people you ever come into contact with are basically supermodels. The people I usually mix with are significantly more ordinary. I finger the hem of my dress. It is new, exquisite and expensive. I bought it after much coercion from Emily. A blue abstract print, fitted, it swirls around my knees in a pleasing way. But when I bought it, I didn't think about shoes and when I put it on this morning, I realized I didn't have any that matched. I'm wearing black platform sandals. They aren't ideal. Emily is keeping a list of things she thinks I need. She's added blue shoes to said list.

"Would you like to follow me? I'll take you up to the meeting room." The receptionist's professional smile reveals pearly white, straight teeth. I run my tongue over my own and hope there's no lipstick on them. Jake chats to the receptionist whilst the elevator takes us to the fifteenth floor. He reveals a deep longing to visit Tokyo that I have never heard mentioned before. I inwardly roll my eyes, mildly irritated by his inappropriate attempt to flirt. I reach for his hand and gave it a brief squeeze. Onlookers would think it was affection, he might understand it's a warning.

The room is full of men, suited and booted. They smile with the same professionalism the receptionist has shown. I hadn't considered that smiles could be professional until recently. I've always thought they had to be warm, broad, sincere or even insincere. The room is paneled in a dark polished wood—mahogany? There are two incredible floral arrangements on the long glass table and a plate of colorful macarons. I just know that no one will eat them. I bet eating is considered frivolous at this type of meeting. I wish I dared ask to take them home for Logan, then I remember I don't need to—if we want macarons, we can buy them. The receptionist hands us over to a young man called Jeb, who is apparently our "host," then she disappears. A vision of loveliness gone in an instant. Jeb offers tea, coffee, water, still or sparkling. Once we are furnished with delicate china cups and heavy crystal glasses, he discreetly sits at the side of the room. He has an iPad and seems poised to take notes. I think he's probably fulfilling the role that used to be identified as secretary when I was much younger. I turn to the suited and booted men, now sitting the table. And take a deep breath.

There is a lot to take in. The financial advisor talks about managing risk while also tapping growth opportunities, words such as trusts, bonds, shares, options, diversifying global growth, equity investors, ISAs are all bandied about. I know what most of these words mean—in isolation—but I'm not absolutely sure I am keeping abreast of the context. My heart is thumping so hard that I imagine people can see it. I am terrified someone is suddenly going to ask how much money we have exactly, and I'll have to confess to giving Toma the three million. I don't regret doing so but I really should have told Jake. I should tell him what I have done before he finds out. Maybe he's more likely to forgive and understand if I do that.

I don't know.

Would I forgive and understand if I was handed a confession rather than having to discover something shocking? Or would I still feel enraged and vengeful? My eyes slide to Jake. He is sitting forward in his chair, eager. He emits a newfound confidence. It borders on arrogance. I stay silent.

The accountant is easier to follow.

"One of the perks of playing lotteries in the UK is that winnings are not subject to capital gains tax or income tax, regardless of how much money you win."

"I thought so!" Jake punches the air. "Winning!"

"Isn't that weird, when you think about it? You know, up until now we've earned a combined salary of fifty-six thousand a year and had to pay a big chunk of that in tax and now we get given, just *given*, this money and no tax is due," I comment.

"Are you seriously complaining because you don't have to pay tax?" asks Jake. He is laughing. At me.

"No, of course not. I'm just observing," I say defensively.

"Don't look a gift horse in the mouth," he mutters.

"I'm not, I'm just... Well, I've always believed people should pay tax. It's almost a privilege, isn't it? It means you're gainfully employed and that you are meaningfully contributing to society and..." I trail off because I've lost Jake's attention. He is shaking his head, grinning at the accountant, who is holding his face in a polite, neutral expression.

"Ignore her, go on," he urges.

The accountant throws an apologetic look my way. I don't think he is the one who should be apologizing for my husband's rudeness, but I don't want to get into it in front of strangers. I force myself to smile at the accountant to smooth waters, giving him permission to carry on.

"However, once you've deposited the winnings in your bank account, any money earned through interest is subject to income tax."

"Okay, happy now?" Jake challenges. I ignore him.

"It's very natural in circumstances such as yours that you start sharing and gifting."

Jake interrupts. "Yeah, too right. We're not tight!"

"So, it's a good idea to understand how that works in terms of tax." Jake shrugs, unconcerned, certain that whatever the tax implications are, we can afford them.

"Go on," I urge grittily, my throat tight. The words just squeeze out. I hadn't thought about the tax implications of gifting. I need to listen carefully, in case there's anything I have to tell Toma.

"You can give away three thousand pounds' worth of gifts, every year, without the recipient becoming subject to tax. This is your annual exemption."

"Three thousand pounds? That's like pocket money to us now, isn't it?" Jake laughs again, shaking his head. "Loose change, down the back of the settee." Jake claps his hands together and rubs them gleefully. I should be relieved he has such an easy come, easy go attitude to three thousand pounds. Maybe gifting three million won't rile him, either.

"Some small gifts, such as Christmas and birthday presents, or those that you can afford out of your normal income, are also exempt. To avoid complications in the event of your death, it is a good idea to keep detailed records of any gifts you give to friends and family, so that they don't unduly receive a hefty inheritance tax bill."

"Okay." I nod slowly. "And what about bigger gifts? What are the implications there?" I cough.

"We're paying off my brothers' mortgages and getting her sister a place." Jake beams, proud of his own largesse, unable to resist bragging about it.

"Right. Well, they need to know, if you were to die within seven years of handing out gifts in excess of three hundred and twenty-five thousand pounds, the recipients of those gifts would be subject to an inheritance tax bill of up to forty per cent."

Oh.

"I've no plans to die, mate," laughs Jake. "I'm going to live to be a very, very old man. I'm going to make the most of this. This has not only changed my life, it's given *meaning* to my life."

The room feels heavy. The awkward silence slips down the walls. Leave it, I tell myself. Leave it. My heart overrules my head. "Weren't me and the kids meaning?" My voice is quiet but determined and therefore powerful.

Jake colors. "Well, yes, of course. You know what I mean." He laughs again, but this time there is a distinct lack of bonhomie. He reaches out and takes my hand, squeezes it, brings it to his lips, kisses it. I let my hand go dead in his, a weight. Resistance. "But now there's no struggle. Imagine that. We're going to be okay for life and the kids, too. We've changed their lives, too."

The accountant continues to talk about a sliding scale of tax. He tells us what the laws are between spouses and much more, besides. I do my best to take it in, but all I want is for the meeting to end. For people to stop talking about money. Just for a few minutes.

Finally, we are outside, on the busy London street. The wind whips at the skirt of my dress and bits of rubbish scuttle across the road with pedestrians. It's a chilly day, the air pinches. It's been a weird spring weatherwise. Bright one minute, wet and nippy the next. Sometimes we have all four seasons in a day. It seems the mercurial weather is reflecting our situation. Unprecedented. Unforeseeable. Gillian says goodbye and Jake hails a cab. Once inside, he asks the driver to take us back to Bucks.

"I can do, mate, but it will cost you a few hundred quid."

"Let me worry about that," says Jake. He taps his breast pocket.

A flair of frustration slaps me. He is behaving like a dick. "Don't be insane," I snap. "Please just take us to Marylebone Station," I say to the cabbie. The cabbie nods, seemingly unconcerned about missing out on a huge fare that would have taken him far out of his usual zone. Most likely he is relieved. He probably thinks no amount of money is worth sitting on the A4, M4, M25 and A41 on a Friday afternoon, breathing in traffic fumes.

We sit in silence. I fiddle with the air-conditioning. I suddenly feel hot inside and out. I stare out of the window, not wanting to catch Jake's eye but unsure why. Shouldn't we be constantly celebrating? If Jake had his way, we'd be popping open a bottle of champagne in the cab, have it on tap. Anyone would. Right? My eyes fall on one grubby sleeping bag after another, legs poking out of cardboard homes. Many homeless people set up camp on the busiest London streets.

Jake sighs. His thoughts are clearly traveling along a similar path. "Why are you resisting this?" he asks.

"I'm not resisting anything, I'm—" I can't explain it to him, I can't explain it to myself.

"Don't you remember what it was like, Lexi?" Jake's voice oozes an attractive mix of emotions. He sounds sincere, concerned, reasonable. The brash, overly confident, idiot-man who was annoying and confusing has apparently slipped out of the cab. "How many times have you woken up in the middle of the night, worried about money, about our future?"

I sigh. It's true. I remember the helpless black, when my worries chased and chased around my head. Snowballing until I felt immobilized, unable to think, a panic-induced brain freeze. Last year we'd agreed that Emily could go on the school skiing trip to Norway and, to ensure things remained fair and even in our home, that Logan could go on a geography field trip to Italy. I lay awake for many nights, running the numbers through my head, over and over again. How come the trips were so expensive, considering the kids were traveling by coach, and flying on airlines that were little more than buckets with an engine? What about group discounts? And another thing, my kids were flying in *buckets*! This worry also kept me awake, but it wasn't related to money, or was it? Does money increase safety and security? I think of Toma, Reveka and Benke. Yes, of course it does.

When the kids came home from their trips, they both reported that the accommodation and food turned out to be dreadful. Not that they cared because they had been with their friends, joining in, not the ones being ignored or left out. Left behind. But I had cared because I value value for money. I knew I could have created the exact same holidays for a fraction of the price. And besides the outlay for the holiday—which we'd scrimped for—there was the cost of the equipment and kit. I'd bought Emily's ski jacket and pants from TK Maxx and yet it still came to hundreds. Logan had needed waterproofs, climbing boots and a backpack. I sold clothes on eBay to raise a bit extra. I've never told Jake, but I started to buy from there, too. T-shirts and stuff, mostly for Logan. From about the age of eleven he wanted Nike like everyone else, Superdry and Jack Wills. They were brands that I could only justify if I picked them up secondhand. Logan believes me when I say I always prewash shop clothes before he wears them to "soften them up." I've never tried the same trick with Emily. Emily needs the security of price tags. We paid for the school trips in instalments. The final payment for both trips happened to fall in the same week. I sold the ring my grandmother had given me for my twenty-first birthday. No one noticed when I stopped wearing the little ruby. No one other than me.

So, yes, I do remember the dark nights of worry. We weren't starving, we weren't living on the street, but we had to be careful. We were a family that made do, that managed.

And now that is all gone. That is all over. I am safe. We all are. We can pay off our mortgage, and we will never again see a red demand bill. It is bliss. I should be feeling something pure and uncomplicated. Joy. Happiness.

"Haven't you always wanted to be rich, Lexi?"

"Well, yes, of course. Everyone wants to be rich, don't they," I reply, trying hard not to make it sound like a question. It is obviously true that money solves a lot of problems, that is a given.

The news is, it creates some, too.

CHAPTER 25

Emily

Monday, May 13

Dad's idea of throwing a party is inspired! Just what I need. A great distraction. A way of not thinking about it. I don't like thinking about it. Even when I try, I can't. It's like I leave my body. I float above myself and theoretically think, what should that girl have done? What should she do now? And I don't *know*. So I'm not doing anything about it. Staying in the moment is the best. That's what I have to do. Not think about what has happened or what might happen next. Hey, basically I'm practicing mindfulness for screwed teens.

Dad has hired a party planner because, even though Mum doesn't have a job anymore, she wasn't really getting into the party. She constantly asked what things cost and insisted on us getting three quotes for every single thing! It was getting tiring. Plus, I don't want to be mean, but I'm not certain Mum has the vision to pull it off the way Dad and I want to see things go down. For instance, Mum agreed that it would be nice to have a moment where we cut a celebration cake as a family. She even suggested it should be tiered "to make sure there's enough to go around." But then Dad said we could have a cake with a false top tier and get a magician to pull a rabbit out of the hat or something. Better yet, a monkey in one of those cute little red showman jackets. I mean, *that* is vision. You know. But then Mum started going on about health and safety and animal cruelty and kept insisting we "consider the practicalities." Another example—Mum thought she was being flash when she gave the nod to us having loads of helium balloons, then Dad said we should get an actual hot air balloon and have it tethered to the ground but people could go up and down on it, just for fun. You know, *vision*. Let's just say Mum set a budget that she described as "generous." We've quadrupled it.

So now basically me, Dad and the party planner, Sara, are doing everything, and Mum spends most of her time dealing with the charity requests that are rolling in thick and fast. She seems pretty happy with this division of labour. Logan went back to school. He said he wanted to finish this term with his old mates and was bored at home. It's not that he's a super nerd or a saint, it's just that he never worked very hard at school before. He might as well be there, messing about with his mates and having people high-five him in the corridors than here, on his own playing video games online with complete strangers who are sweaty losers at best, but most likely potential pedos.

This party is going to be amazing!

I can't really emphasize that enough. Sara is awesome. If I ever thought I might need to get a job, I think I'd want to be a party planner, maybe. But I'm never going to need a job now though, am I? She's really creative and yet efficient and businesslike. We've plumped for *The Greatest Showman* as our theme, so basically circus with a nineteenth-century lean. She found us a field that we can rent about five miles from where we live. It doesn't look like much at the moment, just a big field, overgrown with grass and wildflowers, backing onto a frankly spooky-looking area of woodland. Behind that there is a pond that's dank and sullen. However, Sara's Pinterest boards promise the space is going to be transformed!

We are having a Ferris wheel and merry-go-round, like Dad said, and we're hiring actors to wander around pretending to be magicians or bearded ladies or whatever. We're having actual trapeze artists and a tightrope to entertain the guests. Dad said he wants to wear a red jacket and a top hat and I think he likes the idea of Mum wearing a cancan dress—ugh, perv, gross. Mum said we should all wear red, so everyone knows we're a family, but that's mad, everyone *does* know we are a family. This is why it's best she doesn't get involved. Besides, I'm more thinking I'll take my inspiration from Zendaya's costume, not the purple glitzy number but the simpler one she wears when she's rehearsing—hot pink hot pants and a blush camisole. I want to look cool and stand out, but as though I haven't tried at all.

Like we first talked about, we're going to have popcorn machines, candy floss and festoons of colorful lights everywhere! Dad's coming good on all his promises. We couldn't find a red-and-white-striped marquee and so we are having a white one customised. There is going to be a hog roast plus a selection of cabins with other food options, like crepes, hot dogs and burgers—although I'm not sure exactly how nineteenth century they are. I'll Google. There is going to be a cocktail bar and a massive champagne tower. You know, a stack of those round tit-shaped champagne glasses piled high up and you pour champers from the top and it flows into all the glasses. Sticky, I bet, but so glam! I think it's time I started to drink. Why not? Logan is right, basically I'm a freak. What's the worst that can happen if I get drunk and I lose control of my mind and my knickers? I mean, really? How much worse can it get? When we were about thirteen, Ridley started sneaking alcopop into socials by pretending it was a slush puppy. I just didn't feel ready to get behind it then. I don't know, maybe it was because Logan was often out with me and he'd definitely have snitched me up to Mum and Dad. They'd have gone ape—hypocritically, I might add, as they both can knock it back. Then suddenly, Ridley and Megan and everyone I've ever met were drinking vodka straight, hard-core. They seemed to skip the beer and cider stage.

Mum says I can't invite Megan and Ridley to the party. I get that, I know why she hates them. I hate them, too.

Sort of.

I want them at the party, though. I want Megan there because she has to see it all, to see my life and know what she could have shared with me, but she couldn't let herself because she is boiling in her own jealousy and she just can't be happy for me. It's so weird that I'm not sharing this with her considering everything we shared up until this point in our lives. Like secrets, chicken pox, crushes, hairbrushes, homework, lip gloss. The list is endless. We created things, too—memories, friendship bracelets, rose perfume in jam jars. And Ridley? Well, we've done so much together. We've curled up on a sofa watching Disney movies, telling ourselves we were only enjoying them in an ironic nostalgic way, but in fact loving them for real, in an authentic way. We've played Chicken Wing Roulette at Nando's, we've Christmas-shopped in London, we went to our first gig together.

We've made a baby.

I need to talk to Ridley, I suppose. Although how am I going to say what I have to? It kills me, but I miss him so much. It's so uncool of me not to just straightforward kick-him-out-of-bed-hate-him. I didn't know until now that it was possible to hate and love a person at the same time. I miss the way when I'm with him I feel strangely light-headed. The way he moves, effortless and loose, thick hair, dark and curly. Backpack flung over his shoulder. I used to cling to his other shoulder as casually, as intrinsically. I miss the feel of his hands on me. I miss the way he throws back his head when he laughs, exposing his lumpy Adam's apple. His laugh is the best if I've caused it. I miss the conversations we had. "What's your greatest fear?" He asked me this as he trailed kisses up and down my thigh and hip. His lips were gentle, tender and yet also hot. Right then, I had none. No fears at all. He made me fearless.

"Weird question," I pointed out.

He smiled. "Yes, I guess it is. I was hoping you'd say, losing me." He looked shy, sheepish. I grinned.

"Yeah, that's it," I replied, indulging him. He came toward me and kissed my mouth. Through his kisses, I murmured, "Losing you and not doing this again are my fears."

He momentarily stopped kissing me and stared at me with a fabulous intensity, his dark eyes boring into me, like he knew me inside out. "Then you are totally safe. Which is all I want. I want to protect you and keep you safe forever."

This was quite caveman as an approach, but it bothered me less than it should.

The conversations we had were the sort you can't have with anyone else, not even Megan. I miss the musty smell of his balls. Obviously, I hate him, too.

Or maybe not obviously. Not at all.

"Dad, are you going to ask Jennifer and Fred to the party?" I ask as we are examining Sara's map and timing plan of the evening's flow.

"Your mum isn't keen."

"Yeah, but they've apologized, right? And set the record straight about them not being in the lottery."

"You think I should forgive them?"

Dad keeps his eyes on the plan. He marks up a suggestion in pencil, swapping the crepe stall with the taco cabin, so that the sweet options are all on one side of the big marquee and the savory on another. I'm not sure it should be regimented, but don't want to get into it with him as we might get off track. It's because he seems caught up in something else that I feel I dare admit, "Maybe."

"What if they bring Ridley along? Do you want to see him?"

"God, Dad, no. No way." Yes. Yes, more than anything. "I mean, if they bring him along, I'm cool with that, but I don't *want* to see him."

Dad looks at me now. Steadily. Unblinking, he searches my face for something. Whatever he was looking for he must be satisfied as he says, "I might ask them, then, if you are okay with it."

I shrug. Dad gets me.

CHAPTER 26

Lexi

Monday, May 20

I look out of the window and see that the dark gray cloud, which has hovered all day, has now swollen to stretch across the entire sky. Rain is imminent. I wonder how much progress my family has made today. Jake, Emily and Logan are all at the party site helping pitch the marquee. Actually, if only that was true, then I'd be there with them lending a hand. To be accurate, they are standing about watching other people mow the field, pitch the marquee, lay the dance floor inside the marquee. I haven't joined them because I don't want to endorse our children's idleness and increasing belief, encouraged by Jake, that they can pay someone else to do everything for them.

We now have a cleaner and she does our ironing, too. She's a lovely woman and I'm sure Jake's right, I probably will get used to the idea of someone throwing bleach down my loo and emptying the bathroom bin. Eventually. I can't deny that our house has never been tidier; in fact, it's immaculate as it has benefited from two thorough goings-over this week, the first one done by me before our cleaner arrived.

As much as Jake loves his brand-new Ferrari, which he took delivery of last week, he doesn't clean it himself. Yesterday he got someone to come around to do a specialist inside-and-out clean, even though it's only a whisper away from pristine. Certainly, a far cry from the state we used to allow the old family Volvo to get into. The inside of that always reflected the fact it had served years of hard labor ferrying us around. A foot deep of crisp packets, banana skins and Diet Coke cans was the norm. Whenever I drove it, I kept the window down an inch to try to disperse the stench of rotting food, sweaty sports kits and dried mud. Jake has got rid of the Volvo. He's bought a new Audi Q7. In metallic brown. It's undeniably gorgeous. He says it's my car.

"Mine?" I wouldn't have chosen brown.

"Well, the family car. You know, because we can't all fit into the Ferrari."

I haven't had a chance to drive the Audi yet, but I have been a passenger and it definitely smells better than the Volvo.

Jake and the kids have been at the party site all day. Emily keeps sending me photos of the props and rides arriving and being unloaded from huge vans and lorries. Her photos are pretty good, and I want to show that I'm interested so I reply with a series of exuberant messages. Awesome!! Amazing! Wow! And a string of overly jolly emojis. Sometimes I have to admit emojis are a godsend—they save us from ever having to articulate anything tricky. Emily has yet another new phone, the second in as many weeks. She told us that she dropped her first one when she was trying to carry a takeaway coffee and Snapchat someone at the same time. "Why weren't you more careful?" I grumbled when she finally admitted this to be the case. I could hear my father's voice singing in my head, *easy come, easy go*, a reprimand that carried such force when I was a child. I had instinctively known that nothing had come easy to my parents, who worked long hours at hard jobs to provide for me and my sister.

"I just dropped it, Mum. I didn't do it on purpose," Emily muttered sulkily. "What do you want me to do—chain it to me?"

"Well, you could buy a case," I suggested. She seemed okay with that suggestion. It gave her something else to buy online. She has spent a lot of time online buying stuff. I can't bring myself to tell her off about that. What else is she supposed to do if she's not at school and isn't seeing her friends or boyfriend anymore? Until recently Emily defied the stereotype of a teen. She served on the school student council for three years, she was an active member of the debating society, she sang in the school choir, and last year she was the only student in her year to receive the Gold Award of Leadership Through Service at school. It was a scheme that a keen member of staff set up, which monitored just about everything the kids did: attendance, participation in sport and clubs, volunteering work, etc. It was pretty much the most hated thing in Year 9 because they all felt their every moment was clocked-in and clocked-out. That said, Emily did everything that was required. Never put a foot wrong. I remember at the time Ridley and Megan teased her, saying she had an unhealthy respect for rules considering she's a teenager. They, and a handful of others, got the silver award. Getting up on a Sunday morning to coach lower school hockey games was the deal breaker. I was so proud of her enthusiasm and her community spirit.

She doesn't seem interested in anything other than shopping now.

I am not a big shopper so when I was asked to leave work, I had worried that I would be bored, but in fact as one door closes, another opens. As Gillian told us to expect, we are now receiving a lot of letters requesting charitable donations or asking if we are interested in investing in different ventures, some no doubt real, others appearing deeply suspicious. We are not unlisted. A fact that we had entirely forgotten because that decision was made when God was a boy, and no one had ever really heard of data protection, privacy issues, etc. Certainly, none of us could have imagined a scenario whereby people we didn't already know might want to contact us. Within just hours of the public announcement of the win, we began to understand what that historic decision meant. The phone started to ring nonstop. Most of the calls were from family, friends, neighbors and some vaguer acquaintances congratulating us on our luck; others were from complete strangers wanting to help us spend our cash. We unplugged the landline pretty sharpish and I put the handset in a cupboard. If only everything could be cleared away so easily. As we didn't opt out of the telephone directory, this doesn't just mean people could call us. It also apparently means that our address is easily tracked down online. We are now inundated with letters that Jake scathingly refers to as begging letters.

"They are not begging letters."

"Right, some of them are scams."

"They are just overtures from strangers."

"And I suppose strangers are just friends you haven't yet met?" he says with something that seems close to a sneer.

"Maybe," I mumble sulkily.

"Is there a single letter that doesn't ask for money?"

"Well, no." He makes a sound of victory, confident that he's proven his point. "But most of them are asking for money on other people's behalf. It's actually fascinating to see the breadth of charities and enterprises that exist in order to make the world a better place. If you watch the news or go online, it's easy to imagine the world is going to hell in a handcart, but reading through these charity requests reminds me that there are countless good people out there trying to make things better, not just for themselves, but more often than not, for others. There are a number of interesting projects that—" I looked up and noticed he'd left the room. The kids seemed embarrassed for me.

Unfortunately, the flip side of beginning to comprehend how many charities and aid projects there are in the world is that it drives home the fact that there are endless people who are suffering and in need of help. I sit at the kitchen table and let my fingers trail over the words that have been sent my way. Most of them are sprawled across printed letters, or even professional-looking pamphlets and brochures, but some have been handwritten. Florid, loopy requests made in ink; fast, urgent pleas in pencil, even some desperate, rudimentary ones in crayon. They all say the same. Help me.

I'm not sure how I will decide which causes to support.

...We work in twenty-two countries, helping communities to lift themselves out of poverty through education, training and supporting livelihoods...

Donate safe in the knowledge that it will be used where it is most needed...

...Be the reason for improved livelihoods...

...Your donation means we can continue funding vital research into heart disease, strokes and...

...Just a small donation could support a PhD student starting their career in research in vascular dementia...

...Become a sponsor today, and you'll see a child's life change for the better. By sponsoring a child you'll help them have access to safe, clean water, health care and education...

At first, I approach the letters haphazardly. I pick them up, read them, paw them, put them down again. It's only after I have read about twenty and I pick up one I recognize that I realize I need a system. I sort the requests into three piles. One for charitable requests, another for investment requests in businesses and a third for scams. These letters—from people asking for my bank details, a PayPal transfer or urging me to invest in wine, land, carbon credits, gold or diamonds—all go in the bin.

I put the more genuine-looking investment opportunities into a file—I'll look at those later. It's the charitable projects that interest me the most. The extraordinary wealth is weighing heavily on me, but at the same time it affords me a tremendous opportunity. I can do a lot of good.

I realize that many will think impulsively giving Toma, a relative stranger, three million pounds was an act of insanity.

Maybe it was.

I should have told Jake by now. I really should have. I know that. But I haven't. The right moment hasn't presented itself. I'm beginning to think the right moment doesn't exist. Jake will be livid, that's for certain. He'll see it as a betrayal. Maybe even cruelty or spite. I wonder how long it will take him to notice. Whilst he is very keen on spending the money we won, he hasn't yet shown any interest in investing it or monitoring what is in our prestige bank account. He spends, spends, spends, safe in the knowledge that we have enough, we have plenty.

Jake and I are not seeing eye to eye on much at the moment. Whilst I'm dealing with all the correspondence regarding charitable endeavours, he's dealing with the party RSVPs. As he left the house today, he oh so casually said, "You know, the Heathcotes have said yes to coming to the party."

"Have they?"

"Which is a good thing."

"Is it, though?"

"Lexi, they changed their statement. We got what we wanted."

"Their son beat up our daughter."

"Well, technically, he didn't beat her—Megan and her cronies did."

"Jake! Can you even hear yourself? Okay, technically, he stood by and watched as our daughter, his *girlfriend*, was beaten up."

"They've been buffeting one another around since they were toddlers. Fallouts, scraps and makeups are a way of life to them. Emily is fine with this. Kids will be kids," says Jake with a shrug.

"You know this is nothing to do with kids being kids."

"I think it's important we make a clear and public statement that all that nonsense about them claiming to be winners is water under the bridge."

I glared at him. "We don't need to make clear and public statements about anything. We're not running the country. How do we know something won't kick off again? What if they hurt Emily again?"

"Tensions were high. Things have calmed down now."

The one thing I know about parties is that nothing ever calms down at them.

I sigh, check the clock. I should put on some dinner. They'll probably be home soon. I decide to prepare a lasagna. We've been eating out a lot recently, still too high to consider anything as mundane as cooking. Maybe we're ready for some home-cooked food, and lasagna is a long-standing crowd-pleaser in our family. Good, solid, comfort food that I regularly serve up when the kids are feeling overwhelmed with schoolwork or after an important sports match or when Jake has had a long day at the office. Often on Tuesdays. He always used to work late on Tuesdays.

None of the above apply, but I find I have a need to eat lasagna anyway. Reading the letters has been emotionally exhausting. I heat some olive oil in a frying pan, the gas is up too high and it snaps and spits. I pour myself a glass of red wine and put on the radio as I like to listen to Classic FM when I'm cooking. I don't listen to classical music at any other time. Usually, I prefer listening to Sara Cox on Radio 2, but somehow the fugue and rondeau lift browning meat and onions from a mundane chore to something a little more special. I add the passata, beef stock and grated nutmeg. I leave the dish to simmer for half an hour and then put a WhatsApp message on our family chat asking what time I should expect them. I hold the phone for a few minutes until the blue ticks appear that tell me my message has been read by everyone. I wait a little longer, hoping for a response—none comes. I see that all three are online, then Logan isn't. A message tells me Emily is typing. And then she is not. She goes offline without giving me an ETA. I wait for Jake to pick up the mantle. I send another message. Just an estimate will do.

No response. Charming.

The kitchen suddenly seems moody and morose. The gloomy clouds have thickened and although it's only seven o'clock, it's much darker than it ought to be on a May evening. A dark shape slips along the low back fence: the neighbor's cat. Another shadow slinks on the ground. A wily fox.

Flicking on the electric light, I swallow the lump of irritation that sticks in my throat and continue with the prep regardless. Maybe they are just heading home and didn't think it was worth telling me as they'll be here in ten minutes. I spoon the meat sauce into the warmed and greased ovenproof dish, then cover with some fresh lasagna sheets and then cheat a little by layering on ready-made white sauce. I get great pleasure in repeating this process three times, scattering torn mozzarella and prosciutto over the top and popping the entire dish into the oven to bake. There's something lovely and reassuring about producing a big slab of food where, just a short time ago, there was nothing.

I become aware that not only is it dark in the kitchen, but a chill is sweeping through the house. A door slams shut upstairs and makes me jump. The wind is getting up outside and I have all the bedroom windows open. In the garden the trees are shuddering, their leaves rustling as though they are whispering and chattering among themselves, passing on slippery secrets. The sky is charcoal. Raindrops splash onto the kitchen window, fat and determined, the type that suggest an oncoming deluge. I run around the house closing windows. Last year we had a heat wave, and either because we're an optimistic nation or a dumb one, I think we were all expecting the same again despite the fact that the heat wave before last was in 1976. We really ought only to be hopeful every forty-two years. Funny thing, I made this jokey observation to my next-door neighbor this morning, a woman in her eighties who I have always pegged as a sweet old dear.

We have rubbed along side by side for over a decade, passing pleasantries, helping each other when needed. She is tolerant when the kids make a lot of noise in the garden, and Jake puts her bins out.

"I think all your summers have come at once, haven't they? And your Christmases, too, come to that. You can't complain about the weather. You can't complain about anything ever again," she said. Then she chuckled, but it wasn't a nice old lady chuckle—it was a fake laugh, spiked through with aggression.

"I didn't really mean a good summer would be nice for me specifically," I stuttered. "It would be nice for everyone." She glared at me over her glasses. The message was clear: I am no longer entitled to want anything, not even a sunny day.

The downpour is relentless now. I listen to the rain slap the garden patio, our roof, the windows. A drum roll, a constant growl. It's drowning out my classical music so I turn that up to an uncomfortably high volume. I wonder how far they have got with putting up the marquee. This rain will be a problem if the top and sides aren't on yet. Although, however much of a problem it is, I'm sure the party planner will have a solution. She'll buy electric fans to dry the place out, heaters to warm it up. She'll buy carpet for the fields. Money can't solve everything, but it certainly helps when it comes to party planning. I send Jake another message. How's the progress with the tent? I've made a lasagna. Are you on your way home?

His response. We are all in the pub. Sheltering from the rain. We'll grab something to eat here.

A thought jabs my mind, I wonder who "we are all" is referring to exactly. Him and the kids? The party planner? Other people? Who else? I didn't used to be a jealous woman. I never watched Jake the way some women feel the need to watch their husbands.

I never anticipated infidelity. Even when we were very young and both quite striking, when we had chances and choices, I trusted him. We felt solid. Recently, I've felt we are on shifting sands.

I carefully take the piping hot lasagna out of the oven. The delicious smell of cheese, beef and tomatoes floods the kitchen. Seems like a waste to cut into it just for me. Never mind, it will be better tomorrow anyway because it will have settled. I open myself a tin of baked beans and put a couple of slices of bread in the toaster. I suppose I could go and see them at the pub, but it's too wet to walk, I'm not insured on the Ferrari and they have the Audi. Anyway, Jake didn't suggest that I join them, so I feel it might be strangely intrusive. They all—whoever they all are—have spent the day together party planning, and it will be awkward if I muscle in now. Besides, I still have the letters to plow through.

I decide the best way to try to keep track of the requests is to input the details into a spreadsheet. I can log whether funds are for research or relief, education and ongoing development or emergency aid, animals or people, elderly or the young, home or abroad. It still strikes me that it will be a near-impossible job to rank one worthy cause above another, but it feels like a start. It doesn't take long for me to become absorbed. The next thing I know, I look up and see that it's late. It's pitch-black outside; as the lights are on in the kitchen, my image reflects back from the black windows as though I am staring into a mirror.

I am alone.

I mean, obviously I am alone—the others are at the pub—but I am shocked by my reflection. I'm a small woman; however, I've always thought of myself as strong, centered. The reflection that shines back at me exposes a woman who looks isolated, frail and intense. So much has gone on in the past few weeks. I think I'm managing everything, but am I? My hair needs a wash. I should have a blow-dry. I love a blow-dry, and it's not as though I can't afford to treat myself. The truth is I've been avoiding going to my hairdresser's, avoiding all the fuss that will inevitably ensue. All eyes on me, the same barrage of questions. "I bet you can't believe your luck?"

"No, no, I can't."

"What are you going to spend it on?"

"We haven't quite decided yet."

"A house? Car? Travel?"

"Probably." I have encountered this script sixty, seventy, eighty times in the past few weeks. I know I disappoint people. They want me to be more effusive, more committed. They don't understand my reticence. I am wearing jeans and a T-shirt, the same ones I wore yesterday. I should do my nails, too. They are bitten and chipped. I do not look like a lottery winner. The party is in five days' time. I'll have to up my game for that. I can't present myself like this—it's not what people are expecting. Jake would be disappointed. Jake likes painted nails.

As I stare at my reflection, which I fear appears wizened, even vulnerable, rather than wild and winning. It strikes me that anyone outside might see me this way, as well. If they were looking.

I shiver at that thought, unsure as to where it came from.

The rain is still falling persistently. I hear the sound of the plastic recycling bins being scraped along the side path. The wind most likely blew them over and now that fox I saw earlier will be hungrily rooting through the smelly food bin. There will be a mess to clean up in the morning. I think the shed door must have blown open, too, because I hear that swing and bang, swing and bang.

Then something about the light in the hallway changes and catches my attention. Our front door is partially glass plated, and light from the garden lamp floods onto the hall carpet. A momentary dimming, a flickering, suggests someone has just walked up the path. I walk into the hallway, but something stops me putting on the light in there. I see a shadow at the front door. At first I think it's Jake and the kids home at last, but I didn't hear the car and there's none of their familiar chatter heralding their arrival. The shadow looms as whoever it is approaches the door. I wait for the knock, and it doesn't come. I watch as the door handle moves. The door is locked, but I'm turned to stone knowing that whoever it is on the other side just tried to come in without knocking.

And then it is gone. The shadow. The person. Did I imagine something? Conjure someone? I rush to the kitchen window, instinctually wanting to drop the blinds, block out whatever is there in the blackness and cocoon me in the warmth of my home. I scream as I see three faces at the window. Two men and a woman. They smile and wave. The woman is in her late forties, and she has a gap where a bottom tooth is missing. I think I recognize her face. Maybe I've seen her at the CAB. The two men are big and brawly. They have no hair or necks. The younger one is covered in pockmarks that advertise he once suffered badly with acne. They continue to smile and wave, and one of them puts up both his thumbs in an old-fashioned gesture that I only ever see on emojis now. His hands look huge, and despite the gesture I think they are threatening. Did those hands turn the handle on my front door?

"All right, love, can we come in?" the older guy shouts through the window, over the sound of the rain. I shake my head. My heart is pounding—I can feel it in my mouth—and my chest is going to explode. "Come on, love. We're getting drenched out here."

"I don't know you," I mutter. "I don't know you," and then I drop the blind.

I hear them grumble among themselves. I'm shaking, ashamed to have literally drawn a blind down on a fellow human being and also terrified. They might be perfectly lovely people, but I don't know. I can't judge. One of them bangs hard on the window.

I grab my phone and then wonder who to call. Jake? The police? No crime has been committed. They are not really trespassing, just calling round. I wait and nearly collapse with relief when I hear the footsteps move away from the window. The next moment my back door swings open. Jake and the kids must have forgotten to lock it. I should have checked it.

"Come in, can we?" asks the woman, but they are already in the middle of my kitchen and we all know I didn't invite them. She shakes herself, like a dog does when it comes out of the rain. She isn't wearing a coat and she looks blue with cold. Her thin, worn leggings and scruffy hoodie not offering much protection against the elements. She's wearing flip-flops. They are muddy. Her feet are misshapen, no doubt from years of wearing poorly fitting, cheap shoes. The men are bigger, fatter and seem insulated, yet they still wear an air about them that suggests a lack. A need. I've seen this exact demeanor many times at work. Neediness edging into desperation and anger. Although it shouldn't feel shocking, it does because it is in my kitchen. My home. My body is stiff with dread. I wait to see what they will ask for.

"Have you got a towel? To dry off my hair?" asks the woman. I open the drawer where we keep the tea towels. It sticks a little, and I wobble it aggressively and then hand her a bundle. She starts to squeeze the water out of her long hair. I hand towels to the men, too; they use them to rub their bald heads and make jokes about buffing boiled eggs.

"What do you want?" I ask. My voice comes out challenging, awkward. I wanted to sound confident or polite. Either strategy would be better than appearing difficult. I do need a strategy. These people are not my friends—what are they doing here? Are they going to rob me? Threaten me? Hurt me?

"A cup of tea would be nice," says the slightly younger guy. He holds himself up tall. He's at least six feet two, maybe sixteen stone. I slowly move toward the kettle, fill it with water and then set it to boil.

"Why are you in my home?"

"You're the lottery winner, ain't ya?" I consider denying it, but what's the point? My face and those of my family have been all over the local press and news. Around here we are celebrities. At least the children aren't at home. At least they are safe.

"Seventeen-point-eight-million pounds, weren't it?" asks the other guy. I don't reply. I see the rain that has run from their clothes and bodies puddling on my kitchen floor. "That must take some spending." He stares at me. I find myself nodding in agreement. "Them are letters asking for a cut, are they?"

"Some." My voice cracks in my throat, I cough to clear it. We all listen to the sound of the water heating up in the kettle. Could I use that as a weapon, if I had to? Do I have that in me? It's a crazy, drastic thought. I glance at the kitchen knives displayed in a wooden block on the surface. I quickly pull my eyes away, not wanting to draw attention to them. I'm not in a TV show. I know any weapon I try to use is most likely to be used against me.

"The thing is," says the woman, "I came by to see you at work. I was queuing with a lot of other people actually. You ran off. You said you'd be back, but you weren't." She stares at me reproachfully. And even though I was told to leave, effectively sacked, certainly without choice, I feel accused, condemned and guilty.

"What did you want help with?" I ask.

"I owe money." She glances at the floor, suggesting a sense of shame, or maybe it's just exhaustion. "I only borrowed one hundred and fifteen quid but now they are saying I owe nearly two thousand pounds." I notice that she's shaking, too. "They'll hurt me if I don't pay." My heart lurches in sympathy. This woman is slight, defenceless physically and most likely mentally, too. I don't even waste my breath suggesting she try the official channels to fight back against this loan shark. That sort of justice and recourse is simply not available to some—it's an impossible dream, like a unicorn jumping over a rainbow. The chances are the loan shark is part of her community. There would be repercussions.

"And you two?"

"We're just here to get her and the cash home safely." I realize that these men are as much of a threat to her as they are to me.

"I don't have that sort of money in the house. I can't give you it, even if I wanted to."

He does it slowly, deliberately, so that I understand it was a conscious decision and not an unthinking reflex. The younger of the two heavy men slaps the woman in the face. His substantial paw leaves an angry print on her cheek. She keeps her eyes on me, pleading.

"I could write a check." I move to the drawer above the one where we keep the tea towels and pull it open. My checkbook is in there because usually the only checks I ever write are ones for my kids' school stuff: class photos or a random piece of sports kit, and normally those checks are demanded at breakfast time as one of the children is heading out the door.

The man laughs and holds his hand up as though to strike her again. Of course they are not going to take a check—it was crazy of me to suggest it. They know a check can be traced; they know I would cancel it as soon as they left. My guess is they want to be quickly in and out. I'm nothing to them, just a means to an end. I don't know what to do. I don't want them to hurt her, but can I really stop them? I consider walking to the cashpoint with them, but they might do much worse out there in the storm. To either or both of us. I have my phone in my hand and wonder if I can call 999. This woman may not be in a position to call out a loan shark, but I certainly am. "Please, please," she begs, keeping her eyes on me.

Then suddenly there are car headlights on the street. The two men and I look nervously at the door. I don't want my children walking in on this. The men don't know who might be arriving. My husband may be returning with a gang of friends for all they know.

In a flash the older man picks up my laptop and says, "This will cover it." The next moment he is out the back door. The second man and the woman follow him. "Don't go with them. Stay here," I yell after her. She keeps running. As they scarper down the back path, the front door opens wide, and Jake, Emily and Logan come into the house. They are chatting and laughing. They are wet, but on them the rain looks luminous, pearlescent. Emboldened by Jake's arrival, I dash along the back path and scream again, "You don't have to go with them." I think my words have been picked up and tossed far away by the wind until the woman turns around. I feel a sense of joy that I can intervene, I can after all rescue her. Then she flicks me the V sign. "Fuck off, rich bitch," she yells. I can hear them all laughing. For a moment, I stand on the path, rain drilling down on me, confused, and then I understand it was a scam. She was in on it with them. I go back into the kitchen, slam the door behind me, lock it and pull the bolt across.

Jake looks concerned when he sees me dripping on the kitchen floor. "What's going on?" he asks.

"We're moving," I reply.

CHAPTER 27

Lexi

Tuesday, May 21

I want to move into a hotel right away and stay there until we find somewhere new to live, but Jake says I'm overreacting.

"Easy for you to say. You weren't the one face-to-face with them in the kitchen." I haven't slept, not surprisingly, so his normal everything-will-be-all-right manner isn't reassuring me—it's annoying me.

"We'll hire security guards. I have a contact. The people who are doing the security at the party might be able to help."

"People who routinely search teenagers' bags for vodka and know how to put a puking adolescent into the recovery position might not cut it," I mutter crossly.

"They are big guys, ex-army. We'll all be fine."

I want to talk to someone who will sympathize and reassure me, but I don't know who to call. That thought is sobering.

Cold. I don't want to ring my parents because I know I'll make them anxious if I tell them about the intrusion. As people who grew up poor and brought a family up on not much at all, they are dwelling in a happy, uncomplicated bubble, staunch in the belief that our lottery win is the answer to all problems. I consider calling Ellie, but we haven't spoken since she asked me to leave the office. We've exchanged two or three emails, the tone of which have been remote, strictly professional. Whilst Ellie said it was just a temporary leave of absence, I'm not sure there is a place for me at the bureau anymore. Not for the first time I grieve for what I had with Carla and Jennifer. For so many years they were my go-to friends. The people I shared every thought, feeling, crisis and triumph with. Then I feel such a huge wave of ferocity, it nearly swipes me off my feet. As though truly underwater and out of my depth, I kick and flounder and try to find firm ground. I never really knew either woman, despite the fact we have been friends for fifteen years. In the end I call Gillian from the lottery company. I liked her from the moment I met her. Right now, she feels like the only person in the world who won't want something from me and therefore might just be in a position to give me something.

Gillian doesn't let me down. Sensible and serious, she acknowledges that the incident must have been incredibly frightening.

"Can we meet to talk about it?" I ask, feeling weak and silly, but knowing I really need her.

"Of course."

"Today? Can I take you for lunch?" And then, so I don't sound hopelessly cloying, I add, "I'd like to thank you for everything you've done."

"We can certainly meet today, but you can't take me for lunch, I'm afraid. We're not allowed to accept any gifts from winners. We can go for lunch if I pay my way. Would you like to do that?"

"Yes, please, I really want to get out of the house."

We arrange to meet in a pasta chain restaurant in town. I

appreciate her choice. It's low-key and straightforward. We'll be able to chat freely without any overly officious waiters—understandably keen to score a big tip—constantly interrupting to ask if our food is good, if there is anything they can do for me, anything at all. Honestly here, we'll be lucky to catch the attention of the waiting staff when we actually want it; the staff are much more interested in huddling in a group, talking about eyebrow shapes, than they are in attending to us. I oddly like it. It makes me think of work—standing in a gaggle with Rob, Heidi and Judy in the grubby kitchenette that passed as a staff room, talking about what we watched on TV on the weekend.

Gillian is already at the table, and as I approach she stands up, draws me into a big hug, which lasts longer than most. She's a curvy, motherly woman and I enjoy sinking into her. Then she breaks away and produces a small bunch of orange gerberas, tied with an elastic band. She hands them to me with a broad smile. Over the past month we have received at least twenty bouquets of flowers from people congratulating us on our win. Maybe more. I've lost count. We didn't have enough vases and, in the end, put them in glasses and buckets. Every bouquet was beautiful; flowers are an undisputed joy. Many of them came from family, and I massively appreciated the thought of my sister, Jake's brothers and sisters-in-law wanting to celebrate with us; others came from people I hadn't heard from in years, people that had fallen off the Christmas card list. I meant to take the flowers to the local old people's home, but things were so busy that before I got around to it, their stems began to rot. The house was flooded with a pungent, slightly sweet fetid smell of dead foliage. The bouquets were all significantly more elaborate than these five bright blooms, but I think this is the bunch I appreciate most.

"There's nothing in the rule book that says we can't buy you a gift," explains Gillian with a smile. "I'm so sorry about what has happened. You've been very unlucky. I checked with all my colleagues who've worked with numerous other lottery winners and, as far as we're aware, no one in the past has endured anything similar."

"I imagine it's because I work with people in very difficult situations. They are more vulnerable, and therefore the small minority of them might sometimes be reckless. I suppose that has left me exposed."

We order, and as we eat Gillian asks, "What did the police say?"

I sigh, it's awkward. "Jake said there was no point in going to the police."

Gillian looks shocked. "But of course there is. You said you recognized the woman. I'm certain they'll be able to track them down."

I shrug. "He thinks we have had enough upheaval and we should just focus on moving forward." Obviously, she already knows about the Pearsons and Heathcotes making a claim on our win, and I explain that I've been asked to take a break from work, that Jake has resigned and that we are going to change the kids' school. I don't tell her about Emily's beating. It's not as though she can do anything about that situation, and it would be a case of a problem shared, a problem doubled, not halved. We are not her responsibility.

Gillian understands that it is almost impossible to continue living in our home. There are no walls, fences, not even a gate. What if those three from last night are just the thin end of the wedge? Should we expect to be inundated with people just turning up asking for money? Some might ask politely, or there may be more threats. Either way it will become impossible, intolerable.

"If you move, though, can I recommend you consider staying close by, at least to start with? We've found that really works for other lottery winners," suggests Gillian. "Keep your support system around you, just pick somewhere less accessible for strangers. Maybe somewhere less remote." She reaches for her iPad. "I've taken the liberty of doing a bit of a search on the internet. Just to give you some ideas. There is a new development in Great Chester that's almost finished. A gated cul-de-sac that might be worth a look."

Gillian shows me photos of five lovely new houses on a private road. I am aware of the development as Jennifer, Carla and I have been closely watching the building project progress over the last year. We were planning on having a mooch around the showhouse together as soon as it was open to the public. At the time none of us had any intention of moving, but we all like a nose because you can get some inspiration on how to do up your own home—it's a good way to spend a Saturday afternoon. Although the show house opened up Easter weekend, we never got there. The houses in the photos are certainly grander than ours. They are all basically the same with a few cosmetic differences. For example, you can choose your own kitchen units, and the tiles and carpets vary throughout. There are two different sorts of front doors to pick from. According to the listing, all the houses have five bedrooms, three with en suites, a reception room and a snug—whatever that is, somewhere for the kids to hang out, I suppose. They each have separate garages and huge kitchens. I could see myself living in one of these houses, happily. They are not too impossibly grand, but they are elegant, spacious, aspirational.

"You'd get a level of security without feeling cut off," points out Gillian. This search is thoughtful of her and so close to an act of friendship that I feel tears sting in my eyes. The fact I notice the kindness somehow draws attention to the lack of it in my life at the moment. I used to want to live in Great Chester, if we could ever have afforded it. I wanted to be able to walk to my friends' homes, knock on their doors and have impromptu get-togethers, but since I'm no longer friends with Carla and Jennifer, Great Chester has lost its appeal. I don't say this to Gillian—

it would sound ungrateful. Instead, I thank her, tell her I might take a look, although I won't. Then I change the subject and start talking about the party.

We pass a pleasant hour and a half. I want to linger longer, but Gillian has to get back to the office. I envy her sense of purpose and business. As she stands up to leave, I feel a flush of embarrassment at being the rudderless person who does not have to be somewhere. Anywhere.

"I don't want to get overinvolved and push my beak in where it's not wanted," she says with an apologetic grin.

"What is it? Honestly, all advice welcome."

She looks uncomfortable but earnest. I recognize the expression because I sometimes wore it at the CAB when I overstepped a guideline. "Even if the development at Great Chester isn't for you, can I urge you to just maybe think twice about buying somewhere too far away, or too grand, or too—" she searches for the word "—isolated."

The first thing I spot when I arrive home is the for-sale sign standing tall in our front garden.

"That was quick," I comment to Jake.

"Your safety comes first. Why would I delay?" he replies. His comment is somewhat at odds with the one he made this morning about my overreacting, but since it would be very churlish to grumble since he has come around to my point of view I just nod, smile. "I've also booked security guys who will start work this evening at six. They are going to stay overnight."

"Where will they stay?" I ask.

"On the sofa."

"They agreed to that?"

"People agree to anything for the right price." His comment is throwaway—his easy, firm belief. "Anyway, it won't be for long, we're moving out tomorrow."

"You've found a hotel? Great. Then why can't we go tonight?"

"Not a hotel, I've found a home."

I had been edging out of my shoes, busy shrugging off my jacket and looking for a vase to put the gerberas in, but this news makes me pivot to face him. I expect him to be wearing a huge triumphant grin, an expression I've become accustomed to seeing when he arrives home with his latest booty. I'm more concerned that he is not smirking goofily; he simply looks decisive, firm and matter-of-fact. Choosing us a home isn't a matter of joy for him, it's his prerogative. I struggle to process this shift in the dynamics between us. We used to discuss everything from what we were going to have for tea to what we should watch on TV. Certainly, where we live would have been a matter of intense debate. In the past. Why aren't I involved in these decisions anymore? He checks his watch, then smiles smoothly, as though nothing is different or wrong. "Come on, hurry up. You'll need to get changed. An agent is arriving in fifteen minutes to take us for a viewing."

"You haven't seen it? You've bought a house and you haven't even seen it?" I splutter.

"I saw it online. There's nothing to worry about. It's out of this world. Anyway, we're just renting it at the moment, but it is up for sale so if we like it, then we can buy it. How great is that?"

I guess it is great; he has at least only chosen a rental, not our next lifelong home. I allow myself to feel some level of relief, though I'm far from reassured or relaxed. I feel rushed. Bulldozed. "You've already signed a contract?"

"You are going to love it, Lexi."

"Where is this house?"

"Just a few miles past Hurtington."

Hurtington is thirty miles from where we live now. Twenty-five miles from the school Jake has just enrolled the kids in. "How will they get to school every morning?" I ask. "Is there a bus?"

"We'll hire a driver."

"But is there a bus?" I insist.

"I have no idea. How would I know?"

I want to point out it will most probably say on the school website, or the estate agent might possibly know. This is the sort of question people ask when uprooting their family, but I stay silent. I would have asked that question if I had been involved in selecting their school or our home. I feel disconnected. Cut off. The kids are really excited about viewing the new house and specifically bagsying their bedrooms so they chatter throughout the journey. I'm grateful that their noise masks the silence that squats heavily between Jake and me. The slim, blonde professional estate agent has a perma-tan and a perma-smile. She drives us along a winding road that I have never traveled on before and had no idea existed.

"Nearly there," she chirps. I look about; it's all high walls and tall established trees. Their canopies are vast and lush, their purpose not so much to offer shade as privacy, I suspect. All the houses on the road are unique, purpose-built for people who don't think there is a house on earth that fits their specific needs and therefore have to have one designed especially. They are all enormous and elegant, and each one elicits a gasp from the children, who have their noses superglued to the car windows. When we stop at an electric gate, the estate agent opens her car window and then with her long, polished nail jabs in a code that makes the gates open. As they slowly swing on their hinges, I do not feel any sense that we're being welcomed—it's more as though we are stepping inside a monster's open mouth. The gates slowly close behind the car, swallowing us.

"You can change that code, personalize it," says the estate agent. "Maybe to your winning lottery numbers," she suggests with a simpering laugh.

"That would be too long," I point out.

The house is exquisite. Breathtaking. Modern, angular, very much how I imagine houses to be in Los Angeles. It's the exact opposite to our dated, poorly repaired home with flaky paintwork and a weed-pocked garden. This is modern, all white walls, vast windows, and the garden is expertly manicured. Our car inches along the shingled drive and grinds to a halt just outside the vast dark wooden door which the estate agent unlocks. She immediately disarms the intruder alarm by inserting another code into another keypad. I guess I would be safe here. The four of us have dressed up to come on this look round—Jake, Emily and I by tacit agreement that we had to look the part. Logan was coerced, and anyway his idea of dressing up means that he has changed out of a sweaty football top and put on a clean one.

I'm so glad we did.

I get the feeling that anyone who lives in this sort of house has to constantly dress as though they are camera-ready for a shoot with *Hello!* The hallway is cavernous, double the height of any house I've ever been into. There is a glass ceiling that allows the sun to pour onto the floor, which is covered with immense white porcelain tiles that shine like glassy ice.

We dawdle through the vast and numerous rooms. I count them up. There are three reception rooms. I'm thinking maybe one is used as a dining room and another an office, but then we are shown both of those rooms so I struggle to understand why anyone would need three reception rooms. Maybe one for the kids, one for the husband and one for the wife. Oh, dear. The dining room has a huge wooden table running its entire length. I count the seats: twenty. I suppose that would be useful at Christmas. Usually in our home we resort to pulling dressing-table stools and deck chairs up around the table to make sure everyone is seated. Although, other than Christmas, I'm not sure when we'd use the dining room. Like most families we tend to gather in the kitchen, even when we are entertaining. We're unlikely to need an office, either, since neither of us has a job anymore. The kitchen is vast and, yes, there is a huge dining area in there, too. I try to visualize us all clustered around the industrial-looking stainless-steel worktops. The estate agent is good at her job, a people reader. She asks, "Don't you like the kitchen?"

"It's stunning. Very modern." She waits. "Maybe a little clinical for my taste," I admit.

"You can have it ripped out of course, if you buy the place. It is three years old." She rolls her eyes at me and pulls her mouth into a wide grimace; her neck looks like a turtle's. I think I'm supposed to be horrified at the idea of a kitchen being more than three years old.

There are six bedrooms, each with an en suite. There's an extra bathroom on top, which the agent describes as the family bathroom, but I don't understand who would need it because of the multiple en suites. There are a lot of glossy wooden and marble floors and a rich scattering of plush rugs, no carpets. If my parents visit here, the rugs would be a hazard—my dad is always tripping over his own feet. There are a number of lights hidden in the floors, ceilings and recesses, not a dusty lampshade in sight. Some walls are made of glass bricks. I know they're really trendy, but they've been ruined for me because they use them in our local health center. I've sat too often waiting to see a doctor to associate them with anything other than one of my children running a fever. The place is minimalist, furnished with a number of tasteful shades of gray. I suddenly think of Carla. She is the only woman I know who freely admits that she's read *Fifty Shades of Grey*. I imagine her making jokes about the color scheme and the opportunities to christen the endless rooms. I wonder how Jennifer would have responded. She constantly behaved as though Carla's unsubtle innuendo was a bit distasteful. She always seemed to be something approaching sexless. She almost behaved as though giving birth to Ridley had been the result of an immaculate conception. Carla used to say it was because, out of the three of us, Jennifer had the least attractive husband and probably wasn't that into sex with *him*, specifically.

I used to shush Carla when she said things like that. I'd tell her not to be mean. She didn't listen.

"Do we get to keep the furniture?" I ask. It may all be a bit different from my usual tastes—I generally like bright cheerful colors—but I know we don't have enough furniture of our own to fill this place. Everything we own could fit in the one room I'm standing in.

"If you like it and want it. It's from a hire company. I can have it changed if it's not to your taste. We have a range that you can view online."

"It's fine." I'm certain under normal circumstances there's nothing Emily would like more than playing interior designer, but at the moment she's absorbed with party planning. Besides, I'm not sure she needs to feel the buzz of click and collect any more than she already has. I think she's technically addicted.

We are shown around the rest of the house. It's wall-to-wall elegance, the very epitome of wealth and success. I sniff the air and swear I can detect the scent of money wafting about. There is a cinema room, a gym and outside, at the bottom of the garden, a pool room. I mean *swimming* pool, although there is also another room with a pool table in it. The children are beside themselves. They have already picked out their bedrooms, and there were no squabbles because all of them are stunning, huge. This place is the opposite to the sort of place Gillian advised me to move to, but the matter is settled. Jake has signed a contract. The kids like the place. In fact, they love it. And I don't dislike it. How could I? What is there to dislike?

Emily and Logan go into the garden and discover a croquet set. Neither of them has ever played croquet in their lives, the very name of the game a source of derision in the past. Now they are knocking a ball about with a lack of expertise but complete enthusiasm. I stand at the window and watch them.

They giggle and chatter, gently squabbling about whose ball

is closest to the hoop. There are no electronic devices in sight. I'm living the dream. Jake is at my side.

But we're not touching.

The estate agent says breezily, "I've a bottle of champagne in the car. I should have got it out when we arrived and put it in the fridge to chill. Will you excuse me for a moment while I go and fetch it? I imagine you want a moment just to take in all this fabulousness."

A strange thing has happened to Jake and me over the past few weeks. For years we used to talk about anything and everything. The big stuff and the little stuff. The value of my career, how many children we should have, where and how we should raise said children, what we should spend our money on. We discussed, in detail, what we'd do if we only had five minutes left to live and if we have fifty years left to live. Now we only talk about what we—he—wants to buy next. I wish I could keep up with him. I wish I could simply enjoy spending it all. I can't, and somehow that means we no longer know how to reach each other. I've noticed when we are alone together, we seem to be more alone than when we are apart.

"How much does this cost to rent?" I ask.

"We can afford it," replies Jake, which doesn't answer my question.

"And if we did want to buy it, how much would that cost?"

Jake shrugs. "I'm not sure exactly." I stare at him. He looks just above my eyebrows. Doesn't he even care anymore? Has he gone past that?

"A ballpark?"

"No clue."

"Did you ask?"

"We'll ask if we decide we want it."

"What length of lease is on it?"

"Monthly."

I consider this. I'm surprised; a monthly lease offers us the most flexibility. And freedom. It's the careful, considered thing to do. My husband has been the complete antithesis to careful and considered since we won the lottery. Well, since before then, really. "Why, Jake?" He shrugs. "Isn't a six-month rental more usual? Wouldn't it have been better value?"

"That's the point, though, isn't it, Lexi? We are not usual. We don't have to worry about what is better value." He runs his hands through his hair.

"Everyone worries about money. Even the Queen turns her lights out at night at Buck Palace." I'm trying to make a joke because I fear this isn't one. There's something lurking in the murky depths of our relationship. Something that will bite or sting.

Jake shrugs. "I think that HRH's decision is more environment related."

"No, I don't think so. She's trying to be thrifty. I don't think the environment is one of her issues."

"Well, we don't know, do we? Environmental groups probably make her feel she has to switch her lights out. She probably wants to leave them on. I really don't think she cares about spending money. Some people don't care about spending money, Lexi."

"In that case, well done environmental groups. Maybe I should hire them to get you to act differently."

"Jesus, Lexi." He shakes his head. "I'll ask for a discount and take the place for six months, if that's what you want," he says impatiently.

I stand in the vast, cold kitchen and consider how utterly ludicrous it is to be arguing about the Queen's thriftiness or otherwise. We are ludicrous. Then I realize something much worse. We're not arguing about that at all.

I ball up my courage. I grip the side of the table, watch as my knuckles and the tips of my fingers, under the nails, turn a glassy white. "Do you still love me, Jake?"

"Lexi, what a question."

"Do you?" I force myself to look at him. I confront our twenty-five-year history. I see it flashing between us like some sort of kinetic energy. From the moment I realized he was staring at me in the Student Union, his eyes bored into me. Singed me, set me on fire. Just as a ray of sunlight reflected through a lens can cause a forest fire. Our first kiss and fuck. Which happened within about fifteen minutes of one another, such was the strength of our lust. I remember as I pulled up my knickers thinking that I'd broken all the rules and probably lost him because of it. I'd been taught nice girls didn't shag their dates up against a wall in the halls of the student residence. Nice girls at least waited to get their dates into their hard, skinny beds. I thought as his itch had been scratched, I'd never see him again. In fact, he never left my side.

At least not for many years.

I remember our wedding day; it was a big and busy occasion. A blur of beams and best wishes, dreams realized and freshly formed. He carried me over the threshold of our hotel room. Then he stood on my dress and it tore. We laughed and he told me he'd spent all day thinking about tearing the thing off me anyhow. The births of Emily and Logan; one such an easy child, the other a worry and a stress. I see Jake pacing up and down our small sitting room with a squally Logan thrown over his shoulder, his huge hand gently rubbing the baby's back. Covering it. Protecting it. First days at school. Holidays. Sick days. Paydays. I see a string of them bob in front of me like clothes on a washing line being buffeted in the wind. Fresh, buoyant, brilliant. I remember the simple joy of watching the TV, him sitting up straight and me spread out on the sofa, my head in his lap, knowing that *The Graham Norton Show* was good anyway, but all the better because we laughed at the same bits. That all flashes in front of me and I ask for a third time, "Do you love me, Jake?"

"Of course I do." He pulls me into a hug and kisses my forehead, more or less in the spot he's been staring at this entire conversation. "We're struggling because there's been a lot of change. That's all."

I bury my face into his shoulder. I don't want him to see the tears that are threatening to out me. "There's nothing else?"

"No."

"Have you told Jennifer that they are not getting the cash for changing their story?" It's the closest I can bring myself to asking the question I want to ask.

Is it over?

"I think they'll work it out," he replies, pulling his face into something approximating a smile, but he isn't fast enough. I see the wince first and I know then one of two things.

Either it isn't over.

Or it is, and he is sad that it is. Both things break my heart.

Everyone wants something they don't have. A few hundred years ago it was food and a long life. Now it's Insta likes and other people's husbands. My husband does not know that I know he is having an affair with my best friend and has been for at least two years. Two years is her husband's best guess. I suppose it could be longer. I never used to keep anything from him. I'd have sworn that there was nothing he kept from me. Now we share the same secret, but he doesn't know it.

It fucking kills me.

CHAPTER 28

Saturday, April 20

According to the rota, it was Jennifer's turn to host supper that Saturday. Lexi wasn't much looking forward to it, but thought it was essential that the supper went ahead. Considering everything. They needed to keep things on an even keel just a little longer. She comforted herself with the thought that at least it wasn't Carla's turn to host. That would have been trickier. Lexi would never admit it, as she always tried hard to keep the delicate equilibrium of their threesome intact and therefore avoided drawing comparisons or expressing preferences, but the truth was she liked going to Jennifer's home for supper more than she enjoyed going to Carla's. Both women had incredibly stylish and comfortable houses. If anything, Carla's should have been the most welcoming. There was more space, and the kids had their own playroom to hang out in as soon as they were excused from the huge round table that comfortably seated everyone and was certainly designed to encourage conversation. They had a fridge especially for chilling white wine and a selection of cut-glass decanters to allow red wines to breathe. But the luxury and excess had become the problem.

Lexi had never been particularly hung up on the fact she was the least well-off of her three friends. It was just a fact. Even when Patrick made the occasional snobby comment about the temperature of her house in the winter (too cold) or the wine in the summer (too warm), she let the gibes wash over her like water off a duck's back. Lexi didn't blame Carla for her husband's boorishness. She actually felt a bit sorry for her. All the money in the world didn't compensate for a husband who could behave like a prat.

But, over the past few months, Lexi's perspective had changed. She had started to find Patrick's flashy ways annoying, even cruel. He had so much, and she worked with so many people who had next to nothing. She tested him, talked in general, nonspecific terms about her cases at work to gauge his reaction. He was dismissive, derisive. She hadn't cared too much that the man was a snob, but now she realized he was so much more dreadful than that. He was heartless, callous, pitiless. Now, she found his constant talk about his wealth, his profits, his business actively repulsive.

An awkwardness had sprouted up between her and Carla as Lexi started to look at things differently. She used to be so good at compartmentalizing, but now one thing bled into another. In these past few months Lexi's work had become increasingly all-absorbing. Certain cases had burrowed their way into her head and heart. Toma Albu, for example, had leached into her home and social life. She knew very well that she shouldn't have been investigating his claims privately and with such vigor. She was overstepping. She couldn't tell her boss what she was up to because she knew Ellie would rein her in. Remind her of the proper channels that ought to handle the matter. But Lexi doubted the proper channels could go far enough—they didn't have the resources. There was only ever a certain amount that could be done. Lexi had wanted to gather hard, empirical evidence. She couldn't let this atrocity go unpunished. And now she had it and didn't know what to do with it. She hadn't confided in Jake, either. He wouldn't approve of her casting aside the bureau's guidelines, not that he was a stickler for rules himself, but he would be worried for her safety if he knew she was running around town with Toma, a desperate, emotional and vulnerable man.

A sexy, single and handsome man. What would he say?

And because she hadn't told Jake what she was up to, she hadn't told Jennifer or Carla, either. Lexi was self-aware enough to understand that the fact she was keeping quiet about something that was so important to her had probably contributed to the unease between her and her friends. The unpleasantness about the buying of the lottery ticket that had occurred last week hadn't helped matters.

Patrick had made things so unbearable for everyone.

It was complex. There was a web of crisscrossing relationships and a shared history that tied them all together. Their relationships and the children's relationships were interwoven; the warp and weft of their lives, which had always been neat and regulated, now was entangled, knotted. She needed things to go ahead as usual. She needed everyone to carry on until she'd thought this through fully. Until she decided on her next step.

Lexi thought perhaps she could talk to Jennifer. Sometimes they did have conversations outside of their relationship with Carla. This wasn't a secrecy thing, or a matter of leaving anyone out. Their particular intimacy had grown over this past year, largely from the fact Emily and Ridley were dating. They saw a lot of one another when they dropped off or picked up the kids. Jennifer was always so interested in Lexi's life. She was the friend most likely to lend a sympathetic ear if Lexi wanted to grumble about the kids, Jake or work. They sometimes did have a small moan about Carla's flashy extravagance, Patrick's arrogance. Only occasionally. They really tried not to. And so Lexi was bitterly disappointed when on Saturday evening, at about five o'clock, she received a WhatsApp message from Jennifer saying that they were making an impromptu visit to Fred's sister and they would have to postpone dinner that week. The message was sent via the group chat. A second later, Carla posted, too. Oh, well, let's skip this week then. I'm exhausted and could do with putting my feet up.

Lexi couldn't remember another occasion when any of them had canceled at such late notice without at least the courtesy of making a phone call. Jennifer didn't even like her sister-in-law; she was always grumbling about her undisciplined children and dirty house. Why had she suddenly decided to visit? Unless there was a family emergency... It didn't add up, and if there was a family emergency she would have mentioned it. Wouldn't she? Lexi told herself that it was perfectly reasonable for Carla to want a night in, although normally if one of them couldn't manage the Saturday-night meetups, the other two would discuss whether to go ahead or do something different. A creeping, prickly sensation crawled up Lexi's spine, and she felt suspicious of the proximity of when the messages had been posted.

She shook her head, trying to clear it. She was being crazy, paranoid.

Maybe, yet she couldn't stop herself imagining them sitting, heads together, planning how to pull out of the evening.

The bleak and humiliating thought swelled in Lexi's head, spread through her like a disease and caused twinges in her gut. Last week, when Patrick had said the lottery was common, she had felt a sting of something like shame. Hurt. Anger? How dare he? The vile man. How dare *he* judge them. Because it was *them*, she realized now. Her and Jake. And it seemed as though it wasn't just Patrick judging and finding them lacking. These messages suggested Carla, Jennifer and Fred were trying to distance themselves, too.

She forced herself to think about things she'd been trying to ignore. It wasn't just the lottery business, not really, not if she was honest with herself. Lexi recalled Sunday outings that they had not been invited to but had only heard of afterward—trips to National Trust properties or for country walks. "Not outings, just jaunts. Impromptu jaunts," Jennifer had insisted, the last time Lexi realized she had been excluded.

"What's the difference between an outing and a jaunt?" Lexi had asked, embarrassed to find herself pursuing the matter, a dog with a bone.

"We don't plan these things in advance, they just organically happen. It's because we live closer to one another, you live farther out." Lexi had thought it sounded almost reasonable at the time. Although, in fact, they only lived five miles away, not what anyone could describe as an insurmountable distance. She wanted to believe they were telling her the truth because the alternative was awful. But then there was the occasion that Carla and Jennifer had gone to London to the Good Housekeeping Show and hadn't asked her to join them. They'd explained it away. "You were working, we knew you wouldn't be able to make it." It would have been nice to be asked, though.

"Honestly, Lexi, Carla never feels left out if we have a coffee when you pick up Emily from our house," Jennifer had added, reasonably. Lexi felt foolish—was she making a fuss?

Why would they be cutting her out, and was it just her or was it Jake, too? Fred and Patrick had memberships to the same gym, and they played squash together once a week. Jake had looked into becoming a member and periodically brought the matter to the table, but the monthly fees were exorbitant, and they couldn't justify it. Had they become the third wheel? Lexi felt confused, rejected. She hadn't felt like this since she was at school. It was a given that kids, teens, did thoughtless and mean things from time to time. Forgot to be inclusive and supportive. They were not fully formed, but coming face-to-face with the same sort of behavior from adults was so much more shocking. It suggested a lack of progress for humankind. Lexi felt depressed.

"Are we not going out tonight, Mum?" Logan asked. It was seven o'clock, and usually by that time Lexi would be on at them to get in the car.

"No, Jennifer canceled. They're going away this weekend so can't have us over."

"Oh." Logan sloped back up to his room, not too concerned. Playing Fortnite at home or on Ridley's console was all the same to him.

Lexi threw a glance Emily's way. She was at the breakfast bar, reading something on her phone. Her head was bent as if in prayer, which struck Lexi as appropriate as Emily worshipped her phone. "Have you any plans tonight?"

"No."

"Not seeing Megan?"

"No."

"Did you know Ridley was going away?"

"No."

"Would you like to watch a movie with me and Dad?"

"No." Emily's phone buzzed. A smile spread across her face. Most likely the message was from Ridley. "I'll be in my room." Emily stood up quickly and rushed out of the kitchen.

Lexi and Jake watched the film in silence for about twenty minutes. Normally Lexi was the sort of person who gave a running commentary when watching movies at home; she only just managed to suppress this urge when they were at the cinema because she feared being shushed. She liked to guess at how the plot might turn out or she would ask, "What's she been in before? It's bugging me." Tonight she couldn't concentrate on the plot.

Jake pressed Pause and said, "Well, as I'm not needed to be

a taxi driver for the kids tonight, I'm going to have a beer. Do you want a glass of wine?"

"Maybe later. Actually, I've just remembered I need to nip out."

"Out? Where? Why?" Jake looked put out that their quiet night in was threatened.

"I said I'd drop off a book at Diane Roper's. It will only take me five minutes in the car."

"You're going now? On a Saturday night?"

"She needs to read it for book club on Tuesday. I promised I'd get it to her today and I forgot all about it. Sorry. Look, watch the film without me. I won't be long, and I'll just catch up." Lexi stood up, hunted out her car keys and headed to the front door.

"Aren't you forgetting something?" asked Jake.

"Like what?"

"The book." He looked questioning, unconvinced.

"Oh, oh yes." Lexi ran upstairs and grabbed a book from the towering pile beside her bed. She took the top one without even checking its title.

Lexi drove along the narrow, winding country roads that she knew so well, a route she had taken hundreds—maybe thousands—of times before. She knew every twist and bump. She was headed toward Great Chester, the smart village where Jennifer and Carla both lived. A village she and Jake had never been able to afford to buy in. It was often featured in articles about Britain's most beautiful places to live. She wasn't planning on stopping, she just needed to drive by. To check. Of course, Jennifer wouldn't be lying to her. Of course, she was at Fred's sister's, just as she'd said. But Lexi couldn't stop herself. She had to see the closed-up house, still and quiet. She wanted to be reassured by the fact that there would only be one car on the drive. Jennifer and Fred had two, but they preferred to use his for long journeys.

She had been planning on driving past at a sedate speed, just taking time enough to ascertain that her friend was indeed away, as claimed. However, she immediately saw that both cars were parked on the drive, the downstairs windows were wide-open and Ridley's bike was propped up against the fence, advertising a confidence in the sleepy, safe, practically crime-free habitat. Lexi gasped, shocked that her fear had been justified, disappointed to be proven right. She stopped her car right in front of Jennifer's home, suddenly aggressive and provocative, she almost wanted to be seen now. She wanted her so-called friends to know she had caught them out in their lie. It was still light, and she could easily see into the house and right through to the back garden. There, she could see Jennifer and Fred. She was sitting at the table; he was pacing about.

Lexi parked up and got out of the car. She was not going to take this lying down. Not after fifteen years of friendship. She was going to confront Jennifer and ask her why she had lied. If it was because she was cozying up with the Pearsons and she and Jake were being left out in the cold, then she would rather know. She might even decide to put a bomb under that relationship and light the bloody fuse. She could.

She decided to go straight around the back of the house into the garden. Catch them by surprise and not give them a moment to come up with some bullshit excuse as to why they weren't driving to Birmingham to see Fred's sister.

She walked up the back path. The moment she dipped into shadow, she regretted leaving the house in such a hurry. She should have picked up a cardigan. The sun was losing its power, and in the shadows the solid chill was the victor. Earlier today the breeze had caressed, now it nipped. Suddenly she lost her confidence in the idea of intruding when she heard Fred yell something or other—she couldn't quite make out what, but he sounded seriously het up. Jennifer hissed something back at him, her tone too low to catch. Ah, a domestic. That's why Jennifer had pulled out of the evening's arrangements. Nothing insidious, just a row. Lexi felt relieved. And then instantly she felt mean for being relieved. She didn't like to think of her friends rowing. An insect buzzed past her ear and she instinctively ducked away from it, then froze, not wanting her movements to draw attention, although they were unlikely to notice her as they were deeply embroiled in their drama. It was not like Jennifer and Fred to fight. Carla and Patrick, yes, they were volatile, caustic. Jennifer and Fred had a much calmer, civilized relationship. Some might go as far as to say that their relationship was so civilized it was borderline dull. A partnership, an economically based partnership. Jennifer had a good life being married to Fred, but not a passionate one.

"You are fucking him," yelled Fred. "Just admit it!" He sounded drunk. His words were slurred but loud, insistent. What was he talking about? "You. Are. Fucking him. Just admit it." This was embarrassing. What could Fred be thinking? Jennifer wasn't having an affair. She'd have told Lexi. How had Fred come to believe something so out there?

"Keep your voice down—the neighbors." Lexi should just turn around, walk away from this private mess, but she crept farther up the path so she could see her friends, not just hear them. She was only human. She saw the couple face one another, like warring gladiators, every muscle tense. Ready to pounce or run. Lexi could see the tension pulse in the tendons of Jennifer's neck.

"I don't care about the fucking neighbors," snarled Fred.

"Then Ridley."

"You should have thought of Ridley before you started fucking Jake fucking Greenwood."

No, no, no. No! Lexi's bones turned fluid. Her body sloshed about underneath her. Jake, her Jake? No. That can't be right. Fred had got this wrong. Jennifer was going to tell him so. This was ludicrous. The moment stretched out to an eternity. Jennifer did not say anything to correct her husband. She didn't say anything at all. Lexi couldn't tear her eyes off Fred's face, which looked swollen with betrayal and despair. She didn't know it, but her own was twisted with shock. The birds tweeted merrily, oblivious to the noxious words that were being thrown, each one a blade, hacking at their lives. A neighbor's dog barked repeatedly, indicating they weren't at home after all. Lucky Jennifer, she didn't have to worry about her neighbors overhearing the domestic. Lucky bloody Jennifer.

"I followed you, Jennifer. For fuck's sake. I didn't want to be right, but week after week the same bill from the same hotel."

"I told you, it's the cost of spa treatments. That's the cost of a massage and a manicure."

"Stop fucking lying, Jennifer. I checked. The hotel doesn't have a spa. It's the cost of a room. I've been paying for the room that my best friend fucks my wife in every Tuesday." Lexi was sitting on the ground. She didn't remember sitting down, but perhaps her body had known she might fall and had protected her. She dropped her head into her hands. She couldn't look at them. This couple who were ripping her life apart with their accusations, their lies. She heard the sound of breaking glass. Maybe Fred had thrown or dropped his glass. She heard him sob. A grown man crying was always a hideously painful sound. Tuesdays? Jake always worked late on Tuesdays. An aphid landed on Lexi's arm. She flicked it off and found herself momentarily concerned for Jennifer's roses; might they get infected? Because that is how it had always been—they were concerned for one another, they looked out for one another. Then Lexi's brain caught up with her instincts and she wished a blight on Jennifer's roses, her home, her family, her whole rotten life.

The adrenaline surge that Lexi had felt as she'd stormed up the back-garden path had vanished as quickly as it had arrived. She didn't feel combative—she was broken. It felt like someone was hitting her repeatedly in the chest. Her knees were shaking as she forced herself to stand and then hurry back to the car, her breath jagged, catching in her throat. She sliced through a cloud of midges that hung in the air. No, no, no. Fred had this wrong. He had to have it wrong. Jake having an affair with Jennifer? She would know *that* about her husband. She would have found out. People who had affairs were always found out, weren't they? The thought was ludicrous because as it formed in her head, she simultaneously realized that was exactly what had just happened. She had found out. She wanted to vomit. She wanted to scream. Pull out her hair. Lie on the road. She flung herself into the driver's seat and fought the urge to bang her head against the steering wheel, over and over again, until she could gain some clarity. She did not. Instead, she slowly turned the key in the ignition and drove away.

CHAPTER 29

Emily

Saturday, May 25

I am wearing a pair of bed shorts that I got from Jack Wills when I was about twelve. Back then, Mum chose nearly all my clothes and she bought everything big and comfortable.

Now they are tight, like a second skin, but I still like them even though they are frayed and faded. I wish Mum had not washed Ridley's hoodie. He left it at my house just before we broke up because he had been kicking a ball around in the garden with Logan and then they used their hoodies for goalposts. He went home in his T-shirt and forgot all about the grubby hoodie. Mum popped it in the wash along with my clothes, but now I wish I had stopped her because I miss the smell of him. I wear it at night anyway. But it doesn't smell of him now, it smells of me. Sweat from restless nights where sleep eludes. Although my smell is strangely unfamiliar to me. Am I imagining it or is there a strange new hormone?

Oh hell.

Oh, bloody hell.

Bloody, bloody hell. How can this be happening?

I can't sleep at night or through the day. In a way I'm glad I can't. If I did, I'd have to wake up and remember the reality all over again. My reality.

The win—yippee! A baby—fuck me!

I can't have a baby. I'm a baby myself. I know this. Not just because Mum calls me her baby, but because I just *am*. But how do I stop having it? I mean, I know about abortions and stuff. I'm not a fucking idiot. But how do I go to a doctor and tell them that's what I need?

I am a fucking idiot.

Will he be prosecuted? Technically underage sex isn't just that anymore, is it? It's pedo stuff. It's a big deal. I don't want Ridley to go to prison, but on the other hand if he was in prison, he couldn't do the things he used to do with me to anyone else. But even so, no. I don't want him to go to prison.

Oh, my God! Oh, my God! I just want this to go away. I can't think about it right now. I won't. I just won't.

I get up, pull off my bedclothes and climb into my costume. I check how I look in the long mirror. In our old house I had to stand on my bed to get a look at my outfit because my mirror was only face height and not very big. Now I have an honest-to-God dressing room with two full-length mirrors facing each other, so there are an infinite number of me—stretching into the distance, getting smaller and smaller until I disappear. My outfit rocks. I spent ages on Amazon trying to source a Zendaya outfit. I wanted a really cool version, not some cheap polyester crap that meant I was in real danger of going up in flames if I stood too close to a hot light. In the end, Sara had an exact replica made for me. It's so gorgeous! A silky tiny cami and velvet hot pants. It's sweet and flattering in a girl-next-door way. Sara thought that I might regret going too subtle, so she also had an exact replica made of Zendaya's purple performance outfit, too. It is so much more glam and sexy! It has a sheer neckline that is cut to the waist, gold boots, even a pink wig. I take off the sweet number and climb into the purple. I zip up the boots, stand tall. Place the wig carefully on my head. Check my reflection again. Transformed. It's a relief to step out of me. Mum is going to hate it. It's awesome! I smooth my hands over my stomach, still flat. I'm not sure when you start to show, but I'm glad it's not tonight. Tonight, I have to be hot and cute and perfect. Which means a flat stomach.

The late-afternoon sun floods into my new übercool bedroom. I only have to flick a switch and the electric blinds would close, but I don't. I like the way the warmth and light falls into the room, onto my body, which is sticky and hot. I move my hands across my hips, my bottom, my waist, remembering the pleasure we once gifted each other that was beyond words. I'd never felt that way before Ridley. I didn't know people could make each other feel like that. What if I never feel that way again? What if no one's touch can ever bring me to life like that again? I knew everything about Ridley's body before we started to have sex. Or so I thought. I had shared bubble baths and paddling pools with him as a toddler. That stopped as we got to school age, but still we were in and out of one another's homes, tents, gardens, kitchens, lives. So I knew that there are tiny blue veins on his eyelids that you can only see when he's sleeping, I knew he had a chicken pox scar on his jaw (right-hand side) and a birthmark on his thigh that looks like a melted chocolate button. I knew he had a line of hair that ran downward from his tummy button and a thatch of dark hair under each arm. I did not know what that body could do.

And now I do, so I can never be the same. We can never be the same. Being friends isn't enough. Suddenly I don't like the heat or the sunshine or anything at all. I can't face the party. My body feels heavy, leaden with memories and consequences. My dad keeps saying life is great, everything is wonderful now and always will be. I want it to be. I want to believe him. But Mum keeps asking if I'm okay, if everything is all right and I feel I might collapse under her scrutiny. I lie on my bed and stare at the ceiling. I force my eyelids to stay wide-open, but a fat tear slips down the side of my face anyway. I brush it away impatiently. I have to go to the party. I have to talk to him. Him first.

CHAPTER 30

Lexi

I tightly grasp the party planner's laminated timetable in my hand, not unlike a toddler grasps a security blanket. The first version was printed on stiff creamy card, but as the weather forecast suggests there might be another downpour later tonight, the planner had the plans laminated so that I could refer to them no matter what the weather. She's very plan-y, I'll say that for her. She considers every eventuality. I can't help but think if she was running the country, we'd probably clear the national debt in the next decade. She's not though, is she? She's arranging parties for people with more money than sense. And I firmly count us in that bracket when I spot staff handing out glittering monogrammed glow sticks studded with Swarovski crystals.

The party is, by anyone's estimation, tremendous. As I've had little to do with the planning, I am surprised and impressed by the props and design. It's not just a party, it's an amalgamation of a funfair, a circus and a movie set. People have understood it was going to be spectacular and have made a big effort with their costumes. There are a lot of girls and women in basques and fishnets, wearing top hats. There are men dressed as bearded ladies, lions and ringmasters, depending on their self-view—funny, cuddly or Alpha respectively. There are a lot of people in random spangly things and endless clowns. This is not the place to come if you suffer from coulrophobia.

I glance at the plan every few moments, but no matter how often I read it the details won't stay in my head. The party planner has listed out where and when each event is going to take place throughout the evening. Obviously, like at most parties, there will be eating, drinking and dancing, but there are also magic acts, performers and photo opportunities that I have to be aware of. I have never encountered a precision-timed party before, and I'm finding it overwhelming. At the children's parties we've thrown in the past, the only clock-watching we did was because we were counting down the minutes until the bedlam ended. We have hosted Christmas parties before. We'd invite all our friends and neighbours to bring a bottle/drink a bottle at our place. If I was feeling very efficient, I sometimes stuck a few mince pies in the oven. I'd expect thirty-odd guests to those parties; tonight, we are expecting just over three hundred. I had no idea we knew so many people. Having read over the RSVPs, I'm still not convinced we do. Jake made good on his promise to invite everyone and anyone we knew or have ever known, however vaguely, and we've had an extremely high acceptance rate. Only a handful of people have said no and that was because they're out of the country. I'm surprised, but Jake was right—even the kids from the new school have said yes.

"You can't overestimate just how thrilling our win is to other people," commented Jake smugly this morning. We were lying in bed, perusing the guest list. His attitude to the response was unadulterated joy. Mine was barely disguised panic.

"I'm nervous about the large number of unknown faces that will be arriving tonight," I admitted.

"We have a lot of security. I think they'll spot the difference between a fifteen-year-old rich kid we haven't met but has come to party because they've been invited and a fifty-year-old pierced thug who has come to rob us. Not exactly tricky."

I've never before heard Jake stereotype using a piercing as shorthand for *trouble*. That's the kind of thing Patrick does.

We all arrived at the party together at six o'clock. The early start was Jake's idea. He wants the night to last forever, but that's not possible—even money can't change the space-time continuum. The children disappeared the instant we stepped out of the car. They melted into the crowds, keen to hunt out their friends, old or new, I'm not sure. Jake wasn't at my side for much longer—there were too many outstretched hands that he had to shake, numerous pats on the back to be received. Inevitably, we became separated as people demanded our attention. Everyone appears to be giddy with excitement and overawed. We are repeatedly congratulated on our win, and the party, the cocktails and our costumes are all admired. I'm wearing a Pierrot, sad clown costume—loose white blouse with large pom-pom buttons and wide white pantaloons, a frilled black collar and skullcap. I've completed the look by painting my face white, I have black lips and I've drawn a fat tear on my cheek. Jake disapproves of my costume. He doesn't like that I'm dressed as a man. He wanted me to wear a figure-hugging, sparkling something or other. He derisively refers to my outfit as my "monotone mime costume." But Jake is missing the point. The Pierrot has been a stock character in circus and pantomime for centuries; he creates pity in audiences as he pines for the love of Columbine, who usually breaks his heart and leaves him for Harlequin, the colorful one. The defining characteristic of Pierrot is his naivete. He is seen as a fool, often the butt of pranks, yet nonetheless he is loved. His redeeming feature is that he's trusting.

I thought about my costume long and hard.

The baggy getup and the white face offer me some much-needed anonymity. Once I'm not by Jake's side, who is dressed as a ringmaster—no make that *the* ringmaster)—I am not easily recognized. I am able to drift through the gentle din of polite early-party chatter and clinking glasses. I breathe in the heady perfume of the sun-scorched meadow and delicious food aromas without anyone really bothering me.

There is no denying it—the entire party looks amazing. I have never attended anything so stupendous in my life, and I don't suppose many, if any, of the guests have, either. Every detail has been stage-managed to create an awe-inspiring, magical spectacle. The waiters, dressed as acrobats, are all incredibly fit and attractive. Bulging biceps and taut abs are everywhere I turn. They are carrying trays of brightly colored cocktails, poking out of which are slices of toffee apple or candy floss and red-and-white straws. There are dozens of primary-colored light bulbs hung in festoons crisscrossing between the trees. It's still too early for them to be anything more than eye-catching, but they are most definitely that. There are ice sculptures of roaring lions and seals balancing balls on their noses dotted about, and enormous beanbags surround firepits and chocolate fountains that have encouraged pockets of teens to cluster. The teenagers are even enjoying themselves. I see this because they are not sat in a line, heads bent devoutly over their phones. They are talking to each other, laughing, shoving and then hugging one another. There are a lot of similar-looking girls in tiny, glittering outfits with dyed blond hair and dark roots that extend to about the ear. I understand this is deliberate and fashionable because when I once commented that it looked careless, unkempt, Emily rolled her eyes. "That's the point, Mum."

Their young faces are still taut and keen. Later this evening I imagine they will be flushed with drink, maybe drugs, maybe sex, but right now they ooze innocence and hope.

I scan each teen group for Emily, Megan or Ridley. Habit. I've done this since they were babies. Checked their whereabouts, their comfort levels. Swooped in if one of them needed taking to the loo, feeding, or if there was a dispute to be managed.

Of course it's different now, everything is. I can't manage their disputes. I can't do anything to help.

Megan isn't invited and it would take some cheek for the Pearsons to turn up under the circumstances, but they have that in spades so I'm not completely ruling it out. We haven't heard anything from them since I called Carla. Their silence is partially disconcerting—they were so loud in our lives for such a long time—but mostly a relief. A triumph. What can they say? What can they do? I feel a small glow of pride that I have managed to deal with them so effectively, so conclusively. The Heathcotes? They are a different beast. Emily says she's not bothered about whether Ridley comes or not, but I watched her patiently sit while a professional makeup artist spent three hours doing her makeup and styling her pink wig in preparation for tonight, so I don't believe her. She cares. Far too much.

The volume has cranked up considerably and carries across the field in every direction. There are clashing tunes from the dance floor and the funfair rides, laughter is more boisterous and committed. People are talking over each other, everyone convinced that they are funny and interesting, more so than when they arrived, more so than the people they are talking to. From time to time I pass a cloud of the familiar smog that used to pop up at parties when I was younger. It was weed back then. Now it's hash. I never partook. I stare intently at the kids and eye them suspiciously, but I can't catch anyone with so much as a cigarette let alone find the source of the stale haze. They are quick and devious. People are.

"Hello, Lexi, lovely party." Jennifer beams at me. I haven't seen her since the press conference. Weirdly, my first instinct is to hug her. That's my body betraying my mind, muscles and nerves collaborating because of the long and intimate past we share.

Drawing one another into an easy hug or honest conversation was normal for so long. Now I should slap her. I squeeze my hands together behind my back to avoid that. She lunges at me and kisses the air on either side of my face. As we pull apart, I stay stony silent and simply stare at her. I look at this woman who has lied and hurt me. Tried to steal from me. "Are you enjoying yourself?" she asks. "Sometimes it's hard to relax at one's own parties."

I don't respond straightaway. I want it to be awkward. I want the intimacy we had to be missed and grieved for. I want her to feel guilty and ashamed. Although I must be an idiot to think she has any depth that way. Our past was tissue thin. Our future is tumultuous and confused. My mind is struggling to catch up to the fact that she's had the nerve to turn up. I know she was invited, and I know she accepted, but a tiny part of me thought that when it came to it, she might have the good grace to realize that she ought not to be here.

No. She's ballsier than that. More threatening than that.

I try to understand what it means, her being here. Does she know yet that the bribe Jake offered her is never going to get into her bank account? What must she think about that? Then I notice her costume and I understand completely. She is wearing a skintight silky catsuit that is a clash of primary-colored diamonds of fabric, an elaborate ruffle framing her face and a cute pointy hat. She is the Harlequin. Pierrot's competitor for Columbine's heart. I am left wondering how it's possible that I have been Jennifer's friend for so many years and not been especially aware of her figure. She's tall, a good five inches taller than I am. I've always known she had long legs, but now I notice the swell and curve of her breasts, her ramrod posture, her tight waist.

"Who told you what I was wearing?" I ask. I don't see that there's any point or room for dissembling.

"I think Jake let it slip," she says with a smile that is as dishonest as it is broad. I want to know when. When she spoke to him and what else was said. But I won't give her the satisfaction of asking. Her costume is a challenge. Defiance. A declaration of war.

"What was wrong with your own husband?" I ask suddenly. This just burst from me. I wasn't planning on pushing the matter out in the open.

"Wrong with him?" She doesn't catch my meaning at first or at least pretends not to. She must have known I'd find out sooner rather than later, considering Fred knows. I was going to keep quiet forever, pretend it was beneath my notice, their sordid little affair, but if I facilitate the secrecy I might be adding to their drama, the thrill. Calling her out is not the same as giving Jake up. Once the secrecy is taken away, this thing they had—or even have—won't be as exciting. It will fall apart. I'm culling it. Whatever it is. Love or lust.

"Why couldn't you just stick to him?" I challenge.

"Fred? There's nothing wrong with Fred. I love Fred."

"No, you don't," I say wearily.

She shrugs. "Well, maybe not. No. But I did, once, I think. I mean, there is nothing wrong with him exactly, but your husband is simply better. Don't you agree? It was clear from the start that you had the catch. Except for the money thing. He just couldn't hold down a job, could he?"

"That never bothered me."

"Yes, it did."

We speak with hideous honesty. A pair of women who have been the very best to one another and now the worst. We have known each other at our most courageous and magnificent and at our most vile and depraved. "Well, money problems are behind us now," I point out.

"Yes." The sudden intimacy of such cruel honesty only accentuates the void between us. "He's a very wealthy man now. That lottery ticket win of yours has made him very wealthy."

That's a ridiculous understatement. From anyone other than J.Lo's point of view, he is obscenely rich. I'm not naive, I know what this could mean. Wealthy men are catnip to women like Jennifer.

"You know, I never thought you were the one I had to watch. I'd always have thought Carla was more Jake's type. She's so much more—"

"Obvious?" interrupts Jennifer.

"I was going to say glamorous. Oh, well, they do say the quiet ones are the worst." I didn't watch closely enough though, did I? I can't continue this conversation. I can't pretend to be cooler, calmer, more in control than I am for very much longer. "Have a lovely time. Go easy on the cocktails, I understand they are really quite lethal," I say, and then turn to melt into the crowd.

CHAPTER 31

Emily

The party is off the scale! I'm almost sick with excitement as I watch everyone's reactions as they drive up and see the big top, the dance floor—it's awesome. And when they hear that Radio 1 DJ Greg James is actually going to be gigging tonight—their faces! Scarlett, Liv and Nella are all over me. They stick to me like glue and even though I know I'm moving schools and according to both Mum and Dad (in a rare moment of agreement) I ought to be digging out new friends, I cling to my new—old ones, gratefully.

We hang around the vodka luge that Mum in her infinite naivete described earlier as a "really striking ice sculpture." Ostensibly, the luge is for adults only and there's even a member of staff standing by. He's supposed to be policing who drinks from it, but he looks bored and only a smidge over eighteen himself so—big surprise—he doesn't ask four scantily dressed girls how old we are. I do three shots in quick succession. The first one is disgusting. It burns my throat and makes me want to gag, but the second and third are easier. I realize that under the circumstances, this is the worst time for me to start drinking.

And also the best.

I shouldn't be drinking because I'm pregnant. I need to drink because I'm pregnant. The thought makes me want to vomit with panic. I push it out of my head.

I watch as guests gather in concentrated, random groups that cluster together then effortlessly float apart as if their movements are part of an elaborate dance. Loads of people come up to me and say they are happy for me and when they do, Scarlett, Liv and Nella clap or bounce about, basically just act like cheerleaders because they just hear words, but I hear feelings and I'm not sure there's not something dark behind the smiles and congratulations. Jealousy, bitterness, resentment. I taste it on my tongue, although it could just be vodka. I smell it in the air. Or is that hash?

I constantly scan the crowds, straining my neck almost, in a none-too-discreet hunt for Ridley. Normally, a girl being this desperate would lead to her mates taking the piss, but the girls pretend not to notice. They are cutting me a lot of slack because there are different rules for rich girls. Eventually, I spot Ridley. And when I see him, I hate it that my first thought is shoulders back, boobs out. I check on my phone that my makeup is still good, no mascara smudges under the eyes. I was depending on his excessive gall. The girls kept saying he'd never have the nerve to turn up, especially without Megan, his sidekick, but I knew him better. He's not short of nerve. Ridley hurls himself at life. That's why, when we got together, it was the gentleness that I valued, that made what we had better than what anyone else had. Megan, his parents, his mates, they could all have his enthusiasm, but only I got the tender ache of him.

Until I didn't.

He arrives with his rugby friends. The gang of boys all ooze swagger, they are used to being noticed and valued. Other boys hunch and slouch as a matter of course. Ridley ought to be cowed, but he isn't. It's not the same when the hockey girls arrive. Despite coordinating their outfits to create maximum impact, it strikes me that they are noticed in a way that undervalues them. The girls are measured and, often as not, they are found lacking and even if they pass the test of scrutiny, the prize is just being admired by a guy. I'm not saying it's fair, I'm just saying it is. Maybe if we all notice how it is, we can start to change things.

He is wearing a strong man costume. It's pretty ludicrous as it has fake muscles and stuff, but as Ridley is more muscular than most boys his age, he pulls it off. I take a cocktail off the tray of a passing waiter. Holding a glass gives me something to do with my hands. We used to play dress up together. I don't mean recently in, like, a sex game way—we're not a sad couple in our forties! I mean, we played dress up when we were kids. The three of us. Mum had a huge wicker basket that was the designated dress-up box. There were endless costumes from World Book Day, Halloween and themed parties stashed in there. But when we played, only Megan bothered to hunt out a complete and matching kit. Jake and I preferred to rummage and pull together our own mad mix-ups. A fireman's helmet, a Roman breastplate, a ballerina skirt. We'd roar with laughter as we layered one another up in ever-increasing ludicrousness. A multicolored wig, neon bangles, angel wings.

He doesn't look ludicrous tonight. He looks hot. And cool. My insides billow as though someone has just blown life into me. And I know for a fact I'll take him back in an instant if I can because wanting beats dignity every time when it comes to people you love. But then the rugby lads jostle about a bit and I notice Ridley isn't alone. Besides the lads, there is a girl.

Evie Clarke.

In the moment I relax because it's not Megan he's here with, then I start to boil with jealousy. I hate Evie with her fake Michael Kors tote. I think of her yanking at my hair, kicking my shins in that nasty loo cubicle. She was not invited. Dad and I deliberately avoided inviting Megan and any of her cronies. What is she doing here? I watch as Ridley casually flings his arm across her shoulders.

It could be a gesture between mates. It could be more. I down the vodka I'm holding. I need it. Something to blunt it, blot it up, this hemorrhaging of feelings, this extreme pain. I think, *Fuck him, I'm rich now*, then I think, *Imagine not wanting me now when I'm this rich. He must really not want me at all*, and that makes me feel so sad, so pointless.

"I'm going to get Evie Clarke kicked out," I tell Scarlett. I expect her to nod, but she doesn't. She just puts her hand on my arm, tentatively, gently. Since this is the first sign of opposition she's shown to anything I have suggested since we became friends, her caring gesture is all the more powerful. I want to cry.

"Let's go and see some more of this party, hey?" she suggests lightly.

I try. I try to just enjoy the party. I mean, it's phenomenal, I've been so excited working on it with Dad and Sara, it's all I want to care about, but I can't stop thinking about Ridley. I am constantly aware of his presence. He is currently the closest he's been to me for four weeks now. I thought it would be a good thing, but it's torture. Like Mum said it would be. She said boys are preprogrammed to lose focus, but that's not right and I hate her for generalizing. My pain is particular and absolute. No one understands. I keep putting my hand on my stomach, cradling the bunch of cells that are threatening to ruin my life. That may make my life brilliant. I don't know. Scarlett notices. "You doing okay? Does your tummy hurt? Do you feel sick?"

"A bit," I admit. She assumes it's the alcohol. Better that than she has any real idea.

I don't mean to, but I find myself moving in roughly the same direction as he does as we explore the party. When he goes on the Ferris wheel, I get in the queue. When he's eating at the pulled pork cabin, I'm just in the next cabin along, picking at candy floss. The loss of the fluency, ease and intimacy between us is catastrophic, incomprehensible. Evie Clarke is where I ought rightfully to be, tucked under his arm, sharing his jokes, his drink, his space. I look at him and I think of the places we did it and I think of the places on my body that he has touched. My insides lurch.

"You have to stop stalking him," groans Scarlett. "Let's go and dance." I stare at her, or at least try to. The cocktails taste way better than vodka shots. These are sweet and fruity. They go down pretty easily.

Drink is beautiful and it is my friend because it makes things not matter, not to me. Maybe they matter to the person I was or will be tomorrow, but right now nothing matters. I'm floating.

Drink is awful. I've had too much. I'm wedged painfully between desperation and yearning. I pretty much love Scarlett right now because she's really trying to be a proper best friend, not just a rich person's best friend, but I'm going to ignore her. "I don't want to dance yet." The dance floor is in the opposite direction to where Ridley is standing.

"Then how about some water? We should all have some water. Nella, Liv, go and get some. I'll stay with her."

Then a miracle happens. Ridley walks away from Evie Clarke and he walks toward *me*! He keeps his eyes trained on me as though there aren't three hundred other people in the field. I hear Scarlett make a low whistle sound and Liv laughs, but then they fall away. Vanish. Poof. Just like that. As does all other sound and sense. There's just him, walking toward me, holding eye contact. He has remained certain of himself, that's because he doesn't know what I know. He thinks he's a boy on the cusp of GCSEs, A levels, university, a future. He doesn't know what

I know and the thought cheers me because for a moment, maybe I have more power.

"Hiya."

"Hi."

"Nice party."

"Thanks." I say thanks automatically because it's the same script that I've followed about fifty times tonight. He didn't give the compliment with as much enthusiasm as some. In fact, maybe it had a sliver of sarcasm, but maybe not. The vodka and the cocktails mean I'm finding what people are saying is a bit blurry. Their faces aren't staying still, either.

Ridley glances at the others that are hanging around us—Scarlett, Liv, Nella and three or four of his mates, too. Liv and Nella have not gone for the water. No one is going anywhere. All eyes are on us. They are not even bothering to pretend to hold their own conversations. It's quite cool, it's like we're Kim Kardashian and Kanye, but it's also awful because I know Ridley won't be his best self in front of others. His best self is when he's alone with me and mucking about doing daft stuff like throwing Maltesers in the air and catching them in his mouth or shooting hoops and stopping to kiss me every time he gets ten in a row (which was often, because he's really good at sport). I finish off my cocktail because I don't know what else to do.

"You drink now?" Ridley sounds surprised but pleased.

"Things change," I say with a shrug. This is like the opposite of true. Because yes, I drink now, and yes, my family are millionaires, and yes, our parents have fallen out, and yes, he took photos of me with my pants down, peeing.

But I love him. That has not changed and that's the only thing that matters.

"How many have you had?" he asks.

"Not enough," I reply, giggling. Again, most likely the opposite of true. But it sounds pretty cool, like we're in a film or something. Nella put her hand straight in the air and actually clicks her fingers at a waiter. The others all laugh and one of Ridley's friends says, "You didn't just fucking do that for real, did you?"

Nella shrugs. "My girl wants a drink." She pouts and we all laugh again. The guy with a tray of cocktails appears and lets us all take one even though he looks unsure about it.

"You're all eighteen, right?"

Liv points at me and says, "It's her party." Not really answering the question, but also very much answering the question. We clink our glasses and then drink. The boys make jokes about cocktails being for "bloody girls" and ask where they can get a beer.

"There's a bar," I say, pointing to one of the tents.

"It's free," adds Scarlett. Immediately, all the boys dash off. I hold my breath. All the boys but Ridley. He stays. And I breathe again. He chose me over a free-beer tent. That's massive. He looks over his shoulder to where he left Evie Clarke standing. She's still waiting for him. I see her sort of floundering about in space. Not sure what to do with herself, not sure where she fits, and I almost feel sorry for her. Almost. He turns back to me and I instantly forget her. He stayed with me.

"Cool costume," he says. I wore the purple in the end. Sara was right, this isn't the moment to undersell. I'm glad I wore the one that made Mum mutter and demand of Dad, "You're happy with her going out dressed like that?" It's pretty obvious Mum's losing her shit, though, because in the past she ultimately made the decision on what did or didn't happen in our house. I kind of get the feeling that Dad decides now. I don't really know why.

"I like yours, too," I comment. Then I want to punch myself in the face because it's not really a very imaginative comment. He grabs hold of my hand. "Come on, let's get some privacy." And now I want to sing and clap and dance and kiss him.

Mostly, I want to kiss him.

CHAPTER 32

Lexi

I'm glad the party is outside. I have seen four steaming pools of vomit already. At least if the forecasted rain does come tonight, it will be washed away or maybe the foxes will get to it. Horrible thought. I search about for the party planner. I want her to check that the staff really are confirming ID and not serving cocktails or spirits to anyone under eighteen, but I can't locate her. I go and speak to as many members of staff as I can personally; however, they don't look too interested in my instructions. I try to explain that I am the host, although as they've dealt with Jake and Sara they seem reluctant to listen to me. Glancing about, I see a fair number of quite wasted teens, but I can't definitively blame the bar staff. As the drinks are free many are left half drunk, so even if a teen didn't ask for alcohol at the bar they could easily minesweep.

I'm not drinking. I feel a need to watch over the guests, specifically the younger ones. I spot one girl who looks as though she is managing to sleep vertically. Her friends cluster around her, propping her up between them. She's wearing a barely there clown's costume that is streaked with vomit. Her thin, spindly legs drop into chunky wedged heels. She's swaying about like a rooted tree. I fear if she falls, she'll twist her ankle, or maybe she'll just snap. Her friends are nervous when I approach, fearing she—and they—might get into trouble. I don't judge, but I do suggest we call her parents. They seem relieved that I've taken responsibility. I sit with the girl until her parents arrive. I fully expect them to have a go at me for letting their daughter get into this state. I know if I was called to collect my teen from a party at eight o'clock and found she was barely conscious through alcohol, concern might cause me to lash out. I steel myself, but in fact they simply compliment me on the beautiful party, congratulate me on the win and say they look forward to seeing me again once Emily and Logan start at the new school. They bundle their daughter into their car and throw one last wistful glance over their shoulders. I think their greatest regret is that they weren't invited.

I haven't seen Jake for a while. I call him, but he doesn't pick up. I'm not surprised, he often has his phone on silent. And whilst planning the party over this past week or so, Jake has said the reason it's been difficult to reach him sometimes is that the reception in the field is patchy.

I've nothing to worry about. I've nothing to worry about. It's over.

I scour the partying people for Jennifer's colorful costume. There are two or three other Harlequins that catch my eye, but I don't see her. Involuntarily, my gaze is drawn to the woodland at the back of the field, the perfect place for people to disappear into if they wanted to be alone, if they didn't want to be found. I shake my head. It's a stupid, destructive thought. Jennifer is probably at the champagne stack—she does enjoy a glass or two of champagne. Jake is most likely watching the magic act, which according to my timetable, is happening right now in the big top. The party site is vast and the throng thick so it's actually very hard to find anyone.

I haven't seen Logan since we arrived, although he has at least replied to my texts saying he's having a "wicked time" and that he is with his friends, yes, they are staying together, no, they are not causing trouble. This is unlikely to be absolutely true, but it's enough to be reassuring. I can't help but note that his phone seems to have better reception than my husband's. I haven't spotted Ellie, Judy, Heidi or Rob from the bureau yet, either, and I really want to see them. I want to ask about a couple of my old cases. There are people who I have been thinking about, and I'd like to know how things are progressing. I know they are here because Judy has already posted about twenty pictures of herself on Facebook: her face poking out from behind a great big candy floss, her face open with a roar of laughter as she rode the Ferris. I checked at the Ferris wheel, but I couldn't see them, already having moved on by the time I got there. I decide to make another circuit of the party in the hope of catching them, but my progress is almost immediately interrupted as I am stopped by some old work colleagues of Jake's. Not from his last job, but the one before that. I smile and nod along with their conversation, although not a lot is being said. Mostly, it's a repetition of the mantras.

"Who would have thought it?"

"What are the odds?"

When my phone vibrates in my pocket, I'm grateful for the excuse to cut it short. "I'm so sorry, I have to take this." I throw out an apologetic grimace and duck away from them.

"Lexi?"

"Toma?"

"You recognized my voice!" He sounds happy and noting as much reminds me that it's not an emotion I usually associate with him. I think of him as sincere, troubled, determined, angry, thoughtful. A complex kaleidoscope of sentiment that is tight and knotted.

"Your name came up on my phone," I reply, matching the smile in his voice.

"You have me programmed in your phone!" He's buoyant. Almost playful.

"Everyone has everyone programmed in their phone nowadays, Toma."

"Where are you? You sound like you are at a party."

"I am, actually. My own."

"You are throwing a party, without me? How is that possible?"

I laugh. "Have you been drinking, Toma?"

"Some." If I was having this conversation with anyone else, I would go so far as to call his tone flirtatious. I suppose that's what happens when you gift a man three million pounds. I mean, how is he supposed to read that signal?

"Why are you calling? Is everything okay?"

"You should not always think everything is a problem with me," he says, his tone changing abruptly, sobering.

"It's not that. I don't." I falter because I do. I met the man when he was sleeping in the street outside my office. It's hard to disassociate him from a feeling of concern.

He quickly dissolves the awkwardness. "Well, I am calling for a stupid reason now. You make me feel stupid because you haven't asked me to *your* party and I am calling to ask you to mine." There's no real irritation or anger in his voice, just amusement. It warms me. It makes no sense, but my stomach hiccups a fraction, a small glimmer of excitement at the idea that Toma is having a party. That he is inviting me. "My going-away party." And then my stomach plummets.

"You're leaving the UK?"

"Yes, because of you."

"What did I do wrong?" I joke, but it's forced. When I gave

him the money, I hoped it would help him move on. That's what I wanted to enable, what I suggested, but now that it has come to it I feel a faint breath of loss.

Toma laughs. "You are the most right person I have ever met, Lexi." His words slice through me. It's obviously a translation thing that makes his compliment seem so moving. The words seem real and raw, although I know they are not. I am not a right person. Jake doesn't even know about the money I gave to Toma yet. "I have no idea why you decided to give me that money." He pauses, waiting for me to explain, no doubt. I'd like to one day, but I can't right now, so I stay silent. He doesn't push me. Then I hear him breathe out deeply. "Okay, so whatever the reason, it is a miracle. At first, I think it is a joke but then the money arrives in my account. I do not spend it. In case you change your mind. Have you?"

"No, I haven't changed my mind." My voice comes out in a whisper, and I grip my phone. Sweat prickles under my arms.

"Okay, then it is a miracle. I am going home, Lexi, you gifted me that."

"What will you do?"

"Something good. Something that will honour Reveka and Benke. I plan a—how do you say it?—a sponsorship of education. I'll give another child the life I would have given Benke. What am I saying? With that much money I will give many, many children a good life." I gasp. The air builds in my throat and I can't breathe. It's the first time since we won the lottery that I've been genuinely excited about how the money is being spent. "I give it a lot of thought. I make a trust. Make the money work hard. Go back to home and find kids who need help to flourish. It will be a full-time job if I do it right."

I'm in awe of his certainty. I have spent hours poring over endless charity petitions and numerous proposals for beneficial projects. I've been paralyzed. Unsure where and how much to commit. I am impressed by Toma's assurance and clarity.

"When do you go?"

"Tomorrow."

"Tomorrow? So your party is happening—"

"Right now," he interrupts to confirm. "Lexi, don't think I am rude. I wanted you to come, but I didn't know how to ask you, and then I have two beers and realize I ask you as I ask everyone. So, I ring you up." He laughs. "But it's too late. You have your own party."

"Where is your party?" He gives me an address in town. It's not too far from my office. I look about me. We've quickly arrived at the point of the evening where everyone is too drunk to keep track of anyone else. Plus, the party is spread over a massive field, so no one would notice if I slipped away. He is going away. After tomorrow I might never see this dignified, decent man again. "Okay, I'll be there as soon as I can."

I calculate that if I drive back to the new house to take off my makeup and change outfits, then drive back to the address Toma gave me I will lose almost an hour and a half just getting there. It's already approaching nine o'clock, and somehow this sacrifice doesn't seem worth it. I decide to drive directly to Toma's in my costume. I should feel foolish and self-conscious, but oddly I don't. I realize that all that matters to me is getting there as soon as I can.

There is a field that has been turned into a car park. I'm frustrated to find that our car has been blocked in by dozens of others. When I challenge the young guys who are working at the car park about this, they point out that they weren't expecting us to leave until the very end of the party. It's a fair comment. I check my watch, see that there's a bus due in four minutes. I run, if I catch it that will be faster than calling an Uber. Now that I've made the decision to go to Toma's party, I can't get there soon enough. There are not many people on the bus when I get on it. Just two lads at the very back and an old lady sat near the front, within shouting distance of the driver. The old dear says she likes my costume and the two boys ignore me altogether. Of course they do. A middle-aged woman, even one dressed as a brokenhearted clown, is invisible to them. As the bus gets closer to town, a handful more people get on. Couples mostly, who look as though they are going to spend the night in a pub or maybe at the cinema. They are all dressed up, and laugh and chatter between themselves. I'm reminded of Saturday nights, long ago, when Jake and I used to enjoy a night out in town. The memory should make me smile because we had such great times, but it doesn't. I shiver. The memory is too distant to warm me. I get off at the last stop and a plastic bag, lifted in the wind, gets caught around my ankle. I kick it off, glance at Google Maps on my phone and then set off in what I hope to be the right direction. I move away from the smell of bus diesel and fast-food fat and head down a badly lit street where the strongest aroma is overflowing bins. It's about a ten-minute walk until I'm approaching the house that I was given the address to. The party is not happening at the lodgings where I know Toma lives—that's not this part of town—so I can only assume a friend is hosting this goodbye party for him. How lovely. Even without the address, it would have been clear to me that this is where the party was being held. One house in the middle of the terraced row has its windows flung wide. There is music floating out of it, old pop songs that seem never to go away, but no one can ever remember when they were genuinely fashionable. Lots of chatter and laugher ebbs and flows onto the street. There's cheap, cheerful bunting hung inexpertly from the gatepost to the doorway. I ring the bell, wait, wondering whether it will have been heard above the noise of the festivities.

Toma flings open the door, a bottle of beer in his hand and a beam on his face. For a moment he looks startled to see me on his step and I am concerned that he's forgotten all about inviting me, then I remember what I'm wearing, that my face is painted white. I wonder, can he see my blushes through the makeup?

"You dressed up!" he says with a laugh.

"My party is a fancy-dress party," I explain with a shrug. "I didn't want to waste the evening going home to change."

Toma's beam widens a fraction more and I know I made the right decision. He steps forward and flings his arms around me, enveloping me in a huge bear hug. This is the first physical contact I've ever had with Toma. I'm generally a tactile person, and I tend to squeeze a person's arm to convey sympathy, solidarity, encouragement. However, I'm strict about not doing so at work as it can be construed as unprofessional. I don't remember my fingers so much as brushing Toma's as I've passed him a cup of tea, or my shoulder rubbing against his as he's held open a door for me. His sudden physicality ought to feel unfamiliar, maybe awkward, but I find my body smudges against his with ease and we fit. He's tall, I slip under his arms, which are raised to embrace me. As we separate, I suddenly feel a lack, notice that my hands are empty.

"I'm sorry, I should have brought a bottle." I think of all the bottles of champagne, wine, beer, spirits that are stacked at my party and I am embarrassed that I didn't think to pick one up to bring here.

"Lexi, you don't have to bring anything other than yourself."

I nip to the bathroom and wash the makeup off my face. Toma might not think it's odd I have arrived in full fancy dress, but I'm sure others will. There's nothing I can do about my costume. When I emerge from the bathroom, Toma is patiently waiting for me. I follow him through to the sitting room where about twenty people are pushed into a small space. All the seats are taken, and floor space is at a premium, too. Everyone is talking to someone. No one is lurking gauchely in the background. As I walk in, everyone turns, smiles, give small nods and waves. I have been to small dinner parties where there have been only a handful of guests, and sometimes those guests have ignored the arrival of a new person. These people seem extraordinarily inclusive. I smile back shyly. Toma leads me to a group of three—two women and a man, all about my age or older, I guess. Of course, the first comments are about my costume. I explain I've come from another party but don't mention it was my own as I fear that might require more of an explanation than I can offer. Why have I left my party of three hundred guests to come to this gathering of twenty people?

Toma touches my arm—it's startling. "Drink?"

"Yes, please. I came on the bus." He goes into the kitchen to get me a drink. He returns with a glass of white wine, and by then I have jumped into the conversation that his friends were having about the books they are reading at the moment. They talk passionately about the plot and characters. By chance I've also read the book that is at the root of their discussion so I can agree that the ending was deeply satisfying.

The thin woman in the flowered dress, Dita, puts her fingers in her ears and makes loud "la-la-la" sounds. "I haven't finished it, just two more chapters to go," she says, laughing.

"Wasn't it a bit predictable, though?" asked the bearded man, Mandek, looking genuinely concerned about this.

"Well, sometimes a little bit of getting what you expected is just what you need," I point out.

"Very true," he agrees. I try to establish which one of them works in publishing or as a librarian because I can't imagine why they would all be so informed and opinionated about books otherwise, but I discover Dita and Mandek work at the laundry with Toma. Sabina, the youngest of us all, is a cleaner at the local police station.

"Good jobs," explains Sabina, "fit around my family. I never take worries home with me." I nod, that's undeniably true. I also discover that it is Dita and Mandek's home that I'm in. I thank them profusely for inviting me.

"Any friend of Toma's is our friend," they tell me. No one mentions the lottery win. Notable because people rarely talk to me about anything else nowadays. I don't think Toma has told anyone about my luck or his good fortune. I feel relieved. If he had, I could not have been just another guest.

I move around from one group of people to the next. A mixed bunch, they remind me of the sort of friendship groups Jake and I used to make on holiday when we were much younger. Transient people from many different walks of life. All with stories and histories, and none of those histories are shared. It makes an interesting party. There is a freedom in talking to these people who have been brought together through chance and circumstances. They did not go to school together; nor do their children. They did not meet at child birthing classes. They don't even live in the same neighbourhood, but are scattered across the town and county. Their lives aren't intrinsically entwined through years of responsibility or habit; there is a sense that they are choosing to spend time together because they value the moment. Within the first hour of being at the party, I encounter people from five or six different birth countries. Yet, despite having come from different places, we have all arrived in the same spot this Saturday night. A terraced house in a small British town, and everyone seems happy about it. Their viewpoints may not have originally been the same, but they have found commonalities, unity and harmony. They want to make the most of it.

We want to make the most of it. I count myself in among this melange of people who wish to harvest joy tonight.

The air has a sense of energy and delight. People excitedly try one another's dishes—it appears the catering was a case of everyone bringing the dish they most like to prepare. No one was given instructions as to whether that dish ought to be sweet or savory. However, as cling film and tin foil lids are peeled back it seems that the rich thick stews, spicy meatballs, pretzels, strudels, dumplings, buns and breads were designed to complement each other as precisely as if Sara the party planner had written up elaborate directions. There's a big bowl of punch. If anyone knew the ingredients at the beginning of the evening, by the time I try it, the mix is certainly unclear. It's sweet; I can taste pineapple and rum, and then I witness someone add a bottle of vodka. It's careless and crazy, but I couldn't be enjoying myself more. Toma also catches his friend Vladislav adding the vodka. "Good man, fulfill our cultural expectations," he says, slapping his friend on the back. He turns to me. "You better eat plenty of syr smazeny," he warns.

"What's that?"

"Breaded fried cheese."

"Sounds perfect," I comment, and dive in. I meet the couple Toma lives with, Joan and Frank. An English working-class, salt-of-the-earth pair. Frank has brought his slippers with him to the party. Joan rolls her eyes at this but doesn't seem too disgruntled. "It's a party, Frank, you are supposed to dress up."

"Like this one?" he asks, pointing at me. I just laugh because his ribbing is well meant.

Joan is concerned about the washing up and spends most of the evening in the kitchen, rinsing glasses and moving food from one plate to another to "clear some space." It seems every time a dish is finished, another one lands on the table as more guests stream through the door. Not only does each and every one arrive with food and drink, but their entrance precipitates ever-increasing cheers of excitement. "Probably 'cause they've brought drink," comments Frank with a grin.

Joan tuts, rinses another plate under the tap and says to me, "I hear it's you we have to thank for finding us our Toma." I smile, sip my wine. "He's like a son to us. We're going to miss him."

"Yes." My voice sounds gravelly, as though I'm chewing sand. It feels that way, too. I put down the wineglass I'm holding. It's empty. I've lost count of how much I've had to drink, which means too much. I should check my phone. See how my own party is going. I should really return to it. But I don't because it feels distant and I feel detached. I can hear music playing here and that grabs my attention, holds it fast, more than the thought of my own party. It's not the pop tunes, blasting from a phone and a speaker, that had people jiggling in the sitting room earlier, but someone has actually started to play a guitar. Requests are being made and whilst I don't recognize the song that is being sung, many do and lots of people join in. Raucous and tuneless in some cases, as though self-consciousness had never been acknowledged. I stand at the doorway nodding my head, never more aware of my limiting British reserve. Then Toma taps me on the shoulder, takes my hand and leads me away from the singing, through the kitchen and out to the back garden.

He took my hand. I let him.

I hold tight and tell myself it is natural, normal, not in any way wrong. Even though I am a married woman. Even though his thumb is caressing my hand and the warmth of him is shooting through my body like a firework.

The back garden is only a few metres wide, but it is surprisingly long as it falls away to the railway track. There are a number of people smoking and vaping on the small patio near the house. Toma cuts through them with polite determination. We head toward the bottom of the garden. There has been enough rain this spring to mean the grass on well-kept lawns is lush and green. The grass here has bald patches that suggest children's robust play; the plastic playhouse and stray football confirm as much. There is a washing line, trailing the whole length, where plastic pegs perch, waiting to secure a new load of clean clothes. There are closed dandelions, buttercups and less attractive weeds sprinkled everywhere like freckles on a redhead. We head for two beat-up white plastic sun chairs at the very bottom of the garden.

I suppose this is where Dita and Mandek sit and relax after work. I notice there are two old-fashioned tartan travel blankets slung over the backs of the chairs. It's not the most peaceful place on earth, with trains thundering by, but I can see the appeal of looking out over the urban scene: train tracks, factories and warehouses. It reminds me a little of London. Maybe Dita and Mandek came from cities and miss them.

As we reach the bottom of the garden, Toma is still holding my hand. I glance at our fingers interlocked and then wish I hadn't because he suddenly seems to notice and lets go. We sit down. Side by side, but with a proper distance between us. I pull one of the blankets over my lap. It could be the wine, the balmy night, the varied company—I could find any number of excuses—but I can't pretend to myself there isn't an atmosphere between us. Something shimmering, stretching between us, because there most definitely is. There was drink at my party, it was the same balmy night and, yes, there was varied company—I felt I hardly knew a soul—yet I did not feel this sense of alertness when I was with Jake. I did not feel my skin prickle, the sky did not seem so black, the stars so bright.

"Are you enjoying yourself?" he asks in a tone of voice that suggests this is the most important thing on earth for him right now. That I am his priority. My happiness is his obsession.

"Very much so."

"Don't you have to get back to your own party?"

"I should, yes." For a few moments we don't say anything else. It's half past eleven. I ought to reach for my phone. I should call an Uber. Not so much to transport me back to reality, but to take me back to the unreality that is now my world. Instead, I comment, "I liked your friends."

"I've met some good people. Some recently, some from my days with Reveka and Benke. I wanted them all here tonight."

I nod.

"What time are you flying out tomorrow?"

"Eight a.m."

"All packed?"

"Yes." Toma turns to me and leans very close. For a mad moment I think he is going to kiss me, and I wonder what I will do if he does. Will I kiss him back? I have been completely faithful to Jake since the moment our eyes collided in the student union, over twenty years ago. This isn't a matter of self-discipline or even an admirable and conscious act of loyalty. It simply hasn't ever crossed my mind to be unfaithful. I haven't found anyone else attractive enough to be disruptive. I have only ever seen Jake. And, yes, I made vows and promises.

So did Jake.

I don't think a broken promise can ever be mended. Not really. And I do find Toma attractive. However, he does not kiss me. My hair falls in front of my eyes and he leans forward, tucks the strand behind my ear. He stares at me for a length of time that should be embarrassing; it's not. It's nice. "I have to ask you again, Lexi, before I commit the money to the trust. Are you sure?"

"Absolutely," I say firmly.

"Because I haven't spent any of it yet. It's done a job already, without being spent. Already I have life again. I don't have to take the money."

"But you are going to do such good with it," I urge.

"And your husband is in agreement?"

I consider lying to him and can't. There are too many lies swilling about my life as is. I can't add another. "He doesn't know."

"Isn't that going to be a problem when he finds out?"

"Maybe," I admit with a sigh. "But we're facing a number of problems at the moment."

"I don't want to be an extra one."

I take a deep and determined breath in. "The way I see it, worst-case scenario is we have nine million each to spend as we like. This is what I wanted to do with my portion. I'm most likely going to give more away. I don't really know what to do with it. Other people need it more than I do. That much is clear." Toma stares at me with unadulterated admiration. It's the best look one human being can give another. He looks at me with respect, approval, gratitude and eagerness. As though I have shown him something new in the world. It's embarrassing and also wonderful. Something flickers, boils and melts beneath my breastbone.

"How do you manage it?" he asks.

"Manage what?"

"Caring so much for people you don't even know? In my experience, it's cruel enough caring for those you do."

"I know you, Toma," I reply. My voice comes out as a whisper although I didn't mean this to be a secret.

He replies in a bolder tone. One that shakes and sobers me a little. I think maybe because of the alcohol I'm having a moment here, but he is not. I'm being dreamy and romantic. He wants to check that he's not going to get sued for accepting my gift of three million pounds. "Yes, but it's not just me. You care for everyone. I'm just one in a long line of people," he insists firmly. I find his comment infuriating, hurtful.

"How can you say that? I didn't split my winnings with everyone. In fact, I didn't split my winnings with anyone other than you."

"You gave me 2.976 million exactly."

"Yes."

"A very particular number."

"Precisely a sixth of what we won. Your share."

"My share?"

I need to change the subject. "You are going to make a new life, Toma. You are going to give many people a new life."

"For a long, long time all I could think of was my old life. The one I lost. I imagined Benke growing up. Playing football with him in a park, walking him to school, sitting with his teachers whilst they tell me he is a smart boy, a kind boy. And I think of more babies. Another son, maybe a daughter. She'd also play football or, if she didn't want to, I'd sit with a plastic cup and pretend to sip from it at tea parties. I'd look ridiculous. I wouldn't care." Toma's gaze is on the grass a foot in front of him. "Also, if Benke didn't want to play football, if he was into music, theater or drawing, that would be good, too. Tea parties! This kid could be anything he wanted to be. I wouldn't care. And Reveka." He rolled her name around his tongue, around the dark night, and I could hear the longing as clearly as I could hear the happy singing drift from the house. "She'd pass her exams and become an accountant. She'd be very good. Very dedicated. She'd become a big boss. She might come home and be angry with me because I didn't do the ironing, didn't make supper the way she wanted. And I'd apologize. And I'd try harder to do more in the house. Even though this is not our tradition, we'd adopt a more modern and fair way." He turns to me now. I look at him even though his pain is hard to witness. "I'd have thrown myself at all the bright possibilities of the world, exposing myself to anything that might blow in, a kid that needed expensive dentist work, an exam badly failed, a teen scraping the side of my new car, even finding a stash of drugs in their room. The stuff that happens to my friends. I'd have borne it all because those cold winds would have ruffled, possibly brought down a fence or two. But nothing more."

I love the way Toma talks. He tries harder to grasp at what we mean, what life means, than most people bother to do. I don't know if it's because he comes from a different culture or language, or because of what he's shouldered in losing his wife and child. I just know I could sit here and listen to him all night. He sighs. "I spend a lot of time thinking about that life and being angry with my different life. The one with storms—hazardous, brutal storms, where I try to numb myself. Where I became a man who drank too much and took antidepressants. A man who ended up living on the street." He shakes his head. "Reveka would have been so sad to see that. Or angry. She could be fierce. She hated waste."

I smile. "I'm certain I would have liked Reveka."

"Yes, you would, but you would never have met."

"I suppose not."

"When they died, I lost everything. Them, yes, but also the glorious impulse to be better. Without them I had no one to let down but myself. Which I did." He sighs, shakes his head. "You gave me a chance, Lexi. I can't live that life. It's gone. But you gave me a chance to live a different life. You gave me back the wish to be better. I think you have given me the chance of a very, very good life."

"I just gave you money, Toma. You are deciding what to do with it." I shrug.

"Question." Toma taps a finger against my hand to get my attention. He has it anyway, but his touch sends a pulse ricocheting through my body. "Do you think less of me, Lexi, because I stopped searching for the people who owned the property? The people ultimately responsible?" I shake my head. "I thought maybe now I have all this money I should stay and hunt them down. The records are obviously purposefully confusing, but now we could hire private detectives."

"What then?" I ask. "The man won't be brought to justice because Winterdale took the fall. It's a dead end."

"If we found him, we could hire thugs to kill him." My eyes widen and Toma laughs. "I'm joking. I'm not a killer. There was a time when I raged that way, but you poured oil on those waters, Lexi."

"It's better that you move on. That's what I want for you. That's why I gave you the money."

Toma stretches out his hand. His thumb touches the bit of forehead above my eyebrow, and he strokes me there. I close my eyes and allow the caress. It is slow and gentle; it is as though he's just found that bit of my body and it is the most erotic part of me. Or precious. He soothes away my cares. I feel my body slacken. He pulls the blanket up to my chin and I feel his firm hands tuck it tightly around me, so I'm snugly cocooned. He pauses, looks me in the eye and then moves forward, kisses my forehead. Chastely, but not really so. Tenderly. I can smell the cold night air clinging to him.

"I should call an Uber," I murmur.

"Yes, you need to go back to your party."

Back to my life. Or whoever's life I am leading now.

CHAPTER 33

Emily

Ridley keeps hold of my hand as he strides through the party, across the field and toward the woods. He's walking quickly, I can hardly keep up. The boots I'm wearing are high and even though the heels are quite chunky, I fall off them two or three times, hurting my ankle a bit. Every time I do, he rolls his eyes and says, "Seriously, Emily, how much have you had to drink?" And I like it that he's concerned for me. Even if his concern comes out sounding a little like a condemnation. He's right. I am drunk. I like it. It's as if my fingers are candy floss, all malleable and melty, vapid. My fingers, my head, my body.

The neatly mowed grass gives way to longer, wilder stuff and then soon a tangle of brambles, twigs, foliage. I'm glad of the boots, otherwise my legs would be ripped to bits. Ridley only lets go of my hand when he pushes me up against a tree. The bark scratches my bare shoulders and back, but I don't care because his tongue is down my throat. He's kissing me hard and I know what this sort of kissing means. I'm glad. I kiss him back. Just as hard, our teeth bang and our tongues clash as though they've forgotten how to move with each other, but I don't stop. I tangle my fingers in his hair and pull his head toward me so he can't stop, either. His hands are running up and down my body. It seems neither of us have forgotten how good that is. His kisses make everything else just fall away, as though there is just us up against one of those green screens they use in movie making, our own space to create of it what we will. A moment ago, I could hear the party blaring in the background—the DJ, the fairground rides, shrieking and laughter. Now there is no sound except our breathing, heavy and fast. Someone has hit the mute button on the world's remote, and there is nothing to see, my eyes are closed, all there is is him. His touch. His warmth. His presence.

After a bit, I know I have to ask. I don't want to. I want to carry on with his lips on mine, with his hands exploring my body, but I have some self-respect and so I break my mouth away from his. He just attaches his to my neck, to my ears, to my arms and face. His breath is warm and perfect. I can smell beer and toffee apples on him. His fingers are edging into the leg on my leotard. Panting, I ask, "So, Evie Clarke then?"

He stops kissing for a moment to face me and grins. "Jealous?" I am, obviously, but can't see it would help to admit it.

"Curious," I say. I'm pretty pleased with that retort. I think I sound witty and sophisticated, not quite as anxious and worried as I am. He shrugs. If I didn't love him so much, I'd say he looked dumb. Or maybe embarrassed. I freeze, understanding this even through the haze of alcohol and lust.

I thought he'd say she was nothing. He's not saying she's nothing.

Which means she is something. The latest thing. But then, he was just a second ago kissing me. I block out the memory of him standing at the door of the school toilets while Megan slapped and kicked me. I try not to think about him taking photos of me with my knickers around my ankles. He starts to look about him, he seems confused. Almost as though he's suddenly unsure as to how he came to be alone in the woods with me, as though he's forgotten he was the one who took my hand and practically dragged me here.

"I'm really drunk," I say. I've heard people say this, by way of an excuse, when they've done something they regret or when they want to do something they know they shouldn't and are already making excuses even before it's happened. And sometimes people say it just because it fills a gap in conversation, and they can't think of what else to say. I'm not sure which of these applies to me. Maybe all of them. The ease between Ridley and me has been hacked apart. He's nervous and jumpy and can't look at me. I want him to look at me more than anything in the world, because my costume is cool and I had my makeup done professionally and if ever there was a time for him to want me, it is now.

"I'm pregnant."

So now he looks at me. His head snaps around so damn quickly I think it is going to fall off. I expect to see some level of regret or sympathy, maybe even excitement, or is that too much? All I see is rage.

"You are fucking lying." His voice breaks on the word *fucking.* Which—'cause I'm drunk—makes me sort of want to laugh. Laugh for two reasons, I mean, one, his voice is still unreliable and he's going to be a daddy. Plus two, the word *fucking* is definitely the pertinent one here. We had sex, more than once, now there's a baby coming. It doesn't take Einstein. My brain is thinking this, but lots of other stuff, too. Once again I feel like I'm floating above this conversation, not really in it. It's too much. I guess I'm technically hysterical.

I shake my head, try to focus. "It's true. I took a test."

"Fuck." He drops into a low crouch. Goes down like he's been shot. Balancing on his feet, his elbows resting on his haunches, his shoulders bent, head in his hands, he stares at the ground. It's a familiar stance. He squats like this when his team loses a match. "Fuck," he says again.

"It's okay," I say. Although I don't think it is. I don't want to be a mum. I'm too young. We've just won the lottery and I've bought all those cool clothes. I won't be able to get into them because I'll get fat. But on the other hand, we've just won the lottery and I am sixteen in a few weeks so maybe it could be okay. If Ridley wanted the baby. If he wanted me. I crouch down next to him. Very close. Our heads are almost touching. I want to put my hand on his back. Stroke him. Comfort him. I start to, but daren't, not quite. My hand hovers near his skin but not on it. I can feel the heat coming off him. It drives me mad.

I hear him mumble something, but it's tricky to make out exactly what. I'm swaying—crouching in heels after debut-vodka-chugging is hard. He repeats himself, clearer this time. "I don't want this."

"This?" I ask, dying.

"You. A baby. This." He looks straight at me now. Arrows fly from his eyes and literally pierce me. "I don't want you at all." His words knock me over. I fall back onto my bottom. The ground is damp.

I look at Ridley, he is shaking, his hands and lips are quivering. I think he's going to cry. He hasn't cried since he was eleven, not even when his grandad died, and he loved his grandad. He looks really scared. Really sad. I feel bad that I've made him feel this way. That not wanting me is weighing so heavily on him. I know this is weird and I should just hate him, but I don't. I love him. All I ever wanted was to make him happy. To be happy with him. I've known him since before I can remember knowing anything. He is so familiar to me. He is the boy for me. I watch him withdraw. It hurts as though I am being split in half. "How can I mean nothing to you now?" I ask. When we were that. All that.

"I dunno, but you don't." He stands up and looks longingly back at the party. I know he wants to be there. Probably with Evie Clarke. He does not want to be with me, or to be a dad.

"Have you told anyone?" he asks. I shake my head. "You need to tell your mum. She'll sort it out. You have enough money to fix everything now," he says over his shoulder as he strides away.

I can't watch him walk. I turn away, and clamber onto all fours, like an animal. I start to puke. My vomit is cocktail-colored. Red. It looks like blood is pouring from my mouth. I'm sick and sick and sick until I'm just retching and spluttering and there's nothing more to bring up. I don't know if I'm being sick with the pregnancy, or with the alcohol. I know, lousy combo. Maybe I'm just sick because of life. My eyes are closed as I can't face the world. But then I hear footsteps behind me, scrambling through the brambles, twigs and grass. I freeze.

Ridley has come back! My heart lifts again. He's come back! Maybe to apologize, maybe to hold me close. He's come back and it will be okay. I quickly wipe my mouth with the back of my hand. He won't want to kiss me if I'm covered in vomit. I don't want him to see me crawling on all fours, surrounded by puke and self-pity. I need to get up, look a bit dignified, look a bit sorted. As I move, something hits me from behind. Really hard. Sudden and unexpected, I think a log has fallen from a tree above and bashed me. It's like accidentally belly flopping into a swimming pool when you are trying to dive. Hurt and shock invade, but the pain is not on my belly but in my bottom as though I've literally been kicked up the arse. Instinctually, I scrabble away from the pain. As I do so I put my palm flat into my vomit, which causes my arm to slip and give way beneath me. Whack, another hit. Terrified, I think the sky is falling in. I cannot control my limbs. I crumple and fall flat to the ground.

Instantly, frenzied hands are all over me and I understand it's not logs falling, not the sky. It's more ordinary than that. I'm being assaulted. It's a man, or men. I'm a young girl in a leotard. This sort of thing happens all the time. I start to scream, but a hand is clamped over my mouth. I wriggle, I struggle, I try to bite the hand, but tape, thick blue tape, is wrapped around my mouth and eyes. In just seconds, I'm made blind and dumb. I still kick out and try to push them off me but there's two, three, maybe more of them. Men. Not boys. I can smell them and feel their rough hands gag and bind me. My heart is thumping against my chest cavity, and I think I'm going to split wide-open in fear. They tie my feet together, they tie my hands behind my back. It's fast and unspeakably terrifying. I'm powerless. They straddle me and I think they are going to rape me, but realize that they are just subduing me. At least at the moment. They are probably going to take me somewhere else to rape me. I'm sobbing but neither the tears nor the sound can escape. I think I might suffocate. I am so utterly petrified, more petrified than I have ever been in my life. This is a million times worse than the beating in the loo, this is a million times worse than the blue tick on the window of the pregnancy test. This is the worst thing I can ever imagine. I beg them to let me go, but they can't hear me because of the tape. And they don't care. I'm hauled up and two people carry me between them. I think I'm going to die.

"Shut the fuck up and stay fucking still or you'll regret it," says a man's voice. I believe him. I want to be quiet now because he could hurt me more, but I sob and kick, my body flaying and bucking uselessly. Then someone punches me in the stomach. I'm too winded to shout out. Then I smell something odd, like at a dentist.

CHAPTER 34

Lexi

In the Uber, the effects of the wine and the punch start to wane, and I immediately feel the responsibilities of my family, of my life, settle back on my shoulders. I shouldn't have just taken off without telling anyone where I was going. What was I thinking? Just because I felt a bit lonely and neglected at my party isn't a good excuse to bail. I check my phone, feeling guilty that I hadn't looked at it whilst I was with Toma. However, there are no messages for me. Irrationally, the guilt is immediately shoved aside, and I feel a flare of irritation. It's eleven thirty and apparently no one has missed me. My reaction makes no sense. It's better that I wasn't missed. I'm behaving like a teenager. I call Logan and he picks up after the third ring.

"Hi, having fun?"

"It's awesome, Mum! Where are you? I've been looking for you."

I smile, grateful that after all I haven't been completely forgotten. "I had to go out, do something, but I'm on my way back now. Five minutes away. Meet me at the dance floor?"

"We are not dancing together, Mum." I can almost hear him roll his eyes in despair.

"No, I know. I just want to see you." I want to hold him, my baby who is now only a couple of inches shorter than me. I suddenly feel a very keen need to be reassured by his solidness, his simplicity. Things are so complicated right now. "Have you seen much of your dad tonight?" I feel wrong asking. I can't really expect Jake to have been too hands-on, considering I dashed off to be at another party. With another man.

"He's with me now. We were looking for you and Emily. Neither of you turned up to do the cake-cutting photo thing."

"Oh, sorry, I forgot all about it."

"You forgot about a metre-high cake!" Logan is still young enough to have an unashamedly sweet tooth and the four-tier cake has been a source of endless discussion for him over this past week. He was the one who had the final say over the layers—red velvet, chocolate, coconut, lime and carrot.

"Does Dad want to cut it now?"

"No, it's okay, we did it. Jennifer and Fred and loads of other friends just piled in. It's like a big gang photo now. Not a family one."

I seethe, but bite my tongue. "Okay, well, nearly there with you." As I reenter the party grounds I swiftly help myself to a glass of champagne from a tray. Hearing that Jennifer crashed the family photo op somehow means I require liquid fortification. I know it is partially my fault for not being there, but really? Did it have to be Jennifer who stood in for me? The server holding the tray looks bored, and I see her casting longing looks in the direction of the loud party. She's only about nineteen. I flash her a sympathetic smile. I did a lot of waitressing work for extra cash when I was young—it was basically an exercise in managing older men's roaming hands and older women's unreasonable dietary requirements. I hope she hasn't been met with too much rudeness tonight. I hope everyone has smiled, made eye contact, said thank you.

I head toward the main marquee where the dance floor is. The costumes make it harder to pick out faces I know. Most people are happy in their own cliques now, dancing, drinking, chatting, and no one turns to say hello as I thread through the crowds.

The dry ice smoke swirls, catching the amalgam of lights—dazzling blues, perky greens, loud reds—that are clashing and dashing through the hot, fused bodies. The DJ knows what he's doing, the songs he's picking are clear favorites with Emily's friends, who are all on the dance floor and thrashing their bodies around with wild abandon. Logan's friends look less sure, many lined up around the edge of the tent, trying not to look self-conscious and therefore looking exactly that. I spot Jake and Logan by the cake and make my way closer. The music blasts at a volume I've long since identified as too loud. It reverberates through my chest and spine.

I drop a kiss on Logan's head. His scalp is sweaty and familiar. He looks about him, checking none of his friends have seen me. It's just a truth universally acknowledged that parent affection is uncool. I have no idea why being loved is deemed embarrassing. In my experience, loving is the thing most likely to lead to humiliation. I look around for Emily and don't see her. "Where's Emily?" I ask Jake.

"What?" he yells back.

"Have you caught up with Emily yet?" I yell again, louder this time. A flicker of annoyance skitters up my spine when Jake just turns to me with a broad, obviously drunken smile.

"Not for ages."

"You should be keeping an eye on her," I snap.

"Why?"

"She was drinking earlier."

"All the kids are drinking." Jake makes a big, benevolent gesture with his arm, which takes in the entire area. He's right, no one is sober. Me included. The beer he is holding slops over the glass rim and splashes on the floor.

"Yeah, but it's her first time. She won't know when to say when."

"Anyway, where have you been?" he asks.

"What?" I am playing for time; I can't tell him the truth. He would never understand why I had to say goodbye to Toma. I hardly understand myself. The memory of the man stroking my forehead with his thumb scalds. I can still feel his fingers tapping on the back on my hand. I rub over the spot he touched, as though trying to wipe away words off a blackboard. Jake doesn't even know Toma's name. I really need to tell him about the three million pounds. I'll do that tomorrow, after we've cleared up from the party.

"I saw you take off a few hours ago. I've been looking for you all night. Where have you been?" Jake is showing an interest in me that has been lacking of late. However, it doesn't feel as though it's coming from a place of concern.

"Oh, we ran out of limes. I thought I could go and get some." I stop. It's nonsense. If we had run out of limes—which is unlikely as Sara thought of everything—then why would I be the one to go for them? It's not that sort of party where the hosts pop out to the corner shop to get more crisps and alcohol, something that did happen fairly regularly at our old parties. We have staff now.

Jake is incredulous, too. "Limes."

"For the margaritas." I'm bluffing. I'm not even sure they are serving margaritas. I'm not just bluffing. I'm lying. I'm a liar. "Where is Emily, do you think? I need to speak to her."

Jake shrugs. "Have you called her?"

"Straight to voice mail. And I have texted now, three times throughout the evening. Nothing back." I pause. "Will you call her?"

"Me?"

"Yes."

"But you've just said you've tried," he points out. I glare at him.

For all his incredulity, I know he understands perfectly. I think she might be blocking me. Ignoring me specifically because I am the parent most likely to call time on drunken exploits. I'm the one who will want to know if she's cold, and if she is, then I'll be the one to make her change into something warmer. Her outfit is ridiculously skimpy, and whilst I'm not an idiot I realize most of the girls' outfits are equally tiny and I get the importance of making an entrance. I also think being comfortable enough to have fun is important, too. I insisted she pack a pair of leggings and trainers to put on as the night wore on. I just think heels, a skimpy, plunging leotard, alcohol and fair rides are a combination that amount to an accident waiting to happen. The leggings and trainers are purple and sparkly and go with her costume, but still she wasn't keen. They remain in a bag behind the bar. I know, I've checked. The fact is Emily is more likely to take Jake's call than mine—she might think he's calling her about some party-planning issue. He smiles obligingly and presses her number. We both listen as it rings and rings.

I look around me at the crowded dance floor and spot the three girls who got ready at ours tonight: Scarlett, Liv, Nella. They are dancing with a bunch of boys, writhing around like eels in a bucket. I think the boys must be from the new school because I don't recognize them. They are all tall, handsome. They have floppy hair, loud laughs and ooze confidence as though their raison d'être is to fulfill the stereotype of what it means to be a private schoolboy. I realize that if I go and talk to them I'll be killing their mood, but I do need to know where Emily is. It's after midnight and I'm not sure when anyone last saw her. Apprehension skitters up my spine.

I squeeze my way onto the dance floor, and although it is rammed, somehow a space opens up for me. The girls are all shiny and sticky, their makeup has run and smudged, but they still look gorgeous because they are young and are clearly having a lot of fun. That combo makes for gorgeous. I'm glad for them. "Have you seen Emily?" I yell above the music. They exchange a look that tells me they have, but are weighing up whether to tell me. My first thought is relief.

"She's not in trouble, I just haven't seen her for a while," I say to encourage them.

"I think she went off with—" Liv doesn't get to finish her sentence because Scarlett nudges her in the ribs. It's a forceful shove, effective but indiscreet.

"With whom?" I ask firmly.

Liv looks nervous. Her eyes drop to the dance floor. The boys snigger and then start to melt away into the crowd, not interested in girls who attract parental attention. Nella stares at them, something close to anguish in her pretty, plump face. I watch as she makes a quick calculation. She does not want to lose the boys—she needs to wrap up this conversation and get rid of me. "She's probably just somewhere with Ridley," she garbles.

With Ridley? I try not to alter my expression. "Are they back together?" I hope my tone is lighter than my heart. The girls shrug and move away from me to chase after the boys they were dancing and flirting with. That's far more important to them right now than Emily's goings-on.

I return to where Jake and Logan are standing. Logan is looking tired. Pale and shadowy. I suggest he go home. "One of the security guys could go with you in the taxi." He just scowls at me, unimpressed by the idea. I know he wants to be here until the bitter end. We have a licence to play music until 1:00 a.m. I guess with all the sugar he has undoubtedly consumed, he'll manage to push through until then.

"Her friends think she might be with Ridley," I inform Jake. "I think she might have got back with him."

He nods. "Most likely."

"Why would she want to do that?" I demand, thinking about how Ridley stood by and allowed Megan and her monsters to beat Emily. I should never have agreed to him being here.

"Because she's still in love with him," replies Jake simply with a sigh.

"No, she isn't!" I say this forcefully because I want to be right. "She'd have told me," I insist. But would she? Emily and I haven't been having many heart-to-hearts of late. "Did she tell you?" I demand.

"She didn't have to. I know my daughter."

It's an accusation. I hear it loud and clear. When did that happen? When did Jake start to know what was going on in Emily's head better than I do? I check my phone, but there are still no messages. "Have you tried that find my iPhone tracking thing?" We all have this app on our phones; I can't tell you how many times it's saved the day when one or the other of us has believed we've lost our phone.

"It won't be specific enough in a field this size." Jake takes a big gulp of his beer, lets his gaze fall on the dancers.

I try it anyway. Knowing she's on the field would be some sort of reassurance. I mean, of course she must be. Why would she be anywhere else? Even so, I'd like the matter confirmed. "No joy. It just says her phone is off-line."

"She's probably out of power."

"She was fully charged when we left the house."

"But she'll have taken loads of photos and been posting on Snapchat all night. That drains the battery." Although it's a brand-new phone with a huge capacity, I grab the thought anyway. I quickly look at her Instagram account. She last posted when the sky was still light. I tell Logan to check Snapchat, which I don't have and I don't understand. He does as I ask him, and I stand by, watching intently.

"Nope, nothing," he says.

"Most likely she's just switched off her phone," says Jake.

"I told her to keep her phone on tonight." The anxiety begins to swell and solidify. It grows into a throbbing apprehension, cementing in the base of my back, pulling me to the ground. I stagger a bit, prop myself up against a bar table. Legs and hands shaking, my brain behind my body. I breathe in, deeply.

"So our teenager doesn't want to be found," Jake says, grinning. "That's not exactly breaking news. My guess is she's sneaked off with some of her new friends. Probably trying dope for the first time."

"And that doesn't bother you?" I snap.

"Of course it bothers me. I'm just saying most likely whatever she is up to, it isn't Armageddon."

Jake has always taken a looser position on drugs than I have. He sees them as inevitable, experiential. I really do see them as Armageddon. I force myself not to sound too frantic, but can't stop myself asking, "So you do think something is up?"

"I didn't mean that. Look, have a drink. Try to enjoy yourself, Lexi."

"I can't enjoy myself," I insist.

"That's half the problem," he sighs.

I want to ask him what the other half is. I want to *tell* him what it is. I shiver, despite the sticky heat in the tent. The heat is intensified by the sentences that also hang in the air, half-formed. Too lethal to commit to.

"We should call Ridley and her friends, everyone in her school year. Everyone we invited from her old school and the new one. We have the new class list. I think I have it on my phone."

As I scramble to open contacts, Jake places his hand over my phone. "Just take a breath, Lexi. She's just out there, drunk and sleeping it off. Let's not make a fuss. Blow this out of proportion. What sort of first impression are we going to make on the parents at the new school if we call and say she's missing at her own party? If we call at this time of night, they'll all worry about their own kids, half of which have gone home with different friends, et cetera. It would cause a panic."

I glare at Jake, but reluctantly accept he might have a point. I leave Logan in the dance tent with Jake and go outside to look for Emily. I tell myself that most likely there is nothing seriously wrong, but my years of mothering mean that I do know one thing: if a child doesn't want to be found, they probably should be.

The weather forecast was accurate. The night air has turned cold, and rain starts to splatter on the ground, mocking the British optimism in summer. Many people abandon the outside attractions and head for shelter, others call it a night and start falling into minicabs. Like a salmon heading upstream, I walk out into the blackness, scouring the crowds and the shadows for my daughter.

CHAPTER 35

Lexi

"Emily, Emily!" My voice pierces the night, and the sounds from the party fall away into the distance—the laughing, the noise from the fair rides, the music from the DJ. I don't hear any of it. I only hear my heart beating against my rib cage, and my ears strain as I wait for her to yell back a response. I've scoured the entire party site and there's no sign of her. I've asked everyone I've bumped into if they've seen her recently. I'm met with nothing other than blank shrugs and vague apologies that, no, they haven't. Most people just want to get out of the rain, and I don't think they really give my question much thought. "She was dressed as Zendaya as she appeared in *The Greatest Showman.*" A shrug. "You know, purple leotard thing." I lose patience with their glassy eyes, their dumb indifference, and rush on with my search. I start to run. I'm not as fit as I should be. I've spent too many long hours behind a desk. My breath never makes it to and from my lungs; instead, it harbors in my throat and I'm suffocating.

I imagine her unconscious, choking on her own alcohol-induced vomit. I imagine her cold, wet, alone. The woods loom in the background of my every thought and breath, shadowy, threatening, overpowering. She's nowhere to be found at the party—I need to head into the woods next and search there. The trees are dense, some fat and ancient, others scrubby and slight, saplings, really. Their combined canopies block out any moonlight that the clouds haven't already stolen. I stumble around, possibly in circles because there are no clear paths, and even if there were, I wouldn't know how far to follow one, or in which direction. Brambles rip at the thin cotton of my costume and soon my legs and arms are scratched. I wish I was wearing jeans. I wish I'd just spot her lying asleep under a fat tree. I wish I had kept her by my side all night. I wish we'd never had a party. I wish so many things. My slashed calves are the least of my problems.

Even using the torch on my phone, it's too dark to see anything much. I decide I need to go back to the party and rouse security. They can help me search—we need to do this systematically. I run back to the dance tent. I only realize how long I've been searching when I notice that the music has stopped. The DJ has packed away, is probably back on the motorway by now. The dance floor looks like a crime scene, pocked with spilled drinks and shards of crushed plastic glasses. The colors from the party popper streamers have bled into the puddles caused by wet and muddy footprints. With the lights up, the scene that had seemed thrilling just a short time ago now has the dank, grubby quality of a public toilet. No one is tidying up. The staff are too exhausted to bother to paint on smiles when they see me. They sag and slouch, suppress yawns and reach their arms into coat sleeves, no doubt very glad of the decision we made to clean up tomorrow in daylight. The guests have thinned out to a few stragglers. Jake is still deep in conversation with one of them. I don't recognize whoever it is he's talking to. I spot Logan, asleep I think. He is slouched on a tall stool, his head resting on the bar. "I can't find her," I yell. "Jake, Jake, we need to get security. We need to call the police. I can't find her."

Of course, this draws everyone's attention. The staff immediately swap their exhausted demeanors for ones of alertness, curiosity or panic. The laggard guests fight through their drunkenness and stare at me with confusion and the sort of ghoulish interest rubbernecks give car accidents. Jake walks swiftly toward me. He moves me away from the fray by placing a determined hand on the base of my spine. In the past this gesture has felt tender and territorial—now I feel the manipulation. His first priority seems to be avoiding causing a scene. Avoiding anyone else becoming upset or alarmed. Anyone other than me, that is. I don't give a damn. All I want to know is where Emily is.

"I've looked everywhere for her. No sign."

"She'll turn up." He smiles. If he's trying to be reassuring, I just find him arrogant and annoying.

"When?"

"Everything's fine."

"It's obviously not."

We are talking in splintered sentences that stutter out like gunfire: abrupt, deadly. Jake takes a deep breath. Waves goodbye to the last few guests, tells the staff they can go. Why is he letting people slip away? We need these people to help us search for her. I feel drained and powerless, a flat, sputtering battery because I don't throw out contradicting instructions. I let him have his way. "You know what, I'm sure it's nothing to worry about. I bet our first guess was right. I bet she's with Ridley."

I want this to be true. I wouldn't care. I really wouldn't. Him or any boy. The rich, pompous ones who arrived with vodka and attitudes, or the scruffy, meaty ones who arrived with bad haircuts and acne. Right now, I'm desperate for it to be this level of deceit. Praying for it. "Have you seen Ridley?" I demand of no one in particular, but the entire room.

"Someone asking for me?" I turn, and there he is, head hung, looking for all the world as though he wants to vanish rather than be brought into the limelight. I pounce on him.

"Have you seen Emily?" He shakes his head slowly.

"Not at all? Not all evening?"

"Well, a bit. Earlier." He's clearly reluctant.

"When? What time?" His eyes are glassy and red. Drink, drugs, tears? I don't really care. I just want him to answer my questions.

"About eight." Over five hours ago. My heart sinks.

"What's going on?" asks Jennifer. I'd been so intent on interrogating Ridley, it's only now that I notice he is flanked by his mother and father. He looks protected, defended. My daughter is absent, Jake's and my inadequacies bite. And although I hate Jennifer, loathe her with a base, visceral certainty, at this moment I just remember that she's known Emily since she was a baby. Thoughts clash about my head, pleading for attention. Jennifer once drove us at breakneck speed to the hospital because Emily had fallen out of a tree that she, Ridley and Megan had been climbing. Jennifer makes separate gravy for Emily because Emily is veggie; so few people bother to do that. She has always sewn the name tags onto Emily's and Logan's school uniforms for me, because she has a sewing machine and it takes minutes, whereas hand sewing swallows hours. She has driven to my house with medicine because my kids were running fevers, Jake was away and I was housebound. She's plunked a sunhat on my daughter's head when she's spotted her running in the garden unprotected. She taught Emily to sail. Jennifer might have fucked my husband, but right now I don't care. All I care about is finding Emily, and I think that will happen sooner if the people who love her are galvanized. So I tell her, "Emily is missing." I see

Jennifer's face crumple in horror. I feel vindicated that she sees the agony as I do.

"Has someone taken her?" she asks.

I gasp. A new horror. "You think that's possible?" I had not thought of that. My fears just ran to alcohol and accidents.

"Well, you are so wealthy now. She might have been kidnapped." My knees start to shake, and I stagger. Someone lowers me into a chair. I let them.

"I'm guessing she's just passed out somewhere," adds Jake. I see Jennifer's face change, suddenly relieved.

"Well, that would be better," adds Fred.

I know it would. A teen in turmoil, a teen in a sulk, a teen drunk and lawless is infinitely preferable to a teen who's been kidnapped and held for ransom, but I suddenly feel a deep despair crawl through my being and I'm certain Jake is wrong.

"Yes, that will be it," says Jennifer. "I noticed she was drinking earlier on tonight. I'm sure it's nothing serious at all." I hate Jennifer for instantly siding with Jake, for instantly accepting his version of events and diminishing my fears, dismissing them. But of course she would. Sucking a man's dick trumps putting a sunhat on a child's head in terms of allegiances and commitment. I feel sick with anxiety and can't be bothered with either of them. Now that Jennifer has put the thought of kidnapping in my mind, I'm delirious with fear. Even whilst I looked for Emily and imagined her choking on her vomit, cold and unconscious, part of me doubted it, couldn't accept it. She's not the sort to allow herself to get into that much of a mess. She would have found help, and even if she didn't want us to see her hideously drunk, she could have gone to her friends or her brother.

"Where is she, Jake?" Jake doesn't respond or move. I want to rip his head off with my bare hands. Why isn't he more concerned? "Where is she?" Obviously, he doesn't know. I realize that, but I want something from him. Anything! "Who has taken her?"

"We don't know anyone has taken her," he mutters impatiently, dismissively. He clearly thinks I'm being hysterical. He moves toward Ridley. "Ridley, mate. I know you think you are being a friend to her by covering, but you're not," says Jake. I am embarrassed for my husband that he called Ridley his "mate." On no level is this appropriate, and it's so obviously a desperate attempt to ingratiate himself and pretend he's somehow cool and down with the kids. Embarrassment flourishes into disdain when I consider that, specifically, he wants to be down with the kid who broke his daughter's heart. "Just tell us where she's hiding out and we can all go home to bed. Where is she?"

"I don't know."

"You do. You're just not telling us," says Jake a little more firmly.

"I don't." Ridley's gaze is bolted to the floor.

I sigh. I fear he probably doesn't. I watched him during the earlier part of the evening, and from what I could gather he didn't seem in the least bit interested in Emily. She trailed after him like a devoted dog, but he kept moving along. If he was at the Ferris wheel, over she'd saunter, only for him to leg it to the bouncy castle. When she turned up there, he went to get something to eat. Always with the girl he brought along. He seemed pretty focused on her, not interested in Emily at all. It was heartbreaking to watch. I was fuming with Jake for inviting him here and allowing him to rub Emily's nose in his new relationship or fling or whatever it is. I believe him when he says he doesn't know where Emily is. It's just not what I want to hear. My desperation makes me focused, hostile and disapproving all at once.

I glare at him, every centimetre of my body emitting loathing.

"Are you sure you haven't any ideas, son?" asks Fred, his tone jovial, too. We're the sort of parents who have read all the books telling us not to get riled with our teens because they simply shut down and you hit a wall. Better to create an environment that suggests safety and belief. Right now, I want to climb down

Ridley's throat and haul out his tongue to force him to spit out any words that might help.

"I'm not her babysitter," Ridley mutters sulkily.

But I am. His response slaps me. Because, in fact, I am more than that. I am her *mother*, not even a substitute. I should have been here. Watching over her. Taking care of her. Not with Toma. At that second my phone buzzes. I think it's going to be a message from Toma, that I've somehow conjured him up by thinking of him. I glance at my screen. At first I don't understand what I am looking at. But then I do.

It is a photo of Emily. I can't see much of her face—there is duct tape wrapped around her eyes and mouth, leaving just her nose free. Her neat little nose is slimy. Tears, snot. Her hands are tied behind her back, her legs are tied at the ankles, her long coltish legs look bruised, battered. She's still wearing her purple leotard. It clings to her body and I am beaten by the thought of her vulnerability. "We need to call the police," I say, my voice barely a whisper.

As the words leave my mouth, another message comes through. Don't involve the police or we will hurt her. There's an audio clip. I play it.

"Mum, Mum, please." She's sobbing, gasping. "Do what they say. I'm frightened, Mum, please." Then there's the sound of a scuffle. Then nothing. It goes dead.

CHAPTER 36

Emily

I can't see anything! I can't see anything so everything I feel, smell and hear is magnified and terrifying. I feel a man's rigid grip around my forearm. It's too tight. He's hurting me. I can smell his sour breath. I freeze. Recoil. You think your instinct is going to be to kick and fight. But I don't. I can't. How can I, blindfolded and bound? How can I escape? Then another man roughly picks up my legs and I have no chance. I know I have no chance. They carry me between them as easily as a bag of shopping.

Are they going to kill me? They are going to kill me.

The second man's hands on my bare legs is like a slap and suddenly I am flinching, writhing, but the more I struggle the tighter he grips. I'm not thinking straight. A vision of Logan and Ridley as small boys poking caterpillars with tiny sticks for no other reason than the amusement of watching them loop and coil, crashes into my head. They were not usually cruel boys, but I always hated it when they did that. It was nasty. The prodding could hurt the caterpillar, injure it, kill it. I wanted to see it left alone to become a butterfly. Just let it become a fucking butterfly! I force myself to go limp even though every instinct is screaming to do the opposite because I think they might want me to struggle. For me to writhe and wriggle in their hands. For my leotard to ride up my backside. For them to get to feel my bare thighs, arms and the thin silkiness of my costume, which only just covers the rest of my body. They are talking to each other. Foreign voices, speaking a language I don't recognize, which makes it harder for me to work out how many there are. There are two carrying me and there's another man who has the tone of someone speaking on a phone. Sometimes he seems to bark out orders at the two carrying me. The boss. The worst one. They are going to kill me.

They throw me into the back of a van. I land on my shoulder. I'm winded and sore everywhere, but the pain I'm feeling doesn't frighten me as much as the pain I'm anticipating. The metal doors slam behind me. Then I hear them climb into the front. They set off at speed.

Because I'm tied up and there are no seats, let alone seat belts, I roll around the floor of the van every time it goes around a corner. I bang my head, my back, my knee. Eventually I orientate myself enough to sit up, I crawl backward on my bottom, shuffle into a corner. Then I consider a van's layout. By pushing myself into a corner, I am either moving closer to the seats they must be in, or the door. I think of leaning against the door and somehow opening it, it swinging open and me falling onto the road. Would that be better? Probably not at this speed but I don't know. I might die but there are fates worse than death, aren't there? Mum would say not. She always says you can come back from everything but that. So I lie flat again and get thrown from one side of the van to the other.

I imagine the men looking at me, smirking at my struggle, my lack of direction or coordination. The thought of them looking at me makes me want to heave again. I smell of my own vomit from earlier. I don't feel drunk anymore. I wish I did because maybe that would numb the fear, but my terror has punched the alcohol out of my system. I wish I was wearing more than I am. The thought of the leotard, which leaves little to the imagination, horrifies me. What are they going to do to me? I wish I had changed into the clothes Mum made me bring to the party. I think of the trainers, the trackies behind the bar. I want to cry. I think of my mum and I do cry. I sob for the whole journey, panting for breath. And although my nose isn't obstructed, I feel certain I am going to suffocate. I can't get enough air. My gasps are shallow, strained.

After some time the van comes to a sudden stop. The back is opened again, and I am pulled out. This time just one man carries me. He throws me over his shoulder. I can tell he is taller than my dad, broader. It's raining. I can smell trees and wet grass but it doesn't smell fresh and spring-like. The ground smells of decay. Dirt.

Death.

CHAPTER 37

Lexi

I freeze for a moment. Never, ever so completely destroyed with fear. I vainly try to find the number from where the message just came from, but of course it's withheld—kidnappers are hardly likely to give out their contact details. I look at Jake and see if he can make any sense of this. If he can do anything about this. But what? I feel I've just been thrown off a high-speed train. What's going on? Jake's face mirrors my own: confusion, terror. I start to hit the numbers 999 on my phone. Before I manage to touch the nine for a third time, Jake snatches the phone out of my hand. "What are you doing?" he demands angrily.

"I'm calling the police."

"We can't, don't be a fool."

I lunge to retrieve my phone, but he holds it above my head. As I stretch to reach it, he calmly passes it to Jennifer. She takes it from him and then passes it to Fred. Fred shakes his head at me and puts my phone in his trouser pocket, keeping his hand on it. I stare at him, disgusted. Fred, too? Ganging up on me? Siding with these two? I sense that he's not going to budge and have no time to argue with him. I turn my attention back to Jake, Emily's father. *Surely*, he'll see sense. "We have to, Jake. This isn't a matter of choice."

"You saw the message, they told us not to."

"Well, they are bound to tell us not to, aren't they? They are criminals. Kidnappers!" The word strikes me as disconcertingly inadequate, almost comical. They may be rapists, torturers, murderers. I can only bring myself to say kidnappers. "The police will help us. That's what the police are for."

"We can't afford to have them sniffing around when the kidnappers specifically told us not to call them."

"Sniffing around? Jake, they'll *find* her. That's their job. We *need* them."

Jake's face curls into a snarl. "And what if they don't find her? Crimes do go unsolved, you know, Lexi. The police aren't infallible. What if we call them, but they can't retrieve her and yet the kidnappers know we've called them. Then they'll hurt her. Is that what you want?"

"No, but—"

"Don't. Call. The police." His instruction is icy, fearsome. I stare at him. I have known this man for so long and he is a stranger. I see the same dark brown almost black hair, feathered with a breath of gray around his ears. I recognize the strong, square jawline that is cloaked in a fashionably shaped, neatly trimmed beard, but I don't have a clue who he is. In the past five weeks, there have been surprises—shocks. The way he has behaved since we won the money, his affair, are not things I would have expected of him, but they were things that I managed to accept are in the realms of possibility. But this? This thumps me in my solar plexus. I can't breathe. I stare at him, this strange man. Obviously we have to go to the police. We can't follow the instructions of kidnappers because they are fucking *kidnappers*. Criminals. They will outsmart us. They will out-wicked us. They will think of doing things that we can't even imagine in our worst nightmares. Our daughter is in serious danger. There are no words. There are no limits. What the fuck is he thinking suggesting we don't call the police? Something awful, *unthinkable*, might be happening to her right now and I am powerless to stop it. I glare at Fred and then at his pocket, where my phone is nestled.

"You are siding with him?" I demand. Fred won't meet my eye. He doesn't so much as nod. He just pushes his hand further into his pockets, as though securing my phone a little more tightly. "You weak bastard," I mutter. No one responds. It's as though I haven't spoken.

"Let's get Logan home, we'll decide what to do from there," suggests Jennifer. What in God's name has it to do with her?

I try to hold it together in front of Logan. He was asleep when I received the photo of Emily so when we wake him, the first thing he mumbles is, "Where's Emily?"

"She's sleeping at friends'," replies Jake. I let the lie roll. I just can't bring myself to tell him what is going on. It would terrify him. What good would it do? We walk in a numb, ominous silence to the car. I am shaking so much that I can feel my organs rattle inside my body; I think it is a miracle that one foot finds its way in front of the next. I am undoubtedly in medical shock, but no one attends to me. No one slips their arm around my shoulders, hands me a hot sweet drink, squeezes my hand. Maybe they don't bother because they know any gesture will be simply that—a gesture, empty and useless. No one can make me feel better when my daughter is God knows where and God knows what is happening to her.

Jennifer, Fred and Ridley climb into our car with us. I'm horrified. I don't want to be anywhere near them, and Jake is acting as though this makes perfect sense and this somehow means

I can't find the words to stop it happening. I can't waste energy on them. Once we are at home, Logan goes upstairs to bed, mumbling something about us not waking him in the morning. When he is in the bathroom peeing, I check that the windows in his bedroom are locked. When he climbs into bed, I tuck the duvet around him and remind him about the panic button next to his bed. He is too sleepy to ask why I'm now giving the device a sense of gravitas. When we moved in, just a few days ago, Emily and I joked that it was crazy to have a panic button so close to Logan's bed. Emily said he'd constantly be hitting it when he wanted my attention. The police would be called every time he wanted a glass of water. It abruptly occurs to me that I could hit the button now. The police would respond. It's more dramatic than calling 999, but my daughter is in serious danger, things *are* dramatic. I can't call 999. I feel like a prisoner in my home as my phone has basically been confiscated. To underline that thought, I hear Jake on the stairs, then he is in the room, close behind me. "Night, champ," he says to Logan. Of course, it's natural he wants to check in with his son, especially tonight, considering everything, but his presence means I can't lunge for the panic button. Had he, too, suddenly remembered its existence? Was he saying good-night to Logan or was he checking up on me? Stopping me from getting the help I think we need.

We go downstairs where the Heathcotes are gathered around the kitchen table. It's un-fucking-believable, but I notice Jennifer's eyes swivel greedily around the Poggenpohl units, I see her check out the expensive worktops, the enormous state-of-the-art fridge. I see her nostrils widen a fraction as envy flares. She is envious of me? A woman who has a child bound and gagged, abducted, missing, lost. I can't begin to understand her. I have always tried to understand people. Not because I'm intrinsically kind or think that I value empathy any more than anyone else. It's simply an urge, an instinct, to get to the bottom of human behavior. I thought I'd be safer then, if I understood people, but people are infinitely unknowable, mysterious. They have smiley talk, but give hard stares. They kiss you, but hurt you. Tell you they love you when, really, they hate you.

"Where are the security men you hired?" I demand.

Jake glances at his watch. "They've knocked off now. Gone home."

"But I want someone here, right now, outside our door, outside Logan's bedroom door. Twenty-four hours."

"This house is perfectly secure. You know it is, and anyway we need to keep a lid on this, like the kidnappers said. Security guys would quickly pick up on the problem." His words are infuriating. Too considered and reasonable in light of what is going on. I glare at him, but then my heart swells and slackens. I see that he's not indifferent. There's a milky white sheen on his skin that puts me in mind of meat sweating on a buffet on a hot day; he is trembling. He is more stressed and terrified than I have ever seen him before—we just don't agree on how this should be managed. Naturally, we don't. We agree on so little nowadays. The problem is Jake is far too used to getting his own way now. But this is not the same as going along with a choice of car or even house or school. This is a matter of life and death. Doesn't he see we need all the help we can get? Jake asks, "Anything, Fred?" Fred reaches into his pocket and hands Jake my phone. Jake checks my phone, presumably for another message.

"We need to get her home!" I cry, frustrated. "We need help. I want you to call those security guys," I blurt. "Someone, do *something*!"

"They are basically glorified bouncers. They can't do much in a situation like this."

"But that's not what you said when we first employed them. You said..." I trail off. What is the point? Jake is not consistent. I know that much by now.

"Shall I put the kettle on?" offers Fred. No one answers him.

"Coffee then?" Fred starts to play around with the Krups coffee machine. He doesn't have to take our orders, knowing who drinks cappuccinos, lattes or Americanos. We all know that—and so much more—about one another. Jake places my phone in the middle of the kitchen table. I suppose he thinks I've accepted his commands and I suppose I have, at least for the moment. If I reach for the phone, they will only grab it from me again. They all seem so clear that not calling the police is the correct thing that I'm becoming confused, overwhelmed. Maybe they are right. Maybe we should follow the kidnappers' instructions. I don't know.

We pull up chairs, sit around the table and stare at the phone. Waiting for it to ring or beep. We look ridiculous in our fancy-dress costumes—Pierrot, Harlequin, a lion, a strong man, a boy pretending to be a strong man. I pull off my cap, but I don't want to go upstairs to shower and change. What if the kidnappers call and I miss it?

Fred places the mugs of coffee on the table. I notice only the Heathcotes manage to drink theirs. Fred eats a couple of biscuits, too. Jake and I let our drinks go cold and slick. We don't reach for a biscuit. The phone does not ring. Jennifer is the first to comment she wants to change out of her fancy dress. She asks if she can borrow something of mine. I agree but don't go upstairs with her to dig anything out as she's more than capable of rooting through my wardrobe. I don't care what she purloins, not anymore. I just can't leave my phone. She returns thirty minutes later, showered, fresh faced. Men would think she's not wearing any makeup, but I can tell she's applied mascara, blusher and even lip gloss. At a time like this. Unbelievable. She's wearing a denim skirt and a clingy emerald shirt. I know both things were still in a shopping bag on my bedroom floor. I hadn't hung them up because I bought them for Emily. I just hadn't got around to putting them in her room. They fit and suit Jennifer. The men and Ridley also shower and change.

It comes to my turn. They are all insistent that I'll feel better if I follow their lead. I think of Emily, wearing a purple leotard and high gold boots. She doesn't have the comfort of a shower, the relief of slipping into joggers. I refuse to change.

"You don't need to be a martyr about this, Lexi. You are not helping her by being uncomfortable yourself," comments Jake. I don't respond. I hate it that he doesn't understand me.

"How do you think they got my number?" I ask instead.

"I don't know, Lexi—who do you give your number to?" Jake stares at me, cold and challenging.

I flush, although I don't know why. "Just regular people," I mutter.

"People that you help at work?" probes Jennifer.

"No, I'm careful not to do that." Toma is the only person I've ever helped at the bureau and then given my number to. I don't tell her that. It isn't any of her business. None of this is. She shouldn't even be here.

"Do you think this might be connected to those desperate people who broke in and stole your laptop?"

I didn't tell her about the laptop, so I assume Jake has filled her in on that. Clearly, they are still seeing each other. That doesn't necessarily mean they are still sleeping together, but it might. It probably does. I find I don't care. I don't care where my husband is shoving his dick; I can't imagine why I thought that him sleeping with someone else was a tragedy. It doesn't matter to me now. I just want my daughter home. I glance at Ridley. I keep forgetting he is here with us. He probably shouldn't be. He should be in bed. Sleeping off the party excess or excitedly messaging friends about how much fun he had at the out-of-this-world party, like a normal teenager. Nothing about this is as it is supposed to be. I notice he is sobbing, silently. Tears roll down his face, leaving a snail's trail of sadness.

I almost reach across the table and squeeze his hand—he's just a kid—but can't bring myself to. This boy crushed my daughter and now my daughter is gone. He is here. Normal things like decency have been wrung out of me. I almost hate him and everyone around the table for being safe and here. I would change places with her in an instant. But he is sobbing, and Emily would want me to comfort him. I make myself behave like a proper person—I lean across the table and pat his arm. However, my gesture doesn't help. Ridley flinches, withdraws from me. "You should try to get some sleep, Ridley. You can take a bed in one of the spare rooms. I think they are all made up."

He shakes his head. "I won't be able to sleep. I'd rather be here." I nod, respecting his decision. I keep checking the wall clock and my watch; they agree. Time is passing. The last time any of us saw Emily was at about eight thirty. It's now three in the morning. I don't want them to, but my thoughts start to traverse down dark and disturbing paths.

You are a winner.

Four words and the whole world shifts. I can't find her.

Just four more words. But they are the ones that shove me from fortunate to damned. She was there in front of me. All hopeful and sulky and glorious and angry, and then she was gone. It's strange that the good news—the winning—took time to sink in. This horror I accept instantly. I've been waiting for it. I wish more than anything that she was here by my side being annoyed by my clinginess and what she calls righteousness. Resenting me for being her buzzkill.

I should have known that we'd pay. I did know. I would have paid in any other way. I've never felt so alone in my life. I want to be doing something, to bring her home. I want to be out there looking for her. It's not enough to just sit and wait, wait and see what happens. I go and dig out Logan's laptop, start to Google the procedure and statistics around kidnapping. It's a mistake. Like most things on the internet, facts are drowned by hysteria and cruelty, worst-case scenarios. I try not to click and wander down the rabbit warrens of despair and dread, but I can't help myself. I feel sick, faced with videos of men in hoodies, men on CCTV cameras, men driving vans into the distance. I am immobilized by the fuzzy, faded pictures of smiley young girls never recovered; instead destined to stay forever in school uniforms, not allowed to grow up, grow old, to live. I see pictures of heartbroken parents at press conferences, at tombstones. My eyes slide from one article to the next, but I am too much of a coward to read anything properly. Words morph on and off the screen; like ants at a picnic, they won't stay still. Often the word "kidnapper" is linked with the words "teen" and "murder." The Wikipedia definition—the unlawful carrying away and confinement of a person against their will—punches me in the gut. Carrying away where? Confined where?

I read that the police consider the first few hours often to be the most vital in offering up clues in a missing person case. Again, I am swamped with doubt that Jake's decision not to involve the police is the right one, but I don't challenge him. I don't trust myself—or anyone, come to that. If the kidnappers hurt her because they somehow find out I've contacted the police, I'd never forgive myself. How would I live with that? Soon they will send a message. They will ask for money. We can give money. That, we can do. I Google the word "ransom." It's a silly habit of our time. Something is wrong—a rash, weening problems, sleeping patterns—we Google it. Something is unknown—school catchment areas, inoculation guidelines, dates for the Topshop sale—Google it.

Someone is lost—what then?

I Google it. I am hoping for some advice on how to handle this impossible, unimaginable situation because I'm clueless, alone. Maybe we all are, trapped in a terrible space where there are only digital responses, digital solutions. Pixels on a screen, placed there by strangers. I want to talk to my husband, but I don't have the words. I want to talk to my friends, but I don't have any of those. In a way, the search does help. I am stunned that the first thing that comes up is adverts for companies that insure people against ransom. I feel a peculiar, uncomfortable relief that we are not alone and yet a profound, distinct terror that this is a business. Hostage situations, kidnapping and extortion occur often enough for people to insure themselves against it. I have insurance for accidents in the home, for luggage lost on holiday. I should have known things were bigger now. I should have protected her more. "Jake, did you know that there are companies that work to cover monies lost to ransom?" I call through to where he is still sitting in the kitchen.

"Too late for that," he bites back.

"No, I didn't mean we needed cover," I mutter impatiently. "Of course not, but my point is if it's a business, then..." I quickly add a few more words to the search engine. "Look here!" Jake swiftly walks over to where I'm sitting and bends over me to read the screen. For a moment I feel it again, the old intimacy between us. I feel shored up, hopeful. Perhaps I can lean on him. Perhaps we can make it through this. But then Jennifer and Fred crowd around the screen, too, and the intimacy is loosened, lost. I push on. "There are companies that say their aim at all times is the safe return of a kidnap victim, that they can help with that."

Yes, there are specialists. I should know that by now. There are specialists for everything: accountants, lawyers, florists, image consultants, party planners. Whilst planning the party I learned there are people who make a living out of being hummus specialists, balloon sculptors and adding edible glitter to jelly. Of course there are people who specialize in safely returning your kidnapped child. It's just a matter of money. And we have money. "We should get in touch with these people." I click on the link, but again Jake stops me.

"Just wait. Don't do anything rash. We have to research these sites. How do we know we can trust these people? They might be scam artists."

"We don't know if we can trust them, but as our daughter is currently bound and gagged God knows where, we have to do something."

"Let me do some reading," offers Jennifer. It's an eminently sensible suggestion under normal circumstances—due diligence and research before employing someone is a good plan. I want to stab her. We're so far from normal circumstances. She is close at my side, her hand hovering over the mouse. I realize she's expecting me to relinquish my control of the laptop. I'm not sure I can. So much seems outside of my control, I need to cling to this. Jake puts his hands on both my shoulders, gently helps me to my feet and leads me away from the laptop back to the kitchen table. He guides me into a chair, and when I resist, the pressure exerted increases fractionally. I flop into the chair and he releases me. The moment he does I leap to my feet. "I can't just sit here." I rush into the hall. All eyes are on me. They look concerned and a bit exasperated. They are looking at me as though I'm a crazy woman, but they are the crazy ones, just sitting here, accepting this, waiting.

"Where are you going?" demands Jake.

"I don't know, I need to be out there. To comb over the party site again. I need to find her."

"I'll come with you," says Fred. I nod, grateful, willing to enter another truce with him even though he collaborated in the seizure of my phone. People are not queuing up to help me, and I'll take what I can get. I am aware that it should have been Jake offering. Jake who wants to be with me, hunting for his daughter.

Instead, he says, "I can't imagine it will do any good, though. If we are dealing with professionals, which I think we are, they are hardly going to have left a big arrow pointing to where they've gone."

"We have to do something!" I scream.

At that moment my phone buzzes. We all rush back to the

table. I'm the most determined. An animal, I snatch at it first and answer. "Hello."

"Have you called the police?" The voice is not recognizable. Whoever is speaking sounds like a robot. I remember from some spy film or other that you can get apps and devices that can be attached to your phone that disguise your voice. I could be talking to a man or a woman, someone with a posh London accent or someone speaking in a second language—it's impossible to tell. I curse the person with the mind dark and clever enough to invent this app.

"No, we haven't."

"Don't, or else." The mechanical way the threat is delivered in no way diminishes its power. I don't need to know what the "or else" is. I can imagine it, but still—in order to underline the point—I hear my daughter yell out in pain. Her voice is not disguised. I don't know what caused her to yell. Did they hit her, kick her, pull her to her feet by her hair? Worse? I start to cry. Jake impatiently gestures to me that I should hand over the phone, but I just move farther away from him, glad the table is between us and he can't snatch it from me again.

"We want ten million pounds." The robot again.

"Okay." It doesn't cross my mind to argue the point. I'd give them every penny I won and every penny I had before the win. I would.

"Bank transfer. We'll send details. When we have the money, we'll tell you where she is."

"Okay."

The line goes dead.

CHAPTER 38

Emily

I don't know how long I have been here. I'm too terrified and disorientated to be able to keep track. I wish I could sleep, let some time pass without this horrendous, impossible to describe fear, but I can't sleep. I am trying, really trying, to stay calm. That's what Mum and Dad would want. If they were here, they'd tell me it was going to be okay. They'd tell me I am brave and strong and that it will all be over soon. Mum would be the one to say, *Don't think about the pain, Emily, don't anticipate it, you make it worse. Try to think about something else.* That's what they said when I had to go to the doctor for injections or had to visit the dentist. It's almost laughable that I was once scared of those things. Now I see that those things are nothing to be scared of. Nothing at all. I also see nothing is laughable and that maybe it's not all going to be okay.

I wish my mum and dad were here.

Where are they? They will be coming for me. I know that. I cling to that. They will come for me soon. They will have called the police and there will be a massive search for me already underway. Mum will be insisting that helicopters with big beaming lights scan the dark night, Dad will be walking through fields searching for me with gangs of other people, too, everyone who came to the party will be looking for me. We have friends, we have resources, they will find me. I listen hopefully for the sound of a helicopter engine or my dad calling my name. Nothing.

I think we are in a barn or farm building of some sort. The ground is uneven and doesn't feel tiled or wooden, it feels like earth, but I can't be sure because I'm too woozy—shock, drink, dehydration, plain old-fashioned terror. All this combined has left me confused, unsteady. I'm sitting on a hard plastic chair, my arms tied to it behind my back and my legs splayed, tied to each front leg. The rope is thick and hurts my wrists. I am freezing cold and my feet have gone numb. I'm parched. When they tied me to the chair, they took off the tape from my mouth.

"Don't scream. No one hear you. I hit you if you scream. I hurt you. Understand."

I nodded. I understood. Totally. Still, I thought as soon as they take the tape off, I'll scream, but ripping off the tape was so painful I didn't scream, I was too shocked. Stunned. Then there was a moment where a plastic bottle of water was put to my lips. I chose the water over yelling. It wasn't really a matter of choice. It was about survival. Instinctually, I gulped it down, a lot of it running down my chin and neck. Before I'd had enough, the bottle was snatched away. "Make a message for your mother," one man instructs in a heavy Eastern European accent. "Mum, Mum, please. Do what they say. I'm frightened, Mum, please." I didn't get chance to say any more before they gagged me again, this time with a scarf. The thin fabric of the scarf means I can breathe a bit better than I could through the tape, but it holds my mouth open unnaturally, cuts into the edges of my lips. I think my mouth is bleeding.

No one has interacted with me since then. Maybe an hour ago, maybe four or five. I don't know. I can't tell. From time to time, I can hear the three men talk between themselves. They don't say much. I think they are waiting for something. I gather at least one of them is playing a game on his phone because intermittently he throws up a small cheer and the other men laugh at him.

They are playing games. I am shaking, bruised, bound.

I try not to panic or, you know, *despair.* I think I finally understand that word as I fight it. I used to use it a lot with Megan when we were about thirteen. "Megan, I despair of you!" I'd say if she, like, mucked up her eyeliner or something and we'd both laugh so hard. Now I know what despair might mean. What if my parents can't find me? What if these men are going to rape and kill me? That's like, what men do, right? I feel my body tremble so violently I make the chair rattle. I don't know if it's cold or fear. Both are ripping through my body, squeezing every internal organ. The rope on my wrists and ankles rubs painfully.

No. Stop. I can't think that way.

They play games, that makes them human, right?

Or maybe just psychopaths. Maybe they play games and then rape and kill.

I think that most likely I have been kidnapped for money. If these men were going to rape me, they would have done so by now. But they are waiting for something. A message from a boss, word of a drop-off. I allow myself a moment of hope. They won't hurt me if they want money for me. Then I hear movement. They are coming closer. All three at once. They are untying my feet, my hands. I should run, fight, kick, but pins and needles, numbness—something—stops me. I collapse like a sack of potatoes. I hate my body for not being as strong as my mind. I don't want to give in, but I have no ability to fight. One man picks me up. I start to cry. No, no, no. He throws me, like I'm a doll, and I land on a mattress, on the floor. The mattress is thin and cheap and as I land, I feel the impact of the ground underneath. No. No. Please no.

One of them takes my right hand and ties it to something solid. I pull, but there's no give. I can't sit up. I can only lie down on the mattress. I scramble about, thrashing, wriggling, trying to dodge them, but I don't know how, I don't know where they are. They are not touching me yet. Just watching me I suppose. Checking I'm secure and can't escape. I realize I am wetting myself. I try to clench and stop, but it just comes, I feel it on my thigh. A warm gush. The smell of ammonia.

"Piss, piss," yells one of the men. I can hear his disgust. Neither of the other two responds. I am crying, but the tears can't escape, the tape on my eyes is so tight. I think I am going to go blind. I think I am going to suffocate. I am going to die rolling around in my own wee and maybe that's the best I can hope for, dying now.

Someone kicks me in the stomach. I scream and pull up my legs to protect my baby.

CHAPTER 39

Lexi

Terror is leaking in, a drop at a time. Drip, drip. The clock tick-tocks and the hours pass. Now there is enough terror that we can drown in it. No one suggests we change into our pajamas, clean our teeth, get some sleep. I'm glad, because doing something so automatic and familiar and ordinary would be a betrayal. Ridley, Jennifer and Fred all nap for periods of time on chairs and the sofa in the kitchen. Every time they wake with a start, they look guilty, embarrassed that their frail bodies have overwhelmed them with the need to sleep. They rub their eyes, mumble, "Any news?" As there is none, they fall back to sleep. I can't blame them. Their being awake doesn't help anything. I'm glad that Jennifer in particular isn't hovering around Jake, looking concerned, patting his shoulder, squeezing his arm. I'm under such extreme pressure I don't know how long I can continue to turn a blind eye to the way she searches for a connection with him, tries to assert her special place with him. Has she always been that way? How have I missed it for so long?

Neither Jake nor I get a wink. I can't stand the idea of sleep, the passing of the night and a fresh day because I want to halt time. Turn it back, ideally. I want her home *now.* But it doesn't matter what I want. Some things can't be changed. Time trundles on, insisting that now is later and later, further and further away from when I last saw her.

Then and now. An unbridgeable chasm. Then, when she was in my care, when I had choices and chances. Now, this fresh hell. Jake and I stay upright on the kitchen chairs. A personal penance for being the sort of parents who lose their child at a party. We stare at the ceiling, the table, the walls—we can't look at each other. If I did look at him, what would I see? I wonder. Fear, undoubtedly, but what else? Regret? Accusation? Jake aggressively rubs his eyes with the heel of his palm, as though he wants to scrape them out. The silence sits about us like a storm cloud, dense and heavy. Menacing. Foreboding.

Eventually I force myself to break the impasse. Maybe I want to hear the thunder. "I wish I'd never won the lottery."

"Well, we did."

"But look where it's brought us."

"It will be okay."

"You don't know that."

Jake stands up and walks over to me with real purpose. For a crazy moment I think he's going to hit me. This makes no sense as he's never hurt me physically. It makes much more sense that he puts his arm around me and pulls me close to him. Him doing so doesn't offer the comfort I imagine he hopes it would. It just underlines the fact he hasn't touched me since we discovered she'd been kidnapped. I breathe in the smell of his sweat and fear. The smell of human frailty. I could nuzzle into his neck, feel the warmth of him, be eased, but I think of Emily. Wherever she is, she has no one to console or support her. Allowing myself the luxury of being soothed by Jake is a betrayal. I break away.

We sit in silence. Unable to think of a single thing to say to one another. Eventually, I say, "I'm going to check on Logan."

I nip upstairs and pop my head around Logan's bedroom door to reassure myself that he, at least, is in his bed, sleeping like the proverbial baby. He is. Then I look into her bedroom. It's crazy, but as I edge into the room, a tiny part of me imagines she's going to be there, curled up, under her brand-new White Company duvet, waiting for me to talk about the party, to discuss costumes—whose was the best, whose was the worst? To gossip—who had too much to drink, who danced with whom? Although of course I don't know the answers to most of these questions because I was at Toma's party. I was not where I was supposed to be. I was not looking after my family. A wave of shame threatens to knock me over as my eyes scan the teenage girl debris that litters her room: abandoned clothes, glossy magazines, makeup, the cables of her hair dryer and curlers are tangled. The room is chaos even though she's only lived in it a few days. I nagged her about it this morning. That thought nearly kills me. I can smell her hair spray, body spray and perfumes dawdling in the air. Ghostly.

"I need to tell you something, Lexi."

"Jesus, Ridley, you scared me half to death." I jump and turn to him. Actually, he looks scared half to death himself. His face is so pale it is translucent, and I can almost see the wall behind him. Normally, he's one of those teens who is forever flush with a dewy tan that shouts hale health and happiness. There are dark clouds under his eyes, which are bloodshot with lack of sleep and crying.

"Do you think Emily is okay?" he mumbles.

"Well, she's been kidnapped, Ridley," I snap. "So not exactly, no."

He looks stricken. "I know. I just meant—"

I soften. "I know what you meant. Do I think she's okay under the circumstances?"

"That's it. That's what I meant. Well, do you?" He stares at me hopefully. He wants me to reassure him, fix things. Take away some of his guilt and torment. I wish I could. I remember when he was a small boy, he was the last of the trio to give up his belief in Father Christmas. How they teased him. He asked me if Santa did indeed exist, or if the others were right. I remember his wide, bright eyes shining up at me and I told him he was right, the others were mistaken, they'd get coal for Christmas. I couldn't resist his innocence, his need to believe. Now I find I can.

"No, Emily is not okay. You saw the photo, Ridley. She's terrified and in danger." I know I'm punishing him for standing by when Megan beat her. For abandoning her. "We just have to hope we can get her home soon."

Ridley nods. Looks at the floor. "We did talk tonight. I wasn't, I wasn't—" He breaks off.

"What weren't you?" I ask, although I think I know the answer.

He wasn't very nice to her. He didn't want her. "I wasn't very supportive. Or brave."

"Brave?"

He has color in his cheeks now; he's flushing, embarrassed, stammering, nervous. "She told me something. She wanted my help, but I didn't help her."

"What did she tell you? Had she been threatened? Did she tell you something that might be to do with this kidnapping, Ridley?" I've grabbed hold of his elbows. I don't mean to, but I'm shaking him as though I'm trying to spill information out of him, like seasoning from a pepper pot.

"No, nothing to do with that. She told me she's pregnant."

CHAPTER 40

Emily

The men don't rape me. They don't touch me at all. Maybe because when I wet myself it disgusted them or maybe all they were going to do was move me from the chair to the mattress.

I don't know, but I lie still on the soiled, thin mattress and thank God I'm being left alone. Even though I'm hungry and thirsty, hideously uncomfortable, it's better when I am left alone. I literally thank God. I pray. Something I've never done since junior school, and I beg and I bargain. I can't believe this is happening to me. I want my old life back. The life before the lottery win, when I didn't have designer clothes, or a cool house or holidays, but I did have a boyfriend, a best friend and no one wanted to beat me up or kidnap me. My life is so fucked up. It might get worse. It might even end. I don't want to die. I'm too young. I have too much I want to do, and see, and feel, and be. I want my mum. Where are my mum and dad? Why aren't they here yet? Will they come? I don't want to die. The thought ping-pongs around my head, sending me mental with fear.

Eventually, I must fall asleep although it isn't restful. My nightmares are so close to my reality I can't tell when I am asleep or awake. My head aches with dehydration, my limbs ache because I've been tied up so long and because of them beating me when they captured me in the woods and flung me in the van. I can't gauge how long I slept for. I only realize I'm definitely awake when I hear new voices. Different ones. English ones and I listen really carefully, maybe a woman? Is it my mum? Is it the police, has someone found me? The hope vanishes, almost the moment it bloomed. The voices stay outside the barn, no one comes to save me. Whoever it is, they are angry, rowing.

I close my eyes again, too weak to resist sleep. Someone lifts my head. Rough hands, fast and careless, cradle my head and then hold a cloth under my nose. I smell that funny smell again. The dentist. I realize I'm being drugged and I'm glad in a way, because unconscious I can't feel pain or worry.

The next time I wake, the hands on me are much softer. A woman? If so, I wonder if she owns the voice I heard earlier. I don't know because she doesn't speak. She takes off my gag, she gently brings a plastic bottle to my lips and I sip. The water is cold and fresh. She then slips some chocolate in my mouth. I think I'm dreaming again, but this time it's not so. Yes, I am because I can smell her perfume and I can hear Megan, too. She's swearing, and upset, like when her mum won't let her go to a party or something. I wish Ridley would come to me in my dreams. I wish my mum would, and Dad. I need them. Where are they? Where are the police? I will myself to stay in the dream, but I think I'm weeing myself again, and that wakes me. The wet stickiness between my legs.

CHAPTER 41

Lexi

Sunday, May 26

We have heard nothing more from the kidnappers. I watch as the sky turns from black to an early-morning pink, the promises of a warm day. The light pulses its way into the kitchen, but it can't bring any cheer. The glossy, perfect space is somehow exposed for what it really is: harsh and cold, impersonal rather than reassuringly expensive. The place is pocked with tea and coffee cups, half-full of forsaken slimy drinks that couldn't warm or console. Jake puts on the lights, but they can't seem to chase the gloomy shadows. Logan's laptop is droning quietly. I don't know what else to Google. I don't know where to find answers.

At seven o'clock, the Heathcotes, who have slept, wake up because the sun is now fiercely shining in through the wall of windows. This was one of the features the estate agent pointed out to us. She said it was "very LA." It's hot as hell, and the heat combined with everything else makes me drowsy, cloudy, unfocused. I need to focus. I need to get my baby home. My pregnant baby. Not that this is my home. The house is something other. Without Emily it is not any sort of a home, it's nowhere in particular. I look outside and see that the grass is wet from yesterday's downpour and the early-morning sun rays make it look as though it is dripping with diamonds. It is beautiful, but I can't feel the beauty. Until I get Emily back, I can't taste, smell or feel beauty. I'm numb, sitting in a glass house, waiting for people to throw stones.

Ridley and Logan are both being archetypal teenage boys and sleeping like the dead. I'm glad I could finally persuade Ridley to go to bed after he told me everything he knew about the pregnancy. I don't want him around when I tell Jake. Our circumstances are extreme and peculiar, but this news is age-old and no father ever shakes the hand of the fifteen-year-old who impregnated his daughter.

I have nursed one cup of coffee after another all night. Making it, if not drinking it, is at least something to do, and once we admitted to ourselves that we were awake and never going to find sleep, we needed things to do. I made coffee; Jake has been on his phone all night. When I asked him who he was messaging, he said he is sending texts to friends and family. Holding the pretence that the big news in our life was how the party went. He shouldn't be wasting his time disseminating false news. He should be doing something real, although I'm not sure what. Certainly not comforting me—I don't think he can do that. I imagine calling Gillian or Toma. I crave their sensibleness, their steadfast sympathy, but I know they'd both insist we call the police, so it's impossible.

I suppose I could have told Jake about the pregnancy when the light first eked into the kitchen, when it was just the two of us. I could have made it our thing, about our daughter, but I know that's not how he sees us anymore; otherwise, the Heathcotes wouldn't be here. Jennifer means a lot to him. She's not just a fling, a dalliance. I see that now. I'm going to tell them about the pregnancy at the same time, not because I respect her position in his life, but because I couldn't bear the pain and humiliation of watching his first response be to look for her, hunting her out, wanting to share the news with her. This way I keep things on a more even keel. Anyway, this pregnancy is technically as much to do with her as it is to do with him.

The Heathcotes and Jake shower and dress. After being asked multiple times to do the same—"For God's sake, Lexi, you are still in your fancy dress!"—I haul myself upstairs. I don't shower, I don't want to waste time in case the kidnappers call again. I pull on the first thing that comes to hand, something I was wearing before the party that never made it into the wash basket. It's not quite clean. I possibly smell. I haven't the energy to care.

Jennifer, Fred and Jake eat breakfast. It's all I can do to swallow down more strong black coffee, which I force myself to in order to sharpen my day. I need to push through this fog of fear. I watch Jake chew, his strong, confident jaw moving with purpose. I only just resist hurling my scalding coffee in his face. I'm enraged at his ability to carry on. Watching him bite into his toast used to turn me on. I thought his appetites were sexy; now they disgust me. I loathe his greed, his hunger. The man who wanted it all.

I wait until we are all sitting around the table. There has been a surprising amount of normality this morning. I find it irritating, offensive. There is a lot of "Pass the butter, please" and "How would you like your eggs?" It's unbelievable to me. There should be no semblance of normality. We are waiting to hear from kidnappers who want us to deposit ten million pounds in an offshore account. Why are they pretending a choice between marmalade or jam matters? I take a strange, secret pleasure in knowing that I have the information and power to destroy this facade of ordinariness they have created. I won't be comforted and they shouldn't be, either. This situation is dire, why would they try to minimize it? I'd respect everyone more if they were wailing and panicking.

I take a deep breath. "So, we have even more in common than ever now." I throw this comment on the table, landing where they can all make of it what they will, but I keep my eyes on Jennifer. I've always thought she's been a little overprotective of Ridley. Let's see how this bombshell blows up her perception of her precious innocent son. I know I am behaving like a basic bitch—fear can do that. My child is gone. No one seems to be doing anything to get her back and they are stopping me doing what I want to. They are just munching whole wheat toast. My child has been ripped from me. I am going to take Jennifer's baby boy away from her and deliver a procreating man back in his place. It doesn't take even four words, just three.

"Emily is pregnant."

Jaws and spoons drop, clatter on the breakfast table. "What?" demands Jake. He turns so white he's almost blue, like snow on a field.

"Ridley confided in me last night. Naturally, he's terrified for her." The color empties from Jennifer's face, too. Fred reaches for her hand, and she snatches it away. "I take it you didn't know?" I ask faux sweetly.

"Well, nor did you," challenges Jake, even though I had directed my question at Jennifer. I move my focus to him now. I see that there are deep lines of panic scratched onto his forehead. He's shrunk inches in just moments. I imagine I look equally terrible, but I don't have the will to put myself in front of a mirror.

"Ridley told me that Emily planned to tell me after the party. She only told him yesterday." Honestly, delivering this information doesn't give me any satisfaction. Even though I am accurately retelling what Ridley said, it breaks my heart that Emily hadn't turned to me first. She must be terrified. Why didn't she tell me? I feel a surge of horror and adrenaline swamp me, suffocate me.

"I didn't even know they were having sex," mutters Jennifer.

"People do tend to be very secretive about sex," I point out.

And then, although I think it might choke me, I bite into a slice of toast. With my mouth full, I won't be able to blurt out everything else I know.

Suddenly, Jake jumps up from the table. "Where are you going?" I ask.

"To look for her," he yells back over his shoulder. I hear dread and horror in his voice. I wish I didn't because he has insisted that everything was under control, that everything was going to be fine. He said we'd get through it; we'd get her back safe and well. Although I've thought his perpetual optimism was delusional, exasperating, deep down I was seduced by it. I longed for him to be right. I've believed and trusted Jake forever. He is that sort of man, a man that might just be right. Now, he's afraid, too, which is horrifying. I feel a tsunami of anxiety swell, threatening to wash me away, but I know Emily needs me to be calm now, not distraught. Jake is already in the hallway with the car keys in his hand and now he's through the front door.

"I'll come with you, I can—" The door slams behind him, cutting off Jennifer's offer.

I stare at her, and she understands. I'm not jubilant. How can I be, under the circumstances? But I am somewhat vindicated. As much as the evidence of her precious only son having had sex will be bothering her—she'll be mourning her place as his number one woman—her emotions are unlikely to compare to Jake's. A father's protectiveness of his daughter is fierce. Emily is underage, she's pregnant, and now she's been abducted. Emily has never needed her father more. Her pregnancy will change everything for Jake. Maybe now he'll find a way to get her home. I just want my baby home.

I stand up and start to clear away the pots. Jennifer rushes from the room; I presume she's gone to wake Ridley. I feel a bit sorry for him, but a dressing-down is inevitable under these circumstances. Fred and I listen to her feet clatter as she runs up the stairs. Fred looks apprehensive, unsure what to say next.

"A baby, hey?" he offers eventually.

"Certainly a pregnancy."

"You're saying she might not keep it. I mean, they are very young." He looks hopeful.

"I have no idea what she will decide. Obviously, I haven't had time to discuss the matter with her," I snap. It doesn't surprise me that Fred's first thought is to have this tidied away. Apparently, it was Ridley's, too. He confessed as much to me last night. A confession hiccuped out between tears of panic, regret, fright. I can't imagine how horrendous things must be for Emily right now. An unplanned teenage pregnancy would be enough for any fifteen-year-old to cope with, but she's been abducted by strangers, too. She's tied up like a badly treated animal. I feel faint with fear every time I think of her and I'm thinking of her constantly. All I want is to hold her, comfort her, tell her everything is going to be all right because whatever she decides I will make sure that much is true. We will be all right. I just need her home. She might be having a baby of her own, but she is my baby still. My job, until she is home, is to protect her right to choose her future. I know Jennifer and Fred will be pushing for a termination, sweeping this under the carpet. They want Ridley at Cambridge. I can't even begin to think what I want for Emily, beyond wanting her to walk through the door. I ache for that.

Fred looks uncomfortable. He coughs as though clearing his throat. I expect him to start talking about the fact all teens are curious, but that doesn't mean they are ready to be parents. I expect him to give me statistics about the slim chances of teenage parents going to university.

"Will I still get my cut?" he asks.

"Wow. You are asking this now?" I drop back into the chair and glare at him.

"I'm owed it, Lexi. You know I am."

"No, Fred, I know no such thing. I'm being generous in offering you a share." My tone is steely.

"And you'll still do that, even though the kidnappers have

asked for ten million? I mean, you promised me three if I changed my statement for the inquiry and I did so."

Funny that Jake thinks he sorted this with his bribe to Jennifer—he never really asked why Fred might have changed his statement in advance of being offered the one million. I suppose he thought Fred was doing it to spite Jennifer, considering everything. He didn't know he had me to thank. Ten to the kidnappers, three to Toma, three to Fred. That would leave us with just under two million. It's possible that Jake has spent most of that already—on the cars, the party, clothes, the house rental, the holidays he's booked and canceled, his brothers' mortgages, my sister's house. I find I don't care. "I said three. You'll get three," I tell Fred with a sigh.

He looks relieved. "You don't think it's over between them, do you?" he asks.

"I don't care whether it is or it isn't." I realize that there is a chance Jake will leave me anyhow. When he discovers I've cleared out our bank account, that there is no more money, I think he will leave.

"I think they are done," says Fred firmly.

"Are you thinking of staying, then?"

"Isn't a condition of the 'gift' that I leave her?"

"I never said that." Not in so many words, but if I've learned anything from the lottery win, everyone has their price. Stylists, security guards, bar staff.

Husbands.

I wonder what Jennifer is worth to Fred. "The way I recall it, Fred, is that you said you wanted to divorce her, but were worried she'd 'take you to the cleaners' despite her being the guilty party. As your friend, I promised you that when you did divorce her, I'd help you with setting up a new home, living expenses, securing custody of Ridley, et cetera." Of course, three million pounds does this and more. Fred's eyes widen greedily.

"I've already spoken to a lawyer. I'm not staying with her."

CHAPTER 42

Emily

"Oh, my God. Oh, my God. What have they done to her? We need to get her to a fucking hospital."

Dad?

"Jesus, Jesus. It's okay, baby. It's okay. I'm here. Daddy is here." My dad hasn't called himself Daddy for ages. I'd laugh at him, usually. I think I want to laugh, but I'm crying. He is stroking my head and my face like he does when I'm ill. Is this real? Please let this be real. He usually smells of instant coffee, my dad, but now he smells of something darker and richer. His aftershave is different, too. Is it him? Is this difference since the lottery win? "I'm sorry, I'm sorry I let this happen to you." It's not like he could have actually stopped them. This isn't his fault, but his words make me cry harder. Tenderly, as though he doesn't quite trust himself to touch me, he carefully takes off my blindfold and my gag. "Oh, my princess. What the fuck have they done to you?"

I guess I must look pretty bad.

CHAPTER 43

Lexi

Just when I believe the longest day of my life will never end, it does so with a sweet, sudden abruptness. At ten o'clock on Sunday night Jake does exactly what I need him to do—he finds our girl.

I had not even noticed, until it was too late, that when he'd strode out of the house this morning, he'd taken my phone with him. He must have discreetly pocketed it, knowing it was the way the kidnappers would communicate. When I realized, just ten minutes later, I was wild. I felt thwarted, infantilized. Isolated. I had no way of reaching him and, more importantly, no way of hearing from the kidnappers. In frustration, I threw a plate at the kitchen wall. It smashed satisfyingly. The shards splintered in every direction. The discarded jam toast that had been on the plate clung to the pristine white wall for a moment. I watched in fascination as it slowly loosened and then slipped, smearing jam, the color of blood.

"How dare he!" I yelled.

"He's trying to protect you, for fuck's sake," snapped Jennifer. I saw that it hurt her to acknowledge as much. She was defending a man that she—what? Loved?—to his wife. She was pointing out her lover's kindness and responsibility to his wife. Not an easy position to take. She must have been wondering where she stood now.

I had no choice but to accept the situation Jake had left me in, but I clung to my dignity and a semblance of control. "Send him a text. Tell him he has to keep me informed," I instructed. "He needs to give me updates regularly or I'm calling the police." She texted swiftly. Almost instantly, her phone pinged in response. Wherever he was, he clearly didn't struggle to receive her messages, the way he struggled to receive mine all the time. "He says okay, he'll text updates and he'll call on my phone when he has news." Jennifer placed her phone in the middle of the kitchen table, just where mine had been. I fought the urge to think the replacement was symbolic. The day passed at a snail's pace. On about a thousand occasions, I reached for Jennifer's telephone to check to see if I had somehow missed a call from Jake. Time after time I was faced with a blank screen. He didn't keep his promise to keep me informed. Why did I think he would?

"I'm going to call the police," I said more than once.

"No, you are not," replied Jennifer or Fred, sometimes forcefully, though as the day mooched on, they were less forceful, more bored, as though they had identified my threat as empty, dull. As though they knew I was ultimately weak and would do what Jake had asked.

When the phone finally rings, it is like an ambulance siren. It fills the house with dread and promise. Threat and hope. Jake cries out, "I have her. I have her. Lexi, I have her."

The relief is so overwhelming, it feels as though my body explodes into a million pieces and then in a fraction of a second pieces itself back together again, sharper, more focused, euphoric. I have never in my life felt such happiness.

"Is she okay?" Tears are in my throat and eyes. I rest my forehead on the kitchen table, which feels solid and steady. It might shore me up when I hear his answer. What they could have done to her has played around and around my head and heart for nearly twenty-four hours.

"Yes." He pauses. "Mostly. We're on our way to the hospital."

"I'm coming."

"Yes, come at once. Meet us there."

"Can I talk to her?"

"She's not herself." I hear the catch in Jake's throat.

"Please put the phone to her ear if you can." I assume he has followed my instruction and I murmur down the phone, "I'm coming, my baby girl. I'm coming."

"I think she understood," says Jake. "She's not fully conscious." I don't want to talk any longer. I just need to see her. I hang up. Naturally, Jennifer tries to muscle in on this deeply personal family moment. "You shouldn't be driving, you are not in a fit state," she says. "I'll drive you."

"I'm perfectly capable, thank you."

"Which car will you take? Jake took the Audi. Are you even insured for the Ferrari?"

"Are you?" I challenge. She might be for all I know. "I'll get a taxi. Please stay here with the boys, keep an eye on Logan for me." Logan is still oblivious to what we've all been going through. He's spent the day playing video games with Ridley. I'm not sure whether Ridley showed impressive maturity in protecting Logan from the reality of what was going on or whether he simply wanted to keep out of his parents' way but, whatever his motivation, I'm grateful. I'm a fast learner and, copying my husband's trick, I pocket Jennifer's phone unnoticed. I call an Uber and then I call the police.

CHAPTER 44

Emily

Monday, May 27

When I open my eyes, I am beyond relieved that everything is cream and light, not black and shadowy. I can hear the beep and hum of hospital machines, Mum and Dad are at my bedside. They look like shit and from the look on their faces I guess I must be worse. Mum looks as though she's bruised. I squint a bit to try to focus, the bright lights are a bit much after the darkness. I realize Mum's face is swollen, red, purple and blue through crying, not because she's had a beating. I try to move a bit. My body protests loudly, suggesting I might have taken a beating.

"Hello, darling, how are you feeling?" murmurs Mum. She has hold of my hand, she leans forward and kisses it, like I'm royalty or the Pope or something.

"Okay," I mumble back. I don't feel okay. I ache from head to toe. It's more than pain, it's like a fragility—if I move, I'll fall apart. I'm in a private room. Of course I am, we are rich. I'd forgotten. When we won the lottery, I thought being rich meant I'd be indulged, protected. I guess it can mean that, but it can also mean I'm exploited, threatened. "I'm thirsty." Mum reaches for some water at my bedside. She drips it carefully into my mouth, like a bird feeding a chick. It reminds me of something.

Something to do with the abduction, but I can't remember what. "What happened?" I ask.

"You were kidnapped," says Mum. "Some very bad people held you hostage for money." I almost want to laugh at Mum's words "some very bad people." That doesn't get close. They kicked me, starved me, bound me and drugged me. Yes, I think I was drugged. I guess she will know all this now, there will be medical evidence. I suppose she's trying not to distress me by being too explicit. I'm far too weak and weary to point out that she can't protect me—I was the one who lived through it.

"Hey, Dad." It shouldn't be up to me to cheer things up, but Dad looks literally done for. Like battered. Suffering.

He stands up and kisses my forehead, then says, "I'll go and get a doctor, tell them she's awake."

I get the feeling he's making himself scarce, as though he's finding it a struggle to be around me. I glance at Mum, afraid. Dad often leaves the tricky stuff to her. Like when me and Logan really wanted a dog and they'd more or less agreed we could have one and then they changed their minds—Dad left it up to Mum to tell us. Or if we aren't allowed to go somewhere like a gig, or buy something—you know, before the big win—Dad would avoid answering the tricky questions and just say, "Check with your mum."

"What is it, Mum?"

"You've lost your baby, angel." She just says it like that. Like we both knew there was a baby before. She makes it uncomplicated. "I'm sorry, my darling. I'm sorry," she whispers.

"Don't cry, Mum. I'm not sure I wanted it, anyway." I try to make it sound like I've just lost out on buying a dress because they didn't have it in my size. But then suddenly I'm sobbing. Ridley's baby is gone. Ridley's and my baby is gone. "I didn't look after it. I didn't keep it safe," I say.

Mum jumps up and wraps her arms around me, buries her face into my neck. All this hurts, but it's worth it. She tells me over and over again that it's not my fault. None of this is my fault. Eventually, she tells me the police want to talk to me when I'm ready. "We are going to catch these bastards that did this to you." I agree to be interviewed, but ask Mum to stay with me. She immediately understands it's not the police I am afraid of. Obviously, I'm actually safer if there are a couple of coppers in my room, but I don't want Mum out of my sight. "You are safe now," she says firmly.

"What happens if someone does it again?" I demand.

She smiles ruefully. "That's unlikely. There's no money left." I wonder whether they've given her some sort of tranquilizer drug, a happy pill because how come she's not acting like that's the end of the world?

CHAPTER 45

Lexi

Tuesday, June 11

We have paid to stay in the rental house for six months and the money is nonrefundable so there's no point in suggesting we leave it and find somewhere more affordable, although there's no more talk about buying it. Jake now knows that there's only just under four million left in the bank: "I thought we had more." He groaned on discovering the balance.

"I gave a lot away," I admitted.

"Away?"

"To charity." I'm vague, and whilst he looked shocked, confounded, he didn't pursue the matter. I had expected him to be more challenging. I'm disturbed by his passive acceptance; it seems just a smidge away from indifference. "Okay, well, we have four million, Lexi. We don't need to panic. It's a substantial amount of money, it just seems less substantial because not so long ago we had almost eighteen." He's right, four million is a huge amount of money. What he doesn't know yet is that I have promised Fred three of it after he divorces Jen. That's not a conversation I can find my way into.

Things are not great between the two of us. I don't know if Jennifer has told him about what I said to her at the party. Is he aware that I know of their affair? We should probably get it all out in the open. Fight, say dreadful things to each other, hurl hurt and abuse and then move on. Or at least around it. But could we move on or around? I don't know. Bringing the matter into the open is too risky. I'm hideously aware that once it is out of the bag, I won't ever be able to put it back in. I will forever be the woman who accepted his affair and whilst initially he may be grateful for that, somewhere down the line he might feel smug about it, invincible. He might have another affair, assuming I'll stomach that one, too. Or, worse yet, once it is an acknowledged thing, he might confess to loving Jennifer. He might just leave. The tissue-thin veneer of family life carrying on as usual shrouds us for now. The children have been through so much lately. I can't bear the idea of putting them through anything more. We just need some time to let things settle. We are still a family.

Although I'm not sure we are a couple any longer.

We sleep in the same bed, but have consciously uncoupled, as the A-listers might say. We are tremendously careful never to make any physical contact, not even an accidental banging together of feet. We cling to our own bed edge, like bookends with invisible fat volumes between us. We are giving each other space, and I'm able to hide the three-million-pound gift to Toma in that space. Luckily, the police are more tenacious in the matter of investigating the kidnap and trying to recover our ten-million ransom money than Jake is about understanding how our bank balance came to net out as it has. I understand the police carried out a forensic search of the place where

Emily was found and all the surrounding area. The criminals apparently weren't quite as professional as we first assumed: they have left a raft of physical evidence. Fingerprints on casually discarded food tins and drink cans, tire tracks that will help the police identify what vehicle they used to abduct her, and even a jacket from which they can collect DNA. Besides this physical evidence, the police have fraud experts pursuing the paper trail. They took our phones, and I presume they might have ways of tracing calls that we thought were impossible. We only had our phones returned today. I've been managing without one; it's actually quite liberating. As long as my kids were close beside me, I found it peaceful to be out of reach, off-grid. It gave me some thinking time. Jake disagreed; he was really narky about giving his up. Apparently, he can't go without a phone for a matter of hours, let alone days. He went out and bought the top-of-the-line latest model.

We have all been interviewed at length. Emily was brilliantly brave as she recounted her ordeal as well as she could. Her medical exam confirmed she'd been sedated, and that she was beaten, restrained, starved and severely dehydrated, so it's no surprise that her memory is patchy. The police are encouraging. They say everything she recalls, no matter how small a detail, is a help. Jake and I sat in on her interview. It was harrowing to hear exactly what she had gone through. Jake actually wept. I stroked Emily's back, held her hand. Whispered that I was sorry. I feel I let her down. How did I let this happen? I should have been more vigilant. I should have anticipated this threat and guarded against it. Whilst she was missing, I had imagined every possible degradation and torture that she might be enduring, but that still did not prepare me for hearing my child talk about what actually did happen—her absolute fear, her pain, her humiliation. When Jake sobbed, Emily took hold of his hand and said, "Don't cry, Dad. It could have been worse." This only made his shoulders shake more, because no grown man imagines his baby girl will one day have to be comforting him about her own misery. It's an unnatural perversion of order. Still, I'm glad I know exactly what she has endured. We shouldn't be protected from it, and maybe I can support her most effectively now I know.

Jake's interview took a long time as he is potentially very useful, being the one who had the most contact with the criminals and the one who recovered Emily. I found my interview excruciating, especially when asked, "Why didn't you call the police straight away, Mrs. Greenwood?"

"I wanted to. I thought we should, but I was too scared. They said they'd hurt her."

"They hurt her anyway," pointed out Detective Inspector Owens. I can't resent the man for stating the truth. She was kicked and punched in the stomach. That's most likely how she lost her baby.

The police seem confident that they will find a lead. Whether we ever recover the money or not, which Jake deposited into an offshore account as demanded, I don't know, but I do want those monsters who hurt Emily brought to justice. I want them to rot in a prison cell for years.

Emily constantly assures us she is fine. She's certainly being strong, but that is often different from fine. She was in hospital for three days and she's been home a week now. Mostly she stays in her room. She hasn't started at the new school; she isn't ready for it. Logan has used her nonattendance there this term as an excuse for him to return to his old school. We've all agreed we can discuss the matter of which school they will settle on over the summer holidays and make a final decision then. I have put the idea of returning to their old school back on the table because first and foremost I think they'd both benefit from having their old friends around them, and also because I know that after I have paid Fred the promised money, we probably won't be able to afford private school. Jake has not railroaded this through his preference for the private school. I guess he's aware of Emily's fragility. As far as I know, she has not been in touch with Ridley since she was rescued. I told him that she'd lost the baby; he was palpably relieved. An uncomplicated, understandable response. I envy him because I fear things may be a little more complex for Emily as she carried the fetus. Bloody biology curses women every time. This evening, Logan went to Scouts as usual and I was delighted when Emily emerged and announced she wanted to visit her friend Scarlett. It's great that she's feeling robust enough to venture out of the house and to gently kick-start her social life. I immediately drove her there and Scarlett's dad kindly offered to bring her home by ten.

I'm not sure where Jake is. He's often out and I don't ask where exactly. That space thing again. Or, more honestly, that fear of having all the cards laid out on the table. I plan to spend the evening drafting an email to my old boss, Ellie, at the CAB asking whether I can have my job back now that we aren't multimillionaires. My plan is to make a public announcement that we have given all the money away to charity; obviously, we can't admit to paying kidnappers.

I sit in front of the family computer painstakingly perfecting my note when suddenly the screen turns black. A fraction of a second later the lights flutter and then turn off. I had music playing, but silence now throbs all around me, and not even the fridge is humming. A power cut. It's just a power cut. Isn't it? The blackness settles and I wait. Has someone cut the power? Is there someone here with me? I'm so glad the kids are out. I used to think being alone was frightening; now I know there are far more horrifying things.

I wait, straining my ears for a creaking floorboard, a door opening or closing. I glance about for my phone. Where did I put it? I should keep it close to me at all times the way the kids do, the way Jake does, but as I've been without one for a few days I've got out of the habit of keeping it close by. I tend to pick it up and put it down wherever I happen to be standing.

Tentatively, I begin to edge around the house. It's pitch-black. The blinds are down, blocking out the streetlight, and I can't open them manually because, of course, they are designed to rise and fall at the flick of a switch. The combination of privacy, security and convenience renders me powerless. Even if I could rid myself of the fear that there is an intruder, which I can't quite, I am not familiar enough with my surroundings to walk confidently through the house, so I creep and steal. I feel my way, painstakingly.

An inch-by-inch blind search reveals that my phone is not on the kitchen table or counters, not on the hall console or on any of the coffee or occasional tables in the sitting room. I carefully edge upstairs, trailing my fingers along cool, unfamiliar walls, finding my way around corners and through doors. There is no sign of an intruder, but they wouldn't advertise themselves, would they? My phone is not by my bed, or in the bathroom by the basin. Eventually, I find it in my dressing room, the last place I searched because I'm not used to having a dressing room and it didn't pop into my head to look there.

I'm relieved to have the phone in my hand. It feels like a lifeline out of the blackness and silence. I could call an engineer, or Jake. Maybe even the police. I don't think there's anyone here, but perhaps it's better to be safe than sorry. I call Toma.

"Lexi!"

"Toma."

"How good to hear from you!" The joy in his voice floats across the miles that separate us, it fills my room, even lights up the room and—I can't deny it—my heart, too. "What are you doing with yourself?"

"Well, right now, I'm sitting in the pitch-black."

"What?"

"We've had a power cut." Suddenly, I'm certain that's all it is. Hearing his voice has made me feel more secure and rational. The fear that was causing my shoulders to hunch, my pulse to race, ebbs away. Although my pulse remains speedy, I sigh. "Oh, Toma, I have so much to tell you."

"Then tell me, Lexi."

"You have time?"

"For you, always."

Jake doesn't come home until after midnight. By the time he does I have already called the mother of one of Logan's Scout friends to explain about the power cut and make arrangements for him to have a sleepover. I have also called Emily who, unsurprisingly, didn't want to return to a pitch-black house. She's staying at Scarlett's. The power cut is an inconvenience, but the silver lining is that both the kids will enjoy their impromptu sleepovers. Jake strides into the house, using the torch on his phone to light his way. I heard a taxi drop him off, and the slight heaviness in his step suggests he's had a fair bit to drink. I wonder who with.

"I pressed the buzzer, why didn't you let me in? I had to climb over the fence. I ripped my trousers." Then, almost an afterthought, he demands, "Why are you sitting here in the dark?"

"Because we've had a power cut."

"A power cut or has a fuse flipped?"

"I don't know."

"You didn't check?"

"I don't know where the fuse box is," I mutter. Jake laughs at this, as though it's amusing rather than what it is: humiliating or frustrating. I should know where the fuse box is in my own house. "Anyway, I think it's bigger than a fuse because everything is out," I mutter defensively.

"Why didn't you call me?"

I hesitate. "My phone was dead." How do I explain that I called Toma first and that we chatted all evening, until the battery of my phone drained to almost nothing and I could only make the two calls pertinent to the kids' arrangements? I told

Toma about the kidnapping, walked through every moment of horror; it felt good to talk about it, almost like therapy.

"Why did you let your friends bully you?" Toma asked. "You should have called the police. You know it was the right thing to do."

"I was weak. I regret it. I let Emily down. I just thought, as they all believed one thing and I was the only one to believe another, I had to be wrong. I was scared I'd make things worse."

"I would think this Jennifer, she is your friend, yes? I would think she would support you, not your husband's decision." And so I told him about the fact Jake is having an affair with Jennifer. "Or, at least, he was. I don't know if it's still going on, but maybe that complicated things on the night. Maybe that's why Jennifer agreed with Jake. I can't quite explain it."

Toma went silent. I could almost hear his brain ticking over through the telephone.

"You don't have to stay with him, Lexi."

I felt suddenly ashamed. As though I had betrayed someone. Jake, perhaps, for telling Toma about his torrid affair. "People have affairs, Toma, they make mistakes. We've been together for so long. I'm not throwing in the towel on my marriage after just one mistake."

I do believe that, so I'm not sure why—now that Jake is finally home—I seem to be picking a fight with him. "It was really scary. At first, I thought it was an intruder and then I felt trapped. I couldn't get the car out of the garage because the garage has an electric door and our gate is an electric gate. You know we are overly dependent on our gadgets, I didn't know what to do with myself without the computer or TV."

"You could have had a swim," points out Jake. "Our pool is not electricity dependent." This is not actually correct—the heater and filter are both dependent on electricity—but I know what he means. The truth is it hadn't crossed my mind to have a swim. I haven't quite taken on board the fact we have a pool—or a gym or a cinema room, come to think of it.

"So what did you do all night?"

"I read a book," I mutter sulkily. The truth is, I didn't miss the computer or TV—I had Toma. I feel guilty lying to my husband. I almost ask him what he's been doing all night, but I guess he'll just deliver up a lie, too.

Jake picks up his phone and calls the electrician or, at least, he calls the property manager, who I assume will call the electrician. It only takes fifteen minutes before the electricity is restored; it's managed remotely. I feel like an idiot for sitting shivering in the dark for so long.

"The police have a lead," Jake announces.

"They do?" I sit up, excited. "Who? Have they said?"

"Yes, it came off the back of Emily describing the kidnappers' voices. And something to do with suspicious movement in our bank account. They didn't really explain it to me, but they are looking for a man called Toma Albu."

CHAPTER 46

Lexi

Wednesday, June 12

I call the police station at the crack of dawn and ask to speak to Detective Inspector Owens. They tell me I can come to the station at once. As I dress, Jake asks where I am going; when I tell him, he says he wants to come with me. I shrug. He can if he wants. I just want to get there as quickly as possible and put the record straight.

We are shown into a room that has a small, chipped Formica table and three plastic chairs in the center of it, nothing else. There is no window and so the air feels stale, as though it has been inhaled and exhaled too many times. I can't help but think of who else might have sat in this room: hardened criminals, vicious or desperate types, the guilty and innocent. I think I can smell their fear, and maybe remorse, that has to have dripped onto the tiled floor. The chairs are arranged so that there is one chair on one side of the tatty table and two on the other. The setup is stark and intimidating. I'm glad Jake is with me as we sit side by side. My previous interview took place at our home; this one feels much more serious. The inspector comes into the room with a junior policeman. Presumably, two police officers generally interview one person, so the younger policeman has nowhere to sit. He stands against the wall, close to the door. Admirably, he resists the temptation to slouch.

"Do you mind if I record the interview?" asks DI Owens. I am instantly reminded of the inquiry held by the lottery company a few weeks back, a lifetime ago. Now, as then, I agree. "And you want your husband to attend this interview?" I nod. "And you don't want to call a solicitor?"

"No. Why? Should I?"

"Entirely your decision." DI Owens has a very dour face, the sort it's hard to imagine ever breaking into a smile. When I first met him, I liked his no-nonsense approach, thinking he might be the person to get results. Now I feel his face is daunting, almost threatening. Dour people rarely like admitting to making mistakes. If he is spending time pursuing Toma, he is wasting time, time that should be spent pursuing the real kidnappers.

"It wasn't Toma Albu who kidnapped Emily. He has nothing to do with it," I state firmly.

"How do you know?"

"Well, firstly, I was with him at the time of the kidnapping so he has a watertight alibi."

DI Owens sits up a little straighter, looking excited. "He was at your party?" Placing Toma at my party would strengthen their case against him.

"No, I was at his. The other side of town. There are a lot of people who can vouch for that." I don't look at Jake. "Toma is my friend."

"A friend?"

"Yes." I pause. I understand the inference and decide to take it full on. "Just a friend. We met through work. The night of my party happened to be the night Toma threw a leaving party so I left mine to go along to his for a bit."

"Where is he going?"

"He's gone. He went the next day, very early, back to Moldova."

"He's skipped the country!" shouts Jake, banging his fist on the table.

I turn to him. "No, don't be stupid, he's just gone home."

"He's from Moldova? Emily's captors were foreign."

"That's quite a broad range. Toma wasn't in the country most of the time she was captured."

"He didn't have to be there in person, he could have masterminded it from a distance," insists Jake.

"He didn't! He wouldn't." I lose patience with Jake and turn back to the DI. "I have Toma's telephone number. You can speak to him yourself if it helps clear this up."

"Oh, we will be, don't you worry. We have his number already. In fact, we knew you were—" the DI pauses "—friends. We have your phone records."

I blush and hate myself for it. "He knew nothing of the kidnapping until I told him about it last night. He was horrified by it."

"You spoke to him last night?" demands Jake. "Why?"

I don't answer his question but press on. "Secondly, the money he has, that came from our bank account—there's nothing suspicious about that. I gifted it to him."

"You gifted 2.976 million pounds to your friend?"

"Yes."

"Why did you give it to him?"

"It was his share."

"What do you mean?"

I squirm uncomfortably. Jake throws me a complex look: anger, warning, anguish? I answer carefully, hoping he'll understand. "If the lottery numbers had come up a week before they did, my friends would each have been entitled to a share of the win. Each couple would have got just under six million pounds or each individual would have got 2.976 million pounds."

"Of course that didn't happen, on account of them dropping out of the syndicate," adds Jake.

"What has any of this got to do with Toma Albu?" asks DI Owens.

"I gave him Patrick Pearson's share."

"Why?"

"Because Patrick Pearson murdered Toma's wife and son."

CHAPTER 47

Tuesday, December 23, 2014

Reveka carefully handed Benke the glittery star that they had made together earlier that afternoon. Then she hoisted him onto her hip. He was getting heavier, but still fitted quite comfortably into the side of her body, like two jigsaw pieces snapping together. Benke hooked one chubby toddler arm behind her neck and then confidently lunged forward toward the tree, excited to be placing the final ornament, trusting she would hold him steady, keep him safe. He propped the star up against a branch, but couldn't manage to secure it in place with the ribbon. He turned to his mother, eyes wide and gleaming with pride and excitement. She kissed his face enthusiastically, breathing him in. The star was fashioned from tinfoil and cardboard from a cereal box, things they had in the house. Reveka had bought glitter glue, which Benke had joyfully and inexpertly smeared everywhere: the star, the tiny kitchen table, his clothes. There was more glitter on his hands than on the decoration, and that had delighted him. He clapped and repeatedly yelled, "Me have kissmas magic, me have kissmas magic."

"You have indeed!" laughed Reveka. She gently lowered Benke down to the floor. They both took a step back to admire their handiwork. "Beautiful!" she enthused. Reveka had brought about half a dozen Christmas ornaments with her from home. Benke had been besotted with the jewel-colored glass trinkets. He'd teetered on the verge of a tantrum when she wouldn't allow him to handle them. The tantrum had only been diverted because she persuaded him that he could instruct her as to exactly where they ought to go, that he was in control overall. All six decorations were currently huddled at Benke's eye level, and the rest of the tree looked a little Spartan. She'd rearrange them tonight, spread them about a little, after he was in bed. Reveka had bought colored Christmas lights from the pound shop. They cost two pounds, not one, but still. She knew a lot of people only ever bought white twinkling lights, but Reveka liked color. She'd also bought tinsel. Five streamers, all different colors, they filled up the tree nicely. It looked wonderful. Reveka loved the pound shop. She had once watched an old film called *Breakfast at Tiffany's.* The beautiful actress was supposed to be poor and she felt happiest, safest, at the jewel shop Tiffany's. Reveka didn't think the actress seemed very poor. Although she was very thin, she was beautiful thin, not penniless thin. Still, Reveka understood the film, liked it even. The pound shop was her Tiffany's. Tonight, when Benke was in bed, she would wrap up his Christmas presents in the paper she had bought there. It had cheerful little reindeers on it. She'd taken ages deciding which wrapping was the most perfect. She had not bought ribbons. Ribbons were lovely, but even at Christmas Reveka had to make choices and she didn't need to spend the extra pound.

She drew the bath, tested the temperature and lowered her chattering son into the warm water. It was always the same; a busy, full day did not make him tired, just more excitable, more buoyant. He babbled on nonsensically, happy in his make-believe world where an empty washing-up liquid bottle passed as a rocket, a rocket that could *whoosh* to the sky and land on a star.

"Do you think you might want to be an astronaut when you grow up, Benke?" Reveka asked her son, knowing perfectly well that he had no idea what an astronaut was. He nodded enthusiastically. "Or maybe an engineer?" He nodded again, compliant. Happy to see his mother smile. "You can be anything and everything you want to be, Benke," Reveka whispered. The emotion caught in her voice. She believed this, but she also believed that the more often she said it, the truer it was. "This is why we are here, Benke. For the education. For the chances. You can be anything and everything."

And for the first time in a long time, it seemed possible that this was true. Now the flat was usually warm. Thank God the landlord had finally had the boiler fixed. For the first two years of Benke's life, the only heating they'd had was from one small electric fire that they moved from room to room, depending where the baby was sleeping. It was expensive to heat a flat, even one this compact, with an electric fire. Every time the orange bars glowed Reveka was torn, partially relieved that the icy air would thaw, mostly anxious about the money they were burning. More often she would put on another layer, another jumper, a second pair of tights under her trousers. During last winter the baby wore so many layers he looked like a little boiled egg! She put the fire on when they were all at home; when it was just her and the baby, she tried to save money by walking the streets to keep warm. She pushed the stroller from shop to shop, where she would wander round with no intention of buying until a security guard started to follow her, or the fourth, fifth, sixth stiff inquiry from a shop assistant, "Can I help you with anything?" embarrassed her into leaving. Then she would walk to the library, her favorite place! Free books, comfortable chairs, warm air, but crying babies were not welcome in libraries for sustained periods of time. Her feet often felt like blocks of ice. She was sometimes so desperate to warm up that she'd stand in the public toilets at the Civic Centre, where she'd learned to ignore the smell. A flat as cold as theirs had been was not a home.

But this year there was Christmas magic! Benke was right! Now the boiler was mended, the air was warm, the water was hot. This winter, since the heating had been fixed, they stayed at home more. Today they had not had to venture out at all. Better to stay snug and safe than walk the streets. The man who fixed the boiler had been very young, not much more than a boy, really. No overalls, no badge. He had drunk the tea she offered, eaten three biscuits off the plate. She had only put three biscuits on the plate, so she and Benke went without. The boy talked a lot. She didn't understand everything he said. Maybe he said he was still in college. Still training. Maybe he said something about cash in hand. Beer money. He did jobs for Mr. Pearson often. "Anything really, I can turn my hand to anything," he said confidently. Reveka had no idea who Mr. Pearson was. She didn't care. Her flat was warm.

The glitter had loosened from Benke's hands and floated on the bathwater. Reveka yawned and Benke caught it, opening his mouth wide, flashing his tiny, pearly baby teeth. The bath seemed to have calmed him. She hauled him out, wrapped him in a towel. Her head hurt. Benke was pulling at his ear, something he did when he was in pain. Maybe a toothache. She hoped they hadn't caught a cold or flu. No one wanted to be sick at Christmas.

She dressed her boy in soft cotton pajamas, and he was almost asleep before his head touched the pillow. She leaned over the cot to kiss him good-night. He really ought to be in a bed. They might find one in a charity shop after Christmas. As she straightened up, the room slipped. She felt dizzy, a little nauseous. She had so much to do. Besides wrapping the gifts, she wanted to finish the ironing, make a dish for Toma's return. It was important he came home to something good. He worked so hard. Double shifts at that factory were gruelling. Noisy, demanding, he was on his feet all day. He never complained.

She went into the kitchen, picked up a knife. Onions, potatoes, carrots, they all needed chopping. But the pain in her head was so fierce now. Maybe she should sit down. Or even lie down. Just for a few minutes. She was so tired. All she wanted to do was sleep. Reveka dropped the knife, which narrowly missed her foot. She looked at it, lying on the floor, and was surprised. What was wrong with her? Why was the room swimming? Reveka collapsed onto her hands and knees. What was wrong? Something was very wrong. She started to crawl to her son's room. Fear shot through her body. She needed to see him. She was sick. Was he sick, too? She placed one hand in front of the other, dragged her knees and legs along behind her. She just wanted to sleep. Lie down on the kitchen lino, but more she wanted to check on her baby son. She dragged her body into his room, lit by the cheerful golden glow of the tractor lamp. There he was. Sound asleep. So still. Perfectly still. She had thought he might be dreaming. Dreaming about stars and gifts and Christmas treats, but when he dreamed his eyes usually flickered. Tonight, he was stone.

Reveka stretched to put her hand through the bars of the cot. Exhausted, she knew she couldn't make it into her own bed, didn't want to. She must have a bug. Her head screamed from the inside. So much pain. Toma would be home soon. He would get her Tylenol. She couldn't get it herself. Didn't want to be that far from Benke. She lay down on the floor next to him. Close by if he woke and needed her.

CHAPTER 48

Emily

Thursday, June 20

Oh. My. God. Patrick Pearson has been arrested for kidnapping me! Mum and Dad are reeling. I don't know if they were even going to tell me. Well, they'd have had to at some point, but I guess they were going to struggle to find the right moment to drop that one. At is happened, I overheard them talking in the kitchen.

"DI Owens has been in touch," says Mum.

"Oh, yes," replies Dad. My parents have a weird way of speaking to one another at the moment. It's all sort of stiff and narky. I don't know if it's the stress of me being kidnapped or what. I think it was there a bit even before then. Not sure. Anyway, when they talk to one another now, it's like they're constantly waiting for bad news or are about to deliver it. Something like that. I miss them just being—I don't know—*themselves.* Sort of relaxed and nice to each other.

"The police have checked out Toma's alibi and since the funds he has in his account are a certified gift from me, there is no case against him." Who is Mum talking about? Who is Toma? I sit at the top of the stairs that lead straight into the kitchen. My parents have their backs to me, so they don't know I'm listening.

It's a funny thing. We now live in a massive house but honestly, because it's all open plan, there are no secrets. Or rather, there are *loads* of secrets, apparently, but it's easier to find them out now than when we lived in our small house when everyone had a door they could close. I'm guessing Dad didn't take that into account when he picked this place.

"So, what now?"

"They said they had someone else in for questioning."

"Who?"

"Patrick Pearson."

"Patrick Pearson?" Dad sounds stunned.

"Yes. They haven't arrested him, but I think it's only a matter of time." Mum sounds satisfied with this, vindicated.

"Shit." Dad takes a step backward, staggers a bit, rests his hands on the kitchen counter, as though he needs something to keep him upright.

Mum snakes her arms around his back and rubs him, like she's comforting a child. "I know, this is huge, isn't it? DI Owens said there is a paper trail to enormous sums of money in various offshore accounts that can ultimately be linked back to our account. Well, a digital trail, I suppose."

"How much money?"

"He didn't say."

"And you didn't give him the money? It's not another one of your gifts, is it?"

"Ha-ha, Jake," Mum says drily. "I'm serious. No, of course I didn't give him any bloody money. I hate the man."

Dad nods but doesn't look at her. Mum is staring at him, trying to make eye contact, trying to read him. She used to be very good at that. She used to say she knew his every thought, then she'd joke that it wasn't tricky as all he ever thought about was food or sport. I think he has a lot more on his mind nowadays.

"Must be hard for you to process the betrayal. It's a massive shock," she says.

"No, it's not that. Well, yes, yes, obviously. But—" My dad shakes his head. He seems bewildered.

"I mean, it's also a relief, right? Now that we've found out who did it, the kids are safer." Mum sounds shrill. I can see her face side-on. She looks hard, furious. Then her face sort of collapses and she starts to cry. This is her thing. She behaves aggressive and tough just before the moment she shows her vulnerability. I think she needs to take some evening primrose or something. "I am devastated, too," she admits. "I've known for months that Patrick is a vile, despicable criminal, but I never imagined he'd hurt *our* daughter, a child he has known since she was born. I suppose that's self-absorbed of me. After all, he killed Toma's child through greed and neglect, so actually planning an abduction isn't such a jump." WTF? Patrick killed someone? A child? Mum goes on. "The man disgusts me. You saw her, Jake. You saw the state she was in."

"I know, I know." Dad looks like he's going to cry again. He's been like an emotional wreck since I was kidnapped. They both have, but Mum tries harder to tough it out, it's like she doesn't want to worry me. Dad's eyes follow me around, scarred, scared, sorrowful. I wish he wouldn't. It's hard enough dealing with my own crap. Dad turns to Mum and pulls her to his chest. She sort of collapses against him. I shiver. I mean, I'm home now, right? Safe. But yeah, Mum is correct—I was in a state. Totally fucked up. It was so, so beyond awful. I rub my stomach. I feel empty. Since, you know. I wasn't even sure I wanted it. I probably didn't. So why am I so sad? It's a relief, right? That I didn't have to make a decision. The doctor said I'd still be okay, you know, in the future, when I'm older and I'm with someone. So that's good. Only it doesn't really feel good. Not totally. I feel so, so sad. I try not to think about it too much. Probably for the best. But even though I'm not trying to remember stuff, bits keep coming back to me. Like nothing in a coherent run but flashes of sounds or smells. The memories choke me, deafen me. Like I can still feel the gag in my mouth, tearing at the side of my lips, the actual texture of the cloth, and I keep wanting to spit it out. And the smell of the damp, fuggy mattress lingers in my nostrils, makes me feel sick and faint. The perfume the woman wore hangs about near my hair. I mean, that's not possible. Perfume doesn't transfer from one person to another and even if it did, I've washed my hair, like, five times since then. But the smell won't go away.

"I'm going to go and visit Megan," I yell as I clatter down the stairs.

"What? No. Why would you do that?" asks Mum, breaking from Dad's embrace and turning to me, the habitual look of perpetual worry etched into her face.

"I've just heard you say Patrick has been arrested."

"Well, taken in for questioning," Mum corrects cautiously. She doesn't yell at me for listening in to their conversation or anything like that. Since my abduction, and the baby thing, Mum and Dad have started to treat me differently. Differently from before and differently to each other. Mum and I are closer. She seems to, I don't know, almost respect me as another adult now. Dad seems embarrassed if anything. I guess there's no way either of them can see me as their baby girl anymore.

"Can you imagine what she is going through? Her dad is like a proper crim."

My dad, who is basically a hero—negotiated my release, recovered me, got me to hospital—steps up again and says to Mum,

"I'll drive her, she shouldn't go on her own. You stay here with Logan. We won't be long."

Mum, who was probably going to have, like, a million objections and probably also wants to come with us—not to offer Carla any consolation, just to punch her in the face or something—looks torn. "Mum, we were best friends for forever," I add.

"You can't leave Logan here alone," points out Dad.

Mum is pretty stressed about our security at the moment, understandably. Even if Patrick is behind bars and if he was responsible for kidnapping me, he's hardly the only greedy nutter on the planet. There's no way she'll leave Logan alone. Mum nods stiffly.

CHAPTER 49

Emily

We drive to the Pearsons' house in silence. Dad keeps his eyes on the road, he looks tense, stressed. Everyone does, all the time now. We haven't spent much time alone together since he found me in that barn. Any time, really. If I walk into a room and it's just him, he makes some excuse to leave, says he's looking for a book to read or has an errand to run. He is obviously uncomfortable around me. I get it. I'm not exactly cool with him, either.

It's the pregnancy thing.

Dad hasn't talked to me about it. Not mentioned it once. I get it. He saw my baby bleed out all over my leotard, and he can't hide from the fact his princess had sex. I swallow hard, chew on the inside of my cheek as though I am eating gum. It stops me crying. I don't know if Dad is angry that I had sex, per se. I mean, under normal circumstances he'd be furious, clear-cut furious. But it's so complicated. Maybe he's not angry as such, just sad about how it all turned out. I don't know. Mum says he feels bad, like really, really bad. Daddies are supposed to protect their little girls, right? She says she feels really bad, too. She cried when she told me this. "We're so sorry we didn't keep you safer, that we didn't protect you." She's said this over and over again. It's not like it's their fault. They didn't hit me and bundle me into a van. I think it's a good thing I'm not going to be a parent yet. I really couldn't cope with the constant guilt and self-blame that obviously comes with it.

I can't stand the silence, so I ask Dad, "Do you think he did it?"

"The police obviously do."

"Why would he, though? Why would he do that to me?" Patrick isn't, like, a great dad to Megan and her brothers, the way my dad is a great dad to me and Logan. He doesn't make jokes or hot chocolates when she has friends for a sleepover. He doesn't get up on a Saturday morning and suggest something fun like Go Ape or a trip to London to do some shopping, and he doesn't really sit and talk to her much. My dad does all of this stuff (well, the talking bit is on a temporary pause, but usually!). Patrick was often absent. He left for work before Megan got up, he arrived home late, loosened his tie and asked Carla for a drink in a way that always made any kids that happened to be about—his own or guests—feel we should go into another room, that we were in the way. It seemed he put his work ahead of his family. I know Megan has always thought my dad is better than hers, but Patrick wasn't, like, the worst, either. He bought her cool stuff, he helped her with her maths homework. He wasn't, like, a totally crap dad. Or at least not until now. Kidnapping, false imprisonment, extortion is totally crap. New level crap.

I think Dad has hay fever because his eyes are red and watery. He can't be actually crying, can he? Why now? I get crying in the hospital, when I was all battered and stuff, but why now when the police have basically solved it, caught the bad guy? He still doesn't look at me, but he does answer my question. "Well, he missed out on a lot of money, a lot, and I think that might have sent him a bit nuts. People do a lot of really bad stuff for the sort of money we won. Really bad stuff."

I suddenly get nervous when we pull up at Megan's. I could be mistaken. What if my hunch is wrong and she thinks I'm mental, or what if I'm right and she just doesn't want to talk about it?

And if I'm right? What if Megan was there with her dad and she was the one who gave me that water, who helped me? Because honestly, at that moment it was so dark that I think her kindness saved me. And I don't mean dark so I couldn't see. I mean it was dark in my head and heart. I thought I was going to die. I thought they were going to kill me. I was lying in my own piss and blood. Never more alone or scared in my life.

I remember hearing a car pull up. Voices. Probably she was told to stay in the car. Probably she didn't know what was going on, but Megan rarely does as she's told. She's too nosy to stay in a car when clearly something big was happening. I can just imagine her sneaking out of the car and into the barn wondering who her dad was meeting. She must have been shit scared when she found me. Was she the person who contacted my dad? They haven't told me all the details about how Dad found me. They said they will but only when I'm ready. I do know that he got a tip-off and acted on it. Didn't even call the police, just charged in, unconcerned for his own safety, just desperate to get me home. Sadly, the intel on where I was being kept came after he'd paid the cash, but someone sent him a pin drop of where to find me. Someone was trying to help. To save me. Megan loves pin drops. She used to always send me them if we were going somewhere new. I've never known anyone who loves a pin drop as much as she does. Who knows what might have happened if she hadn't done that? Once Patrick had the money secured in his offshore account, might he have instructed those men to kill me? I don't know, it's possible. But as Dad arrived, he scared them off. Megan saved my life.

Carla answers the door. She doesn't seem surprised to see us. She pulls my dad into this big over-the-top hug, like, hangs on his neck and then she starts to cry. I am getting a bit bored of everyone crying all the time. I just stand there. After about a year she seems to remember I'm there and says, "Megan is in her room." Pretty rude, not even a polite inquiry into my health. On the other hand, everyone is treating me so carefully, it's almost a relief to be treated normally. I don't wait to be asked twice. I bound up the stairs.

On Megan's bedroom door there is a tin sign, it says: "Megan's messy room. Enter at your own risk." I have one that says the same, but "Emily's messy room" obviously. We bought them at Camden Market when we were about ten. We'd come to London because the three mums wanted to take all of us to the Tower of London to see the Crown Jewels. The crowns were flashy, but the best bit of the trip was the market. Ridley sulked that you couldn't buy the room sign with his name on it. We teased him and said he wasn't in our club. I don't know where my sign is anymore; at the back of some wardrobe until we moved, I'd guess, maybe in the loft now, or a bag that ended up at a charity shop. I've always thought it was funny that Megan kept her sign up. In so many ways she's so cool and conscious of being seen as adult but then she'll just do something funny like keep up a sign that basically advertises her kid status. Megan can do that. She can make something uncool, cool, just by her disregard for caring whether it's cool or not.

I've missed her.

The last time we saw each other she was punching me in a loo. Or was she feeding me water and chocolate?

I'm still gathering my nerve to knock on the door, or maybe just open it and go in without announcing myself, when Carla shouts up the stairs. "Your dad is just going to run me to the shops. With everything that's been going on, we have nothing in for supper. He says you are staying."

Megan obviously hears her mother and she flings open the door. I try to pretend I've just walked up the stairs and not admit that I've been hanging about, gathering courage to go into her room. She stares at me but doesn't say anything. It doesn't seem like she's going to answer her mum, so I yell down the stairs, "Okay."

"Keep an eye on your brothers, Megan. Text your mum and tell her you are staying for a bit, Emily."

I guess Dad knows Mum will be less than chuffed with this news, which is why he's letting me deliver it. Cheers, Dad. I decide I'll text in a bit, put it off for a while. Megan and I stay on the landing until we hear our parents leave the house, the door bang behind them and the roar of my dad's Ferrari down the street.

"She's been dying to get in that car," comments Megan, rolling her eyes. "I promise you there is food in the house—she's just looking for an excuse for your dad to take her somewhere in the Ferrari. She is so shallow."

"Total puddle," I add. Megan grins and then grabs me, folding me into a tight hug.

"It is a fucking cool car, though, hey?" she asks.

"Totally," I murmur into her neck. I inhale her and I'm not mistaken. Of course I'm not. Her smell is as familiar to me as my own.

CHAPTER 50

Lexi

Logan and I play FIFA. He is Manchester City and I am Real Madrid. He wins all three games. I get a text from Emily saying she is staying at Megan's for supper. I'm conflicted. Emily needs all the friends she can have around her right now, but how can Megan be a friend when her father is responsible for the kidnapping? It's a lot to process. I decide to let it go. Emily needs her space. Logan and I order a pizza delivery. He thinks he's died and gone to heaven. I grin at my son, glad I can make him so happy so easily. I don't hear from Jake. I guess he could be eating with them, or maybe he's gone to the gym. Or maybe somewhere else. Jennifer's.

The thought keeps creeping up on me. I wish it didn't, but I can't quite shake the fact that for years I thought I knew where he was, what he was doing. I didn't. Logan gets bored of beating me so easily and says he's going to play with his friends online now. I've enjoyed our mother-son time, but honestly, I hate video games and am relieved. I go downstairs into the kitchen and pour myself a glass of wine.

I am not planning on snooping. I'm planning on picking up a book and losing myself in someone else's world, but I find myself in the room that Jake designated as his office. I flick on his PC. A subconscious part of my brain has taken over and my body is just following instructions. Whilst the PC is warming up, humming into life, I open his desk drawers. I idly flick through his paperwork. I don't know exactly what I'm looking for—emails or cards from her, phone records that prove they are still talking to one another. I wonder if he's changed his password. It used to be our wedding anniversary.

CHAPTER 51

Emily

Megan keeps her room really tidy. She always has. Ridley and I used to tease her and say she had OCD, but my mum said we weren't allowed to do that because mental disorders weren't a laughing matter and just because a teenager keeps her room tidy, it doesn't mean she has a syndrome. My mum can be really worthy. Megan sits on the stool in front of the dressing table and I sit on her neat bed that could have been made by a soldier and I wish there was some clutter lying about, something for me to pick up and play with, something to distract us both.

"Do you want to listen to some music?" she asks. I nod. She puts on Billie Eilish's latest release. I downloaded this recently, too. It cheers me that we have continued to listen to the same music, even when our lives were spiraling in different directions. It means something about us, our friendship. "How've you been?" she asks eventually.

I shrug. Where to start? Rich? Euphoric? Lonely? Terrified? I go with, "Pregnant."

"For real?" Her eyes are saucers. I almost want to giggle. It's always felt pretty fun shocking Megan because, out of the two of us, she's probably the most daring.

It's no fun, though, when I have to add, "I was. I lost it, during the abduction." She nods and looks out the window.

"Are you sad?" she asks.

"What would I have done with a baby?"

She shrugs. "I dunno, cuddle it?" It's so true. That's what I could have done. I flop back on the bed and let the hot silent tears fall onto her duvet. She gets up from the dressing table stool and comes to lie next to me.

"Does Ridley know?"

"Yes."

"What did he say?"

"He didn't want it. I guess he's happy now. I think he's with Evie Clarke."

"That won't last," she says loyally.

"I don't care."

"Yeah, you do."

"Yeah, I do."

She holds my hand and says nothing more. We stay like that for ages. The light in her room starts to change, it becomes orange, then pink. The sun is setting. I feel peaceful. Placed.

"I'm sorry about that thing we did to you. In the loos, you know." Megan is mumbling. Embarrassed. She hates apologizing.

"It's okay." It seems a long time ago. So much more and so much worse has happened since. "Why were you so angry, though? You know I would have shared everything with you."

"My mum said it was unfair." Megan shrugged.

"Your mum and my dad are taking ages with the shopping," I point out.

"Most likely gone to the pub. I guess they have a lot to talk about. Or maybe my mum has had a call from the police station." Megan keeps her eyes on the ceiling. I slide my glance toward her. I'm so happy in this moment, bathed in friendship and an orange sunset, I don't want to spoil things, but since she's brought it up…

"It was you, wasn't it?"

"What was me?"

"You were the person who gave me water and chocolate." The words stutter out of my mouth, like a faulty firework that you can't trust because you don't know when it will explode. "I think you tipped off my dad. Am I imagining this, Megan, or am I right?"

Megan doesn't answer straight away. She takes a deep breath. "It was really fucking scary. Seeing you bleed like that. I thought you were going to die. I had to do something."

"So, you were there with your dad?"

I turn to Megan and she's crying hard now. So many tears. "No, Emily. I was there with my mum. And *your* dad."

CHAPTER 52

Lexi

I can't believe what I'm looking at and yet I can. Confirmation of my worst fears. No, more than that, confirmation of a betrayal I couldn't ever have imagined. An email confirming two flights to Acapulco International Airport, Mexico. One way. Leaving tonight. Leaving in two hours.

I call Detective Inspector Owens and tell him what I've found.

"You are quite sure?"

"I'll forward the email to you." I sound calm, dispassionate; the DI probably thinks I'm heartless. I am. My heart has been ripped out. It's as though Jake has plunged his fist through my chest and grabbed my heart, gouged it out bloody and beating, stomped on it. Just as easily as someone might break a window. I am shattered.

The DI says he'll alert the airport, get people there immediately. "They are probably at the gate. We can get the flight stopped."

The doorbell rings. I have no idea who to expect. Not Jake. I hope it is Emily. I've texted her already, and she confirmed she is at Megan's. Even though the app on my phone told me this, I needed to have her confirm it. I don't want her alarmed, but I have to keep her safe. I've told her to come straight home in an Uber, but I guess, even if she follows my instructions to the letter, she'll be another half an hour.

It's Jennifer.

I almost pity her. We were once so close. Ostensibly we were three legs of a stool, equally involved and committed to one another, but we both secretly knew Carla was the most glamorous, the most sexy. The most spoiled. We did occasionally allow ourselves a moment when we shared a look of envy as we noticed Carla's long, smooth, tanned legs or her new designer dress, new diamonds dropping discreetly from her earlobes. That's why discovering Jake's affair with Jennifer had been such a shock to me. I'd have had my money on Carla being the one he fancied. I guess because I was right in the end, I backed the right horse, and I'm holding the winning ticket. It doesn't feel like it. I feel like a loser.

"Where's Jake?" Jennifer demands, crossing the threshold of my door, coming in uninvited.

"Not here," I say simply and honestly.

She throws me a look of pity. I absorb it and wait for the moment I can spit it back at her. "Lexi, I'm sorry, but it's time you accepted the situation. I know you know that Jake and I are—"

"What? What are you?" I demand.

She colors, not a blush exactly, something closer to a flush of irritation. "We're together." I raise my eyebrows, but bite my tongue. "I've left Fred, and Jake is leaving you. We're leaving tonight. It's all arranged. You lost. I won."

"Where are you going?" I ask.

"I don't want to discuss that with you."

"Mexico?"

She looks surprised but nods.

"Wrong, Jennifer—you are not going to Mexico with my husband. Carla is." Understandably, Jennifer looks confused. "He's upgraded, apparently. Having money allows you to do that, doesn't it?"

"I—I don't believe you," she stutters.

"I'm sure you don't, but I'm telling the truth. He played you as he played me. He played us all." Her mouth falls open. I can see her little pink tongue, a tongue she used to lick and suck my husband with. I feel strangely close to her and loathe her, too. I remind myself she is not the worst. She had an affair with my husband, but Carla is worse. She had an affair with my husband and kidnapped my daughter to secure a ten-million-pound ransom.

And Jake? Jake is the vilest of them all.

How could he have plotted and hurt the way he most surely has? How could he have put his own daughter in such mortal danger? For money? For sex? "The police are on their way to the airport. They'll arrest the two of them there. I think Patrick was in on it, too. The kidnapping, that is. Not the affair. They double-crossed him, too. He's already at the police station."

Jennifer starts to tremble. And now I can throw back that look of pity she was in such a hurry to land on me. She starts to turn away from me, reaching for the door handle. She's shaking too much to manage to grasp it, turn it and leave. I guess she is in a hurry to get home as quickly as she can, tear up the letter she left her husband. I wonder where she left her note. Possibly pinned on the fridge, maybe on the table in the hallway. The letter that says she's sorry, she's leaving him. That she has fallen in love with Jake and wants to start a new life. I am not heartless. I open the door for her, but I wonder when she gets back to her comfortable home in Great Chester, will her husband be waiting for her or will he already have left? Taken Ridley with him. I suppose I'll find out if Fred requests his 2.976 million. I've put that aside in a separate account. It's his, whenever he earns it.

CHAPTER 53

Lexi

Thursday, October 24

It made the papers, naturally. Not just a discreet little piece in the *Buckinghamshire Gazette*—a few column inches, the way Reveka's and Benke's deaths were reported. No, our story was splashed across tabloids and broadsheets for many consecutive days as the trial played out. Of course it was. It had all the elements to titillate the morbidly curious, the wickedly gossipy: a lottery win, an extravagant lifestyle, illicit sex and shocking violence. Our family's pain was trumpeted. We were exposed. Everyone got to know that my husband betrayed me not once but twice, both women ostensibly my friends. Friends for fifteen years. It was revealed that, more horrifyingly, he placed his child in extreme danger for financial gain. He was the one who hired the thugs who beat her, bound her, starved her for twenty-four hours. He cried in court, sobbed, swore that he hadn't given specific instructions for any of that, and that the thugs went too far of their own accord. He had only asked that they hold her. He had thought they were taking her to a hotel, but the thugs had decided that was too risky and made their own plans. Jake had underestimated the vileness, the underlying throbbing brutality, of the people he had mixed himself up with. He begged the judge and jury to believe him. I want to believe him because he would have to be the absolute devil to have planned to put Emily, his own daughter, through such horrors, but even if I believe him, I still blame him and can never forgive him. There's no getting away from the fact that he was the one who was responsible for the loss of her child. The loss of her childhood. And Logan's, come to that.

Jake wanted more. Always more. A wife, a lover, another lover. During the trial it transpired he'd never offered Jennifer and Fred a million to change their testimony. He'd offered Jennifer a life with him and "his" half of the win. But it wasn't enough for him to walk away with close to nine million, which he would have got if he'd divorced me. He staged the kidnap to siphon off ten million. If we'd divorced, we'd have split what was left, and he'd have bagged the majority of the cash.

And he still wanted more. Jennifer wasn't enough, either.

Carla was in on the kidnapping plan. Patrick continued to protest his innocence. He also continued to insist that he was due a share of the lottery win and that they had never left the syndicate. I went along to watch the trial. It was distressing, humiliating, but how could I keep away? I noticed that when Patrick insisted that they had never left the syndicate—that they were due a share of the money all along—the judge sneered. Judges are supposed to keep their faces entirely neutral, but he couldn't stop himself sneering. He seemed disgusted by the whole lot of them. I think that is why he threw the book at them. Custodial sentences. Three years for Carla and Patrick. Seven for Jake.

The judge was a father of three teenage girls himself. He must have been sickened.

Jennifer, Fred and Ridley have moved away. Somewhere up north. Leeds, I think. They want to start again. They want to try again. I wish them well, but mostly I wish them well away from us. I still have an account with almost three million pounds put aside. It's Fred's, if ever he should want it enough. He knows the terms. And if he never claims it, I might give it to Ridley, when he's old enough to manage that sort of wealth properly.

We've put money in trust for Megan and her brothers, too. We wanted them to come and live with us, but the social services decided it was too complicated. They are living with Carla's sister in Surrey; apparently, she's a lovely woman. They are settling well enough. I know they will be taken care of, looked after and loved. Emily has stayed in touch with Megan. Their relationship isn't as tight as it was—how could it be? But they send one another snaps and messages. There's talk of a meetup in London. I don't know if it will happen. Time will tell whether they can remain close, after everything. It might be better if the friendship fades. If they move on. Like the social worker said, it's complicated.

My children are doing okay. Considering everything, they are doing brilliantly. They have had to deal with so much. They've been hurt and horrified in a way that will take years to heal properly. They'll never get over what's happened, but I think they will get through it. I'm impressed by their courage, their resilience. We spent the summer in Moldova at Toma's school for underprivileged kids. It was just what we all needed. To get away. To climb out of our own lives and skins for a while. The work he is doing there is astonishing. He's genuinely making a profound difference, offering opportunities through education. Lives will be changed for the better. I love him for it.

I love him for many reasons.

The kids have returned to their old school. Logan was delighted. He has a great friendship group and simply slipped right back into it. Emily seems to be getting along very well with Scarlett, Liv and Nella. They are sweet girls.

Sadly, I never went back to CAB. Our family name has been dragged through the mud and I'm basically a reluctant celebrity. Ellie couldn't in all conscience sanction my return—it would be too disruptive. I miss the bureau, but I understand. You can't have everything in life. Besides, I want to offer the kids as much stability as I can, and being at home helps with that. I don't need the money. The police recovered the ten million Jake pretended he'd given to the kidnappers. It was spread through various accounts: most in his and Carla's name, about a million in Patrick's account. The money in Patrick's account suggested his guilt, no matter how much he protested his innocence. I don't know if that money was his cut of the kidnapping or Carla leaving him a bit of money to assuage her own guilt. Or was it crueller than that? Did she and Jake frame Patrick? I guess that will remain a mystery forever. The money has been returned to me. Emily, Logan and I have spent a lot of time talking about what we might do with it next. Following the experience in Moldova, they both seem keen to set up something similar here in the UK—a trust that gives opportunities, creates light where before there was only despair.

"Not all of it, though? Right, Mum?" Emily asked. "I mean, we can spend some of it on clothes and stuff."

"Of course, I promise."

We ended up staying in the rental longer than I expected. It seemed sensible to stay somewhere gated throughout the trial, to avoid being stalked by hungry journos, but we're moving back into our old home. Whilst we've been here, we've had some work done on our old place. An extra bedroom, a sunroom. I'm looking forward to going home. To getting back to normal.

CHAPTER 54

Saturday, April 13

"Not this week," announced Jake, looking up from his phone, his face pulled into an expression that approximated a comedic take on disappointment. "Not a single number."

"Situation normal," said Lexi. No one else responded at all. The lull in conversation seemed heavy. Fred had been talking about, oh, something or other, Lexi couldn't recall, his car engine? Tire pressure? It hadn't been gripping, but Jake's interruption to announce they weren't lottery winners had created an atmosphere. No one liked to be reminded that they'd lost at anything, even if there was never any real expectation of winning. "Oh, by the way, it's time to chip in to the kitty again," she said.

"Why are we even doing the lotto?" asked Patrick, his face flushed, his voice booming. "What's the bloody point?"

Lexi couldn't understand why he was suddenly grumbling. He'd hit the bottle of red hard that he'd brought with him. Polished it off before she had even served the main.

"Well, we do it because we've always done it, haven't we? Since we first met. It's our thing, our gang's thing." She smiled coolly. "Do you remember, we used to say if we won, we'd invest in twenty-four-hour childcare?" The absolute dream of all exhausted, shell-shocked new parents.

"That would still seem like a good investment," commented Carla with a wry grin. "Perhaps not a nanny but a private detective, someone to follow Megan around—I never know where she is or what she's up to nowadays."

"Or a clairvoyant," added Jennifer. "To read Ridley's mind. You are so lucky, Lexi, to have a chatty girl. I don't get more than a grunt out of my son—typical boy."

"Is that the best you can come up with? Spending the dosh stalking your kids?" Jake challenged. "If I won the lotto, I'd have much more fun spending it."

"You'd buy a Lamborghini and a yacht, I suppose," said Fred with a grin.

"Absolutely," Jake beamed. "You?"

"A bigger house. Several bigger houses, actually. One here, one in London."

Jennifer joined in. "South of France."

"California," added Carla.

"What about you, Patrick? Would you invest in property?" Lexi couldn't stop herself sounding challenging. Not considering all she knew. Patrick had a lot of property already, most of it unfit to keep an animal in. Lexi had found it difficult to sit at the same table as Patrick tonight, to feed him. Considering her suspicions. She now was fully aware that he was a slum landlord—her investigations with Toma had uncovered as much. She was waiting on one more piece of information to discover if he was *the* slum landlord. The one that murdered Reveka and Benke. She would know for certain next week. Everything would change next week.

"Maybe," said Patrick, and he yawned. He looked bored.

"Or would you perhaps just make improvements on the places you already own?" she asked hopefully, desperately. Part of her wanted to keep the show on the road. They had all been friends for so long. If they weren't friends, what would they be?

"Oh, no, not that," he chuckled. His big belly, the result of too many indulgent work lunches, shook. "Don't want to spoil the tenants." Lexi felt sick.

"I think I'd send Ridley to a posh sixth form. Marlborough or Eton," chipped in Jennifer.

Jake excitedly took up the mantle. "I'd want swimming pools in all my properties. I'd only ever fly first class from then on in."

"I'd dress entirely in haute couture, even to do the housework," said Carla.

"You don't do the housework," muttered Patrick. "We have a cleaner."

"Wouldn't any of you do anything good with it?" All five pairs of eyes swivelled to Lexi, who had asked the question.

"Good?" they chorused.

"Give to charities? Sent up trusts or foundations?"

"Oh, yes, yes, of course," they hurried to reassure her.

"I'm just saying it would be great fun to spoil oneself, you know, totally," commented Carla. Patrick looked irritated. As far as Lexi could tell, he did a good job of spoiling his wife as it was; the woman could be so greedy. Did she have any idea how others lived so she could wear Jimmy Choos, so her husband could get fat? Surely not. Lexi hoped not. If Carla knew about the state of the properties, that would be too much. That would be unbearable.

"I'd buy a really decent watch for every day of the week," said Jake. "You know, a Patek Philippe for Monday, a Chopard for Tuesday, a Rolex for Wednesday—"

"Oh, for God's sake, man, grow up," Patrick snapped.

Startled, Lexi and Jake turned their heads toward him, and

the others all dropped their eyes to their plates. Lexi felt something in the air, a chill.

"Will you cut the crap. All this talk about lotto wins is doing my head in. That's not how you make money in this world. You need to graft."

"Patrick, playing the lotto is only a bit of fun," said Lexi, in what she hoped was a placating tone.

"It's crass," he muttered aggressively. Lexi felt the hairs on her body stand in revolt. Crass? Coming from him? She wanted to slap him. But she also wanted to preserve what they had around this table. Fifteen years of friendship.

"It's a few quid, man, what are you making a fuss for?" Jake asked with a laugh that may have been designed to mollify but sounded a bit insistent.

Patrick looked uncomfortable, shifted on his seat, fingered his collar as though his tie was too tight, although he wasn't wearing a tie. "It's not the money, of course it's not the money." He paused and then added, "It's what it says."

"What it says?"

"About us." No one was making eye contact. Lexi thought about offering dessert or another drink, but she didn't bother.

"What does buying a lotto ticket say about us, exactly?" challenged Jake. He held his smile, but it didn't reach his eyes.

"Come on, mate, you know what I'm saying."

"I really don't."

"It's for losers. Even the winners are losers," Patrick sniggered to himself. "You know how it goes. Someone wins a huge amount and they buy a big house or two, fancy cars, just as you've described. They snort a fortune up their nose, go on flash holidays and in less than a few years they are back riding the bus, living in a rented house. They can't hack it, these people."

"These people?"

"And the sad thing is, they're not as happy as they were before, because they've tasted the high life, seen how the other half lives." Patrick reached for the whiskey bottle that Lexi's mum had given Jake for his birthday. Patrick poured himself a generous measure.

Then with some bitterness, he added, "The wrong sort always wins. Statistically they have a better chance because it's idlers and doleys that buy tickets."

Jake snorted. "Does anyone say doleys anymore?"

"I just did," replied Patrick seriously. "It's such a waste. Those people aren't used to having money, they don't know how to deal with it. How to invest, how to spend, how to save, most importantly. Losers."

"Well, dreamers," Lexi suggested.

Jake laughed. It was a strained, overly dramatic laugh. "If you think this way, why have you been doing the lottery for fifteen years?"

"To humor you." Patrick grinned coldly. "You seem to enjoy doing it. You like a flutter." He paused over the word "flutter," his tone mocking, derisory.

"Well, you don't have to be part of the syndicate," said Lexi. "You're under no obligation."

"Fine. I don't want to be a killjoy, but…"

"But?"

"We're going to pull out."

"Okay." Lexi nodded. She felt a flush of shame rise up her chest and neck, and she hoped it wouldn't reach her face. She wasn't absolutely certain what she felt ashamed of. Something intangible. She suddenly felt accused. Accused of what? She wasn't sure. Had she and Jake press-ganged their friends into coughing up every week? Into doing something they didn't want to do? But it was just a few quid. Why wouldn't they want to do it? It was fun. And for it to be Patrick of all people to judge her. He had no right. Yet she felt insulted, hurt.

"It's not as though we're ever actually going to win," chipped in Carla.

"No, but—" Lexi clamped her mouth shut. She didn't want to say that she valued the tradition, the fact it was a thing, *their* thing. A bit like watching the fireworks together on Guy Fawkes Night or seeing in the new year—something they'd always done. If it needed saying, it wasn't true. It wasn't "their thing" if only she believed it to be so.

"It's common, like taking your shirt off in public or having a tattoo," Patrick said.

Jake bristled. Jake had a tattoo on his shoulder. They all knew as much. It had been the center of discussion when they first went on holiday to Lexi's mum and dad's place in Spain years ago, and in fact the tattoo had been center of discussion every holiday since.

The silence throbbed.

"Oh, for fuck's sake. It's just a few quid, if it makes you happy," said Carla. She reached for her handbag, scrabbled about in her purse. "Here's our fiver. We're in." She hated it when her husband became pigheaded, caused a scene. Patrick rolled his eyes. "All right, Patrick," said Carla, her voice steely. "We're happy to carry on with the lottery, aren't we?"

"If it makes you happy," he said, and then downed his whiskey.

Fred quickly followed suit. His jacket was hung on the back of his chair. He dug out his wallet, threw in a tenner, picked up Carla's fiver as change. "Us too, Lexi. It's just a bit of fun, isn't it? No need for us to fall out about it."

Jennifer smiled, her eyes on Jake. "You never know your luck, our numbers might come up next week, and then all our lives will change forever."

*****

AUTHOR'S NOTE

Dear Reader,

Prepare yourself for gratitude overload. I am always pretty profuse with my thank-yous, but on the publication of my twentieth novel I have an especially huge amount to be grateful for.

Thank you, Jonny Geller, for years of continual support, advice and true friendship. How lucky that we found each other, way back when. Mark Twain said, "Success is a journey, not a destination. It requires constant effort, vigilance and reevaluation." That's certainly been our journey. I'm glad we have walked every step of the road together.

I never know where to start with my thanks to my publishers, Kate Mills and Lisa Milton, who are two of the most incredible women I've ever had the joy to work with. You are quite simply brilliant, oozing resolve, enthusiasm, ingenuity and business acumen. I'm so incredibly fortunate to have you. I have such enormous respect for you both.

Thank you to Charlie Redmayne for being an interested, encouraging and inspiring CEO. You captain a great ship!

I've always believed that if a book is lucky enough to be successful, then that's because there's an enormous number of people doing their jobs incredibly well. I'm so delighted to be working with such fantastic teams in the UK and across the globe. I am thoroughly appreciative of the talent and commitment of every single person involved in this book's existence. Thank you so much for all your support and dedication—Anna Derkacz, Georgina Green, Fliss Porter, Sophie Calder, Izzy Smith, Joanna Rose, Claire Brett, Darren Shoffren, Becky Heeley, Agnes Rigou, Aisling Smyth, Emily Yolland, Kate Oakley and Anna Sikorska.

I want to send another massive thank-you across the seas to the amazing James Kellow, Loriana Sacilotto, Margaret Marbury, Leo McDonald, Carina Nunstedt, Celine Hamilton, Pauline Riccius, Anna Hoffmann, Eugene Ashton, Olinka Nell and Rahul Dixit. There are many others who I have yet to meet, but I know I'm so lucky that incredible professionals worldwide are giving my books their love and attention. It's so ridiculously exciting. Thank you.

Thank you to all my readers, bloggers, reviewers, retailers, librarians and fellow authors who have supported me throughout my career. I couldn't have done this without you.

Thank you to my mum, dad, sister, nieces and nephew who are continually supportive of everything I do, who love me and my books whether the sales are good, bad or indifferent!

Thank you, Jimmy and Conrad. No woman could ever hope for more support from a husband or son. I really did win the family lottery.

Finally, I'd like to warmly thank Guy Rudolph and Andy Carter for giving their time and expertise explaining what happens when a person wins the lottery. It was so kind of you!